Praise for

"Meticulously researched . . . the book succeeds in forcefully illustrating the lessons of the French Revolution for today's democratic movements." —*Kirkus Reviews*

"Devotees of Alexandre Dumas and Victor Hugo will devour this tale of heroism, treachery, and adventure." —*Library Journal*

"*Where the Light Falls* is a sweeping romantic novel that takes readers to the heart of Paris and to the center of all the action of the French Revolution. Following the lives of three different people—a determined lawyer and family man itching to join the cause, a young widow determined to break free from her uncle's rule, and a denounced nobleman-turned-soldier—this fascinating novel weaves a compelling tale of love, betrayal, sacrifice, and bravery. Compulsively readable, *Where the Light Falls* is one summer adventure you won't want to miss." —*Bustle*

"This is a story of the French Revolution that begins with your head in the slot watching how fast the blade of the guillotine is heading for your neck—and that's nothing compared to the pace and the drama of what follows." —Tom Wolfe

"A beautiful novel that captures the spirit of the French Revolution and the timeless themes of love and truth." —Steven Pressfield

"While not stinting on gorgeous detail, Allison and Owen Pataki know exactly how to write a gripping historical novel: concentrate on the intimate stories playing out against the epic background of the French Revolution. And *Where the Light Falls* is exactly that, a gripping historical novel of both intimacy and scope."
—Melanie Benjamin, author of
The Girls in the Picture and *The Swans of Fifth Avenue*

Where the Light Falls

Where the Light Falls

A Novel of
the French Revolution

ALLISON PATAKI

AND OWEN PATAKI

The Dial Press | New York

2018 Dial Press Trade Paperback Edition

Copyright © 2017 by Allison Pataki and Owen Pataki

Published in the United States by The Dial Press, an imprint of Random House,
a division of Penguin Random House LLC, New York.

THE DIAL PRESS and the HOUSE colophon are registered trademarks
of Penguin Random House LLC.

Originally published in hardcover in the United States by The Dial Press,
an imprint of Random House, a division of Penguin Random House LLC, in 2017.

Title page art from an original photograph by FreeImages.com/gselmes
Part title art, map of Paris, 1792, provided by www.RareMaps.com—Barry
Lawrence Ruderman Antique Maps Inc.

LIBRARY OF CONGRESS CATALOGING-IN-PUBLICATION DATA

Names: Pataki, Allison, author. | Pataki, Owen, author.
Title: Where the light falls : a novel of the French Revolution / by Allison Pataki
and Owen Pataki.
Description: New York : The Dial Press, 2017.
Identifiers: LCCN 2016053057 | ISBN 9780399591709 (trade paperback) |
ISBN 9780399591693 (ebook)
Subjects: LCSH: France—History—Revolution, 1789-1799—Fiction. |
BISAC: FICTION / Historical. | FICTION / Action & Adventure. | FICTION /
Romance / Historical. | GSAFD: Historical fiction.
Classification: LCC PS3616.A8664 W44 2017 | DDC 813/.6—dc23
LC record available at https://lccn.loc.gov/2016053057

Printed in the United States of America on acid-free paper

randomhousebooks.com

2 4 6 8 9 7 5 3 1

Book design by Virginia Norey

To our family: Mom and Dad, Emily and Teddy

For encouraging our imaginations and believing in big dreams.

"On this day and at this place a new era of world history has begun."

—Johann Wolfgang von Goethe, Valmy, France,
September 1792

"The ship of the revolution can arrive safely at its destination only on a sea that is red with torrents of blood."

—Louis de Saint-Just, the "Archangel of Death,"
political and military leader during the French Revolution

Where the Light Falls

Prologue

Paris, Winter 1792

He hears them before he sees them, a swell of thousands, young and old, male and female, clamoring from the other side of the prison walls. They sound impatient, shrill with the heady prospect of fresh blood to wet the newly sharpened guillotine blade.

His skin grows cold where the rusty shears touch his neck, creaking and groaning as they clip his locks. He watches as the limp wisps of gray float to the ground, harbingers of what is to come for the head that had grown them. He would be sick, but nothing remains in his stomach to be emptied.

"Can't have the hair getting tangled on the blade." The old jail keeper's sour breath reeks of wine as he makes quick work of the prisoners' hair, snipping the line of ponytails in brisk, well-rehearsed succession. Most of the hair, even that from the young heads, is laced with gray. Funny, he thinks, how terror ages a man much more quickly than any passage of time.

"This way, old man, move along." The guard jerks his pockmarked chin toward the far end of the hallway, and Alexandre de Valière, now shorn tighter than a springtime lamb, shuffles his chained feet one final time down the dark corridor. The inmates whose names weren't called peek through the small slits in their doors, watching the march. Grateful, for the moment, to be on the other side of their doors. Their tiny square cells feel safe, even cozy, compared to the brown courtyard toward which Valière now walks.

And now, he waits. Standing alongside the others in the courtyard, he cups his hands and tries to blow some warmth into his cold, aching fingertips.

"Must be thousands of them out there." A nervous-looking man at least thirty years his junior looks at him with wide, unblinking eyes. Valière nods in reply.

"You think this lot are loud, wait 'til you hear them gathered on the other side of the river," one of the other prisoners grunts, spitting on the frosted ground. He was already bald and therefore hadn't required the same shearing as the rest.

The crowd had come out early this morning, as they had for several weeks now, assembling just beyond the walls of the prison that had once been the residence of the ancient kings. They'll line the entire route: across the small island that sits in the middle of the Seine, over the bridge in front of city hall, lining Rue Saint-Honoré before opening into the great square of Place Louis XV, recently renamed La Place de la Révolution, where a deafening roar would erupt from the masses assembled in view of the scaffold.

A guard emerges from the prison. *"All right, it's time. Up you go,"* he says, pointing his musket at the tumbril that awaits. *"Let's not keep Madame waiting."*

Valière recalls Dante's passage, mumbling the words to himself, *"His sworn duty is to ferry the souls of the damned across the infernal river."*

"No back talk, you!" A nearer guard raises the butt of his musket as if to smite the old man across the face, and Valière notices with a flash of bitter humor that he had winced, instinctively, in the face of the threat. As if a beating could do any harm at this point.

Valière waits his turn to climb into the tumbril, helping an old woman before him. When the last of them are aboard, a guard lifts the gate and the driver cracks his whip over the horses. The wheels groan as they slowly begin to turn, stiff like aching bones on this cold morning, lurching the cart forward. Valière steadies himself on the railing, offering a faint smile to the old woman, who had reached for his shoulder to regain her balance. She smiles wanly back at him, her trembling hands betraying her own terror. As the prison gates grind open, the guards posted along the entrance look on, bored, as the human cargo rolls past; the tumbrils passed this way yesterday, and more will pass tomorrow.

Just then the feeble disc of the sun slices through the thick cloud cover and the city is illuminated in stark winter daylight. The old man is momentarily *blinded. He squints, his eyes adjusting as he beholds the great crowd that has come out to witness his final passage through the city. There are even more than he would have guessed.*

The old woman beside him is praying to the Virgin, clutching an ivory rosary that she has somehow slipped past the prison guards. She holds Valière's eyes for just an instant, and he gives her a small, barely perceptible nod.

A whirring noise glides past his ears, followed by a dull thud. He looks over his shoulder at the prisoner immediately behind him and notices the man's gray shirt, splattered with the brown juice of a rotten tomato. A head of lettuce follows, bouncing off Valière's shoulder before it knocks into the old woman, sending her string of beads loose from her hands and over the tumbril railing to the filthy street. She cries out, "My rosary!" The crowd lets out a chorus of jeers and sniggers. One of the more eager onlookers, braving the wrath of the guards, rushes forward to scoop the ivory beads from the grimy street. The old woman mumbles quietly to herself, "My rosary. It was my mother's rosary."

"Ha! Old bitch cares about her necklace 'til the very last!"

A mother clutching a newborn in one arm uses her free hand to hurl a fistful of cabbage that strikes a prisoner toward the front of the tumbril, and the crowd erupts once more. "Rot in hell, you glutted rich pigs!" The guards, some holding old muskets and others armed with newly sharpened pikes, strain to hold back the vengeful crowd.

"Make way, I said!" The driver lifts his whip, and the people clear a path as the mounted guards escorting the tumbril struggle to master their nervous horses. As they cross the river, the crowd lining the old bridge follows behind, running with the procession toward La Place.

The cart rounds the corner and the narrow cobblestoned street opens up into the large, packed square. The mob spots the approaching carriage and erupts. No monarch of France, not even the Sun King himself, Louis XIV, had ever entered La Place to such an uproar.

The noise is deafening as Valière hears voices roar the nation's new anthem. Several men triumphantly wave the new tricolor flag with its streaks of red, white, and blue, the standard of the young nation. Some shout curses, but most of the voices remain an indistinguishable and menacing din to the prisoners quaking in the rolling carriages.

The crowd gathered around the scaffold is so thick that the old man would not be able to see the murder apparatus were it not mounted on its large wooden stage. Raised up, Valière muses, death exalted.

The carriage lurches to a halt. A guard lowers the tumbril's back gate and waves a gloved hand. "All right, step off. Move lively now." For a moment, none of them moves. Valière takes the first step, lowering himself down onto the street.

The crowd jostles to get near them—vying for an opportunity to scratch a bit of noble flesh, pull a strand of noble hair. The mounted guards push back against the onslaught, and a guard on foot swings his elbows and brandishes the butt of his musket to escort the dozen prisoners nearer to the scaffold. Valière ducks in time to miss the assault of a soft rotting apple.

"You first." The guard points at the young man with the wide eyes, the one who had remarked at the large number in the crowd.

The man puts his hands to his chest as if to ask, "Me?"

The guard nods, waving his hand. "Go on up," he says, putting special emphasis on the words that come next: "Best not to keep them waiting, Monsieur le Duc." The young man, whom Valière now knows to be a duke, shuts his eyes and begins to cry, and Valière notices a patch of moisture as it seeps across the groin of the young man's breeches.

Please, don't let me shame myself, Valière thinks. Let me depart with just a final shred of dignity.

The young duke is practically carried up the creaking steps, his thin frame trembling between the guards. His sobs and protestations are audible, even over the noise of the crowd. "But why must I go first? Why me? What on earth have I done?"

"What difference does it make, Seigneur?" The guard is impatient; he's seen enough of this useless pleading to be bored by the last-minute hysterics. He needs to get the show going before the crowd grows unruly.

Valière watches as the man's smooth hands are bound and he is marched to the center of the stage, and notices a woven basket that rests below where the blade will crash down. The duke is forced to kneel, and his neck is taken in the thick fingers of the guard, who settles the prisoner facedown, sliding his throat into a wooden cradle where a smooth semicircle has been carved. A matching wooden plank is placed on top so that the two semicircles form a perfect wooden noose, holding the man's head in place. The nobleman is sob-

bing now, trying to resist, but the base of his neck remains fixed against the bracket. The crowd, witnessing his writhing and his pleading, grows even more frenzied.

Valière stops breathing, but he can't pull his eyes away. A priest makes the sign of the cross over the writhing prisoner, an absolution which the damned man can't see. Finally, when the latch is pulled and the blade flies downward, Valière shuts his eyes. He hears a quick noise, a brief slice, followed by a thunderous roar. In the din, the thudding sound of the severed head dropping into the basket is lost.

"Encore! More!"

"Le prochain! Next!"

Having caught this first whiff of blood, the crowd becomes even more ravenous. The guard calls for the old woman, the frail, praying woman who had steadied herself on Valière's shoulder. He can't watch. He doesn't wish to know what her face looks like as she is escorted up the steps to the jeers and curses of the crowd. Again, he hears that sickening noise that slices through the moment of brief, anticipatory silence, followed by the shrill cries of elation.

"Encore! Encore!"

The guard is looking at him now. Pointing at him. He lets out a slow, long breath. So this is what it means to stare into the face of death.

One foot in front of the other, he makes his way to the stage and up the steps. He no longer feels his own footsteps, nor thinks about how his legs manage to carry him. The roar of the crowd seems to recede, to grow somehow distant, and a strange sensation takes hold of him, almost as if he were floating outside of himself.

He kneels on his own, preempting the guard's gruff handling. On his knees, he glances out over the crowd: a sea of jeering faces, contorting in lusty anticipation. And then his stare lands on one face in particular. Colorless eyes, skin and hair as white as parchment. He's come to gloat, even now? Even in this last moment? In spite of himself, the old man begins to tremble, the pale face of that one onlooker doing more to inspire terror and fury than any guillotine blade could. Lazare. Lazarus. The man whom Jesus raised from the dead; and now, this man sends so many others to their own deaths. Valière holds the man's eyes briefly, swears that those pale lips pull apart in a sinister grin. But then Valière blinks, forcing himself to look away. He won't have that face be the last sight his eyes rest upon while on this earth.

He turns his gaze to the apparatus before him, beckoning him to his death, and his head is slid into the groove. There's the woven basket again, below him now and stained scarlet. The old woman's head is facedown, so that all he sees is her thin, silvery hair, tangled in red and reaching for the body from which it has been severed. But he can't avoid the wide, vacant eyes of the young nobleman killed moments before. They stare at him without blinking, without light, frozen in fear.

The eyes are so distracting that he no longer notices the crowd. He does not hear the droning tap-tap-tap *of the drums. He wills his mind to envision something else, something other than this present hell. To forget the pale hair and colorless face of his enemy. To forget the stunned eyes of the dead young duke beneath him. He thinks of the face of his wife, conjures her image, her beautiful features uncreased by time or worry. And then his mind flies to his greatest source of happiness: two boys, dark-blond curls, happy faces reflecting the lost joy of his own life back to him. He sees them chasing each other in the garden, squealing with childish abandon. At this thought, he smiles one last time.*

His vision turns to black, and he feels nothing as the crowd erupts for the third time, rejoicing in the death of the old nobleman Alexandre de Valière.

PART ONE

1

Paris

September 1792

The heat had finally broken, ushering in what the Parisians were calling *"le répit."* The reprieve. If spoken in another context, it meant grace, though there was little of that to be had in the city that summer. Not now—now that the new invention had been permanently installed in La Place de la Révolution. Crosses had been torn from the altars of churches, cross-shaped pendants ripped from women's breasts and tossed into the filthy gutters that emptied red into the Seine. In many public places, the image of the cross was replaced by the nation's new holy icon: the guillotine.

On the Left Bank, in a narrow street of sunbaked houses, every window was ajar, so that any resident could tell you with some precision about the comings and goings of each occupant in the adjacent flat or home. On this morning, the couple living on the east corner, above the tavern, was quarreling—fighting over money, or the heat, or the stale bread that was supposed to have lasted for days. The couple across from them, based on the sounds issuing from their bedchamber, had made up from last night's quarrel. And a dog on the street, its ribs jutting out from under its tawny coat, had found a prize stew bone, which it had dragged out of the tavern and onto the street, where it now sat gnawing, hoping to coax every last bit of marrow from within.

"Why, you mangy beast, that's where it's got to!" Madame Grocque, the wife of the tavern keeper, lurched out of her door and swiped at the dog with her broom. Seizing on the mutt's momentary shock, she stooped down and snatched the bone with her thick, dirty fingers. The dog, recovered from its beating, jumped at the woman, fixing his teeth on the treat she would deny him.

"You worthless creature, I'll skin you and throw you in the stew alongside this bone! It'd do us good to get a bit o' fresh meat." Madame Grocque kicked at the animal, but the mutt refused to release the first morsel it had scrounged in days.

From a window on the top floor of this dwelling, a young man, not quite thirty years of age, dropped his quill and listened to the raucous activity below. Rubbing his eyes, he sighed. "Soon. Someday soon we'll get out of this neighborhood."

"Jean-Luc?" his wife called from the other side of the door, her voice mixing with the familiar morning sounds of clanging dishes and the crying baby. "Won't you have any breakfast before you leave?"

"Coming, Marie." The lawyer pushed himself away from the desk in the corner of the bedroom. Standing, he rolled up his papers and loaded them into his satchel. He crossed the small room in two strides, reaching for the vest and threadbare jacket that she had set out for him. When he had dressed in his plain gray suit, he checked his reflection in the filmy glass of the cracked mirror. Was that a gray hair he spotted? He leaned in closer, sighing. After the year he'd had, he wouldn't be surprised if there were quite a few gray hairs streaking his dark ponytail. His hazel eyes now stared back at him from within a thin web of unfamiliar lines, a new one seeming to appear each week.

In the other room, the chamber that served as kitchen, dining room, and living room all in one, Marie stood with the baby balanced on her hip. She smiled when she spotted Jean-Luc in the door. "Will you take some coffee?"

"Hmm?" He leaned in and kissed them both, first his wife and then his son.

Marie leaned her head to the side, lifting the pot with her free hand.

"Oh, right. Coffee, yes. Please." Jean-Luc sat at the table before a plate of black bread, the remnants of yesterday's loaf, and a square of hard cheese. Marie served him watered-down coffee as he cleared the papers that he had left strewn across the table. She had every window open, but the air in their top-floor flat hung stale and oppressive from the months of thick heat.

"You were tossing and turning all night." Marie shifted the baby and sat down across from her husband at the small table. "Trouble sleeping again?"

He swallowed a piece of the hard bread, nodding. Outside, the old Grocque woman still hollered at the dog, the beast yelping in response to another swipe of her broom. Marie looked from her husband to the open window and rose to close it.

"No, leave it open." He reached for her hand and kept her at the table.

"Next time you decide to work in the middle of the night, you might try moving out here to—"

"I know. I should come out here so that I don't wake you and Mathieu. I'm sorry." He sipped the thin coffee as she sat back down. "Will you forgive me for imposing my accursed sleeplessness on you?"

She narrowed her eyes and reached for a piece of his cheese, which she broke off between her fingertips and began to nibble. "I suppose. But it's getting worse, you know."

"What is?"

She leaned her head to the side. "Your accursed sleeplessness."

"I know," he replied. They sat opposite each other in silence, he eating his breakfast, she nursing the baby. After several minutes, he propped his elbows on the table and cleared his throat. "I think I'm going to take the Widow Poitier's case."

Stroking the baby's cheek, Marie lowered her eyes, and Jean-Luc waited for her reaction. After a pause, she said: "She can't pay, can she?"

He shook his head, no.

She looked up at him, her brown eyes serious. "You're a good man, Jean-Luc St. Clair."

He took his coffee in his hands, concealing his grin. Her approval, these days so difficult to get, always elicited that grin from him. He looked at her now, her arms full with his baby, her eyes holding his own steadily. "So then, my beloved wife, you've forgiven me for removing you from your beloved south and bringing you to languish in this cramped garret?"

"Forgiven you?" Her lovely eyes widened, her lashes fluttering a few times, reminding him of the girl who had bewitched him. How glorious she was, still. "Who said anything about forgiving you?" She offered half a grin, and he couldn't resist the urge to lean forward and kiss her.

He had moved her from the south of France just over a year ago, only a few months after they had been married. Her father had a steady, if not excessively lucrative, legal practice just outside of Marseille, not far from the village where Jean-Luc's family had owned a small plot of land since the time of the Sun King, Louis XIV.

The St. Clair family had sustained the comfortable farmhouse on the small but fertile plot for centuries. It wasn't until his father's assumption of the property that the fortunes of the family—and indeed of the region, and all of France—had deteriorated so drastically. They had been forced to sell off most of the property, keeping only a half acre with one milk cow, a handful of chickens, and the house for the widower and his son, Jean-Luc. It wasn't from a lack of industriousness that Jean-Luc's father had lost the family land; old Claude St. Clair had been a faithful steward of his family's assets. He was simply another victim of the droughts and crippling financial circumstances that had plagued the rest of the country under the latest Bourbon king, the heir of the Sun King's heir, the most reviled man in France: Louis XVI. Yet, His Majesty could not be considered the most reviled *monarch* in France; that moniker went to his Austrian-born wife, Marie-Antoinette.

When it had come time for Jean-Luc to plan his own future, he'd taken his father's advice and had applied himself to the study of law. What else was there for him? The land was gone; there was no longer wealth to be had in farming, unless you were a nobleman who skimmed the profits from the peasants and then paid no taxes on that bounty. His mother had died in his early boyhood; his only sibling, a sister five years older, had married at the age of sixteen and had been living an ocean away in the New World colony of Saint-Domingue. Other than the handful of letters he'd received from her over the years, Jean-Luc St. Clair, prior to beginning his legal studies in Marseille, had been occupied chiefly by attending to his elderly father.

Jean-Luc had enjoyed his time at school, which offered more excitement and opportunity than he could find in his lonely, quiet home. Having excelled in his studies at Aix-Marseille University, the ambitious young law-yer sought something greater than the small hometown magistrate's of-fice. He applied for a position as a low-level attorney at a reputable law practice closer to Marseille. Meeting and falling in love with Marie Ger-maine, his employer's pretty daughter with thick brunette curls and quick, pert opinions, had been an unexpected but happy windfall.

Jean-Luc had been employed in his new office, his bride happily in-stalled in their comfortable cottage on her father's estate, when the news reached Marseille that King Louis and Queen Marie-Antoinette had been plucked from their gilded palace at Versailles and moved back to Paris, where they'd been forced to live among their people. Jean-Luc, a budding idealist whose family's hopes had been nearly extinguished under an inept monarch, and who had followed with great interest the crafting of a na-scent republic in the American colonies, had longed to ride to Paris like so many of his young fellow countrymen. He did not hide his desire to join the people and sacrifice his worldly comforts and, if necessary, his life, in the name of liberty. Would it not be shameful, he asked Marie, to be born in this era of history and yet shrink from the glorious undertaking of a free people rising up in the name of liberty, equality, and fraternity?

Mathieu arrived six months after their relocation to Paris, and Jean-Luc had been grateful of it. Marie was less lonely with the dark-haired little boy, who shared her coffee-colored eyes and spirited personality, to fill the long hours while Jean-Luc worked as a low-level administrative attorney for the new government. They had settled in this two-room garret—drafty in the winter, stifling in the summer—as it was all that his modest govern-ment salary could afford. His father-in-law, furious at Jean-Luc for taking his daughter so far north, had refused to support the move. If he could only see how she was living now, Jean-Luc thought, looking around at their cramped quarters. They, being from the south, had never known the bitterness of a northern winter until this past year. Nor had either of them ever passed a summer without the salty sea breezes and shade of the fra-grant citrus trees. It had been a trying year for both of them.

But Marie, bless her, never complained; she never held it against Jean-Luc that he had removed her from her father's comfortable home to this loud, dirty city. A place where, on more than one occasion, they'd had to

choose between food and fuel. She was tough, yes. But that was also because she was, Jean-Luc suspected, as much of an idealist as he was, even
if she would never have dared admit it.

"Mr. Bigwig, you are, with your own carriage this morning." Marie had
risen from the table and was looking out the small window, Mathieu fuss-
ing as she tried to burp him.

Jean-Luc took a last bite of rough bread and drained his coffee. "It's
Gavreau. He plans to send me out on one of his cases. Knows I won't mind
as long as I've got the carriage."

"What's the case?"

"Another mansion. This one belonging to a nobleman who lives . . .
well, used to live, in Place Royale." Jean-Luc collected the remaining papers strewn across the table and stuffed them into his packed *portefeuille*.
"The Jacobins want to use the house."

Marie nodded, arching an eyebrow. "So they've sent the carriage for
you." He was privileged to have the job he had, even if the salary was insufficient. More than half of Paris was starving, and he rode a carriage to
work some days.

His work dealt in cataloging property as it was seized from the wealthy
families, former treasure of the *ancien régime*, now as obsolete as the old
order itself. Daily inventory of seized goods—perhaps it was not as stimu-
lating or significant as the work he had hoped to find; perhaps he was not
playing a tremendously important role in building the new France—at
least not yet. But before they could build the new country, someone had to
figure out the proper way of dismantling the former one. For now, that
was his work, to manage the spoils until the state had decided what to do
with them. As for the former proprietors whose treasures he now cataloged, Jean-Luc rarely heard mention of them, and perhaps he did not
want to.

"What happened to the family?" Marie, as usual, had reached directly
into his mind and plucked out his thoughts with her uncanny insight. She
held his gaze with her earnest brown eyes as the baby began to cry on her
hip.

"Pardon?" Jean-Luc tugged on the hem of his jacket.

"You said you're going out to a nobleman's house in Place Royale to
collect the family's goods. What happened to the family?"

"I'm not sure." He shifted his weight, looking back down toward the papers. "They are already gone, from the sound of it. Prison?" Fortunately, he usually visited the grand houses after the occupants had been dragged from their chambers and thrown in the dungeons at the Conciergerie, La Force, or Les Carmes. He'd heard the rumors—reports from colleagues who had visited the prisons. He suspected that if he were to witness the conditions for himself, his current troubles sleeping would grow much worse. Best not to dwell on such negative thoughts, he reminded himself. Best to remember the noble work they were doing, bringing liberty, equality, and fraternity to a people long subjugated by inept Bourbon despots and their callous aristocrats.

Sighing, he looped his *portefeuille* under his arm and crossed the room toward his wife. "I'm late."

"We could always go . . . back . . . you know." Marie avoided her husband's gaze now, bouncing the baby in an attempt to calm him. "If it's getting to be too much. If it's not what you thought it would be."

Jean-Luc froze, staring at his wife in disbelief; was she really suggesting that they leave Paris? That they give up on *la Révolution*?

"I only mean to say . . ." she stammered, "the troubles sleeping. The work." She waved her free arm around the cramped room. "This place."

He dropped his papers onto the table and stepped toward her, placing his arms around her and the baby. "Marie, please." He was far too tired to have this argument. Not now. Sighing, unsure of what else to say, he spoke softly: "I know you hate this garret."

"It's not just the garret I hate."

"I won't be in this position much longer."

She cocked a dark eyebrow. "That's what you said—"

"But it's true now. I will speak to Gavreau soon. I'll ask for more meaningful work. Work where I can finally offer a contribution and find some higher purpose." His voice sagged as he spoke, and his eyes dropped to the floor. Marie's features softened a little, and she sighed. After a long moment of silence, Jean-Luc inhaled deeply and arched his shoulders back, as if fortifying himself. "Come now, we cannot give up so quickly, Marie. Freedom is a blessing. But before it can be enjoyed, it must be secured, and that battle is not easily won."

The baby's cries grew louder, and Marie turned her focus back to their son. After a pause, she shrugged. "You'd better go. Your carriage is waiting."

Jean-Luc leaned forward and wrapped his arms around her and the baby one more time. She looked up at him; she'd lost the suntanned pink of her cheeks, but she still spoke with the lilting southern accent. Still dressed like a southerner in her white linen, and cooked like one, too, even if she complained she couldn't find a decent jar of saffron in the entire city. He couldn't imagine any of this without her.

"I'll be home for supper." He left the apartment, shutting the door behind him. On the other side of the door, he heard the baby grow calm as his wife cooed, her voice more soothing than music. Jean-Luc looked down and noticed that his hands were empty.

"I forgot something." He opened the door and rushed back into the room. She looked at him, the baby balancing on her hip as she cleared the breakfast dishes. "Your papers," she said, nodding, familiar with his forgetfulness.

"And this, as well." He bounded toward her and planted a kiss on her lips. "Yes, there was no way I could leave without that," he said, his worry and tension slackening as he kissed her again, as he felt her own frame growing less rigid in his arms. She let him kiss her.

"I hate that I'm late, otherwise I would—" His hands traveled to her hips, and he felt the softness of her flesh beneath her starched cotton skirt.

Her hand swatted his. "Get going, you lech, before I go nick that carriage for myself and ride away from this stinking city."

The carriage driver looked up when Jean-Luc emerged onto the sunny street, the man's expression remaining bored as he studied his low-level passenger.

"Citizeness Grocque." Jean-Luc leaned his hat toward his scowling neighbor, greeting the tavern keeper's wife with the title that had recently been mandated by law. Madame Grocque stood hunched over a broom on the doorstep. "Lovely to have a bit of a breeze today, is it not, citizeness?" Sensing he would get no reply, Jean-Luc did not pause as he strode toward the waiting carriage.

"How are the streets this morning?" Jean-Luc asked. The driver, adjusting his leather gloves, pretended not to hear the question.

Jean-Luc noted a lone piece of paper on the cobbled sidewalk, stirred by Madame's angry sweeping. A political pamphlet from the looks of it, one of thousands floating around the city; these days any literate man with strong views and access to a printing press could churn out such political discourse. Nevertheless, some of them proved to be interesting reads, even enlightening, and Jean-Luc leaned over to snatch up the leaflet before opening the carriage door and hopping up the step. He perused the pamphlet's headline: *Citizens of America Rally Around President George Washington for Second Term*. The writer went on to urge his own French countrymen to look to that new nation as an example of a republic that safeguarded the liberty of the people, a place where free citizens with the ballot wielded the power, not brigands and foreign mercenaries. The column was written anonymously, this writer evidently hoping to eschew the glory or notoriety of publication, his screed signed only by the cryptic alias "Citizen Persephone."

Jean-Luc looked up from the pamphlet and out the window as the coach driver raised the whip to spur the horses forward. "Let's avoid La Place. I hate to see . . . well, the crowds . . . too much traffic," Jean-Luc called out. Though it would be treasonous to admit, he had no stomach for the throngs on an execution day, he did everything he could to avoid that blood-soaked square. The driver barely nodded as he directed the horses east, out of Jean-Luc's neighborhood.

Jean-Luc lived among fervent supporters of the Revolution, to be sure, his quarter being one of the last neighborhoods where the students, fishmongers, and prostitutes could afford rent. Perhaps due to all the time he'd spent recently among the confiscated goods of the old nobility, the street urchins who chased after his carriage that morning appeared especially wretched. Glancing out the window, Jean-Luc watched as one little boy in cropped pants and bare feet hoisted himself up alongside the carriage window. Just inches from him, the little boy extended a tiny palm caked in dirt. "Please, monsieur, citizen, spare a *sou* for me mum."

"Off there, you filthy rat!" The driver—eager to expedite his delivery so that he might make his way to the tavern before the execution crowds filed in—brandished his whip, and the child scurried down. As his dreary little frame receded from their moving carriage, Jean-Luc tossed a *sou* in his direction, hoping as he did so that the money would make its way to his mother's palm to buy a loaf rather than a cup of watered-down wine.

The neighborhood improved as they crossed the river to the Right Bank. It was a clear morning in Paris, the sunlight reflecting off the water that lapped the shores of the two small islands: Île Saint-Louis and Île de la Cité. Once over the bridge, the driver followed the quay that hugged the northern bank of the river. They were avoiding La Place. And yet, as the carriage crossed over the Rue Saint-Florentin, Jean-Luc couldn't help but glance down the wide boulevard. There, in the distance, he saw them: brown-clad, dirty figures, men in red caps waving the tricolor flag, women in red caps with their knitting in their laps, as if watching something as mundane as a street play. There were thousands of them. Even after a year in the city, Jean-Luc was still staggered—terrified, if he was admitting the full truth—by the bloodlust of the Parisians.

The glorious tales that had come from Paris to his home in the south had stirred within him an exhilaration and sense of patriotic duty that he had answered—tales that had quickly turned dark and macabre when he beheld the street executions for himself. But the past few weeks had brought rumors of even more sinister events, stories that curdled his blood. Whether or not two thousand prisoners from across the city had been dragged from their cells and torn to pieces in the middle of the night, he could not be sure, but he had to believe that this was just a passing fever. A scourge of bloodletting that would soon be over, replaced by the original ideals of hope and freedom. It was as he had just told Marie: they could not give up on freedom, on the new nation. Not yet.

His law offices were a few blocks north of the Seine and a stone's throw from the hulking carcass of that infamous tower of torment, the Bastille. Indeed, if he needed a reminder of why he was here, Jean-Luc could look to the Bastille for affirmation. For four hundred years that great stone fortress had served as a prison, the physical embodiment of the great and arbitrary power of the *ancien régime* of Bourbon kings. With nothing more than a dreaded royal summons, anyone of common birth, whether guilty of a crime or not, could be accused, seized from his home, and locked away forever. On a hot summer's day three years prior, a massive and well-armed mob had marched from the Saint-Antoine quarter and laid siege to the great fortress. After a ferocious struggle, and with the aid of rebellious National Guard soldiers, the poor men and women of Saint-Antoine eventually succeeded in lowering its drawbridge and seizing the structure. Thus the Revolution had been born out of a desperate struggle, consecrated in the blood of its weary and starved citizens.

Jean-Luc worked in a massive administrative building several streets away. Its long corridors were crowded with legal clerks, bankers, and secretaries—bureaucrats of the new regime, most of them happy simply to have employment, to accept paltry salaries with which they could feed their families and brag of a place in the new government.

It was a busy building, a hive of purposefulness and gossip varying in its degrees of legitimacy. On this morning, however, the front halls were quieter than usual. Nodding a greeting to a pair of guards—"Citizens, good day"—Jean-Luc walked up a wide staircase. On the second floor he clipped quickly down the familiar hallway until he reached the chamber that served as a meeting room for his department.

He paused in the doorway. A small crowd had assembled in the office. Several of the faces were familiar to Jean-Luc, colleagues who worked in adjacent offices. However, there were more than those few in here. From the looks of it, Gavreau, his supervisor, had gathered the entire building for this assembly. Whatever the meeting's purpose, Jean-Luc was late.

"St. Clair!" Gavreau saw him enter and waved him forward. He was addressing the crowd from the front of the office. "Citizen St. Clair, I was just sharing the morning's news with your compatriots."

"What news?" Jean-Luc instantly regretted his response, and how plain he had made it that he had not heard whatever it was that had caused such a stir among his peers. The only thing he had observed so far that morning was that the heat had finally broken and the people of Paris still seemed hungry and angry. The manager, thankfully, didn't note his ignorance but instead continued to address the full room. "As you know, the past three months have seen the people rising up and demanding that their voices be heard with more potency than ever before."

Several men in the office thumped their fists against the desks, grunting their support for Gavreau's assertion. The supervisor ignored the interruptions and continued.

"Every prison in the city is overflowing, and those perfumed dukes and duchesses know, at last, what it means to be hungry."

The crowd muttered and nodded its approval as Jean-Luc shifted his weight, having grown uneasy with rousing talks such as these. He had seen many stirring speeches begin with earnest enthusiasm, only to be overtaken and unleashed as a mob's fury and the thirst for violence.

Gavreau's cheeks flushed red. "Just last month, our fellow patriots stormed the Tuileries Palace, where Louis and Marie-Antoinette—"

"You mean Citizen Capet and the Austrian Whore!" A man whom Jean-Luc didn't recognize interjected with the nicknames that Paris had given to the country's disgraced king and queen.

"Call 'em whatever you want." Gavreau waved a hand. "The point is, as of last month, the Bourbons are done getting fat off our starvation and sacrifice. And they are no longer sitting in the Tuileries Palace, hiding behind their hired Swiss guards, as if *that's* prison enough."

"They're in Le Temple dungeon with the rest of the rats, where they belong," a voice called out. The crowd cheered in response.

Gavreau lifted his arms, attempting to quell the mounting fervor. "Brothers, my fellow citizens, today, for the first time, an assembly of free Frenchmen, endowed with the full power of the people, will sit in Paris. They, like the rebels in America, will draft a new constitution and will begin an era of liberty, equality, and fraternity!"

The room shook now with the sound of yelps and fists landing on the oak desks. Even Jean-Luc, on thinking about this achievement by the French people, could join in the celebrations. *"Vive la liberté!"* he shouted.

Gavreau let them revel in their euphoria a moment, his expression indicating his own deep satisfaction, but when he raised his arms, they went quiet once more, greedy for more news. "It's been a good summer for the people, that is certain enough. Hundreds of our brothers have joined our new government in the National Convention. And thousands fewer of those noble wretches have their heads, thanks to our friend Dr. Joseph-Ignace Guillotin."

Several people in the room laughed and jeered, but Jean-Luc bit his lower lip. His job gave him a front-row viewing to just how many noblemen and women had been toppled, and to think that a severed head corresponded to each of his daily cases made his stomach turn.

"And yet, our Revolution—our very nation—is in danger." Gavreau's face grew somber as the room fell silent. "I told you there was news today, and there is. It seems that all of Europe has taken note of the speed and force of our Revolution. And our neighbors to the east are scared."

Jean-Luc leaned closer; he hadn't heard this news.

"Everything we have fought for could soon be lost, if we don't look to what's happening less than a hundred miles to the east. The enemy is close," Gavreau explained. "The Duke of Brunswick has assembled an alliance of forty thousand Prussians, Austrians, and Hessians and is marching toward our city at this very moment." Gavreau spoke softly, but he no longer competed with any stray voices; the entire room was hushed, all eyes fixed intently forward. "Since we plucked Louis and Marie-Antoinette from their plush palace prison, the Habsburgs and their friends have seen just how serious our Revolution is. And they don't like the look of it. The crowns of Europe are shuddering in fear, and now they've decided to bring their hired swords across our borders."

Jean-Luc felt his chest tighten at the thought of foreign soldiers marching across their land, into their city.

"This foreign duke . . . *Brunswick* . . . has declared, no, he has *vowed*"—Gavreau picked up a pair of glasses from his desk and began to read from a parchment—"to put an end to the anarchy in the interior of France, to check the attacks upon the throne and the altar, to reestablish the legal power, to restore to the king the security and the liberty of which he is now deprived, and to place him in a position to exercise once more the legitimate authority which belongs to him."

At this, the room erupted in outraged groans and roars.

"Let the bastards try!"

"Death to the Habsburg tyrants and their foreign mercenaries!"

"We'll take their crowns next! We'll march right into the Habsburg throne room and show them what we free Frenchmen think of—"

"You're a fool, Pierrot, if you think it will be that easy," Jean-Luc interjected, turning to the loud man beside him, a brash colleague who generally seemed to prefer speaking to listening.

Gavreau nodded at Jean-Luc, allowing him to continue. "What do you think, Citizen St. Clair?"

Jean-Luc paused a moment, clearing his throat. Crossing his arms, he ventured: "Citizen Capet and his Austrian wife were rich and have many powerful friends. The kingdoms of central Europe will not stand idly by as a Habsburg princess is forced to sit behind bars."

"That's right, St. Clair," Gavreau agreed.

"So what is happening?" Jean-Luc asked his supervisor, wondering whether he ought to return home to Marie and take her and the baby from Paris.

Gavreau lifted his chin as if in defiance. "It's come to war."

The room now filled with curses and mutters, boasts and declarations, but the supervisor continued over the din. "Fifty thousand brave French-men stand between us and those promising to wipe out all the liberties we've won these past three years."

Jean-Luc let out a long, slow exhale. Many of those soldiers, he knew, had joined the ranks of the French army only within the past few months or even weeks, as the threat of invasion by the united monarchs of Europe escalated from whispered rumor to bona fide peril. They lacked discipline, training, and, in most cases, proper uniforms. Jean-Luc hoped they might somehow make up for their deficiencies of skill with patriotic fervor and democratic zeal, but he, like everyone else, was unsure.

Gavreau looked straight into Jean-Luc's eyes as he said: "You are all good citizens here. I am honored to work with each and every one of you, and I know we shall all do our part for the republic. If we should hear the tocsins or the bells, it means the enemy stands at our gates. Every man in this city . . . hell, every woman, too . . . will be expected to take up arms and defend our home. We must not forget: it was a band of patriots, women and men alike, who conquered the great Bastille fortress. It was a band of starving mothers and daughters who marched on Versailles and took the Bourbons off their gold piss pots. We will be France's last line of resistance. We will shed every last drop of blood in her defense."

The men offered replies to Gavreau's battle cry with varying degrees of enthusiasm. Jean-Luc considered the possibility in silence. Would he take up arms if the enemy marched on Paris? Against this new force that threat-ened the safety of his family and his nation? Yes, he supposed he would.

Beside him, Pierrot was red-faced and appeared as though he hoped the enemy would make it to the Parisian barriers, so he'd have the occasion to shed his blood. Or perhaps he was simply fuming that Jean-Luc had called him a fool.

Gavreau stuffed his hands into his pockets as he continued. "Right now our thoughts go out to our brothers to the east. Our generals Dumouriez and Kellermann have marched their brave soldiers to meet the enemy near the forests outside Valmy. Very soon or perhaps even this very day, the victory or doom of our Revolution could be decided out in those meadows."

Jean-Luc let the news sink deep into his gut as he glanced out the window. Looking east, he saw the river. Just past the Seine the ancient stone spires of Notre Dame Cathedral jutted skyward. In the distance, past where the walls of Paris ceased and the green began, in the old forest hunting grounds of their disgraced king, his fellow patriots waited. Jean-Luc narrowed his eyes and willed himself to see past the city and into that verdant expanse. He could not tell if it was merely a trick of his imagination, but there, in the distance, he thought he could detect a faint wreath of smoke curling up toward the sky.

2

Bois de Valmy,
France

September 1792

The sun sprinkled through the ancient oaks, casting a dancing shadow over the cool, shady wood. Local rumor held that in this copse, in years of peace and plenty, King Louis XVI had liked to spread his blankets to take his nap and his wine while his men chased the boar, stags, and rabbits that occupied these lands. Later, they would present the spoils of the hunt to their monarch, and he would hoist the dead carcasses over his thick shoulders, boasting to his wife as he rode back into the palace grounds that he'd had another glorious day of hunting.

But on this day, the prey in the forest was not boar, nor stags nor rabbits. These woods were no longer the hunting grounds for royal sport and merriment. Today, men were hunting other men.

It was almost evening when the dragoon scouts returned to the French camp. They flew in, a cloud of riders and hooves churning up dust, their horses exhausted and slicked in a thin coating of sweat. Several dogs barked out a rough volley of greeting as the nearby aides scurried to receive the returning party.

Captain André Valière poked his head through the flap of his tent and looked out over the camp. The soft indigo light of dusk seeped over the area, the last few cooking fires sputtering out after the evening meal, but the postprandial quiet of the coming night had now dissipated. The aides were unsaddling the horses and escorting the returning party into camp.

André strained his ears to hear as the scouts gasped out their reconnaissance.

"Where did you cross the river?" an aide asked one of the riders.

"We crossed at the shallow bend to the northeast, past the crossroads at La Lune. We found one of their horses on the other side." A windswept dragoon officer, his black boots caked in dust from the dry road, handed off his reins as he dismounted and cut a quick line toward one of the central tents.

"Just a horse, no rider?" The aide hurried to keep the scout's pace.

The scout shook his head. "Just the mount. We found their fires still smoking. They left in a hurry."

Another scout was beside them now, panting. "We heard a shout—a Prussian scout, we're guessing. Brunswick knows we're here; we've been seen."

André slipped out of his tent and trailed them from a few steps behind, his interest piqued.

"So they are moving on Paris. Did you exchange any fire?" The aide tried to walk and scribble notes at the same time.

"No, we heard the bastards croaking something in German, so we pissed on their fires and grabbed the mount and came straight back here." The officer who appeared to be in charge took a drink from his canteen and splashed water on his face. "Where is the general?"

"Which one?"

"The commander, you fool. Dumouriez." The officer wiped his face with a dirty hand, blinking several times. He passed the canteen back to one of his scouts and continued, "Or better yet, Kellermann. He at least might have some idea of what is going on here."

"They are both inside the command tent, awaiting your report." The aide turned and led the small group of scouts toward a large tent with a massive, if somewhat tattered, tricolor flag waving from its center post. Two bored-looking soldiers stood at attention outside the entrance. As the scouts approached, the guards crossed their muskets diagonally so the steel of their bayonets clanged together, but they quickly capitulated when the lead scout waved a dismissive hand and walked brusquely past them into the tent. André would have to wait until the evening's briefing to hear the rest.

André sighed now, looking in the direction from which the scouts had arrived. He saw, among the brown warhorses, a lone white Lipizzaner, a Prussian cavalry horse, that whinnied and pawed the ground as if defiant in these new surroundings. André surveyed the rest of the camp. Clustered by the fires closest to the command tents sat men who, like André, were dressed in the white and sky blue of the old Bourbon army; these were the holdovers of the army of the monarchy, the regulars who had been trained when there was a king to fund military campaigns and pay salaries generous enough to draw men from the country's poorest farms and its wealthiest families alike. These men, although their crisp white uniforms still bore the Bourbon fleur-de-lis, had been welcomed into the Revolution and composed well over half of the army's forces. They had sworn allegiance to the new—albeit ever changing—government, and the Revolution needed men with their training and skill. They were respected and revered, if not included in the casual, threadbare fraternity of the revolutionary guardsmen who sat around the campfires a few paces away.

This latter group sat clothed in whatever mismatching attire they had scrounged up from their own scant wardrobes. Most of them had been issued a dark blue coat with bronze buttons upon enlistment, but the remainder of their uniforms seemed to be patchwork and individualized. Some of them had nothing on their feet but dirty soles and cracked toenails. Formed into the ranks of the new National Guard just months earlier, these men walked about in short breeches, prompting their new nickname of *sans-culottes,* "men without long pants." They wore their hair long and unkempt, and cited as heroes the Revolution's up-and-coming leaders, commoners Maximilien Robespierre and Georges Danton. They had left their lives as craftsmen, laborers, and tenant farmers to answer the call of the Revolution. They were anything but professional soldiers.

On the eve of battle, they sat around their fires, passing around lewd sketches of tavern girls and skins of watered-down wine. They played card games and shouted obscenities in stark contrast to the quiet, more stoic regulars nearby. Many of this latter group had faced the formidable Prussian and Austrian lines before, and knew what the sunrise would bring. It was an uneasy alliance, this new French army, and tomorrow would be its first true test.

As André walked back from the command tent to his own, he noticed a rider trotting up from the same direction as the dragoon scouts. He watched as the horseman dismounted, a letter in his hand.

The messenger spotted André and strode toward him, leaving his horse to one of the enlisted aides. "Captain Valière?"

"Yes?" André eyed the messenger and took the note from his outstretched hand. In truth, he was shocked to be receiving any news at all, especially on the eve of a fight. "Thank you."

"Very well, sir." The rider saluted André and returned to his horse. André tore the letter open and read the entirety of its contents in a quick glance. Folding the note back up and tucking it into a pocket of his white coat, he let out a quick grin, muttering to himself: "Remy's here."

"Anything good?" One of his men, a corporal by the name of Gustave Leroux, sat before the fire nearest to André. Leroux had a skin of wine resting precariously on his knee, and judging from the filmy look of his eyes, he had already enjoyed enough of its contents.

"Not enough to arouse your interest, Leroux."

"I don't know about that, sir. Did she send a picture? That might arouse more than just my interest." Corporal Leroux chuckled at his own joke.

André let out a long exhale and scratched the stubble on his neck, stifling the urge to chastise such insubordination. Just years prior a soldier would have been flogged for saying such a thing. But this was a new age— and a new army. Any officer seen to be overbearing or not *démocratique* enough might face a Revolutionary Tribunal or, worse, a mutiny.

Still, Gustave Leroux was the one, André had learned, who had taken to calling him "The Marquis" when André was out of earshot. André couldn't have one of his men regularly calling attention to his noble lineage. The title, though André had renounced it, still constituted an inconvenience, if not an outright danger, these days. André had dropped the "de" that had preceded his last name, the ancient designation of noble lineage, in hopes that the army might overlook his origins. Given the current crisis facing the nation and the need for experienced officers such as he, this was, it seemed, a reasonable hope—but not with one of his men continuously calling him The Marquis.

If Leroux survived tomorrow's bloodletting, André decided, he would deal with him then. He tapped the pocket of his coat and answered: "If she did, it's for my eyes only. The privilege of rank, Leroux." And with that,

André leaned down and swiped the skin of wine from the man's knee. "You'd better be sober by tomorrow, soldier. If you're unable to perform your duties, that's malingering, and you'll be put on a charge as a deserter. And you know what happens to you then."

A distant three-note blast from a trumpet signaled the hour for the commanders' briefing, so André emptied the confiscated wine and crossed camp toward headquarters.

As he walked off, André overheard the exchange at the campfire behind him, Leroux's defiant grunt as he said: "If that rich ponce leads us to slaughter tomorrow, if it takes my last breath, I'll put a bullet in him myself."

"Shut your mouth, Leroux." One of André's sergeants, a steady man by the name of Digne, interjected. "You just concern yourself with your own duties. We've enough work to do with those Rhineland bastards across the way, without bothering ourselves and fighting one another. Got it?"

The heat around Paris had broken, and the woods of Valmy were cooler than the city, but still the air inside the tent felt warm and stale. Upon entering, André saw what he had suspected: that he was one of the most junior officers in the gathering. He had been surprised to receive an order this afternoon expressing General Kellermann's request that he be in attendance.

"André de Valière." Another young captain by the name of François LaSalle appeared by his side, a familiar face from the days of the former regime. Like André, LaSalle was dressed in a crisp white coat with sky-blue piping and lapels. Silver buttons traced a smart line down the front of his coat, and he held his tricornered hat in his left hand, revealing black hair that had been pulled back in a ponytail like André's.

"LaSalle, how are you?" André gave his friend a firm handshake. And then, leaning closer, he whispered: "It's just 'Valière' these days."

LaSalle nodded, understanding. "Well then, *Valière*, when did you get out here?"

"We marched in this morning," André answered. "And you?"

"Just before midday," LaSalle replied. He gestured toward the front of the tent. "Did you see them ride into camp?"

"The scouts?" André nodded. "Yes. I caught a bit of their report, too. Seems they've located the Prussians nearby."

"Any word from your brother?" LaSalle asked.

"As a matter of fact, yes, I just received a letter from him. He's here in camp, somewhere."

"Where is General Kellermann?" LaSalle glanced around the tent, and André did the same. At the front stood an oversized desk covered in papers—division rosters, equipment reports, orders from Paris. Two maps hung at the front of the tent, their surfaces large and marked with ink. The larger map was of eastern France out to the Rhine, where they were currently encamped. The other one included all of the surrounding nations and imperial borders, which were shaded in a light reddish color.

The crowd assembling in the tent that evening was disproportionately dressed in white and sky blue; the few revolutionary officers of the National Guard who were present stood together on the fringes of conversations, tugging on their mustaches, casting skeptical glances toward their stiff-postured colleagues. Perhaps after tomorrow, André mused, once they had all faced the crucible of combat together, the two branches of the French army would be slightly more trustful of each other.

The cavalry scouts in their green coats stood laughing with one another in the front corner as though they had just returned from a successful hunt in the Bois de Boulogne. Their scout force had done its duty that afternoon, and they felt buoyed by their accomplishment and the fact that they had been first to get a sight of the enemy. Just behind them stood members of the artillery forces—a disproportionately large portion of the crowd, André thought, and he made a note to find Remy after the briefing. In the center stood the officers and noncommissioned officers of the French infantry, all of whom appeared more on edge than their artillery comrades. These were the men whose soldiers would stand face-to-face with the Prussian, Austrian, and Hessian enemy tomorrow. This was André's group, and the taut lines on their faces seemed to reflet the nerves that he himself was feeling.

All chatter ceased the moment the tent flap lifted and the small frame of General Charles Dumouriez appeared, flanked by the worn but hand-some face of General Christophe Kellermann and a third man, one whom André did not recognize.

"Who's that?" André whispered as the commanders cut a line to the front of the tent.

"The third one? That's Nicolai Murat, the Comte de Custine. He's a brigadier general," LaSalle answered. André nodded, wondering from where LaSalle always gleaned his gossip and wondering why the name—Murat—tugged on some distant corner of his memory. *Murat.* Had he heard the name before?

But André's musings were interrupted as General Kellermann approached, grinning and slapping the shoulders of his surrounding men. As he neared the place where André stood, he nodded and offered a brief smile. "Captain, welcome to camp."

André was momentarily taken aback that the general recognized him as a newcomer. He managed to sputter out, "General Kellermann, sir," before the commander continued on.

"He's good," LaSalle remarked under his breath. "Must know every man in this tent."

While Kellermann continued his entry, Dumouriez walked in front of him, a mask of stoic calm spread across his features. He was short, but his heavily starched uniform and alert gaze spoke of a power not in any way diminished by his small physical stature.

The third commander, Brigadier General Murat, followed behind Kellermann and Dumouriez. His was an unrecognizable face, even if the name rang somehow vaguely familiar to André. The man's black hair was pulled back into a tight ponytail, offering a full view of a broad forehead and a heavily lidded gaze. His eyes were small, two hard marbles the color of cold seawater, but they burned with a formidable intensity. He was tall, taller than Kellermann and certainly taller than Dumouriez, and he used this height to peer down at the men as he passed. When he reached the front of the tent, he turned and caught André watching him. André swallowed uneasily as Murat's gray eyes held his own for a moment, the hint of a derisive smile pulling on his superior's lips.

"Soldiers and citizens of France." Charles Dumouriez now stood at the front of the tent before the two oversized maps. "Welcome to the Valmy wilderness." He gave a quick jerk of his chin, which sent the fringe of his gold epaulets quivering on his shoulders. "We meet here, finally, on the eve of battle."

The men around André fidgeted; the tent was abuzz with a palpable thrum of nerves and excitement.

Looking to his right, Dumouriez nodded to his colleague. "General Kellermann, you may begin the briefing."

"Yes, sir." Kellermann stood up straight from where he had been leaning on the desk, clapping his hands together once. His chestnut hair was streaked with the first hints of gray, pulled back in a loose ponytail. Wide-set blue eyes shone bright in a narrow face lined with experience and concentration, if not a particularly advanced age. While the threat of the next day's battle had seemed to settle like a heavy cloak of anxiety over so many other faces around the tent, Kellermann's features were alight.

"Gentlemen," Kellermann said, raising his arms in a gesture of almost paternal greeting. "It is good to see you all here with us. As you've no doubt heard by now, our scouts have just returned to camp. Seems they've found the enemy."

LaSalle and André shared a glance as Kellermann continued. "As we suspected, we are not alone in these woods. The Duke of Brunswick and his Prussian legions have arrived."

A series of whispers fluttered through the tent before Kellermann lifted a hand and the side talk evaporated. "Up until now, our soldiers have shown little but fear and panic in the face of our enemies. Untrained and undisciplined soldiers have broken at the mere sight of the Prussian battle line, often without even firing a shot. Gentlemen"—Kellermann paused, clearing his throat, his gaze suddenly stern—"that ends tomorrow."

André and the rest of the men listened attentively while Kellermann conducted the briefing. As André had overheard earlier, the Prussians were, in fact, encamped just a few miles to the west; the French armies had been caught behind the Prussians, so that nothing stood in between the Duke of Brunswick and Paris. The French would make their move the next day, hoping to surround the alliance forces and cut them off from their supply lines and reinforcements before they could march on the capital and strangle the Revolution.

The day's fight would begin early, shortly after dawn, with a heavy artillery barrage. As André had suspected, the French commanders had assembled more cannons and gunpowder than they had in any of the previous battles against the Austrians and Prussians. Tomorrow's battle, Kellermann confided to his gathered officers, was the French army's last chance to prevent an enemy march on Paris.

"Tomorrow's battle will be decisive for our Revolution," Kellermann told them. "If the Prussians take our capital, there is little doubt that they will put Louis back on the throne."

Dumouriez stood by quietly, nodding. Kellermann paused before looking up, catching the eyes of his men as he concluded his remarks. "Not only will every man in this tent be arrested or hanged, but all of the rights and freedoms newly won for the people will vanish as quickly as they have come. It is no exaggeration when I tell you men that not only your lives, but the very existence of the Revolution and the nation, hang in the balance."

When Kellermann had finished his report, a tense silence hung over the tent. André looked around, seeing the stony rumination on the faces of the guardsmen and regulars alike. Beside him, LaSalle thrummed his fingertips against his chin in thought. At the front of the tent, Dumouriez cleared his throat.

"Thank you, Christophe," Dumouriez said with a nod, no expression or sentiment apparent on his face. Then, turning to the third officer, he asked, "General Murat, do you have anything you wish to add?"

Murat, who had been absentmindedly stroking the tip of his tight, dark mustache throughout the entirety of Kellermann's briefing, now unfolded his arms and turned to the bluecoats in the room. When he spoke for the first time, André heard a deep, confident baritone of a voice, perfectly audible throughout the tent.

"We are fighting against an army of hired guns, mercenaries, and royalist butchers. They may have the better training, but we have justice on our side." Murat spoke directly to the ragged guardsmen now, those rough militia members who would face their first action tomorrow. "I have no doubt that our men have the heart."

These blue-coated volunteers nodded now, proud of this individual attention from a brigadier general.

And now Murat cracked a smile, his tone lightening. "Soldiers with wet uniforms, dirt on their faces, empty stomachs, fire in their hearts, and pricks longer than their muskets will relish the sight of an overconfident enemy." The pent-up tension inside the tent broke with a burst of deep belly laughter. General Murat held up his hand for silence, casting his glance across the assembled group, then turned his attention back to Kellermann and Dumouriez. "We are ready to do our duty. Tomorrow our Revolution will spread from the French nation and its people's army, and be heard across the civilized world."

"We will do our duty, Citizen Murat!" called out one of the guardsmen standing toward the front, his tone cocksure.

Murat nodded. "Good. And I don't care how often you want to unload your other guns once we beat the Prussians back over the Rhine. . . . you all know what they say about those German women." Another burst of laughter echoed throughout the tent, even louder than the first.

André leaned in to LaSalle. "He seems optimistic."

"It's an act," LaSalle reasoned. "Just trying to bolster their spirits. He knows that, in spite of their big talk, many of the new lads are trembling in their tattered boots." True, André thought, and perhaps a boost of confidence to wavering hearts was not a bad thing.

General Kellermann allowed the chatter to continue for a moment before he raised his hands to silence the side conversation and laughter. "Let us take things one at a time, gentlemen. Our enemy has yet to be opposed, much less defeated. Tomorrow's task will not be an easy one."

"Simply trying to lighten the mood, Christophe," Murat said, his wry smile dissipating. "I do not doubt the commitment of our brave volunteers for even a second."

"Nor do I, General Murat," Kellermann said, looking out across the assembly to the leaders of both groups. "But it is also important that we know the stakes. There is no shame in feeling apprehension or even fear, but as leaders, we must all do everything we can to master it, never revealing it to our men. Some of them are surely nervous. Make sure they get to sleep. And try, as best you can, to keep them away from the wine."

As Kellermann wrapped up the meeting, André caught Murat's steely eyes once more. The general had been smiling, still pleased by his own bawdy joke and the confidence some of the men clearly had in him, but as he met André's gaze, the cheer fled from his face. André looked away and turned to follow the other officers filing out of the tent. A tremor of instinctual unease passed over him, a shadow of some inexplicable dread.

Outside once more, he breathed in the cool evening air. All was silent except for a few nervous mutters as the officers filed out. André was preparing to return to his men when he heard his name called out.

"Valière!"

André turned and his posture instinctively straightened when he saw General Kellermann approaching. "Sir, General Kellermann." André saluted.

"Good to finally meet you, Captain."

"And you, sir." Of course André had seen the general many times, having served in his legion for close to a year. But he had never expected the general to recognize him in return, much less know his name.

"Dumouriez tells me you are young and unblooded, but have shown promise. We are lucky to have you among our number."

André fought against the flush that threatened to betray his surprise and pleasure; that two generals had ever considered him, much less had a conversation about him, was a flattering thought. "Thank you, sir."

"You served before . . . under the old . . ." Kellermann paused, his face just briefly losing its signature composure and confidence. "You are a graduate of the military college at Brienne, are you not?"

"I am, sir." André stood up a little straighter, surprised at the general's knowledge of his background. "I completed my training there four years ago."

"I am a Brienne man myself. Long live the golden lion." Kellermann offered the hint of a measured smile. "You are from the north, yes?"

"Yes, General, my family comes from Normandy." André left it at that. Kellermann most likely already knew his troubling secret: that André came from landed aristocracy on the northern coast, his lands and title dating back to even before the expulsion of the British from Normandy. But there was no need to advertise the guilt of his birthright. And, besides, Kellermann himself was in a similar situation, having renounced his own lands and title as le Comte de Kellermann at the outbreak of the Revolution.

"I heard of your . . . misfortune," Kellermann continued in a low, barely audible voice. "You know, I had the honor of knowing your father."

Despite his efforts to stay impassive, André's mouth now fell open. "You . . . you knew him, sir?"

Kellermann nodded. "Also at Brienne. He was several years ahead of me, but I admired him greatly. If you don't mind my saying so, he was a good man."

André blinked, struggling as the familiar flood of pain and sadness and a strange new feeling, perhaps guilt, ripped through his insides, searing him like a cruel, hot iron. He couldn't help but see the image of his father's face the last time he had beheld it. The night that his father had sent their mother away to England, the night he had begged his sons to stay in the army and change their last name, hoping that those two actions might be enough to save his boys from his own damned fate.

"But I've upset you with such remembrances. Of course I have. I am sorry," Kellermann said, his tone softening.

"No need to apologize, sir." Taking in a slow, measured breath, André tried to steady his shaky voice as he answered: "Thank you, sir."

"He was a good man," Kellermann said after a pause, repeating himself. "He was."

"But there were two of you, two sons, if I'm not mistaken?"

André nodded. "Yes. My brother, Remy. I've just heard from him. He's here in the artillery encampment with the Thirteenth Regiment. In fact, I thought that I might go and seek him out before final bugle call."

Kellermann nodded, his light eyes showing the hint of sympathy. "You go and do that. And know that we are happy to have two of de . . . Valière's boys in our company. We'll have great need of your brother and his artillery comrades tomorrow. Their guns might make all the difference."

André nodded, relieved to turn back to the topic of battle, easy by comparison.

"So this is to be your first taste of combat, Captain Valière?" Kellermann gestured for André to follow, and the two of them walked away from the command tent. The camp was now aglow with nothing but the light of a thin slice of moon and a dozen campfires, eerily silent but for a few soft murmurs of humorless conversation. A horse whinnied from the direction of the cavalry bivouac.

André paused, suddenly self-conscious as he answered: "Yes, sir. I've marched and drilled for years, of course. But not yet in sight of the enemy."

"I'm sure you are impeccably prepared, Captain Valière." Kellermann looked at André, pausing for a moment. His eyes glassed over as if he were lost in a daydream, and for a moment André was not sure if he should fill the silence with a comment. The general stirred suddenly and leaned forward. "Just remember, Captain, when your imagination begins to fill with visions of horror and your own impending death, your spirit must master it and be the stronger of the two. Otherwise fear will creep in and take root, and you will be unable to act or think. Remember your drills, and tell yourself that victory lies in front of you."

"Yes, sir," André said.

With a heartening grin, Kellermann took André by the hand and said, "Good luck. And don't feel too ashamed if you piss yourself. Though most would never admit it, many who face their first baptism by fire also face baptism by their own piss." With that, the general turned and stepped into the blackness of the new night, leaving André alone.

There he stood for several moments, his mind digesting the conversation he'd just had. That the general had sought *him* out, had known of his father and his family. If only Remy could have been here to witness it; but his younger brother would never believe that it had taken place.

"Valière, I believe it was?" A deep voice startled André, pulling him from his reverie. A tall figure with a dark ponytail approached, stepping out of the dim shadows.

"General Murat." André clipped his heels together and saluted. He made an effort to contain his surprise at having the opportunity to speak personally not only to General Kellermann, but now to Murat as well.

The general returned his salute, and André's stance eased slightly. "I heard some of your conversation with Kellermann. So, you're the son of the Good Man de Valière?"

André winced involuntarily, lowering his eyes; so he was not yet finished with this topic. "I was, sir. He no longer lives." André now resisted the urge to mention that he had renounced his title and embraced the cause of the Revolution. Instead, he let Murat continue.

"Kellermann spoke kindly of your old man. But, then again, Kellermann speaks kindly of mostly everyone. One never knows precisely what is true and what is, well, the charm of his overly generous character."

André shifted on his feet, but kept silent.

"Did I overhear that you've yet to meet the enemy in combat, Captain Valière?"

"That is correct, sir."

Murat exhaled through his teeth, creating a high-pitched whistle. "Take care not to let the songs and poetry beguile you—these men march and sing the 'Marseillaise' with admirable spirit, and yet I wonder, have they seen what a volley of canister shot can do to a man? Battle is not glamorous, nor is it beautiful."

André nodded, pressing his lips together. He guessed—he *hoped*—that the quicker he let this general say his piece, the sooner they might part ways and he might go seek out his brother.

"I recall the first engagement I was in. Near Warburg." Murat's voice deepened. When he spoke next, he looked André straight in the eyes, the gray of his irises catching a glint of moonlight. "A twelve-pound cannonball ripped through the belly of my horse and I slid between the two halves of his body. I was covered in horse guts and shit."

André made an instinctive noise, a grunting sound, and Murat looked at him appraisingly. From under his thin mustache, the general's lips curled upward into a sly, joyless smile. Murat continued. "But then it got even worse. My battalion's commanding officer had had his brains shot out and I was put in charge of three hundred men attacking a Hanoverian battery."

André swallowed hard, trying to maintain a mask of cool composure. Murat's dark eyebrows arched upward now as he leaned closer to André. "The soldiers—they may be simple men, but they have an instinct. They can sense fear. And no man reeks of fear more than the young, untried officer who has never stood before the enemy."

André threw his shoulders back, looking into the cold seawater of Murat's eyes. "Well, sir, I will try to show otherwise."

Murat studied André's features a moment, pausing awhile before he spoke. "Let's hope so," he said eventually, flashing that same smirk he'd shown during the briefing. "Well, get some rest, Captain. Who knows how trying tomorrow shall be."

"Yes, sir." André saluted as Murat turned.

Walking away, the commander paused, glancing once more over his shoulder. "Oh, and, Captain?"

"Sir?"

"Don't piss yourself tomorrow."

André nodded, saluting one final time before turning in the opposite direction of the general. Once he was certain that enough distance and darkness spread between them, André kicked the dirt at his feet. Clenching his jaw, he breathed through his nose and growled. "Piss myself!" André was so jarred by the exchange, by his superior's seemingly inexplicable hostility, that he didn't even see the figure approaching until he'd stumbled into him.

"Mind your step, eh? Clumsy bastard." The darkness obstructed the face of the man throwing the insult but not the voice. André jolted at the slander, his entire body tensing. The figure had turned his back and was walking away, but André couldn't allow such insubordination. "Soldier!" André bellowed. "Stand at attention. Do you realize you've just insulted an officer?"

He strode toward the man, who now stood still. André was close enough that his eyes lit on the features of his assailant. A flash of recognition hit him and André was unable to prevent a stunned laugh from tripping out. "Remy, you stupid, insubordinate buffoon!" He lifted a hand and gave his brother a playful slap on the cheek. As he recovered from the blow, recognition dawned on the other man's face, and Remy Valière lunged at his brother, pulling him into a hug that quickly turned into a scuffle, as the two brothers wrestled each other to the ground.

André slid from his younger brother's arms; Remy may have been the more handsome of the two, but André had always been the superior wrestler. Within several seconds he had Remy in a chokehold, and he held him there for a moment, squeezing tightly enough so as to hold Remy captive but not choke him. "You insulted a captain, Remy. Do you know what I could do to you?"

"I don't know, sir. You're about as new to the captain's uniform as they come. What *could* you do?"

André released his brother and Remy stood up, smiling as he looked at his older brother.

"Won't be so inexperienced after tomorrow," André said, patting down his coat, a tinge of defensiveness in his voice. "We'll all be a lot more experienced this time tomorrow."

"And a lot less sober by tomorrow night," Remy replied.

"If we're still alive, that is." André looked at his brother. Although slightly shorter than André, he cut a handsome figure in his uniform. He was ever popular with the ladies; even their mother had favored Remy, André had long ago admitted to himself. Remy shared their mother's jovial personality and good looks while André resembled their more serious father in temperament and appearance. Though his brother's hair was a light golden color, André's hair was a light brown. Remy's eyes were a clear blue while André had inherited their father's hazel.

"Remy, I'm serious."

"You're always serious."

"Remy, you can't walk around camp speaking the way you just did. If you'd addressed any other officer with such language you'd get twenty lashes. Or worse, thrown into a cell back in Paris."

"Don't fret, big brother, I knew it was you. Who else would walk around with such a brooding expression, deep in his own worries?"

André sighed, supposing his brother was right. He had been lost in thought following his two unusual conversations with Kellermann and Murat.

"Have you heard from Mother?" Remy changed the topic, his face now stripped of its usual carefree expression.

"No. Have you?"

Remy shook his head, sighing. "Not in several months. She was still safe in London when last I heard. Why do you suppose she has stopped writing?"

André lowered his eyes, picking at a piece of dirt on his white uniform. It *was* odd, he knew, to have no word from their mother. Even in times of such upheaval, he believed that his mother would be trying frantically to write to her boys. And yet, nothing. No letters for months.

"It's better for her that way," André declared, a conjured tone of nonchalance in his voice. "She's safe in London, waiting for things to settle down here." Better, as well, for her not to know that her two sons were marching into battle tomorrow, but he didn't add that.

"*If* things ever settle down here. Say, did you get my letter, big brother?"

"I did, and I was on my way to come find you. Where are you camped?"

"I'm with the main battery across this field, up by the western ridge line. You should see it, André. It must be the largest assembly of cannons this country's seen since Joan of Arc."

"That's good. From the sounds of it, we'll need it."

"Yes, what have you heard?" Remy asked, crossing his arms.

"I was just at the briefing with General Kellermann, Dumouriez, and the others. The Prussians are waiting for us to the west."

"To the west? Don't they realize that gives them a clear path to Paris?"

"Seems they want to face us first, to ensure their supply lines are secured before they march on our capital."

"Look at you, getting all high and mighty with generals' reports." Remy smirked, punching his brother playfully on the shoulder. "My brother, attending briefings with General Kellermann himself."

"By the way," André said, shrugging off Remy's punches, "have you ever heard of a General Murat?"

"Nicolai Murat?" Remy nodded. "Of course I have."

André frowned. "Who is he?"

"A hero." Remy cocked his head. "General Mustache, the men call him."

"I may attend the briefings, but you always knew how to find the gossip," André replied. "What's his background?"

Remy shrugged his shoulders. "Killed lots of Brits over in America. He's a count, but no one hates the nobility more than he does."

"How does that make sense?"

Remy shrugged again. "Does anything make sense these days? These are not exactly days of reason."

André absorbed his brother's reply, thinking back to the tent, to his superior's ink-black mustache, his thin, pinched lips, and the harsh, cold stare he had given him.

"He's quite popular among these national guardsmen and the revolutionaries," Remy continued. "Sort of seen as one of them. Dirty humor, too, from what I've heard." Remy flashed a smile.

André smirked. "I did see that."

A bugle call sounded across camp, a signal to put out the fires and bed down, and the men began to settle onto piles of blankets and pallets.

"I better get back over to the artillery billets before I get lost and end up wandering into the Prussian camp," Remy said, replacing his tricorn cap on his head.

"Indeed. Will you be all right to find your way?"

"I think," Remy said. "If you hear a gunshot and some German cursing, you'll know I've stumbled in the wrong direction."

"I'm more worried about you stumbling away to go find the nearest tavern."

"A tavern? Me?" Remy gasped, his voice tinged with mock indignation. "I'd never dream of stepping foot in a tavern the night before battle."

"Good."

"It'll be only the brothel for me tonight."

André let out a short, reluctant laugh, before his features became serious. Putting a hand on his younger brother's shoulder, he spoke in a low tone. "God be with you tomorrow, Remy." Pausing, he tried to steady his voice. Now was not the time to say what he truly wanted to say: *you are all I have left in this world.* Instead, he cleared his throat and said, toneless, "You stay safe."

Remy threw his head back, his features defiant. "Those Prussian dukes appreciate beauty; they'd never kill someone as lovely as me. You, on the other hand, André, might be in trouble."

André laughed in spite of himself. "Just promise me you'll take care." And then, leaning close, he whispered to his younger brother: "And for the love of God, aim true with those big guns."

"We will. Our battery is front and center; can't miss," Remy said, slapping his brother on the back. "Truth be told, tomorrow our guns will unleash hell on earth. The poor bastards don't know what's coming."

"Just be safe, Remy."

"You, too, big brother."

September 1792

Jean-Luc St. Clair looked at the woman seated across from him, hoping that she might soon stop weeping.

"You don't understand, Monsieur . . . *Citizen* St. Clair," she stammered, causing the toddler in her lap to fuss. "Before you, ten lawyers turned me and the little ones down. Flat rejected us."

"Please, Citizeness Poitier." Jean-Luc reached across his desk and offered his handkerchief.

"Thank you, sir." The woman took the cloth in her hands and began to dab the tears that slid down her dirty cheeks, forging lines like a river running through tracts of dirt.

Giving her a moment to collect herself, Jean-Luc feigned a sudden interest in sorting the papers on his desk. After a pause, he looked up and said, "Citizeness Poitier, I am happy to be of service to you and your children. And I have every faith that, together, we shall see justice done."

"Oh, monsieur." The widow looked as if she might recommence weeping.

"If you please, citizeness." Jean-Luc took up his quill, dipping it in the inkwell. His voice remained strictly professional. "Would you be so kind as to further acquaint me with the specifics of your case?"

As the Widow Poitier blew her nose into his handkerchief, Jean-Luc avoided the gaze of Gavreau from across the room. "Perhaps, citizeness, I might begin with collecting some facts about your family?"

"All right." She nodded, resting her chin on the top of her child's bare head.

"You have how many children?"

"Six that are living. Three buried. Like . . . like their father." She raised the kerchief once more, sobs racking her body.

"I am sorry to hear that." Jean-Luc paused his writing, allowing the widow to dab her eyes. "And if you are able to discuss it, citizeness, the death of your husband occurred when?"

"Poor Ole Jacques, he's been in the ground three years. Died as I was carrying this one in my belly, right before the storming of that bloody fortress. Oh, I keep thinking, if only he could 'ave held on for a few more months. . . ." And now the widow buried her face in the wet handkerchief, hugging her toddler closer to her bosom.

Jean-Luc fidgeted in his seat, still avoiding his supervisor's stare from across the crowded office. He pressed on. "I do regret that this interview causes so many terrible remembrances, Citizeness Poitier. But the sooner I collect the facts, the sooner I may begin the work of getting you and the children back in your rightful home."

Citizeness Poitier nodded, nibbling on a dirty fingernail as she looked up at her lawyer. "And haven't we waited right long enough, sir?"

Jean-Luc reached behind him and pushed the nearby window ajar, allowing in the hint of a breeze. "If you could, citizeness, please be so kind as to take me through the circumstances of your husband's death, and the subsequent removal of you and your children from your home."

The widow lifted her shoulders, as if fortifying herself to recall those odious events. When she spoke, her words were marked with the accent of the working class, but she gave her testimony in a direct and authoritative manner.

"Jacques and my two eldest boys worked the land of the Marquis de Montnoir. My Jacques was a tenant farmer for the lord, like his father 'fore him. We had a cottage on our bit of land. It were nothing fancy-like, but it were ours. Had been in my husband's family for ages and ages."

Jean-Luc scribbled furiously as he transcribed the interview. "Go on, please, madame. I mean, citizeness."

"One day three years ago, my eldest boy comes running through the door, screamin' like he seen the ghost of St. Paul resurrected. He's hollerin' 'bout Pa being trampled. So, not having the faintest idea of what he was goin' on about, I handed my babies over to one of my daughters and I took off down the fields. I couldn't run awful fast, you see, because I was pregnant with this one 'ere." The widow gestured at the little child squirming in her lap. "But when I get there, I find my Ole Jacques . . ." Now the widow paused, bringing the handkerchief once more to her eyes. "There he lay, flat on his back on the ground, dead from a horse's hoof to the heart." The widow paused, making a sign of the cross. Jean-Luc did not find it necessary to tell her that such Catholic gestures were now very dangerous.

"Citizeness, I am so sorry to hear it." Jean-Luc sighed, his voice quiet. "But how did it happen?"

"My boys saw it happen, not me. They been down the fields, the three of 'em. It was April, so they had just set about with the sowing. Down from the house in a great hurry come the marquis and a number of his lackeys. The marquis were always riding by, snooping about on his way to the hunt or into town, so my Jacques don't think much on it, and he tell the boys to keep working. Strong lads they were. But then the marquis halted his horse right before them and started bothering my Jacques, going on about rent, claiming we was late on our payments. That was a bald-faced lie, you see. My Jacques never missed a payment in his life. We was honest folk who paid our dues, and the marquis knew it!"

Jean-Luc nodded slowly. "Understood. Please continue—what happened next?"

"So, my husband gets to defending himself before the marquis and his ruffians. He weren't one for getting harassed by a good-for-nothing nobleman who toys with his tenant farmers for sport. So, the way my sons tell it, the marquis gets to shouting, and so my husband starts shouting back. Only defending hisself, mind you. Next thing they knew, the marquis has his whip flying, begins beating my husband and my husband's poor farm horse. My sons tried to stop the seigneur, but his guards held 'em back." The widow again paused, collecting herself.

"The marquis must have hit the farm horse one too many times, because next thing they know, the old cob is rising up, hooves in the air like he's just been visited by the devil himself. Pretty close to the devil, that marquis, if you ask me. My husband tried to calm the beast, before he took off across the fields and caused some real trouble for him. But you see . . . when the horse landed . . ." Her voice trailed off. Jean-Luc gave her a moment, but he needed to hear it, for the legal record.

"The horse trampled your husband, Citizeness Poitier?"

"Aye." The woman nodded, her voice feeble as Jean-Luc recorded the exchange.

After a pause, the widow looked up, her eyes steeped with moisture but fierce, as if inflamed by a growing thirst for vengeance. "But you see, the whole business were made up—the charges that we was late on payments."

"Yes, you mentioned that your husband had never been late on his payments. Can you please explain that matter a bit further? Why do you believe that the Marquis de Montnoir would have leveled those false charges against your husband?"

"I know exactly why he done it." She nodded. "The Marquis de Montnoir were a cruel man by nature. Always had been, to hear my husband tell it. But his meanness aside, the lord was angry at us that spring season. Ask anyone on the land; he had it out for my poor husband."

"Why would the Marquis de Montnoir have targeted your husband in particular, Citizeness Poitier?"

"My husband had married our eldest girl, Sylvie, off to her sweethcart without telling the marquis. Did it while the marquis had been away the previous winter. You see"—and now she leaned close, making sure that none of the other clerks in the room might hear what she had to tell—"we often heard rumors. Nasty, filthy rumors."

Jean-Luc's pulse quickened. "Rumors of what sort?"

"We'd heard from more than one tenant farmer that the marquis claimed the *Droit de Seigneur*." She paused, her eyes full of meaning, and Jean-Luc realized in that moment that she was not an unintelligent woman. Unsophisticated, to be sure. But this simple woman had known life and the world in a way that undoubtedly made her more accustomed to cruelty and hardship than he, or anyone else in this office, was. "You know, Citizen St. Clair, about the 'Lord's Right'?"

Jean-Luc lowered his eyes, nodding. He knew of the ancient tradition of *Droit de Seigneur*. But he had always believed it to be an antiquated legend, a horror story told by those who despised the noble classes and sought justification for the recent bloodletting. He had never imagined that it was still practiced so recently, and certainly not this close to Paris.

"Well, my Jacques weren't going to let the Marquis de Montnoir defrock his own daughter. He was a lecherous man, he was, always tormenting the farmers' daughters, and certainly he took no pleasure from that cold fish of a wife. But my Jacques wouldn't stand for it. So he married Sylvie off and never told His Lordship." Now the Widow Poitier pressed her forefinger onto the desk between them. "So, you can reckon how roiled Seigneur was when he found out he'd been denied Sylvie's wedding night."

Jean-Luc lowered his quill, his mouth suddenly dry like starched cloth. "Citizeness Poitier, I think I shall go fetch us some water. Can I bring you some?"

"I would not turn down a spot of wine," the woman answered, shrugging her shoulders. Jean-Luc nodded and rose to fetch them their drinks. When he returned, he also carried with him the latest rolls of prison records.

Offering the widow her cup of wine, he placed the book between them and opened it. "So, you believe that the Marquis de Montnoir is recently removed from his lands?"

"That's what I heard. 'Course, he ran us out of our cottage the day Ole Jacques died. We've been drifting about, living off the mercy of relatives whenever we can. But there are just too many mouths to feed, you see. We don't want to scrounge off the charity of others. My sons, and my daughters, too, we just wish to work for someone who would have us. To make an honest living, that's all. And we was hoping, now that His Lordship is no longer haunting those lands, that we might have the good lord's blessing of returning to our rightful home."

"I see here, from the prison intake records, that you are correct, Citizeness Poitier. The Marquis de Montnoir has been transferred to the prison at La Force. It says here that his home and lands are now in the possession of the Republic."

"So what does that mean?"

"It means that the lands and château once owned by the Montnoir family are now the property of the French people."

"Well, does that mean they will let us back into our home?" The widow's brow crumpled in childlike hope. Jean-Luc felt a swell of anger at the fact that such a woman and her children had been so unjustly treated.

"To be honest with you, citizeness, I'm not certain," Jean-Luc answered, slamming the book shut. "But I intend to do everything I can to get you home."

The widow sighed. "You know, Citizen St. Clair, our Revolution has allowed for a strange wind to shake the trees, if you take my meaning. Oh, if Ole Jacques could imagine this. A lawyer, giving the boot to a seigneur and his rotten family and making way for common folk like us to return." The old woman took a small sip of wine, offering Jean-Luc a timid smile.

Jean-Luc's eyes narrowed as he looked at the woman across from him, her words uncharacteristically sage. "Well, it is the purpose of our Revolution, citizeness, to bring the sacred ideals of liberty, equality, and brotherhood to this land. And I do believe your family has every right to move back into your home." He paused, folding his hands before him on his desk. "But, if you don't mind my asking, madame, er, citizeness. How is it that you came to know of me and seek out my services?"

The widow nodded. "I stood outside this building for days, knowing it to be full of lawyers. I asked—begged—so many men, fancy types in wigs, to take my case up. They all shrugged me off. Said, 'The only man in this building who'll take on a charity case is that Jean-Luc St. Clair.' And so I found you. Knew you were my only chance for justice."

Jean-Luc nodded, lowering his eyes, noting silently that he'd have to tell his fellow lawyers to stop sending such cases his way. And yet he felt oddly satisfied as well, hearing that his colleagues believed him willing to fight for the lowest citizens. Marie would be proud, if he could find a way to relate this to her.

"Well, here we are," he said, looking back to his new client. "I trust that, with justice on our side, we have a duty to fight."

"God bless you, kind sir, for trying. And God willing, you shall succeed. Oh, now, I know we aren't supposed to pray to God anymore and do away with the old superstitions . . . trust only in reason and the law, and all that. But old habits, you know. In any event, you've saved us. Given me hope once more in this cruel country. And who knows . . ." She rose from her chair, her stout frame appearing rusty with age and hardship. "Perhaps someday I shall be able to save you."

4

Bois de Valmy,
France

September 1792

André Valière was shaken from sleep by the bone-thumping roar of a distant cannon. Its jarring announcement silenced the birds that had begun to warble around camp just before sunrise, and he poked his head out of the flap of his tent. Looking to the west, he swore he heard the cannon answered by a few barks of musket fire.

And then an eerie silence settled back over the camp. André saw through the gauzy light of early dawn that his men were beginning to stir. They emerged from under their blankets, hair tousled and faces crinkled from sleep, to huddle around the campfires. He himself had had trouble falling asleep and had drifted off into fretful dozing well past midnight. Now, having heard these first preludes of the coming battle, André knew that remaining in bed was futile, and he dressed.

The camp rose with the sun. A bugler sounded the order to rouse the last few slumbering men. André made quick work of a small square of bread and a cup of watered-down coffee. "Eat whatever you have," he called out to his men, wiping away the last crumbs of his breakfast. "No point saving your rations now, lads. By nightfall, we'll be in a new village, where they'll have fresh meat and ale." André paused at a campfire where half a dozen of his men were coaxing a fresh flame from last night's ashes.

"Or we'll be food for the worms," Corporal Leroux muttered, loud enough for André to hear, as he poked a stick at the gray heap of cinders before him.

"I have no intention of dying, nor should you, nor any of you," André answered with a false measure of confidence, remembering Kellermann's heartening advice from the night before.

"Captain Valière, they'll keep you alive for the pretty ransom they'll get on your head." A young Parisian in his company by the name of Therrien, his cheeks smooth and his hair combed neatly, looked up, smiling in an easy, friendly manner.

"No, not today. Those bastards won't be taking prisoners," Leroux said, shaking his head. "Even a marquis would catch the royal treatment." He swiped a finger across his neck.

André ignored the comment as he walked on, making his way past more of his men clustered around small fires to the southern border of the camp. Here, several of his fellow officers had already begun to gather their companies into marching columns. André greeted them and looked out over the landscape, which was brightening under a strong, determined sun. In the distance, open fields of wheat shone golden in the warm late-summer morning. The dewy sheen across the ground was drying quickly and rising up in a soft veil of mist.

"It's going to be a hot one today, gentlemen." An officer standing nearby had his soldiers moving into two crisp lines, as the men bucked and fidgeted like jumpy horses. André turned and was pleased to see his sergeant, the competent man by the name of Digne, inspecting his group's weapons and kit and growling last-minute instruction to those whose equipment was less than perfect.

Where the army had begun assembling, on the southwest corner of the camp, a line of trees marked the entrance to a small forest. A large tricolor banner was now unfurled and marched to the front, the old fleur-de-lis banners of the monarchy having been replaced, and a small company of drummers and fifes played beneath it. Off to the right, a priest in a black robe and collar held Mass. In most parts of the country, God and Christ had been driven away around the same time the king and queen had been imprisoned, but on a day such as this, a few local priests had convinced the generals to look the other way. A boy no older than twelve, dressed in a green overcoat and overlarge blue pants, fidgeted nervously as he stared down at his drum set.

"Captain Valière!" André heard his name and turned to see his two sergeants approaching, fully dressed in their white uniforms.

"Sergeants." André straightened his posture, assuming a mask over his facial features that he hoped adequately veiled his nerves. "Are the men ready?"

The first, by the name of Thibaud, nodded. "Dressed and equipped, Captain."

"Bayonets ready at the waist, each man with thirty cartridges," Sergeant Digne added. "And, er, they've been issued the tricolor cockade for their uniforms, per regulation, sir."

"Thank you, Sergeant Thibaud, Sergeant Digne." Apart from their names, André knew little about these two men who served under him, as they had only just been assigned to his company several weeks earlier on the march into this province.

André looked out over the rows of men that filled the staging area of the camp just short of the woods. "It's time. We'll get the men into formation now."

"Yes, Captain."

To the left a company in tight file formation marched up, dressed in the career white uniform. Beside them the bluecoat militia looked on, attempting to mimic their order and formation. An unmanned horse whinnied loudly, pawing at the dirt and prompting several nearby blue-coated guardsmen to step nervously backward.

"You think they'll be all right out there?" Thibaud jerked his chin toward the growing cluster of militiamen. One of their commanders had just unfurled a large banner that read "Liberty, Equality, Fraternity, or Death."

"We'll know soon enough," André said, looking at their threadbare blue coats and punctured, barely serviceable boots. He removed his hat and wiped his brow.

"Holding against the Austrian line will be slightly different from slapping around an old Parisian warden," Digne said. "The ones who survive will come out with a bit more hair on their nuts—"

"When we reach the tree line," André interjected, steering his two sergeants back toward the morning's tasks, "the company will march double file until we clear the woods. We expect to find the enemy waiting on the far side of this forest, in the open pastures."

Both sergeants nodded, chastened, as André continued. "The wheat will be high this time of year, but dry enough, given the weather. General Kellermann says there is a windmill on the top of the ridge. When the battalion forms into line, we'll make our position in the front, before the windmill."

Sergeant Digne let out a slow whistle. "Christ in heaven, sir, they're putting us in the front? What did we do to piss them off?"

"We won't be passive observers today, that's for certain." André leaned his head to the side, placing his tricorn hat on top.

A pulse of agitated anticipation hummed across camp as the artillery barrage began. André, with his company formed into two tight files, each forty-five men long, looked to the crest of the hill from where the firing originated. Each boom was followed by a burst of smoke and a flight of birds, startled from their nests into fleeing the violent cacophony. For a moment, André envied those birds, able to quit these lush woods and fields before the golden ground became drizzled in red. But then he recalled his courage; his whole career had prepared him for this moment.

André squinted his eyes and focused on the tree-lined crest, where the French artillery barrage originated; somewhere, behind those stately oaks and chestnuts, stood Remy. "Stay safe, brother," André mouthed to himself, as he offered a silent prayer that he'd see his brother that evening.

All around him now, companies formed into their narrow marching files, and André's men folded in seamlessly beside them. When the bugler sounded, André clenched his jaw tight, speaking in a cool tone: "Right, lads, you heard it. Now we move." Sergeant Digne barked the command and the company began marching forward.

As they crossed the wood-line, quitting the open fields of the previous day's camp, the determined morning sun was almost entirely blocked out by the thick leaf cover that hung heavy on the surrounding boughs. In this copse the air was cool and damp, smelling of loamy earth and sap-filled bark. Mingled in with that sweet, pleasant scent was the unmistakable aroma of sulfur, wafting from the nearby cannonade.

André slapped a mosquito at his neck, removing his palm and seeing the first blood to color his skin that day. Already, his neck was lined with a filmy layer of sweat. He took a sip of water from his canteen, knowing that the day would be a hot one and that the heat from a battlefield sapped a soldier's energy as much as combat. "Take a drink if you need it, lads, but no more than a few sips," he said, hoping his men had filled their skins that morning with water instead of wine.

Finally, just when it seemed that the shade and the shroud of smoke around them might prevent any vision at all, André began to detect spears of light ahead, piercing the tree cover. They were approaching a clearing. Behind them now, the artillery barrage had lessened to a dull thud, muffled by the distance and half a mile of thick forest.

André guided his men directly toward the clearing. The soldiers blinked, some of them holding hands up to block the direct sunlight that felt oppressive after the soft, damp shade of the forest. As the company passed out of the trees, André felt as if he had entered another world; he and his men suddenly seemed uncomfortably exposed. His senses were heightened, his focus sharper than it had ever been.

His training forced him to remember the ninety men whose lives were in his hands. He stood tall, clearing his throat as he reached for the sword at his hip. Unsheathing it and raising it aloft, André was aware that every man in the company turned his focus on him now, awaiting the words that would take them forward into battle.

5

Paris

September 1792

"That looked like a sad heap sitting at your desk." Gavreau approached Jean-Luc as soon as he had seen the Widow Poitier out.

"Indeed." Jean-Luc nodded, sitting back down to his pile of papers. "Say, do you happen to know anything about the Montnoir family or estate?"

Gavreau considered the question. "Doesn't sound familiar. Where is it?"

"Just over twenty miles to the south, near Massy."

"What do you care about an estate near Massy?"

"The lands belonged to the esteemed Marquis de Montnoir, who happened to be the tormenter of that poor woman who just sat at my desk."

"The marquis wanted the likes of *that* woman?"

"No, no, no." Jean-Luc shook his head, his boss's impertinence causing him to smile in spite of himself. "Nothing like that. Well, in fact, *something* like that. The marquis wanted the likes of her daughter. But he also happened to cause the death of her husband and evict the widow and her surviving children from their family's home."

"Holy hellfire," Gavreau said, groaning. "I give you the esteemed nobility of our ancient realm. No wonder she was bawling into your handkerchief."

Jean-Luc propped his elbows on his desk, frowning. "He's now in prison."

"What's to become of His *Lordship*?"

"I must check. I do hope the only time he ever leaves his cell is to visit La Place de la Révolution."

"My my, St. Clair, calling for a man to be sent to the guillotine? I never thought I'd hear you speak that way."

"Only because he is, in fact, an egregious criminal—a rapist and a murderer, and God knows what else. His crimes strike me as far more serious than simply being born into a noble family."

"So I take it she's another one of your charity cases?" Gavreau cocked an eyebrow. "Let me guess, she can't afford to pay?"

Jean-Luc sighed, looking up at his boss. "This is the work of our Revolution, is it not? Equality? Fraternity? Who are we fighting for if not people such as this poor innocent widow and her wretched children? Aren't they entitled to a just society, same as the rest of us?"

"You're too clever to simply serve as a nursemaid, St. Clair." The older lawyer smiled wryly at Jean-Luc before continuing. "But I must say your patriotism makes me hungry. Let me buy you dinner."

"No, thank you. I have too much work to do." Jean-Luc looked over his pile of papers, sighing.

"Come now, I insist. I am your supervisor, even if you never listen to a word I say."

"I do listen to you."

"Yet you keep taking these charity cases. And such jobs won't pay for your rent, or your dinner. Come now, we'll make it quick. And besides, I've got some exciting news I want to share with you."

"Oh, all right," Jean-Luc agreed, noticing for the first time how empty his stomach felt. He hadn't eaten anything since the morning's meager serving of bread and cheese. "As long as we make it quick."

"Now that's something I've heard once or twice," Gavreau said, chuckling.

Jean-Luc ignored the comment, rising from his desk. "Just don't expect me to share a bottle of wine with you."

"Virtuous Citizen St. Clair, doing God's work, even if God himself has been kicked out of our Republic," Gavreau said, smirking. "Meet me downstairs. I need to stop for a piss."

Outside the evening was clear and warm. Jean-Luc and Gavreau detected the distant sounds of the crowd from the nearby Place, but they walked in the opposite direction.

"What are you up for this evening—watered-down potato soup or watered-down carrot soup?" Gavreau smiled as they strolled away from their administrative building near the Palais de Justice. "What I wouldn't give for a bit of meat."

Jean-Luc threw his jacket over his shoulders. "Someplace close."

"Fine, we'll go to La Colombe. The new serving woman there might just have the largest tits I've ever seen." The boss lifted his hands to reinforce his meaning.

Jean-Luc ignored the lewd gesture. "So then, what's this news you wanted to share?"

"News? Oh yes, that's right. I've got someone you will want to meet."

Jean-Luc tossed his head back, exasperated. "Gavreau, how many times have I tried to tell you? I am a happily married man. I don't wish to meet any of your lady friends."

"No, not that." The old bachelor chuckled. "I mean it this time. He arrives in Paris this weekend. Even Robespierre himself is trying to arrange a meeting with him."

Jean-Luc could tell from his manager's shift in tone that this was no jest. "What's his name?"

"His name is Maurice Merignac. He happens to be the personal secretary to Guillaume Lazare."

Jean-Luc halted his step, looking at his boss in stunned silence. After a moment, he repeated the name, unsure he had heard correctly: "Guillaume Lazare?"

Gavreau nodded, a proud smile blooming across his face.

"How do you know the personal secretary to Guillaume Lazare?" Jean-Luc could not conceal the skepticism in his voice, and he instantly regretted it, fearing that he might have offended his friend.

"Ah, so you know who he is, my virtuous young colleague?"

"Of course I know who Guillaume Lazare is. He's tried more cases for the new Republic than—"

"He's *won* more cases for the Republic than any other lawyer," Gavreau corrected him. "I tell you, the corrupt clergymen and nobility of this country fear Guillaume Lazare more than they fear the devil himself."

Jean-Luc thought about this, remembering that Guillaume Lazare had previously worked for the king. Since the sacking of the Bastille, however, the legendary attorney had been hard at work sending his old friends from the royal court to the prisons.

"St. Clair, I'm telling you, you must meet Maurice. You want to be a big lawyer someday—well, it just so happens that Maurice Merignac might be able to introduce you to Guillaume Lazare. The brightest legal mind in all of France."

"And you can arrange an introduction?" Jean-Luc did not attempt to mask his disbelief now as they walked on.

"It just so happens, ye of little faith, that I can." Gavreau rested his hands on his hips and puffed out his chest, defensive. "It helps to be a gregarious man-about-town. Believe it or not, I happen to know a few people."

Jean-Luc was about to inquire further when he noticed the crowd swelling in front of them. Voices were raised in competing hollers, and the windows overlooking the street sprouted clusters of eavesdroppers who leaned out over the crowd.

"What's all this?" Jean-Luc paused, Gavreau halting beside him.

"Paper! Get your paper! News from the front!"

"Hey, you!" Gavreau grabbed the shoulder of the little paperboy, probably eight years old, who was just then weaving his way through the crowd. Gavreau put a *sou* in the urchin's grime-caked hand and took one of his papers.

"What news?" Jean-Luc asked, leaning over Gavreau's shoulder. "Has the battle begun?"

"Looks like our boys have found the enemy in the woods at Valmy," Gavreau said, scanning the page. "The Habsburgs have joined their armies with the Prussians. Seems they still fancy a trip to Paris."

Jean-Luc felt his pulse begin to race. If the Prussians were in fact marching on Paris, he had to get home to Marie. But would it be more dangerous in the city or on the roads leading out of it? "Have we been defeated?"

"Not sure," Gavreau said. "But Kellermann is there to stop the bastards. I fancy he's got as good a chance as anyone to send those German-speaking barbarians back across the Rhine."

Jean-Luc paused. "Say, I had better get home to Marie. To warn her of . . . all this."

Gavreau frowned. "No dinner?"

Jean-Luc shrugged, apologetic. "She's alone at home with Mathieu."

"Fine, fine. Run to your woman. I imagine she's all afright." Gavreau waved him away. "But if they ring the bells, you're coming back here to fight alongside me. I'll need someone to keep me from soiling myself up on the walls when I see those Prussians approach."

"Of course I would come back and take up arms, if it came to that." Jean-Luc nodded, looking once more at his manager, before turning to take off at a trot toward the bridge.

A nervous energy pulsed on the streets of the Left Bank as well, with people huddled on corners, eager to hear the latest news. Jean-Luc turned onto his street and entered his building, bounding up the stairs two at a time. "Marie?" He panted as he entered the garret apartment. It was empty. "Mathieu? Marie?" There was no sign of his family. Alarmed, he turned, climbing back down the stairs. The neighbors downstairs might have seen them.

Grocque's tavern was a hive of activity, and he instantly spotted Marie on the far side. She stood near the hearth, speaking to a small group of women who clustered around her, nodding attentively to whatever it was that she was saying. "Marie?" he called out and she turned, looking distracted. She wore Mathieu in a makeshift sling across her chest so that her hands were free. Beside her, Madame Grocque was piling kindling onto one of the long tavern tables.

Marie waved him over and he crossed the room toward her. All throughout the space were neighborhood women, faces he recognized from the bakery and the butcher. "What is all this?" He kissed his wife on the cheek as she dismissed the small crowd around her and turned back to her task—ripping long strands of cloth into what appeared to be makeshift bandages.

"What does it look like, my love?" she asked, patting Mathieu with one hand as he began to fuss at her breast.

Nearby, women were stacking fire pokers and rolling pins and shovels on the long dining tables. Across the room, several women leaned over cauldrons filled with boiling water. An older woman with broad shoulders was disassembling chairs, as if she intended to use the legs as weapons.

"Excuse me, Citizeness St. Clair?" A young woman approached, holding an armful of firewood. "Where would you like this?"

"Over there, in the kindling pile," Marie said, issuing the order with a comfortable authority. "Thank you."

Jean-Luc looked around once more, slightly amazed. "It looks as if you intend to turn this tavern into some sort of headquarters or hospital?" he said, confused.

She eyed him, not at all frightened, as he had expected her to be. Simply busy. Determined. "We do."

"But . . . what do you mean to do?" he asked, glancing once more around the busy room, the women who worked and chatted with an orderly purposefulness.

"Why, defend ourselves," Marie said, her voice matter-of-fact. "If it comes to it."

She saw the shock on his face, and she smiled. "This thing was started by women who had had enough. Women who picked up their fish-knives and fire pokers and marched all the way to Versailles to demand food for their families. You think that, if the fight comes to Paris, we plan to sit in our apartments while the men take to the walls?"

Jean-Luc's mouth fell open. Then he glanced around the bustling room, heartened by this display, before looking back to his wife. "Well, Marie," he said, leaning toward her, putting a hand on her arm. "I certainly am happy that you're on our side."

6

Bois de Valmy,
France

September 1792

All around André, French soldiers in companies and battalions of vary-ing sizes were emerging from the woods. Their sergeants and offi-cers shouted orders to maneuver them into neat, even columns, three lines deep. A flock of gray geese stood clustered between the two opposing forests, grazing among the tips of wheat as they had each summer day.

The field before André sloped gently downward from the left to the right. On the left was the hillcrest, where French soldiers had begun to line the ridge, their silhouettes barely visible against a shroud of cannon smoke. Slightly behind and to their left, the lone windmill of which Kellermann had spoken pierced the horizon, its wheel barely turning in the hot, breeze-less morning. The hill sloped down to André's right, and soldiers had begun to fill into that low-ground space.

The men had sensed a shift, André noted, seeing some begin to fidget and whisper, unable to suppress the nervous tension that stretched along the front line. Death could, and would, emerge from the distant tree line at any minute.

And yet, though the French waited, no Prussians or Austrians emerged. For a brief moment, André wondered if perhaps the alliance forces had lost their stomach for a fight. Perhaps the French would hold the ground at Valmy without firing a single shot.

But then André peered into the distance, wondering if his vision played a trick on him as he detected the glint of sunlight reflecting off something unnatural, a shimmering surface that did not belong in the forest copse opposite him—a rifle? A helmet? Fifty meters to his left, André saw three men on horseback making their way out in front of the French line. All three of them wore dark blue coats with scarlet piping and gold buttons, the plumes of their hats keeping time with their stallions' steps. They checked their horses. It was the three French commanders.

Kellermann sat in the center, peering through his looking glass toward the faraway tree line. To the right of Kellermann, Dumouriez's horse pawed restlessly at the ground, and Dumouriez tightened his grip on the beast's reins. Murat sat to the left, studying a map. Kellermann slammed his looking glass shut, turning back toward the line of French soldiers.

He said something to his two colleagues, though his words were inaudible to André from such a distance. Dumouriez's bright red sash and golden epaulets shone blindingly bright in the sunlight as he nodded at whatever Kellermann had said. Murat adjusted his hat, lifting it slightly to gain a better view of the far forest.

On André's far right stood a cluster of National Guard companies, recognizable by their tattered blue coats and patchwork leggings. They began to shout and cheer, goaded to a fever pitch by their unseasoned leaders.

"Damned inexperienced whelps," one of André's men grumbled under his breath, but he sounded more anxious than angry.

"Leave it to the grown-ups, lads!" Leroux yelled in their direction, and several of André's men began to chuckle.

André threw Leroux a barbed look. "Steady," he said. "Don't bother with that." He knew that before battle, men often masked their fear with shouts and insults, crutches to fortify their nerves. But his men were trained better than to forget their discipline.

And then André knew he hadn't been imagining things, as there, from the distant tree line, several small figures emerged from behind the veil of the woods. A figure clothed in emerald green and a hat plumed with a single green feather glided out. And then another. And then another. One of the distant enemy held a looking glass, and its funnel caught a ray of sunlight, the reflection glinting off of its polished surface.

"There! Look!" Farther down the French line, one of the bluecoats shouted, pointing. "In the trees!"

André noted with small satisfaction that his men had all remained quiet, still, in their first sighting of the distant enemy.

The Prussian with the looking glass paused for a moment before vanishing back behind the trees. Kellermann, Dumouriez, and Murat must have seen them, too, for they now turned their horses and trotted back from the center of the field toward the French line.

Before his horse passed through the line, Kellermann paused a moment, turning once more in the direction of the Prussians. Almost a taunt, inviting the enemy to come and defy him. And then he lifted his reins and guided his horse back, a hearty grin on his face as he passed his men. "Give 'em hell, boys!" Kellermann lifted his plumed cap from his head.

"*Vive la France!*" a soldier near André shouted, and his voice mingled with the hoarse cries of the other men. All around him, soldiers were shouting the battle cry that had become familiar over the summer: "*La patrie est en danger!* The nation is in danger!"

But this momentary burst of bravery was cut short, as the men realized that they now stood exposed before an enemy that had indeed arrived for battle. A lone Prussian stood on the edge of the wood-line, well out of musket range. He raised his right hand, as if to wave toward the French, and then dropped it as he began to trot forward into the meadow. Still out of range, he dropped to his knees and lifted his long rifle. André saw a puff of smoke and, a heartbeat later, heard a crack that ripped across the field, sending several birds upward toward the sky.

Several other enemy skirmishers emerged, darting along the edge of the woods. They dropped to their knees, concealed partially by the high wheat. Now, intermittent pops of gunfire, followed by small clouds of smoke, rose up out of the wheat in which the Prussian skirmishers knelt. Their bullets were sporadic and shot from far away, their purpose to lure the French.

Suddenly, appearing like woodland ghosts, figures in white and blue began to dart through and past the French line. André watched the French skirmishers run out to challenge the Prussians. They sped past in a crouch, zigzagging to render themselves difficult targets for the long-range enemy rifles.

As the Prussian fire picked up, the French rifles barked in response. It was like watching a frenzied, illogical dance, André reflected—the first awkward moments at the start of a great ball, before partners had been matched and when only a few brave souls ventured out, inviting the other side to engage.

André stole a glance down his line, where his men's faces were rapt, one of them shouting out an encouragement as more of their fleet-footed countrymen joined the skirmishers' dance. None had been hit yet, but the bursts of fire became more constant. On the left, several of the French skirmishers had stopped firing, taking a pause to reload their muskets. The foremost men on each side had now approached within two hundred meters of one another, and André knew that they had now moved into killing range. A lone cry rose up as a green figure, pausing to reload, snapped backward. This sight was met with a murderous cheer that rose up from the French line as the men celebrated the first death of the day—one that had been inflicted by one of their own. But the riflemen did not celebrate, did not pause in the job before them.

André watched as the leader of the French skirmishers dropped to his knee, aimed his rifle, and fired. Before his bullet had found its mark, he heaved backward, a scarlet stain seeping outward from below his hip, where a Prussian bullet had torn through his uniform. Two other Frenchmen were at his side in an instant, pulling the wounded man back behind the line. Several other Prussians were hit. A handful of Frenchmen dropped below the tall wheat, their own bodies catching bullets. And then, just as quickly as it had begun, both sets of skirmishers retreated, receding backward like ocean waves obeying the moon and a retreating tide. The prelude was over.

André stood tall, feeling every muscle in his body go rigid. He noticed that while the skirmishers had filled the field with smoke and a few corpses, he had not yet seen the main body of Prussian and Austrian infantry emerge from the far side of the field. Any second now, he expected those lines to appear. Some of his men began to fidget, cursing under their breath as they heard the deep guttural yells of the distant, unseen enemy. Far-off drumbeats signaled the orders of the enemy to begin moving.

André resisted the impulse to say anything to his men, knowing it would simply reveal his own nervousness. And then he saw them: a wall of green and gold. Two flags hemmed in their formation, and André guessed those to be the banners of the Prussian and Austrian kingdoms. The green-clad Prussian infantry cleared the tree line now and marched into the meadow, their heavily booted feet stomping in unison and giving credence to the rumors that these were the most disciplined soldiers on the Continent.

To the rear of André's formation, the rumble of French drums began to sound, shaking the earth beneath them and signifying that it was time for the French to begin marching as well. Kellermann and Dumouriez, off to the side, leaned their heads toward each other. Murat was beside them, studying a map. Their brief conference concluded, Kellermann spurred his horse, unsheathing his sword as he rode toward the men in the front. All around André now, his men watched their leader, their voices lifting in cheers and shouts.

"Men!" Kellermann rode before the French line, his hat lifted in the air in one hand, his sword raised in the other. André couldn't hear Kellermann's voice over the din of his frenzied men. Let them cheer, he thought, looking at faces that betrayed both fear and exhilaration. He strained his ears, barely detecting the closing of Kellermann's words: "The nation is under attack, but we will not let her be taken. We have answered the call. We here, today, with the whole world watching, fight for liberty, equality, and fraternity!" And then, brandishing his sword high overhead, Kellermann clamored: *"Vive la nation!"*

André made a fist with his hand and lifted it to join the heady cries of his men, his blood rolling with nervous agitation and pride. *"Vaincre ou mourir!"* he shouted, echoing the cries of the thousands around him. "Victory or death!" Those were the only two choices before them, and every Frenchman on that field knew it.

Meanwhile, across the field, the Prussian line advanced, impermeable to this sudden upsurge in French spirit. They carpeted the golden meadow with an unnatural tide of green, white, and gold as their numbers kept coming, marching steadily toward André and his men.

The men were looking at him now, and André felt a tightening in his gut when he saw the anxious expressions on their faces. They awaited his cue. Perhaps they sought confidence from his presence, like a group of mischievous children, so long obstinate, now withdrawing behind their father in the face of a menacing stranger. Only Leroux looked ahead, his features implacable, as though he were willfully avoiding André's gaze.

"All right, lads." André lifted his sword. "Company, shoulder arms!"

André's men lifted their rifles, resting the weapons against their shoulders. He nodded. "Forward march!"

All along the line now, his fellow captains were shouting the same orders, and the men obeyed. As if one body, every man took one fluid stride forward, thousands of left feet taking the first step on the march that carried them forward into the unknown.

Behind him, the artillery barrage started up again. This time, the enemy stood in range and the French cannons were firing not to startle and unnerve, but to kill. For the first time that morning, the Prussian artillery answered back, sending a volley of cannons ripping out from the far side of the forest. André flinched, his body's instinctive response, but he quickly composed himself and resisted the urge to seek protection. The closest cannonball struck wide of André and his company by at least one hundred meters to the right, spewing mud ten feet into the air as it smashed into the damp earth.

To his left, André heard the crackle of a wall of French muskets. The men had grown louder now, too, with officers barking out orders and soldiers shrieking out battle cries. A layer of smoke had begun seeping over the field, so that it filled André's nostrils. He coughed once, turning back to ensure his men were in formation. The enemy was close enough now that he could begin to make out individual facial features from within the wall of Prussians before him. He noticed that one of the men directly opposite him had a thick golden mustache and a wide brow.

"Company, halt!" André stopped his men in their march. Mouth dry, he waited a few seconds, falling back on his training where otherwise his nerve might have faltered. "Company, load!"

While André's men began to front-load the gunpowder and bullets into the muzzles of their muskets, the German officer opposite André barked out an order in words André couldn't understand. At this, the Prussians halted as well, standing with muskets poised in front of them.

A feeling of dread settled over André, but he forced out the hoarse command: "Company, present arms!" André watched as his words turned to action with a quickness that surprised even him. His men were ready to fight.

They cocked back their muskets' hammers. Just before the enemy could open fire, André lifted his sword and shouted: "Fire!"

Forty weapons fired in that moment, deafening André as the musket balls ripped through the field and a wall of smoke enveloped the French line. Seconds later, André heard the crack of enemy fire in reply. But the Prussians were too late. The first French volley had been effective enough to disorient the enemy and obscure their view, so that the majority of Prussian rounds flew high or fell short of their intended targets. André heard a lone, sickening thud, as one of his soldiers grabbed his stomach and dropped to the ground. Farther down the line, several men cried out and fell to the ground as well.

As the smoke cleared, André saw that more Prussians had stepped forward to fill in the line where their comrades had been felled. The brief elation André had felt by unleashing and surviving the first volley was now replaced by the cold, unwavering exigency of his years of drilling and training: he had to get the second round into the enemy before they had recovered from their own initial shock.

"Company, reload!" André yelled. But he noticed, with disappointment, that some of his men were moving unsteadily, numb and dazed after their baptism by enemy fire. The man to André's left, his hands trembling violently, was having trouble sliding the ramrod into the barrel of his musket to lodge the ball and powder into place.

They couldn't delay any longer. "Company, make ready! Fire!" André's men fired off their second volley almost simultaneously with the enemy's. This time, the Prussian bullets proved more accurate and more devastating. To André's left and right, men went down. A bullet flew past his ear, buzzing like an angry hornet, and André saw through the wall of smoke that three men in the front of his line lay flat on the ground. Behind him, Sergeant Digne called out to the men in the second line to fill in these new gaps. The Prussians would not pause their assault to show sympathy for the dying French, André reminded himself, and neither could he.

Behind them the roar of the French artillery continued, adding to the chaos. This was how it had to happen, André knew: they must keep loading and reloading, killing one another until either one of the lines exhausted its numbers or its men lost their will to keep fighting. The best thing André could do for his men was have them send more shots down-range than the enemy.

André noticed that his men were distracted, their attention pulled down the slope toward the right flank. There, a cluster of blue-coated guards-men were shouting like fiends. They had forced the Austrians opposite them into a fighting withdrawal, so that some of the men in the enemy line were beginning to fall back. A handful of the more eager French mili-tiamen were urging their comrades onward to pursue the Austrians, con-fusing the temporary retreat for a rout. The bluecoats moved en masse toward that breach, surging forward in an unorganized frenzy.

When they advanced to within a hundred meters of the enemy, the Austrians halted, regrouping. With machinelike efficiency, they performed an about-face and the front rank dropped to their knees. André saw a flurry of sudden gray as the Austrian muskets fired all at once, pouring their deadly hail into the unsuspecting Frenchmen. The efficiency of this sud-den counterfire was staggering, and the bluecoats fell like stalks of wheat before a scythe. André felt his stomach turn as he heard so many of his countrymen cry out in agony. The survivors, seeing the carnage all around them, turned and fled, leaving their screaming comrades in the grass as the onslaught of Austrian bayonets turned the wounded into corpses.

The enemy leadership sensed the sudden vulnerability of the French right flank, and Austrian reinforcements now marched to that spot like a swollen river pounding a vulnerable dam.

André had to force himself to tear his focus from the carnage and turn back to the more immediate danger facing his own men. He ordered an-other round of fire, wiping the sweat from his face. Still, to the right, the enemy was funneling men toward the weakened stretch of the French line, endeavoring to pierce the space where so many bluecoats had fallen or fled.

"Steady, lads, never mind that," André called out, noticing how many of his men, too, were watching that unraveling swath of their line. What had started as a small hole seemed to be widening, as a torrent of white-coated Austrians now overwhelmed the fissure.

"Company, reload!" André shouted, noticing how feeble his voice sounded amid the frantic elation of the enemy. How in God's name would they stop that breach? André wondered. If the Prussians and Austrians broke through in large enough numbers, they would split the French infantry line and spill into the rear, wreaking havoc and causing a panic that would sap any hope of French victory.

"Company, fire!" André shouted, forcing his hoarse voice to rise up even as this disaster unfolded to his right.

And then André heard three quick trumpet blasts from behind, followed by a roar of cheers. André turned and saw a squadron of *cuirassiers*, the French heavy cavalry, racing toward the line, their thick-chested stallions thundering forward. At the front of the formation rode General Murat, the heavy-plate armor across his chest reflecting the sun and dazzling allies and enemies alike. He held his reins with one hand, directing his horse with his legs. With his sword lifted high above his head he cut a fierce silhouette against the cloudless sky. He reminded André of a hawk, riding in a determined arc, poised to descend upon its hapless prey. And then Murat's sword was slashing and tearing into the line of enemy infantry, cutting down men who moments earlier believed they had broken the French right flank.

Now even André couldn't help but watch, rapt, letting out a savage yell as he watched Murat and his horsemen reclaim the momentum of the battle, driving the Prussian and Austrian infantry back from the previously doomed right flank.

"Sir." Sergeant Thibaud grabbed André's shoulder, pointing at the Prussian infantry line opposite them. "The enemy is advancing, sir! Look!"

André turned to see for himself. Straight ahead, the Prussians had fixed bayonets and were marching forward in a phalanx of men, wood, and steel. The soldiers on both sides began to shout and scream now. The initial fear of death had subsided, and, fueled by bloodlust and the instinct to survive, their desire to kill the enemy had reached its fever pitch. Insults were being hurled from both sides, and André saw it was futile to try to quell the rage of his men. The best course was to harness that frenzied energy and determine the exact moment to unleash it.

"Company! Fix bayonets!" André shouted, his own hoarse voice sounding as mad as the rest of them now. "Company, advance!" André set the pace as he and his men began to march forward to meet the enemy.

Meanwhile, approaching them, the Prussians seemed to be growing taller. And their number seemed to have doubled. André, senses heightened, suddenly smelled the stench of hundreds of sweaty men to his left and his right. Around him, other French companies had begun their own marches forward toward the enemy, and the field would soon be roiling with dead and dying men.

"Company, halt!" André held his sword high. For a moment, there was a crackling, eerie silence as both sides faced each other.

"*Vorwärts Marsch!*" And then the enemy began to surge forward, running toward André's men as they screamed at a bloodcurdling volume: "*Schweine!*"

"Hold positions, lads!" André yelled. His men bucked beside him now, faces grim as they prepared to repel this wave of screaming fighters barreling toward them. And then André lifted his sword, shouting over the wails of the approaching enemy. "Front rank, kneel!" His men obeyed, the front line dropping to their knees.

And then suddenly from behind André, the heavens opened with a terrible wrath, a percussion of noise ripping across the battlefield. The French artillery, which had momentarily fallen silent, now poured out a deadly hail of cannonballs. The advancing Prussian line caught this terrible assault of lead and fire, and scores of men began to convulse and fall to the ground. Clouds of dirt, grass, and smoke flew into the air along with bloody limbs and pieces of shredded uniform. The Prussians cried out in agony and terror, while, across from them, the French erupted in a mighty roar.

The Prussian assault was blunted momentarily but not halted, as the dazed survivors continued to stagger forward. André seized on this momentary confusion. "Both ranks, reload! Second rank, present arms!" André called to the standing men in his secondary line. "Fire at will!" The jarring crack of all of those French muskets added further damage to the decimated Prussian line, and now André told his men to stand and brace. "Prepare to receive bayonets!"

His men braced, their own sharp blades raised and pointed to break the Prussian wave like an impenetrable dike. André bent his knees, chin tucked, as he unthinkingly screamed out his thoughts: "Kill the bastards!"

And then the Prussian infantrymen crashed into his line with a staggering ferocity, the weight of thousands of pounds of men and wood and steel colliding against the lines of the bracing Frenchmen. André held his sword ready to parry the thrust of a steel bayonet that pointed toward his belly.

To his left, a Prussian was impaled as he crashed into the French line. André watched as another Prussian behind the dead man filled in the line and stabbed the Frenchman in the face. The man fell backward, in a bloody tangle with his killer, whom he struggled with until he was stabbed a second and third time.

André received the brunt of a shoulder from a large man who bowled into him, crashing into the second rank of French infantry. When he regained his footing, André turned in time to see the bayonet thrust of a squat, stocky man flying toward him. André dodged the thrust and slashed the man's left shoulder, tearing through uniform and flesh until his blade reached bone.

The smoke from the cannon fire had billowed forward and now settled like a rain cloud, darkening the field with its shadow and stink as the melee unfolded all around him. To his right, Leroux had his musket locked with a Prussian nearly twice his size. André leaped over a body and thrust his sword tip between the Prussian's shoulders. Leroux, under the weight of the dying man, fell to the ground, the corpse crashing on top of him. A moment later he rolled the man off of him, spitting out blood and a loose tooth. Taking André's hand, he rose back to his feet, a stunned look on his face.

"Thanks, sir," was all Leroux could manage, his hands empty of his lost musket. André leaned forward and picked up a gun off a nearby fallen Frenchman. He handed it to Leroux, who nodded, wiping his sweaty, bloodstained face.

André wiped his own brow, panting, as he turned back toward the scrum. As he scanned the throng for his sergeants, his voice rasping out their names, André noticed two enemy soldiers closing in on him. Each of them had bayonets lifted, and he realized that he'd have to face them simultaneously.

André stood with his sword unsheathed, bracing for the assault. The first man lunged from the right, his movements jumpy and undisciplined. André easily parried the thrust and slashed the man's thigh, causing the

Prussian to grunt and stagger backward. In a heartbeat, André delivered a second blow, this time hacking the man's elbow as his assailant fell to the ground, wounded. He crawled away, moaning in agony.

The second Prussian, larger and more methodical than the first, sized up André from a safe distance. Then, with a startling quickness, the man feinted left and jabbed right, his movement causing André to duck and lose his footing. The man then lifted his rifle and slammed its butt into the side of André's head. André staggered, falling to his knees as his vision went blurry. He felt a second blow to his head and dropped flat onto the soft grass. The man stood over him now, blocking out the sun, and André saw the blade of the bayonet held aloft as it reflected the midday light. He rolled to his right just in time to hear his enemy's steel bayonet slice through layers of earth where his head had just rested. The man ripped his blade from the ground, pulling it up covered in dirt and grass, and lowered it in a second attempt, once more just barely missing as André darted out of his way. But the thrust was not entirely ineffective; the blade grazed the side of André's cheek, just below his hairline, and André gasped, feeling the sting of where the steel had ripped his flesh.

In terrible pain now and feeling a fatigue that ached and burned every muscle in his body, André couldn't roll in time to dodge a third attempt. He knew this, and so he clenched his jaw and braced himself for the strike that would surely end his life. He thought of Remy, hoping that wherever he was on this bloodstained battlefield, his brother was still alive. Eyes lifted upward toward his killer and the heavens that he hoped would receive him, André's vision went dark. The sun fled. Would Father be there to receive him?

But it wasn't death that darkened André's world. He blinked, unsure of what he saw. Over him, a massive shadow loomed and he heard the sharp bite of steel on flesh. The large Prussian standing over him began to moan, taking one shaky step forward as he dropped his weapon and fell to his knees, his skull nearly cloven in two.

André looked up at his deliverer and saw a familiar face atop a horse, the man eyeing him as he pulled his sword from the dead man's skull.

"Is that you hiding down there, Valière?" General Kellermann reined in his stallion, which was pawing the earth in an attempt to rear up on its hind legs. Panting, Kellermann lifted his hat and flashed a wild smile down at André. "Better get up. It's ours if we'll take it."

André shivered on the ground, his fingers touching the place where blood seeped from a cut on his cheek.

"Up, Valière!" Kellermann roared now, offering a hand to the young captain and lifting him to his feet. "You don't want to miss the sight of all those devils on the run, not after you and your men did such a damned good job of holding our center."

With that, Kellermann turned his horse, allowing it to rear up on its hind legs. Calling out to the soldiers all around him, the windmill silhouetted on the hillcrest behind him, he raised his sword. "The day is nearly ours. Let's finish this! *Vive la Révolution!*"

Kellermann spurred his horse, charging the ragged lines of Prussians and Austrians who still fought. It seemed to André as if the entire French army took heart, his own breast surging with his last reserves of energy and resolve in response to Kellermann's rally cry. His weary legs found new strength as he stood tall. Around him, the bloodied, grime-soaked soldiers followed the general, racing forward to pursue the faltering enemy. André saw in that moment, his eyes stinging from dirt and sweat, that the soldiers of the Republic—and the Republic itself—would not be defeated that day.

7

Paris

December 1792

The evening's rumors had changed everything.

The ball was to have been a festive occasion, celebrating the dissolution of the monarchy and the victory at Valmy. The survival of the nascent Revolution. But as the chill of night settled over Paris, the snow-flecked Seine glistening like a vein of molten silver, the citizens' hunger for bread was surpassed only by their hunger to hear the latest reports circulating throughout the city: would the king face the guillotine?

Following Paris's bloody summer and the imprisonment of the royal family, the Jacobins had grown in number and consolidated power within the National Convention. The victory at Valmy had, for the moment, halted the threat of foreign invasion, allowing a band of radical and ambitious young lawyers to grab the reins of government, promising expanded suffrage, abolition of noble privileges, and a sweeping new constitution to rival any document that had come out of the Americas. And on this night in late December, all of Paris was humming with the rumors that the Bourbon king himself might face France's new justice.

André had followed the case of King Louis XVI with sharp interest, keenly aware of its resemblance to his own father's trial—if either event could truthfully be called a trial. André had even stood inside the crowded galleries on the final days of the king's prosecution. There he had observed it all in quiet horror: the hostile audience members, all wearing the same red caps and tricolor cockades, their dirty faces angry and their minds decided long before the opening gavel had rapped.

It had been nearly too difficult to watch. The king's cheeks—once fatted from sweets and caked in rouge—hung gaunt and ashen beside trembling lips. His voice quivered as he told the assembly how deeply he loved his subjects—*former* subjects, he corrected himself—and how willing he was to compromise with the new government. The jeers of the angry crowd were so overpowering that there was little hope of mounting a true defense. As the members and audience of the tribunal had sniggered and ridiculed, Louis's eyes had gone vacant. If one had cared to look closely, they would have seen two misty windows into a soul that had been broken. Louis, so coddled and misled since birth, had not seemed to understand such rough treatment.

It had all been too much for André. Through his blurred vision, the pale face of the king became the stony face of his own father, and André excused himself from the courtroom before hearing the verdict.

Several days after attending the trial, André had been startled to receive an invitation to the National Convention soiree, a celebration of the new, popularly elected government. André suspected that Kellermann had arranged the invitation. The general was, for the moment, the most celebrated man in the Republic; he was the man who had defied and repelled the Prussian-Austrian menace, the "Savior of the Revolution." In this mood, even the most radical Jacobin could stomach the presence of a few aristocratic officers for the evening.

Coming just two days after Christmas—or when Christmas had formerly been celebrated—the ball promised to be a festive occasion attended by the leading citizens of Paris. This being Year One of the new French Republic, all Christian holidays had been suspended, all church services canceled. Cathedrals and churches had been seized for the Republic and rebranded "temples of reason." This was not to be a party celebrating Christmas but an event to celebrate the triumph of the ideals of liberty, equality, and fraternity. And André, momentarily excused for his deceased father's nobility, knew this to be an invitation that he would be unwise to refuse.

"Aren't I lucky that my brother couldn't find a date, and I get to attend as his guest?" Remy looked roguishly handsome in his military uniform and, as he stepped out of the rented fiacre, he nodded at a pair of women who walked arm in arm around the street corner. "We could ask those two gals if they'd like to join?"

André smiled at the two women as he stepped out of the fiacre behind his brother. He wore a similar blue coat with the bronze gorget denoting his rank as an officer. Men in blue coats, the adopted color of the French Revolutionary Army, were now ever present in Paris. "Just try not to get drunk and insult anyone important, Remy. We're not exactly the citizens these people hope to see."

"Without a woman, how else should I keep amused?"

André fidgeted with the buttons of his uniform as they crossed La Place de l'Abbe-Basset. "These Jacobins are not necessarily *our* crowd, and they don't sound like the most cheerful bunch. We are here to pay our respects, and then we'll leave."

"I'll drink their wine, dance with a few of their wives. Then I'll leave."

"If you leave it at acquainting and don't take it further than that, then we *might* just be able to leave unnoticed and get on with our lives without these vicious lawyers threatening our heads."

"If their wives take an interest in my head, then what can I do, big brother?" Remy laughed.

André ignored the last comment, tucking his hands into his pockets. The night air was cold and dry as they approached the monumental building on the far side of the square. After months of marching and sleeping in the woods and bogs of the French countryside, André marveled at the size and beauty of the building, even if he had seen it several times before. Despite the winter chill and brutal shortages of food and fuel, the city retained much of its charm.

The evening's event was to be held inside the Panthéon, the colossal structure previously known to Parisians as the Abbey of Sainte-Geneviève; the cross at the front and the sculpture of its patron saint had been removed by the *sans-culottes* and smashed in the street. Perhaps a few glasses of wine would help André forget the fact that the building was now functioning as a mausoleum, the temple where the great Frenchmen of the new nation would be buried. He noted, as they approached, that St. Geneviève's likeness had been replaced with a Greek-style statue bearing the cumbersome name of *The Fatherland Crowning the Heroic and Civic Virtues*.

André nodded at two guards standing at the entry, noting, with a twinge of relief, that their military uniforms gained him and Remy swift, unquestioned admission. Inside, the hall was cool and damp. The high-vaulted dome overhead was designed to wash the place in natural sunlight, but this evening the great hall was illuminated by dim, flickering candlelight.

The hall was sparsely decorated as if it were a Noël occasion: holly strung along the walls, polished candelabras running the lengths of long tables spread with pastries, wine, and punch. Throughout the crowd, André spotted several military uniforms, but the vast majority of men in attendance were dressed in civilian clothing. He saw spectacles, clean-shaven faces, and narrow shoulders that had never worn the uniform of the army. He was, after all, at a Jacobin event, surrounded by lawyers and aspiring statesmen of the new Republic.

The women at this soiree, André noted, appeared entirely different from the women who had frequented the feasts he'd witnessed as a youth. Scarlet satin and violet brocade had been replaced by sensible tones of muted beige and navy. Powdered white hair, curled and piled high atop the head, had been replaced with simple brown buns. Heavily rouged cheeks and cheery, sparkling laughter had been exchanged for serious, even stern, expressions and judicious political discussion. The Jacobins had very different taste in women and fashion, it appeared, than had the former dukes and counts of France.

Remy fixed his eyes on the far side of the party. "There he is, the Incorruptible himself." André followed Remy's gaze and immediately recognized Maximilien Robespierre, the leader of the Jacobin Club and therefore the de facto host of the evening. "He's shorter than I thought," Remy remarked.

André studied the man, agreeing. Robespierre's appearance was, in every way, less impressive than the journal illustrations would have had him believe. The young lawyer had a narrow face, with feline green eyes and a pale, prominent brow. His skin was wan, as if he were in less than perfect health, and as he spoke to the constellation of admirers surrounding him, he twitched his limbs in uneven, jerky movements, as if not quite comfortable with the machinations of his own frame.

Robespierre was known as a great orator, André knew, but not entirely from his skillful delivery. His talent, rather, lay in the complexity of his arguments, the length and weightiness of his addresses to the Convention. André had deduced as much while watching him during the king's trial. When he spoke, Robespierre never resorted to bombast or high volume; his long and circuitous arguments aimed their arrows at a man's brain rather than his heart or gut. And he spoke quietly. So quietly, in fact, that the entire audience was forced to hush and lean forward in order to hear his words. Robespierre's sentences were so long and labyrinthine that one rarely remembered, by the end of a statement, what its initial point might have been. This had the effect, André had realized, of so baffling the crowd that they credited their incomprehension to Robespierre's superior intellect rather than the speaker's meandering message. And thus, he frequently carried the day.

"Robespierre has been pushing for the guillotine ever since the start of Louis's trial," André whispered to his brother, still studying the distant figure. "Said he'd be happy to throw in the first vote."

"I still can't believe you went and watched that circus," Remy said, scanning the hall for a glass of champagne.

"I'm sorry I did," André replied, clenching his jaw. He had suffered more than one nightmare about the trial since that day. Only, in his dreams, it was usually his father who sat on trial before the panel of Convention members. And in one recent nightmare it had been André himself.

"Who is that beside Robespierre?" Remy asked.

André turned back toward Robespierre and his attendants. "Georges Danton, from the looks of it."

"Ah, Robespierre's closest ally." Remy nodded. "He looks like he might have more success with the ladies than his short little friend."

Danton was Robespierre's foil in appearance. Where Robespierre was short and narrow, Danton stood tall and broad, his frame like a massive wrestler's. He had round eyes and fleshy jowls, and when he opened his mouth, the sound of his deep laughter reverberated throughout the hall.

"And there is our commander," Remy said, spotting the uniformed figure of General Dumouriez. "I think I need a drink before I offer my greetings." With that, Remy glided away from his older brother's side.

André stood alone, wishing he had gone with Remy to seek out that drink. Staring around the room, he was startled when he heard his name called out.

"How's that scar healing, Captain Valière?"

André turned and saw General Kellermann approaching, his arm linked to that of a pretty woman of middle age. He, like André, wore his military uniform and his graying hair pulled back tidily by a ribbon.

"You're looking quite a bit more cleaned up than the last time I saw you. I believe some Prussian gentleman was standing over you, trying very hard to lodge his bayonet in your skull." Kellermann paused before André, smiling.

"I had him right where I wanted him, sir," André quipped, and Kellermann let out a cheerful laugh. "But I am much indebted, all the same, sir."

"If that was where you wanted him, I don't think you wished to stay long on this earth."

André's face reddened as he nodded wordlessly.

"Believe it or not," Kellermann continued, his tone light as he glanced at the woman beside him, "I was a young soldier once, too. And foolish. I remember a certain student at the military academy at Brienne. He was years older than me, and so very distinguished. I hoped that someday I might carry myself as he did."

André shifted from one foot to the other, unsure of his superior's meaning.

Now Kellermann's eyes had lost the glimmer of lighthearted laughter, but instead appeared full of earnest meaning. André's own stare slid downward toward his polished boots.

"In fact . . ." Kellermann continued. André looked up, trying to swallow but finding his mouth dry. "The one who *really* knew your father well was"—Kellermann turned—"speak of the devil, and the devil shall appear."

Before André could make sense of what was happening, another man appeared beside him, prompting his spine to stiffen involuntarily. He looked into expressionless gray eyes, a mustached face. "Good evening, General Murat."

"Nicolai, good to see you," Kellermann said. "Doesn't our young captain look dashing, all cleaned up?" He shifted his broad shoulders to make room for his friend in the small cluster of conversation.

"Cleaned up, and hopefully a bit less nervous," Murat said, his thin lips spreading under his mustache into a poorly concealed sneer.

André slowly raised his chin, a small gesture of defiance, and said: "A ball makes some more nervous than a battle. Women can be more dangerous than an army of thousands."

Kellermann laughed, offering his companions an affable grin. "Well said. And speaking of the fairer gender, where are my manners? Allow me to introduce my wife, Christianne Kellermann."

The lady whom André now knew to be Kellermann's wife extended a gloved hand, which he took and kissed. A countess, earlier in her life and her marriage. But now André said: "Citizeness Kellermann, it is an honor to meet you."

"I have heard wonderful things about you, Captain." Christianne Kellermann wore a kind expression and spoke in a soft voice, her manners controlled, almost timid. Quite the opposite of her gregarious husband. "My husband holds a high opinion of you."

"An admiration which is surely exaggerated," André answered, "when your husband has been deemed 'Savior of the Revolution.' You must be proud, Madame Kellermann."

"I believe you mean to say *Citizeness* Kellermann?" Murat's voice had an edge to it, a perturbation that his tense facial features reinforced. André looked to him and stammered, caught off guard by both his hard tone and appearance.

Kellermann interjected, "Any man who stood with us at Valmy is a friend for the rest of my days." Kellermann now looped his arm around his wife's waist in a gesture of comfortable familiarity. "Valière held his line steady while many of the others were breaking. Our center was unshakable that day. Isn't that right, Nicolai?"

Murat answered after a long pause, as if reluctant to agree on the point. "Indeed."

Just then, André noticed a pretty young woman enter. She walked in on the arm of a man who appeared twice her age, her unlined face framed by blond curls pulled back and resting in a loose bun at the nape of her neck. Her cream-colored shoulders were visible above a gown of light blue silk, accented with a modest string of pearls at her throat.

Unlike the other women in the crowd, this lady did not look around at the hall, nor did she speak to her companion as he led her across the floor. Her lips remained pursed, free of either greetings or smiles, tilting downward in the slightest hint of a frown. And yet her sober, impassive face had an almost magnetic quality, drawing the gaze of more than one gentleman as she passed by; her elaborate dress and fine, delicate features caused her to stand out in this room as a lily might appear out of place in a field full of wheat.

The man beside the lady held her arm and now offered her a glass of champagne. Physically, he was in no way her equal. He had rings of doughy flesh lining his ample neck and a few strands of hair the color of ash. He made a quick comment to her and then followed it with a series of short, uneven chortles, and André wondered if he was made more nervous by the crowded party, or the company of the bored, beautiful woman on his arm. André noticed how General Murat's eyes, too, watched this young lady's entrance, fixing on her with an odd, intense expression.

"I think I've lost your interest, Nicolai." Kellermann was speaking, and André noticed that he, too, had not heard a word.

Murat turned back to the conversation, reluctantly rending his eyes from the beautiful blond woman across the room. Then, in a whisper intended only for Kellermann, Murat added: "She's just arrived."

Kellermann nodded. "Should you not go greet her?"

"Oh, yes. In a moment." Murat shifted his weight. "But what were you saying?"

André observed this exchange with great interest, though he forced himself to keep his eyes off the lady in question as Kellermann cleared his throat and continued. "I was asking: what do you make of the trial?"

Murat now straightened his posture, redirecting his attention from the lovely woman in light blue to his colleague. He took a slow sip of champagne before he responded. "I think we did our democratic duty. We gave the man a trial, according him the justice of the law. And now let's be done with him, with all despots, once and for all."

"So, you've been reading Danton and Robespierre," Kellermann replied evenly, his arm still holding his wife close at the waist.

"Send him to La Place," Murat said, with a dismissive wave of his wrist.

"But surely you listened to the defense, Nicolai?" Kellermann looked at André and then leaned toward his friend. "Raymond Desèze was brilliant in stating the king's case, and very compelling."

"Why do you keep calling him 'king,' Christophe?" Murat raised a dark eyebrow.

"Call him 'Citizen Capet,' if you like. Old habits for an old soldier," Kellermann said, shrugging. "But my point is that the trial should be more than just a cursory show of legal proceedings. How can we send a man to his death without a fair and honest trial?"

"And so he had one, Christophe. And now, let's have the verdict. They brought only thirty-three charges against him; they could have easily brought fifty more."

Kellermann cocked his head to the side, considering the argument. André, too, was absorbed in the debate. Murat continued: "On how many occasions has he ordered his hired mercenaries to fire on the people and shed the blood of our patriots? A sovereign exists to protect the liberties of his people, not crush them." Murat's cheeks darkened as he spoke. "We are at war, Christophe."

"I am aware of that, my friend," Kellermann replied calmly.

But Murat continued. "And I haven't even gotten to the fact that he squandered all of our national treasure on dressing and feeding his Austrian wife. All the while, she was holding orgies with half the court and plotting with her brother back in Vienna to seize our kingdom."

Kellermann cringed at the vulgar accusation, casting a sideways glance toward his wife as if to apologize. When he answered, he looked at his friend with a calm expression. "On that score, I think that the journals have drummed up and printed many accusations that are false. Louis and his wife were profligate spenders, that I will grant you. They squandered the wealth of our land and were utterly blind to the needs of their subjects. But I believe Marie-Antoinette wielded far less influence at Versailles than many would have us believe."

"I'd be careful if I were you, Christophe." Murat brought his champagne to his thin lips. "It sounds to me like the—now, what is it that they call you? 'The Savior of the Revolution'?—shares certain sympathies with the monarchy."

Kellermann let out a chuckle, making light of the comment. André, for his part, found it less easy to laugh off Murat's disdain, and he felt as though he were an uninvited spectator at an increasingly dangerous match. What would he say if either man turned to him and asked for his own opinion? Surely they recalled that his own father had been a member of the aristocracy?

But neither man seemed to notice André's presence as they continued their exchange. "Come now, Nicolai," Kellermann said. "That's an absurd charge. I agree wholeheartedly that King Louis—rather, *Citizen Capet*—has forfeited the right to wear the crown and rule our land. I took the oath to the Republic, just the same as you."

"No man deserves a crown."

"On that you have my complete agreement. Our dispute lies not in the virtue of the monarchy, but in the punishment for the fact that he was given the crown to wear. You must keep in mind, Nicolai, that he ascended to the role before the age of twenty and knew no other life than that shown to him inside the gilded walls of Versailles."

"Poor Prince Louis." Murat smirked.

"I don't expect pity for a spoiled prince," Kellermann answered. "I simply mean to point out that Lou—Citizen Capet—executed the job before him with the abilities and experiences afforded by his own sheltered life. The system must come to an end, but must his life as well?"

"We can argue about whether he executed his duties well, but not over whether he executed his own people. We know he did that."

"Are we to take the Old Testament view of justice, Nicolai, or the New Testament? We could say that we must correct past sins with fresh sins of our own, or we can show mercy."

"So you accept the execution of the corrupt nobles, but our spoiled despot should receive preferential treatment?"

Kellermann crossed his arms before his broad chest as he said: "No, in fact I'm not certain that I agree with any of the executions carried out in the name of our Republic." Kellermann paused and breathed out a sigh, his brow knit in thought. He put a hand once more around his wife's waist, pulling her closer.

Murat drained the last of his champagne. "Perhaps that is because you yourself are of noble birth, Monsieur le Comte."

"As are you, Nicolai," Kellermann retorted, his cheeks now flushing a crimson hue.

André's eyes shot to the dark-haired officer, astounded to hear this fact thrown in his face and eager to see the man's reply. Murat waved his long fingers as if swatting a fly. "I swore off my title long ago, before it was even fashionable to do so. I spilled blood for the revolution in America."

Kellermann offered a measured smile. "In a campaign funded by our maligned monarch, might I remind you?"

"The common men of this country know that I am one of them." Murat's mustache twitched as he spoke, a barely noticeable quiver, but the hint of some deeper emotion lurking beneath his bitten-back words. What was it, André wondered, that hid in the man's deep well of feelings? Anger? Envy? Pain? "I am not a . . . what do they call you? *Savior.* . . . I am simply a man. No better than they are," Murat said to Kellermann, ignoring André's stare.

"You know I did not ask for that nickname, Nicolai. Nor would I ever encourage its use," Kellermann declared.

So absorbed was André in this exchange that he had barely heard the uproar behind him. But now, all three men turned to look in the direction of an angry holler. *"Mon dieu!"* Madame Kellermann raised a gloved hand to her lips and gasped. "Christophe, someone must go separate them!"

Just then André saw two men shoving each other, one of them dressed in the dark blue coat of an army uniform. In a flash, he realized the man was Remy. The other was the thick-set companion of the beautiful blond woman.

André cringed as he saw Remy splash a cup of punch in the man's stunned face. And with that, several men had their arms around Remy and were carrying him toward the door. The other man, his cheeks stained pink with rage and punch, shouted at Remy's receding figure. *"Cochon! Pig!"* He tilted his fleshy face toward his date, offering a brief apology before he stomped away.

André felt his face redden, momentarily wishing that he, too, could flee through the door by which Remy had just been expelled.

"Well, it seems your brother has drunk more than his fill." Murat turned his stare on André. "A soldier drunk in public can receive up to thirty lashes."

Kellermann shook his head, looking at André with a knowing smile. "A beautiful lady is always worth the trouble. Now, Christianne, Nicolai, how about we go and refill our glasses? All this talk of politics has made me thirsty. Captain Valière, perhaps your brother has need of assistance?"

"Thank you, sir, I will go see what the fool has done." André, mortified, slipped away from the trio and quickly crossed the room. By the time André had reached the door through which his brother had been escorted, Remy was gone.

Outside, La Place de l'Abbe-Basset was once more empty, showing no sign of his brother or the men who had escorted him from the party. He had clearly been tossed into a carriage and sent home, or worse. André cursed and let out a sigh, kicking the stone step. The last thing he and his brother needed was to attract the attention, and disapproval, of the Jacobins.

Hoping to make apologies for his brother and salvage what had so far been a rather unpleasant night, André turned and reentered the party. There, near the front door, stood the woman who had been at the center of the turmoil. She was alone. Whereas before she had appeared bored, now her features had a taut, agitated quality to them.

"Excuse me, mademoiselle." André approached her, noticing that she was even more beautiful up close than she had appeared from across the great hall. But his thoughts were still preoccupied with his brother and his own embarrassment at Remy's disturbance. "I fear that my brother has interfered with you and your husband, and I must offer my most sincere apologies on his behalf."

She looked at him, her light eyes taking in first his uniform, and then meeting his stare with a blank, unreadable expression. "No, it's quite all right," she said, looking past him and back toward the party.

André shifted, preparing to leave, until she added: "I am grateful for the little bit of excitement."

André paused, looking once more at her, and now he couldn't help but laugh at this curious response. "Well, I'm relieved to hear that. But I'm certain that your husband does not appreciate the punch in his face. I truly cannot apologize heartily enough for my brother's—"

"Don't." She waved her hand. "And please stop calling Franck my husband." She leaned in close, the hint of annoyance now noticeable in her tone. "Can't you give me a little more credit?"

André was taken aback, and he stammered: "Oh, my mistake, mademoiselle."

And then the unexpected happened: a smile bloomed across her features. When she laughed, the noise sent shivers up André's spine; it was a sound from his childhood. The lovely, crystalline sound of female gaiety, an intoxicating ripple, like a first sip of champagne.

"I'm sorry, I don't mean to laugh at your expense." She eyed him intently, and for a moment André involuntarily held his breath, stunned by her gaze. He offered his hand. "André Valière."

Her eyes narrowed to a squint, and André prepared to leave, but she raised a gloved hand and held out her empty glass. "I've finished my champagne." She arched a lone eyebrow. "Would you be a gentleman and refill my glass, or should I wait for my companion to return?"

"I'd . . . yes, all right." André took her glass and turned, crossing the room toward the drinks. He was eager to get back to her before any other man had summoned the courage to approach her.

"Two for me?" She smiled as he reappeared, looking at the glasses he held. "Perhaps *you* are a gentleman, even if your brother is not."

"One for me, and one for you," he said, offering her a glass.

"Well then, *santé*." She clinked his glass and they both took a sip.

"About my brother." André lowered his drink, sighing.

"Please, he was highly amusing. In fact, I think that's the reason Franck got angry to begin with—it was obvious that I was enjoying the other man's company a bit more than his own." She took a long sip.

"And what prompted the quarrel?"

The woman's eyes now scanned the room as she answered, as if she were looking for someone. Perhaps for her companion? Finally, as if she had no other option, she turned back to André. "Oh, he kept asking me to dance. I kept replying that there was no music, and therefore I would not dance. But your brother was undaunted, and merely answered that if there was no music to be had here, then perhaps he should take me somewhere where there was."

She took another sip, turning her eyes back toward André's. They were the same light blue as his mother's eyes, as Remy's, too. But they had a coolness that neither of theirs had.

"I was considering his offer when Franck intervened."

"I would have strongly advised against that, mademoiselle."

"What?" She offered half a smirk. "Leaving with your brother?"

"With him? To be certain. Or any man whose acquaintance you've only just made. These are dangerous times to be taking up with complete strangers."

"Oh, I don't disagree with you, soldier. I was simply ready to accept any offer to leave this party. It's terribly dull." She looked out over the crowd once more, her manner distracted.

"So you don't like your date, and you disapprove of the party. Mademoiselle, why did you come?"

"My uncle is here," she said, her tone suddenly drained of any emotion. "Nowadays he rarely orders me to do anything directly, but, when he does, I've learned it is unwise to disobey."

"I see," André said, to be polite, but wondering to himself what such a comment meant. Based on her uneasy expression, he deemed it best to change topics. "Strange to be at a party at Christmastime without any celebration of Christmas, is it not?"

"These are strange times indeed." She nodded, finishing her champagne.

Just then, the crowd that had been steadily building around the figures of Robespierre and Danton began to call out for quiet. Their hosts wished to address the party. André turned his focus toward Robespierre, looking at the narrow-figured man as he lifted his shoulders and tossed his head back, as if preparing for a performance.

"Say, I'm a bit warm." She was leaning close now, whispering in André's ear. Her breath was sweet with champagne. "Would you be kind enough to escort me outside to get some air?"

André threw a cursory glance toward the crowd gathering around Robespierre before looking back at her. "If you don't mind the cold?"

"But I just told you I was warm," she said, stepping closer to him. Surprised but delighted, André offered his arm and led her toward the front.

"No!" She froze, her eyes suddenly wide with a look that resembled fear. "Let's not go that way. Let's see if there's a side entrance." She pulled him through the crowd and toward the back of the hall, and André followed willingly.

Outside, they leaned against the wall of the building, its cold stone façade shielding them a bit from the wind that whipped across the square. Several feet away, by the front entrance, a crowd of *sans-culottes* had begun to gather. Word had spread throughout the *arrondissement* that Robespierre and Danton were inside, and the people hoped to catch a glimpse of their idols at the end of the evening. By their secluded side entrance, André and his lovely companion stood removed from the growing crowd, their breaths visible in the chilly air and their faces illuminated by the flickering shadows of the fires the crowd had started.

She had claimed overheating inside, but André suspected that that had been only an excuse to avoid someone, perhaps an overzealous admirer. Based on her shivering, he assumed that she was no longer warm. "Take my coat."

She did not protest as he draped his frock coat over her bare, narrow shoulders. "Thank you." She smiled up at him, tucking her hands into the coat pockets.

André looked down at her face, lit up in the hazy glow of the nearby street lanterns. "You know, I haven't gotten your name."

"Sophie de Vincennes."

A noble name. André nodded, studying her delicate features more closely. "I'm not familiar with the name. From where does your family come?"

"Oh, it's not my family's name. It's my husband's."

André felt his whole body slump; so she *was* married.

"Or rather, I should say, my late husband's."

"Late husband?" André repeated; she was too young to be a widow. But then again, the Revolution had no doubt made hundreds of young widows with noble surnames.

She nodded. "Monsieur le Comte de Vincennes did not survive to see this glorious Revolution." She rocked back on her heels as she said it, her tone emotionless.

"I am sorry. It was not my business to pry."

She continued to look up at him, a quizzical smile brightening her previously cool blue eyes. "Bad men have to die as well as good men, don't they?"

A curious statement, André thought, but he did not wish to offend her by inquiring further, so he changed the subject. "Do you live in Paris, Comtesse de Vincennes?"

"Please, call me Sophie. Or citizeness, even." The sarcasm in her voice matched her half smile, and she continued: "The countess was the wife who came before me. She, too, is now expired."

André nodded, looking over her shoulder at the crowd, still growing in number by the front steps. He blew on his hands, his own body beginning to shiver without his jacket.

"I do live in Paris now," she said. "My uncle moved me here when Jean-Baptiste, the *darling* count, died. He said he could better protect me that way."

André turned back to Sophie. "I have rented lodging in the city as well, just a little to the east, near Saint-Paul."

"You mean the Pauline Temple of Reason," Sophie corrected him, another wry smile tugging on her lovely lips. André laughed and then they stood opposite each other in silence for several moments, watching the crowd nearby. One of the men had brought the tricolor flag and hung it outside the entrance. A cluster of several *sans-culottes* began singing the national anthem, while others cried out insults against Citizen Capet and began dancing in a crudely formed circle.

Sophie broke the silence between them. "It *was* strange not to have Christmas this year, wasn't it?"

André nodded, turning back to look into her pale, unblinking eyes.

"I sang carols to myself anyway. I didn't care, and no one else had to hear them." She smirked, shrugging her shoulders. Her frame looked so small in his uniform jacket. "*Maman* used to sing carols to us in the sleigh on the way to Christmas Mass. I especially loved the one about the shepherds who walked through the night to see the little infant."

André knew the tune of which she spoke, and he began to sing from his own childhood memory: "*All through the day, and all through the night.*"

She joined him, their voices weaving into one melody: "*With nothing to guide them but heaven's light.*"

Looking at each other, they both began to laugh at the same time.

"So you know that one?" Sophie blinked, her head dropping to one side. She looked charming, even in his military jacket.

"Of course I do. Remy used to sing carols until my father would lose his temper and send him out of the room."

Remy. André felt a tinge of guilt—he should probably go find his brother and ensure that he hadn't gotten himself into trouble elsewhere in the city. He had known, before they'd arrived this evening, that Remy had been in the mood to fight. But when he looked down at Sophie, her cheeks tinged pink by the frigid night air, her light eyes fixed on his with sudden interest, André found himself not yet ready to leave. Not until she did.

"Remy is, I take it, the man who hoped to dance with me before?"

"I think every man inside that hall hoped to dance with you."

She studied him now, and, as if reading his thoughts, she asked: "Are you worried about him?"

"Every day," he answered. "But somehow, he always manages to sort things out."

A sly grin pulled on her lips, and she asked: "Do *you* wish to dance with me, Officer Valière?"

He gazed at her, hoping that she didn't hear the clamoring of his heart against his rib cage. "Yes, Countess," he said after a moment, his voice quiet.

"I thought I asked you not to call me 'Countess,'" she said, breaking his gaze.

"Oh, yes . . . sorry." He had never been a natural charmer; no, that was Remy.

Perhaps sensing his bashfulness, Sophie turned to him and smiled. Feeling fortified by this encouraging glance, André was just about to take her hand and ask for that dance when he heard footsteps approaching. They were not alone.

"So this is where you've scurried off to."

Though it was too dark for him to immediately recognize the figure approaching, André knew the voice.

"Uncle Nico," Sophie said, just as General Murat's shadowed face became visible in a pool of light cast by the nearest streetlamp. "How wonderful to see you." She attempted, and failed, to bring a tone of cheer to her voice.

"Hello, So-So." Murat leaned down and offered his pale cheek for a kiss. She obliged, appearing so small, suddenly, beside her uncle's tall uniformed frame.

"I see you've met one of my men, André de Valière." Murat turned his stare on André, his eyes two pools of gray ink.

Sophie turned to André, her face confused at the surname he had only partially disclosed. "I . . . yes, I have. He was kind enough to escort me outside for some fresh air. I was feeling a bit overheated in the hall, Uncle."

"Yes, it looked as if you were *quite* warm as I was walking up." Murat's eyes rested on André's jacket, draped over Sophie's shoulders. "My niece is a widow, Captain de Valière," Murat said. "I am her guardian."

"I had just finished telling him about Jean-Baptiste, Uncle Nico," Sophie interjected, shifting her weight from one foot to the other.

Murat kept his cold gaze fixed squarely on André. "So, it looks like one brother tried and failed to gain your attention this evening. And now the other is hoping to . . ." Murat didn't finish his thought. André balled his fists hard, his nails digging into the flesh of his palms.

Murat continued, turning to his niece. "So-So, you left the hall without hearing Citizen Robespierre's address."

"I needed some air," she repeated, her voice quiet.

"Well, I suspect you've gotten quite enough. It's getting late; I shall take you home."

"Uncle, I'm fine, really. I'd like to stay a bit longer, if you don't mind."

Murat spread his thin lips to protest, but just then, a herd of bodies poured forth into the square from the front door of the Panthéon. André turned to look and saw the figure of Robespierre emerging first, with Danton just a step behind him. After them came a dozen other members of the National Convention. General Kellermann, too, was exiting and André saw him running toward a waiting fiacre.

"What's this?" Sophie asked, turning to her uncle.

"Christophe?" Murat called toward Kellermann's retreating frame. André seized this brief opening to lean close to Sophie and whisper, "Can I see you again?"

Sophie turned to answer, but before she could speak, her uncle had slid in between them. "Sophie, come." His jaw clenched, Murat clamped his large hand on his niece's elbow, a gesture that might have signified gallantry if not for his sharp stare and insistent tone. "Come, niece, the night could very well turn dangerous. I will get you safely home."

Glancing once more at André, Sophie hesitated a moment and then accepted her uncle's outstretched arm. With Sophie secure in his grip, Murat called once more toward his colleague. "Kellermann, what news?"

Kellermann turned as he strode quickly toward his coach. "The National Convention has convened an emergency midnight session."

Even from that brief reply, André understood perfectly well his meaning; there was only one thing that would pull the men from their party to the halls of the assembly for a spontaneous meeting. That night, the National Convention of France would vote whether or not to behead their king.

8

Paris

March 1793

Yet again, Jean-Luc St. Clair's colleagues were watching the young law-yer with droll expressions, entertained by the tearful woman sitting at his desk.

"Citizeness Poitier"—Jean-Luc spoke in a hushed tone, hoping to have a calming influence as he did so—"it was my pleasure to represent you. I am just happy that you and your children may, at last, return to your home."

"You don't understand, Citizen St. Clair. If my Jacques was here today, he'd embrace you until he'd half-crushed the life out of you!" She reached across the desk, taking her lawyer's hands in her rough palms. "How can we ever repay you?"

He smiled at her tear-streaked face, his shoulders slackening. "Seeing justice done for our citizens, at last, is reward enough." Though, truth be told, a small financial reward would not have gone unappreciated; Marie had told him just yesterday that they were behind on what they owed both the landlord and the baker.

After several more entreaties, and a few more sobs, Jean-Luc was finally successful in seeing Madame Poitier down to the square, where she bid him farewell with a hearty hug and a promise that, should he ever need accommodations near Massy, he was always welcome in her family's cot-tage.

"Bet you're glad to be done with that one." Gavreau was leaning on

Jean-Luc's oak desk, waiting for him when he reentered the crowded office.

Jean-Luc sighed, taking his seat and sweeping up the scattered documents of Madame Poitier's case. "I'm glad that she can return home. I just hope the government official who has moved into the Montnoir estate will be a better landlord."

"If not, she can always come back here for another round of charity. You can't seem to turn 'em away."

Jean-Luc shrugged off the comment, still sorting the case files for storage.

"Nearly done?" Gavreau had his coat on and buttoned, an eager look on his face.

"Give me twenty minutes." Jean-Luc looked at his manager, who scowled and walked away.

Jean-Luc never organized his papers until he was done with them. Now that they no longer served a purpose, they would be preserved and filed in a precise and logical manner; it was while he worked that he appreciated chaos. Scrawling a quick note to Marie, Jean-Luc called over one of the office errand boys. "Will you deliver this to my wife?" He handed over a *sou* and the note outlining his victory for the Widow Poitier, reminding Marie that he would not be home for supper. Grabbing his coat, he rose from his chair and walked to meet Gavreau.

"So, where are we going?" Outside, in the last moments of sunlight before dusk, the square was packed with men and women of all ages— wine-sipping *sans-culottes,* vendors selling underripe fruit, various laborers taking advantage of one of the first days in which the coming spring seemed not so far off. The lights in the nearby windows and guesthouses were beginning to flicker over a sea of brown coats and red caps.

"It's a small place on Rue des Halles. Maurice picked it," Gavreau replied as they pressed forward into the throng.

Jean-Luc nodded, adjusting his coat and wishing he'd had Marie press his suit before this meeting.

Gavreau turned to his colleague, a teasing grin on his face. "Your first meeting with a big shot of the new government, eh? Don't be nervous, St. Clair."

"I'm not," Jean-Luc lied.

The rendezvous was to take place across from the market square called Les Halles, at a spot aptly named the Café Marché. When they arrived, the hotelier informed Gavreau that the third gentleman already awaited them, and he guided them toward a table in the rear of the dim room, removed from the other diners.

Seated in the corner was a thin, elderly man in a plain black suit, fitted with a tricolor cockade on his left breast pocket. Maurice Merignac stood when he noticed the two men approaching. A ponytailed wig of orange curls framed a pale face—one that didn't appear to often see sunlight. The head beneath the bright wig was, Jean-Luc guessed, bald.

"Citizen Merignac, it is good to see you," Gavreau said, eagerly shaking the older man's hand.

"And you, citizen."

"Allow me to introduce one of my brightest and most promising young associates, Jean-Luc St. Clair."

Merignac turned his small, dark eyes on Jean-Luc as he extended a hand. "Citizen St. Clair."

"Citizen Merignac." Jean-Luc took the man's outstretched hand, which felt cold. "It is an honor to meet you."

The three men took their seats around the small table, and a carafe of red wine was promptly set before them. The attendant informed them that the chef had prepared a fish stew that evening, and they might select either turnips or potatoes to accompany it. All three asked for the stew with potatoes, and then they were left alone in the privacy of their corner.

"So, how is your esteemed boss?" Gavreau asked. "He's the talk of the journals these days. Seems that he's influencing everything from grain prices to the war effort, even to which noble neck should remain and which should be cut off?"

In response, Merignac simply nodded, one slow, reverential movement of the head. The flicker of the lone candle on the table glimmered on his face, illuminating what appeared to be drawn cheeks and tired, deep-set eyes.

"Merignac and I go back—what is it, twenty years?" Gavreau took the carafe of wine and poured them each a full cup. "Back to the days when all we thought about was chasing skirts. 'Course, that's all I'm still thinking about, though Merignac has moved on to much loftier pursuits." With that, Gavreau erupted into a loud, uninhibited chortle and began to gulp his wine.

Merignac offered a curt nod in response, and Jean-Luc thought to himself that he could not imagine such a man ever chasing women. Merignac edged his chair just an inch away from his old acquaintance, as one would slide away from a foul smell, and turned his gaze on St. Clair. "Tell me, Citizen St. Clair, how long have you worked for the new Republic?"

"We've been in the city for a year and a half."

A lone dark eyebrow slid up Merignac's pale, papery brow. " 'We'?"

"My wife," Jean-Luc explained. "And little boy."

Merignac nodded. "From where did you come?"

"The south, near Marseille."

"I thought I detected the southern accent." Merignac nodded. Jean-Luc, slightly embarrassed, reminded himself to curtail the lethargic southern drawl that he thought sounded dreadfully unsophisticated compared to the fast, clipped cadence of the Parisians.

"I, too, come from the south," Merignac said, leaning forward and offering his first smile. "As does Citizen Lazare." Instantly, Jean-Luc felt more at ease.

"And what a year this one has had since coming up from the south," Gavreau interjected, putting a hand on Jean-Luc's shoulder. "Busy from dawn 'til dusk. I can barely tear him away from his desk to dine with me."

Merignac kept his gaze fixed on the younger lawyer. "Are you a member of the club?"

"The Jacobin Club? Yes, I am," Jean-Luc replied. His membership was little more than nominal, a requirement he'd had to fulfill in order to acquire his position in the new government. But the membership fee of twenty-four *livres* had not been appreciated by Marie, to be sure.

"Good." Merignac nodded, and silence spread once more over the table.

Given that it was late winter, and the days were still short, the room began to darken as the sky outside grew black. The server appeared, relighting the candle in the center of their table, which had been extinguished by a sharp draft.

"Let there be light, eh?" Merignac nodded toward the server before looking back at Jean-Luc, his eyes attentive. "Have you ever been over to the Rue Saint-Honoré?"

"To Jacobin headquarters?" Jean-Luc now lifted his wineglass, shaking his head. "No."

"It is no great distance from here." Merignac folded his thin hands on the table before him, not touching his wine. "I could show you in sometime, if you'd like. Citizen Lazare spends much of his time there these days. When he's not sitting through speeches at the Convention or at trial."

Jean-Luc glanced toward Gavreau, whose face betrayed the same surprise that Jean-Luc now felt. And then, turning back to Merignac, Jean-Luc nodded. "That would be an honor. Thank you."

And then, as if seeing with stark clarity the question on Jean-Luc's mind, Merignac added: "My esteemed superior is always willing to meet a bright young man employed in the service of the Republic. He is generous—very generous indeed—with young talent. He calls such men as you"—and now Merignac leaned forward—"*ses petits projets.*"

His little projects.

Jean-Luc nodded just as the server returned, refilling Gavreau's wineglass and depositing their bowls of fish stew. Merignac took his linen napkin in his spindly fingers and tucked it fastidiously into the collar of his suit before he reached for his spoon.

Taking just the smallest, slowest bite of his dinner, Merignac looked up at Jean-Luc. "Robespierre is someone you'll want to meet, as well. But you already know that." He said it matter-of-factly, as if meeting two of the most powerful men in Paris was as easily done as introducing oneself to a neighbor or passerby on the street.

Jean-Luc followed the elder man's lead, hungrily spooning himself a bite of the thin, watery stew. It needed salt and butter, and he tasted very little fish; Marie was correct to complain about Parisian seafood. Turning his focus back to his companions, he said: "I think that a great number of people would like an audience with Citizen Robespierre, as well as Citizen Lazare."

Merignac swallowed, his spoon suspended in his fingers as he spoke. "They are quite sought-after these days."

"Beloved, you might say," Jean-Luc added.

"Indeed, Robespierre is . . . well, he's an interesting fellow. His rise to power was quick. Many believe that he is unstoppable." The room was now completely dark, illuminated by only a dozen flickering candles. The dim lighting gave the orange of Merignac's wig a peculiar fiery appearance against which his pale skin seemed paper-thin, almost translucent.

"Do you know what they've begun to call Robespierre?" Merignac cocked his head. "'The Incorruptible.' But I'm not so sure of that. My employer believes that no man's virtue is beyond corruption. It's simply a matter of finding his weakness."

Jean-Luc looked down at his stew, slightly startled by the remark. Gavreau, perhaps feeling uncomfortable with the silence, slurped his wine and muttered: "I know mine pretty well, you might say." Only Gavreau laughed at his own joke.

"The thing that Robespierre recognized," Merignac continued, ignoring Gavreau, "and that the fool of a king never did, is that anger is so much more potent than love. The Bourbon tried to appeal to people's better natures. He told them he loved them as a father loves his children. They don't want to hear that. They are hungry and enraged and they want someone to tell them that they are right to be so."

Jean-Luc sat silently, considering this.

"We're both from the south, Citizen St. Clair," Merignac continued. "A region perhaps most famed for its maritime industry. I would liken public opinion to the headwinds caught in a great sail. The brilliance of Robespierre is that he has caught the wind of the people's rage and desperation and has directed it with great agility and cunning. True, if managed poorly it can turn on those who wield it—like our ill-fated monarch. But, if harnessed properly, that force can power the machine of progress. As Citizen Lazare likes to say: 'Progress comes from change, and change is generated by force.' Why not harness the power of the people and generate force from all of this splendid chaos?"

"Hear, hear!" Gavreau bellowed, slamming a fist into the table. Jean-Luc turned to his colleague and noticed that he had already drained several glasses of wine, and, from the looks of it, had begun to feel their effects.

Ignoring that interjection, Merignac continued in a quiet tone, looking only at Jean-Luc. "My esteemed patron, Citizen Lazare, believes that the wrath of the people is the true source of the nation's strength and power. The late king may have tried to appeal to the *better natures* of the common people, but, in truth, he feared them. He never understood them, don't you see? Liberty, equality, fraternity." The elder man waved his hand aside, leaning in closer to Jean-Luc. "That is all fine and dandy. But the true origin of this new power is quite a simple thing: pure, unbridled rage. Fury, born out of years of desperation. The man who understands that best . . . well . . ."

Jean-Luc hadn't expected this turn in the conversation. He usually enjoyed discussing policy and how best to serve the people's interests, but something in Merignac's words struck him as more than that. There was an edge of zealous cunning, a base view of mankind that would paint his fellow countrymen as terrifying, bestial, even maniacal. What about the noble work toward which he and his fellow patriots were striving—the Declaration of the Rights of Man? Universal suffrage? Affordable bread and housing? Jean-Luc was about to say as much when there was a loud clamor toward the front of the restaurant.

Two young men wearing the blue coat of the army, their faces so similar that surely they must have been brothers, were being escorted out of the restaurant. One of them, his hair darker, had his arms wrapped around the other, and from the looks of it he was trying to calm him down.

At the table from which they had just been excused, a third man, also in an officer's uniform, was hollering in their direction. He sat before a pile of smashed china, a grin on his face as he sipped from a glass of wine. "Get your drunk arse home, Remy! And next time, I'll stick *you* with the bill."

The younger-looking brother, his hair disheveled from the commotion, yelled over his shoulder. "You're a fool, LaSalle, and I'd punch you if I could!" He struggled against the older man's restraining embrace. The restaurant attendants were insisting that they leave while the darker-haired brother, his grip still on the other's shoulders, offered several coins to the hotelier as consolation.

He snapped at the younger man now: "Remy, that's enough. We're going."

"Agreed, André. They're no fun in this place—take me over to the Left

Bank." The handsome young man's words slipped out, slurred and slow. "I've told Celine I'd visit her tonight."

"Not tonight. I'm taking you home."

The man called Remy lowered his head onto his brother's shoulder as they shuffled out of the café. A stunned silence hovered across the café in their wake. Jean-Luc turned his gaze back to his dinner companions. To his left, Gavreau was chuckling, and to his right, Merignac looked as if he had lost his appetite.

Folding his thin hands on the table, the old secretary propped himself up on his elbows. "They should not allow fools like that into establishments like this. Even if they do wear the uniform."

How undemocratic you sound, Jean-Luc thought to himself. But he simply lifted his spoon and tucked back into his flavorless stew.

Removing a pristine white handkerchief with which he now dabbed the corners of his mouth, Merignac looked up. "Citizen St. Clair, I hear that you just defended a widow. An unfortunate woman who had been preyed upon by a villainous marquis? My employer followed that case, in fact, with interest. He approves of your work."

Jean-Luc nodded, swallowing his stew and the involuntary smile that tugged on his lips, surprised that his drudging work had been noticed by anyone outside his department. "Citizeness Poitier. A worthwhile cause, reinstating her to her proper home."

"Speaking of widows," Merignac said, once Jean-Luc had finished. "Now that Citizen Capet is dead, the question remains: what to do with his Austrian widow? Should Antoinette lose her head as well?"

Jean-Luc, too, had thought much about the question of the deposed queen. He had been shocked when the king had been sent to the guillotine; he could never have imagined, at the outbreak of the Revolution almost four years ago, that the country would go that far in its quest for liberty. But it was treason to say so.

Merignac leaned his chin onto his hands, his face angled toward Jean-Luc as he asked: "Well, citizen? What do you think ought to be done with the Austrian woman?"

Jean-Luc swallowed hard, dabbing the corners of his mouth with his napkin before answering. "I do not wish to see her returned to Austria, where her royalist friends might make more trouble for us."

"What, then?"

Jean-Luc wavered a moment before answering. He recalled the political pamphlet he had read that morning, another installment put out by the cryptic "Citizen Persephone," this one calling for reason and clemency in the sentencing of Marie-Antoinette. Jean-Luc agreed with that argument now as he answered: "I think a life spent under house arrest would be sufficient punishment."

"Come now." Merignac offered a tepid smile, his head leaning to one side. "You are a smart man, Jean-Luc St. Clair. You know she would relish a house arrest. She'd spend her time eating brioches and drinking the finest wines while bedding her guards." He sniggered, looking down to his full bowl of stew, which he still refrained from touching. After a pause, he sighed. "My patron, Citizen Lazare, believes that for her, it must be the blade, just as it was for her husband. While the Austrian consort lives, she serves as a symbol of the monarchy, a rallying cry to inspire our enemies at home and abroad. It is a matter of simple logic: either she dies, or our revolution shall perish. So, send her to the guillotine."

Jean-Luc cleared his throat, lowering his eyes as he took a sip of wine.

"But I think the idea of the guillotine makes you . . . uncomfortable, Citizen St. Clair." Merignac was looking at him appraisingly, his dark eyes narrowed.

Jean-Luc turned to Gavreau, whose lips were stained purple, and held out his glass for a refill of wine.

"Do you know whom we have to thank for the widespread use of the guillotine, Citizen St. Clair?" Merignac asked.

"Joseph-Ignace Guillotin," Jean-Luc answered, turning back to his dinner partner as he lowered his wineglass. "That is from where the name is derived."

"Precisely. *Doctor* Joseph-Ignace Guillotin. And do you know, Jean-Luc . . . may I call you Jean-Luc?"

"Please do."

"Excellent. Where was I? Oh yes, do you know why the guillotine was chosen as our new means of execution?"

"To offer a more humane form of capital punishment."

"Just so."

Jean-Luc swallowed, clearing his throat. "I grant you, the apparatus it-self might be more . . . humane . . . than the gallows, where a man can writhe for upwards of an hour in unimaginable pain. Or beheading by an ax, where failure to land a clean blow can necessitate several hacks before the head is severed. It's just the—"

"Yes?" Merignac was listening intently now, his dark eyes shimmering with the excitement of discussion.

Jean-Luc continued: "I've sometimes wondered about the *expedience* with which our tribunals send men and women—even children—to this device of death."

Merignac considered this, his chin resting on his narrow index finger. "So you would hope for a more bloodless form of revolution?"

Jean-Luc opened his mouth to respond, but nothing came out. All he could think of was the countless hours he'd spent documenting the seized goods of the Revolution's enemies—priests, nuns, nobles, accused spies. Families pulled from their homes in the dark of night. Furniture, china emblazoned with the crests of the former owners, empty beds, some of them no larger than the size of a toddler's little frame.

Finally, his voice faint, Jean-Luc continued: "I suppose I do wish that less blood might be shed. Or, at least, that it would be proven entirely nec-essary before shedding so much blood; I believe our courts could demand more proof of treason before damning one to the guillotine." Jean-Luc wondered if what he was saying was dangerous—he had never before ut-tered these nagging doubts. Not even to Marie.

Merignac looked at him intently as he answered: "In any revolution, there must be blood. How else can the sins of past evils be washed clean in expiation? Monsieur Jefferson himself said as much."

Merignac seized on Jean-Luc's pause to continue. "Citizen Lazare knew our former tyrant quite well, as I'm sure you have heard. He lived with him, and that queen of his, at court. Do you know what our blessed mon-arch wrote in his journal the day that the Bastille was stormed?"

Jean-Luc knew the answer to this question. Every news journal had been sure to print this fact, so that all Parisians knew the answer to this question. Quietly, he answered: *"Rien."*

"Rien." Merignac nodded. "Nothing."

"Nothing!" Gavreau repeated, running a finger along the rim of his empty stew bowl.

Merignac, still ignoring Gavreau, continued. "He wrote *rien*, because he had caught *rien* while out hunting that day." Merignac spoke with a cold, emotionless tone. "What do you think the men and women who stormed the Bastille would have written in their diaries, had they been able to afford ink and paper that day?" His thin black eyebrows arched, touching the border of his orange wig. "Perhaps they would have written a line about how starving they were. Or that another one of their children had died, due to the filth and hunger in the city."

Jean-Luc's heart beat faster now, as he sensed the zeal lurking behind the man's calm, measured voice. He sat there mute, unsure of how to answer, feeling panicked that he had been a fool to advocate for clemency when, clearly, this man loathed the nobility as much as any wronged citizen or citizeness in La Place de la Révolution. But then, to Jean-Luc's utter relief, Merignac cracked a smile. And like a clap of thunder disperses the humidity of a heavy summer evening, the tension at the table was dispelled as Merignac, suddenly, began to laugh.

"Come now, Citizen St. Clair." He reached his hand toward Jean-Luc. Beside them, Gavreau, too, was laughing, for a reason that Jean-Luc could not deduce. "You know, I believe that you love a spirited debate quite as much as my employer does," Merignac said, taking Jean-Luc's hand in his; his palm felt cold. Like a father might soothe a child, Merignac patted the top of Jean-Luc's hand. "What a fascinating conversation. I believe my employer would have enjoyed it! But it's getting late. What do you say, Jean-Luc, shall we retire?" Merignac was suddenly as informal and relaxed as an old friend. "It seems that this one needs his bed." He cast a sideways glance toward Gavreau.

Merignac insisted on paying for the dinner, and the three of them rose from the table. "Where do you live, citizen?"

Jean-Luc felt a moment's flash of embarrassment as he gave his Left Bank address.

"That's too far to walk on a cold night such as this one. I'll see you home in the carriage."

"I thank you for the offer but that won't be necessary, I assure you."

"Come now, haven't you quarreled with me enough for one night? I won't hear your refusal. Besides, Citizen Lazare was gracious enough to lend the coach this evening." And then, turning his eyes on Gavreau, Merignac said: "Gavreau, you'll be fine on foot, no?"

"I'll be more than fine! Might even stop at the tavern on the way for a nightcap, if you two gentlemen care to join me?"

The two of them politely declined.

"Fine, then. But won't let that stop me," Gavreau answered, his words slurred. "G'night, gentlemen. A fine evening."

Jean-Luc cast a glance in the direction of his friend's retreating frame before turning back to Merignac. The two of them stood alone now, outside the café. "Here we are." Merignac pointed toward a halted coach that waited at the end of the darkened street. A footman hopped down and opened the door for them, and they stepped inside. The night was indeed cold, and Jean-Luc was grateful for the covered ride as the carriage sped across the island and south over the Pont Neuf. They sat for several minutes without speaking. It was Merignac who broke the silence. "I enjoyed our little discussion at dinner—and I believe that Citizen Lazare would find you to be quite an interesting fellow."

Jean-Luc looked at the orange-haired man across from him in the carriage. "You are too kind to say so, citizen." Jean-Luc hoped that his reply came out sounding enthusiastic, even if he felt the tinge of irrefutable unease.

"Don't you think you are destined for greater things than counting inventory for a fool like Gavreau?"

Jean-Luc was taken aback by the candor of the remark; by the fact that Merignac spoke that way about an old friend, and to someone whom he'd only just met. Perhaps a bit defensively, Jean-Luc answered: "I am doing the work that is necessary for the new Republic."

The carriage had turned onto Jean-Luc's street, and just then the horses halted. The footman hopped down and opened the door. In the sliver of light that spilled into the coach now, Jean-Luc noticed Merignac's derisive smile. "That may be. But if you ever wish to make something of your talents, rather than defending poor widows and struggling to pay the rent on a Left Bank garret, you know where to find us. I would be more than pleased to introduce you to Guillaume Lazare."

Marie had stayed awake and sat waiting for Jean-Luc. She jumped up from her chair and ran to greet him as he walked through the door. "I got your note about the Widow Poitier's case. Out celebrating?" She planted a kiss on his cheek and took his satchel from his hands.

He shook his head.

"You look exhausted." Her brown eyes now showed concern as she helped him out of his jacket.

In the corner where the roof slanted downward, wrapped in a blanket and tucked into his small cradle, Mathieu slept. Jean-Luc crossed the room and pressed his palm into the rosy, plump cheek of the snoring baby. He remained still for several minutes, staring down at his son, the rounded features soft with sleep.

"Where were you, then?" Marie was beside him now, whispering so as not to wake the baby.

Jean-Luc turned to face her. "At a dinner with Guillaume Lazare's personal secretary," he said, his voice relaying his own confusion at the entire evening. Her eyes widened in surprise.

"What a husband I have. Winning cases and dining with the likes of Guillaume Lazare's secretary." Jean-Luc was too lost in his own thoughts to notice her wide smile.

"I think it was some sort of test," Jean-Luc said, scratching the top of his head as they moved away from Mathieu's cradle.

"And? Did you pass?"

"As a matter of fact, I believe I did."

Marie cocked her head to the side, smiling up at her husband. "Pretty soon you're going to be too important for Mathieu and me and this tiny garret."

"Never."

"Well then, how was it?"

"My darling." He paused, looking down at her as he wrapped his arms around her waist. "It was . . . unexpected. I think that everyone in this world has gone a little bit mad, except for you."

She sighed, but her smile remained. "I went mad long ago. How else could I explain my decision to marry you and move to this dreadful neighborhood?"

He leaned his face toward her now, his lips inches from hers. "If it was madness that caused you to first love me, are you still ailing?"

"Very much." She smiled, balancing on her toes to reach up and kiss him.

"Good," he said, kissing her in reply, his whole body yearning for her. "I would hate for you to ever be cured."

9

Paris

Summer 1793

Back in the French capital, having marched with his men as far as the city of Strasbourg, André took his residence once more in the Saint-Paul quarter, just a short walk from the former Bastille prison. The city smoldered in the summer heat, its narrow cobblestoned streets ripe with the stench of so many close-packed bodies. The fear of both foreign and domestic enemies hung heavy like the humid air, and the free French citizens seemed as determined as ever to witness the murderous apparatus mete out its particular manner of revolutionary justice.

In spite of this, the truth was that André's mind was elsewhere than war or revolution. He cared little for the political assemblies in the taverns or the rallies that sprung up in the squares. His thoughts were heavy with the persistent and secret desire to reunite with the young woman he had met on that strange winter evening, half a year earlier.

When not on duty or busy keeping Remy out of trouble, André had taken to spending his time tramping around the Right Bank, his eyes studying every female figure that passed. As he walked the quays near La Place, André could not help but hear the fiendish roars of the crowds gathered there. He had never seen such bloodlust on any field of battle. But Sophie would not be anywhere near the guillotine and the public beheadings, André reasoned. He sought her in the markets near the Châtelet, among the florists' booths near what had once been the great cathedral of Notre Dame, among the vendors whose carts lined the banks of the Seine.

Maximilien Robespierre had consolidated power in the government, purging the Convention and killing every deputy or ally who could have posed even a shadow of a threat. "The Incorruptible" now reigned supreme, chairing a dictatorial body called the Committee of Public Safety. He called for a fixed price on bread and universal male suffrage—and more noble heads. Always, he said, there lurked the insidious threat of enemies of the Revolution: the Austrians abroad who planned to quash the Revolution from the outside, and the counterrevolutionaries who hoped to destroy it from the inside. And always, this fear fueled the frantic, insatiable need to feed the guillotine.

André was determined that, no matter what occurred within the government and the city, he and Remy would hold tight to their military uniforms. It seemed that their good service in the army was their one thin line of defense, keeping them from the executioner Sanson's exalted podium. And so, as the summer wore on and André heard the rumors from LaSalle that his division would be sent under Kellermann to fight the Habsburgs in the Alps, he began to lose hope of ever again seeing Sophie de Vincennes.

Then, on an afternoon in late August while returning to his boarding-house, André's gaze happened upon a familiar face—a sight that caused his heart to heave in his rib cage. At first, he didn't quite trust his own eyes, recalling how many times before they had deceived him. But there, in the broad daylight, she sat.

Sophie was on the terrace of a crowded restaurant in the Marais quarter, dining with the same man who had accompanied her to the fete at the Panthéon months earlier. "Franck" was the name she had given. André fought to suppress a rush of emotion—a combination of jealousy and frustration. So she *was* involved with this man, in spite of what she had said that night.

And yet, beholding her, he could not stay unhappy for long. She was dressed more casually than she had been for the Jacobin ball. In the heat of late summer, she wore a lightweight dress of white linen, its borders trimmed in lace. Her blond hair, reflecting the golden streaks of midday sunlight, was pulled back in a loose bun. Again, she wore a bored, restless expression, that look that she had shed only after talking to *him*, André thought, indulging in a momentary surge of hope.

"You, come here." André waved forward a shaggy-haired youth, his breeches cut short above scabby knees and bare feet. "Would you like to earn a *sou*?"

The boy's reluctance quickly vanished, and his eyes widened as they fixed on the shiny coin. "Why yes, citizen, I'd love some money."

"Good, then you'll deliver a note to that mademoiselle seated over there. Do you see her? The one in white?"

"That pretty one right there?" The kid pointed a dirty finger, which André shooed down.

"Don't point, little lad," he gently scolded. Picking up a piece of paper from the street, one of the ever-present political pamphlets, André scrawled out a quick note, which he folded and handed to the boy. "Deliver this to her, but don't say anything. Just deliver it and then come back to me, you hear? I'll be standing right around this corner with your *sou*."

The boy nodded, taking the note in his grimy fingers and scampering across the street on his errand. André removed himself from sight, stepping behind a wine vendor's stall. He had scribbled onto the paper in hopes that she had not yet forgotten him, *"If you'd like to continue the conversation we started on the steps of the Panthéon, then offer your regrets to Monsieur and come meet me for a drink at Le Pont Blanc."*

André stood at the front of the café, attempting a posture of casual disinterest that belied the nerves he felt. He was on the verge of ordering himself a cup of wine when he realized, with a pang of apprehension, that perhaps Sophie had no intention of coming. The clock across the room told him he had waited for more than a quarter of an hour. Surely, if she remembered who he was or cared to see him again, she would have arrived by now.

Defeated, André propped his elbows on the bar and cast a forlorn glance toward the door, contemplating where he might go to lift his spirits.

He took a deep breath and let out a long, slow exhale; he would take a walk to clear his mind and go home. He turned toward the door just in time to notice, to his shock and delight, a white-clad figure gliding in from the street. Her cheeks rosy from the walk, Sophie entered the tavern and looked around, pausing her search when her eyes landed on his. She stood still for a moment. André faced her, powerless to conceal the broad smile that spread across his face.

Spotting him, Sophie walked forward, her parasol swaying at her side. She extended a gloved hand toward him, which he took and raised to his lips. Keeping his eyes fixed on her, his gaze not wavering for a moment, he said: "You took your time, mademoiselle."

"Me?" She smiled, leaning her head to the side. "It took *you* long enough. I thought that I'd come across you long before now. It *was* Saint-Paul that you named as your neighborhood, wasn't it?" She lifted an eyebrow, her blue eyes sparkling mischievously.

"I've been away," he said, extending an arm toward her.

"Soldiering?"

He nodded. "Join me for a drink?"

She accepted his outstretched arm and walked with him toward a banquette booth in the back of the room.

"As I was saying, I had given up hope of you coming."

"What would you have had me do—abandon poor Franck before we had finished our meal?"

"Perhaps," André replied, smiling. And then, leaning forward toward Sophie, he continued. "I thought you didn't care for him."

"I don't."

"Then why have dinner with him? The poor man is probably in love with you."

Sophie grinned, covering her mouth with her gloved hand. After a pause, she leaned forward and said: "Franck cares for me as little as I care for him, of that I can assure you." Seeing that André was not satisfied with this answer, Sophie explained further. "It's his steaks and his pork chops that Franck enjoys, and he likes to have me on his arm or at his table—not because he enjoys *me*. I don't even think he enjoys my conversation. At least, not any more than I enjoy his."

André thought about this. "So, then, you admit that you use him?"

"Just as he uses me." Sophie shrugged, her face expressionless. "If it wasn't for Franck, I'd never be allowed out of my home. My uncle permits me to go out with Franck, but no one else. So, you see, he is my only ticket to get out into the world."

André considered this, sitting opposite her in a brooding silence.

"I see you're not convinced, Monsieur Valière. . . . What, do you wish me to go out with *you*, instead?"

"Yes," André answered.

"My uncle would never allow it."

"Your uncle doesn't have to know."

She thought about this proposition, drumming her fingers along the table as she did so. "Well, why don't you buy me a drink for a start?"

André asked the attendant which spirits they had available and was told that all they had was wine from local stores in Vanves and Clamart, so he ordered a carafe and two glasses. When the drink came, he lifted his glass toward hers.

"I was beginning to wonder whether or not you existed, or whether I had imagined meeting you that night," he said. "Perhaps that sounds foolish, but now that I see you, I hope you do not mind my saying that I shall do everything I can to see you as often as I can. At least, before we march out again."

Sophie smiled, clinking her glass against his before taking a sip. The wine was watered down and warm, but at least the place had drinks to offer, and enough of a crowd to give it a mildly cheerful atmosphere.

"Did you return to the city with my uncle?"

"I did." André nodded, sipping his wine. "Were you happy to have him back?"

She pursed her lips but didn't reply. That was all the answer André needed.

"I've lost a husband, so I suppose now my uncle thinks he needs to watch over me. It's always the Revolution he uses as his reason—as if he hopes that fear will convince me."

"How so?"

"I *know* that my name puts me at risk, but he reminds me of it every day. It seems to be his justification in forbidding me from going anywhere, or seeing anyone. *Only I can protect you, So-So. You must not expose yourself to danger. Listen to Uncle Nico. I know best.*"

André thought about this, taking another sip of wine.

"Now can you understand why, on occasion, I allow the one man of whom my uncle approves to take me out to lunch?"

André sighed. "How about we agree not to talk about your uncle? You're here now. With me." He let that last part settle for a moment, enjoying its sound. "I propose a toast: to your freedom."

Sophie nodded her assent. "All right."

"Though you do strike me as too young to be a widow."

Sophie stared at him a moment, her face turning serious. "That's because I was too young to be a bride."

"How old *are* you, if you don't mind my asking?"

She made no reply, and André felt foolish for asking such an obviously rude question. His cheeks grew warm.

She leaned forward, propping her arms on the table. "Let me guess. You, Monsieur Valière, are twenty-five?"

"Twenty-three," he answered, pleased that she had seen him as more mature than he actually felt. "And it's 'Captain Valière,' mademoiselle."

"Oh, I see." She laughed, nodding. "*Captain* Valière."

"I will guess—you are eighteen?"

"And you are smart," she chuckled, "guessing such a low number. That's the way to a woman's heart indeed."

"But you can't be much more than eighteen?"

"I'll be twenty in a few months."

"Then I wasn't so far off the mark."

She looked at him, the smile sliding from her face. "I was fourteen when I was married."

He grasped for words but found none.

"You look as horrified as I felt," she said, lowering her gaze to the table.

"I'm sorry, I didn't mean to—" André stammered. "It's just, well, did you . . . did you at least . . . love him?"

"*Love* him? Ha! I barely knew him. I'd met him once. He himself was widowed, and his children were older than I was."

The attendant appeared, refilling each of their wineglasses.

"The union was not to be long-lived, I'm afraid," Sophie continued once the waiter was gone. "The Comte de Vincennes died just three months after making me a countess. Miraculously, there were no children produced by the short marriage."

André felt his cheeks flush, and he looked down at his now-full wineglass.

"In spite of what you might suspect"—Sophie spoke, drawing his gaze back toward her—"my husband did not perish at the guillotine. No," she sighed, "poor Jean-Baptiste died of nothing more glamorous than old age after a life of dissipation. I think it was the gout, in the end. At least, that's what he most often complained of." She paused, clearing her throat, blinking away some unspoken memory before turning her focus back across the table toward André. "He did, however, leave me with a *very* dangerous surname, as my uncle reminds me often."

André, responding to either her candor or the wine, or both, asked, "But why were you forced, at such a young age, to marry such a sickly old man?"

She peered at him, her lashes fluttering with a teasing gaze. "You seem to be a smart man, Captain André Valière. I'll give you one guess."

"Money?"

"There you have it."

André nodded, understanding, as they both fell silent.

Eventually, she spoke. "Come now, how about you, Captain Valière?"

"What about me?" André shifted in his seat.

"How many hearts have you broken? A dozen at least, I'd imagine."

He shook his head.

"Fine, perhaps you are the more reserved type," she continued, peering at him intently. "Two?"

Again, he shook his head.

"One?" she asked, the surprise becoming apparent in her voice. When he didn't answer, she leaned forward. Now it was her turn to be shocked. "None? Not even *one* lady for a handsome captain?"

André shook his head, noting with a twinge of delight that she had called him handsome. Nevertheless, he hurried to explain himself against her incredulity. "I had the good fortune of *not* being married off to an aged widow, but rather attending military school before the old order fell apart."

Sophie let out a humorless laugh, her gaze remaining fixed on André, steady and appraising. When she spoke, her voice was soft. "No heartbroken lovers for a handsome young officer—well, aren't you full of surprises, André Valière?"

He found this remark curious, but Sophie continued to stare at him. Several moments later she sighed and said: "Shame you didn't come along sooner. It seems that you had the noble title that would have satisfied my impoverished, dying father. And then I might have had a husband who survived. And one whom I could have actually liked."

André's cheeks flushed with heat. "I know that your uncle told you my full name. We were forced to change it when my father was denounced."

Sophie nodded as she considered this, licking lips that had been stained a light purple. When she spoke, it was barely a whisper: "But surely memories aren't that short. Don't people know who you really are?"

André replied in a hushed voice, "This uniform has been a shield, so far. Remy and I will be serving in the army, willingly, until the day that all of this madness has been sorted."

Sophie folded her hands on the table between them, letting out a long, slow exhale.

"Speaking of soldiers," André continued. "Your uncle, the *great General Murat* . . ." André rested his chin on his propped elbows. "How is it that someone like you could share the same blood as someone like him?"

Sophie flashed half a smile but didn't censure André for the slur against her uncle. "He was my mother's brother. You know he was a count, the Comte de Custine, before he renounced the title?"

André nodded.

"That is how it was even possible for someone like me to marry the Comte de Vincennes. My mother was, at one point, nobility."

"Was your mother like him?"

"Not in any way, neither appearance nor demeanor." Sophie paused, and André let her sit in the silence of her memory. When she continued, her voice was quiet, and she seemed years younger. "I didn't know my mother well, as she died when I was a little girl. But I do remember thinking that she reminded me of the angels I read about in my catechism."

As do you, André thought to himself.

"I'm not sure *who* Uncle Nico resembles." Sophie drained the rest of her wineglass. Shrugging her shoulders, she looked up at André, her blue eyes sad. "But as my mother is gone, I'll never be able to ask."

"I'm not sure whom he scares more—his enemies or his own men," André confessed.

"He certainly has that effect on people." She smiled, accepting a refill of wine from the waiter. The crowd throughout the tavern had begun to thicken, and bodies drifted closer to their table, filling up the empty space beside their banquette.

André agreed. "I doubt any man would willingly take on General

Murat." Lost in these troubled thoughts, André was shaken out of his day-dream when he caught a pair of uniformed soldiers enter through the front of the café. He realized, with a stab of panic, that it was Remy and LaSalle, accompanied by two pretty, young women. Remy's eyes had landed on the two of them, sitting together in the back, and he waved, marching with his companions through the crowds toward their table.

"Do my eyes deceive me? Is my brother actually dining in the presence of a woman? And a *very* pretty one, at that." Remy made an exaggerated bow, lifting Sophie's hand to his lips. "Citeness." He flashed a dazzling smile at Sophie before turning to André. "Big brother, hello."

"Hello, Remy," André said, his jaw clenched. "LaSalle."

"So I see you've found her at last?" Remy smirked at them, looping his arm around the waist of his date. "The elusive beauty from the Jacobin ball."

André, the impatience and irritation apparent in his voice, replied, "And we were just about to have dinner, Remy, so if you wouldn't mind—"

"Perfect. Surely a good idea that we eat before we drink any more." With that, Remy pulled up two chairs for the ladies and slid his body into the booth beside Sophie. LaSalle sat down beside André, who felt as though he might groan in frustration. But, to his relief, Sophie did not seem upset by this development. In fact, based on the way she smiled across the table at André, she seemed amused.

"I did not hear your names." Sophie turned to the two ladies who accompanied LaSalle and Remy. "I'm Sophie."

"Please excuse my terrible manners, ladies. Sophie, please meet Captain LaSalle's date, the beautiful Henriette. And this here"—Remy took the hand of the girl seated nearest to him—"is Celine." Turning his gaze back toward his brother, Remy said: "Celine is a ballerina."

"A ballerina!" Sophie remarked, smiling delightedly.

"That's right. I call her *Celine la ballerine.*" Remy leaned over and kissed his date, a pretty woman with thick black hair and hazel eyes. "To have Celine, and my brother, and my brother's . . . friend . . . all together. This calls for a celebration. Raspail!" Remy called over the waiter. "A bottle of wine for my brother and his lovely companion." Turning back to André, Remy asked: "You will join me in a drink, brother, won't you?"

"I see that you intend for it to happen, regardless of my answer," André said, giving Sophie a resigned smile. She seemed highly entertained.

"Dinner sounds wonderful," Remy pronounced. "LaSalle and I just offered to treat these two beauties to a bowl of mussels in exchange for their beguiling company."

"Mussels—that sounds like a splendid idea," Sophie said, turning her gaze toward André. He ordered a bowl for the two of them, as well.

The waiter brought out the bowls just as it was growing dark outside. The restaurant was warm and noisy, and André felt a calm, contented feeling as he sat across from Sophie, even in spite of his brother's uninvited presence. The mussels arrived steaming in a frothy broth of butter, white wine, and garlic. Watching Sophie enjoy the dish, laughing as she did with Celine and Henriette at the foolish banter of Remy and LaSalle, André did not mind spending an entire week's wages on buying her wine and dinner.

Between the six of them, they made quick work of several bottles of wine. Remy signified he was at last full by releasing a loud belch, to which Sophie gasped, laughing as she said: "Remy! You have half the manners of your brother."

Remy glanced sideways at André, his face turning serious for one moment. "That is the truth. There is no better man than my brother."

"Come now." André lowered his eyes to the table. "No need to be serious."

"Says the man who is always serious," quipped LaSalle.

"It's true, though," Remy said. "My brother is the best man you will ever meet." Perhaps sensing his older brother's discomfort at the uncharacteristic flattery, Remy shifted in his chair. "Say, LaSalle and I had hoped to take these two lovely ladies dancing, farther up the hill toward Pigalle. Care to join us, André? Sophie?"

Looking to Sophie, who shook her head slightly, André answered: "Not this time, brother."

"Then we will force you to join us next time," LaSalle said.

Leaning in toward Sophie, feeling a bit more comfortable after several glasses of wine and a warm meal, André whispered to her. "Please allow me to walk you home?"

She looked at him sideways now, her lips stained pink from the wine, and he thought to himself that he had never seen a more irresistible woman. "But, Captain Valière, what would people say if I was escorted home after dark by a man such as you, and no chaperone?"

"You have a better chance with me beside you than if you were to try to walk through this mad city on your own. I promise to deposit you safely before your front door, and that will be all."

They parted ways with Remy and LaSalle outside of the café, walking east along the Seine. In the late-summer evening, the light from the lanterns along the quay shimmered off the river's glassy surface like a thousand diamonds. They strolled slowly, side by side, in silence. André looked up at the stars and sighed, relishing the happy awareness that he was in Sophie's presence. He let the gentle evening breeze add to the already pleasant, dizzying feeling in his breast, the warm flush of his face.

When they reached the old wooden bridge, André paused. "We should go up, have a look out over the river."

"All right." She looped her arm in his as André guided her onto the narrow little pedestrian crossing.

There was only one other person on the bridge at this late hour, a man. From the way he stood—shoulders slumped, chin tucked—he appeared to be either deep in thought or deeply troubled. He glanced up when he saw André and Sophie approaching. In the thin light of the cityscape he appeared only a few years older than André, and dressed like a professional sort—perhaps a professor or a lawyer. His hair, brown with just a few traces of gray, was pulled back in a ponytail, and his facial expression was serious. He accidentally grazed André's shoulder as he passed by on the narrow bridge, so lost was he in thought. "Excuse me, if you please. Good night." And with that greeting, spoken with an accent that seemed to place him as from somewhere outside Paris, he skulked off.

"Oh, excuse me," André said, taken aback by the abrupt encounter. He saw, as he watched the retreating figure, that a small card had slipped from the man's pocket. André bent over, eager to pick it up and return it to its rightful owner. "Pardon me, sir, you dropped your card."

André took a few steps after the man, but either he didn't hear or he didn't care to turn back around. In another moment he was gone, vanished into the dark street where the light of the lamps did not reach.

"How odd," André said, wondering why the gentleman would appear so hurried, in such an agitated state this late in the evening. He glanced down at the card:

Jean-Luc St. Clair
Legal Advocate of the French Republic

André tapped the bridge railing, putting the man's odd behavior out of his mind as he tucked the card into his pocket. He turned back to the lovely companion beside him. He and Sophie stood alone on the footbridge. Below them, the waters of the Seine lapped the stony quay walls. All of Paris stood before them, the city covered in a blanket of velvety evening, pierced by just the tiniest bursts of light that flickered from streetlamps, apartments, and restaurant windows.

"It's something, isn't it?" Sophie said, looking out over the river. "I still remember the first time I saw this city."

"As do I," André said, recalling his own initial impression of Paris. The noise was what had struck him most: sounds so different than those of his rural lands to the north. The city had seen so much since that time—the Bastille torn down, the poverty and the bread shortages, the lootings and killings. He sighed. "Despite it all, she is still beautiful."

Sophie flashed a sad smile, her features reflecting the glimmering surface of the Seine, and André realized in that moment that he might just as well have been speaking about her. "But let's not think about that now," he said, straightening his posture. "We can at least *try* to feel happy once in a while."

She nodded, leaning her hands on the bridge's railing as she spoke. "I remember how, when I first arrived in Paris, I wondered how I was supposed to sleep at night. I heard people below my window at all hours—students laughing, drunkards fighting, lovers returning from dances. I remember hating my uncle. Wishing he'd allow me out, like everyone else my age."

"If you'd like to dance . . ." André took Sophie's hands in his own and began to sway, a slow, languid dance to match the rhythm of the river's current beneath them. He began to sing. It was a song about another bridge, a song his mother had loved to sing to him and Remy when they were young. "*Sur le pont d'Avignon, l'on y danse, l'on y danse . . .*"

Sophie looked up at him and smiled, a twinkle of recognition in her eyes. "The Avignon Bridge song. I know this one."

He nodded. "My mother always loved to sing that song."

"Is your mother . . . gone?"

"Yes," he said, realizing that he wasn't exactly lying. His mother *was* gone. To England, last he knew, even if he hadn't had word from her in over a year. But to tell Sophie the full story right now would be to spoil the beauty of this perfect moment.

"I am sorry to hear it." Sophie rested her head on his shoulder, and he was certain that she could hear the racing of his heart.

"Sophie?"

"Yes?"

André swallowed, unsure for a moment—wondering if perhaps he was too brazen—before deciding to pose his question. "What is it that you want?"

She angled her face upward, looking into his eyes with a curious expression. "What do you mean?"

André raised his hands, fanning them out over the city. "From all of this—this city, this nation. This life. What is it that you want?"

She tilted her head to the side, wordlessly weighing the question a moment. "You know something?"

"What?" he asked.

"You are the first person who has ever asked me that."

André nodded.

"I think you're probably the first person who has ever even thought I had a right to answer such a question," she added. "What I want . . ." She paused. "I suppose I want what so many of us want. To live free. Free from fear. Free from the oppression of my uncle or anyone else. I suppose that someday I'd like to live in a free country. That I'd like to direct my own destiny, raise my own family. That, should I ever have a girl of my own, I will be able to love her and raise her in a manner so entirely unlike the manner in which I was raised. That she'll never be given away at the age of fourteen, sold as chattel into a loveless and abusive marriage. I suppose I will know that I've succeeded in this life if . . . someday . . . my grown daughter may be allowed to marry for love."

André absorbed these words, his mind spinning with the weight of her confessions. After a long pause, leaning toward her, he said: "A life free from fear, and a life filled with love."

She broke his eye contact. "I suppose it sounds silly."

"No." He leaned forward, pulled her gaze back onto himself, and took her hands in his. "Not at all. If I tell you I understand, will you believe me? Will you believe that I know those longings, because I share them myself?"

She nodded, lowering her eyes. In the dim glow of the night, André noted how she turned, wiping her eyes. For several moments she stood quietly, looking out over the water, at the city aglow behind it. She sighed, eventually breaking the silence. "Have you ever seen anything more beautiful?"

André, looking at her, her face shadowed and in profile, answered: "The most beautiful sight I have ever seen."

She tilted her gaze upward. Peering at him, her eyes reflecting the light of the streetlamps and the stars, she appeared expectant, even inviting. And yet so fragile; he couldn't imagine anyone ever wanting to hurt her. He took her chin and cradled it in the cup of his fingers. "Sophie." He said her name, relishing the fact that she stood before him. That he could say it *to* her.

"Yes?" If she felt nervous, her face showed no signs. It was a smooth mask of perfect calm.

The need to kiss her was overwhelming, a compulsion. He took her face softly in his cupped hands and angled her chin upward toward his own lips. "I've been waiting for this for eight months."

She cocked her head, her smile shimmering like the river, reflecting the glow of moonlight off of her perfect features. "I thought you were going to deposit me safely at my front door and that would be all?"

"And I shall. But I didn't say anything about the walk toward your door."

Summer cooled to autumn, the crisp days and chilly nights turning the city's chestnut and plane trees into a bright array of oranges and reds, yellows and golds. Unsure of how long he would remain stationed in the capital, André was determined to spend as much time as he could with Sophie. The thought of an imminent departure weighed on his thoughts, and he did his best to keep both their spirits up.

It was a pleasant golden afternoon in mid-October. André was at Sophie's apartment on the island in the Seine, beating her in a game of *échecs*, chess. It was dangerous for André to visit her here, and they both knew it—her uncle visited her apartment often, rarely giving advanced notice—but Sophie's maid, a graying woman by the name of Parsy, had offered to help them in their forbidden meetings. When André was visiting, Parsy would station herself in the adjacent room, at the window overlooking the building's small walled courtyard. If she saw the tall uniformed figure of General Murat approaching, she had orders to alert Sophie at once. This would afford André enough time to slip down the back stairwell and out onto the street before her uncle had finished crossing the court and climbing the front stairwell to his niece's rented rooms. They had not yet been forced to enact this escape plan, but all three of them knew exactly how it was to work, when the time should come that it would be required.

On this afternoon, Parsy was stationed at her perch beside the window, her knitting in hand, while the two of them sat in the adjacent salon. The door was shut and André was hoping to remain at Sophie's apartment until a dinner he had to attend later, with LaSalle and some of the other officers.

"I'm about to take your queen," André threatened, propping himself up on his elbows as he surveyed the board.

"Queen?" Sophie gasped. "Shouldn't you call her my "Citizeness of *la République*?""

"Call her what you wish," he said. "Once I take her, the game is up."

"Just promise me that you won't send her to the scaffold, should you capture her."

"If I promise that mercy, might I have a kiss?"

"If you want a kiss, you'd better take it now," she said, smiling, "since I'm not yet mad at you for taking my queen."

"If you insist." He rose from his seat on the carpet and sat beside her on the silk sofa. Scooting his body next to hers, he said: "I seem to have entirely forgotten my move. If I *don't* take your queen, then how many kisses do I get for that?"

She smiled and he leaned forward, his heart exultant. When his lips met hers, she sighed, a barely audible sigh, and that sound only increased his longing for her. Raising his hands, he rested the back of her head in his grip, kissing her hungrily. He loved so many things about Sophie, but perhaps best of all was that when he kissed her, she kissed him back. Not timidly, not reservedly. She kissed him with a passion that told him that she, too, longed for him.

Their bodies were beside each other on the couch now, and Sophie reclined, looking up at him. The expectant look in her eyes was torturous for him, and he lowered his body down beside hers. Pausing a moment to meet her gaze, he whispered, his breath grazing her ear: "You do know how beautiful you are, don't you?"

"Only because you tell me every day," she whispered back, bringing her finger to just lightly touch the warm skin of his cheek. The place where he still bore the scar from the enemy's blade at Valmy. "Battle scar?" Sophie asked.

He nodded, taking her fingers to his lips and kissing them. Then he brought his lips to the ridge of her collarbone, tracing a line to her shoulder, and then up her neck. When his lips found hers once more, she parted her mouth and began to kiss him with a fervor that he thought might drive him wild.

Feeling warm, and longing to press his body even closer to hers, he removed his coat. She helped him out of it. Taking his hand in hers, she guided him to her breast, which he cupped over the burdensome folds of her gown. "Sophie?" He paused to look into her eyes, to make sure that he had not overstepped a line, had not made her uncomfortable. But she only groaned, frustrated that he had stopped kissing her.

Now his hands seemed to have taken on an agency of their own as they began to wander toward the hem of her skirt. She assisted him, hoisting the folds of fabric so that he might be unencumbered. Propelled now by a force larger than either one of them, André began to touch her soft, goosebumped skin. He shut his eyes, consumed by his desire for her. And then the door to the salon burst open.

André jumped up, looking toward the door, where he saw the panting figure of Parsy. The old woman's face was ashen, her lower lip falling away from her mouth.

"Is my uncle coming?" Sophie, too, had bolted upright on the couch. André reached for his discarded coat.

"Not him," Parsy said, eyes down, her cheeks aflame with embarrassment over the scene she had interrupted. "But a message from him, madame."

Parsy held a letter, the name *Brigadier General Nicolai Murat* written on the front in the man's upright cursive. Seeing the name, and the letter that had come from that man's hands, thoroughly quashed any last remnants of the romantic ardor André had felt just moments earlier.

"Bring it here." Sophie waved the maid forward, taking the note from her hands. She tore the red wax seal and read, her face growing pale. When she finished, the note slipped from her hands and she began to weep.

"What is it?" André crossed the room toward her, kneeling to retrieve the note from the floor. He read it quickly. The paper was marked with the day's date: October 16, 1793.

The note was brief, emotionless.

> *The former queen, Marie-Antoinette of Austria, has been found guilty by the Republic of France. The widow of Citizen Capet is charged with plotting alongside the foreign enemies of the Republic to overthrow the government; attempting to escape from prison; wasting the riches of the country which were not her own; committing adultery, having relations with many at the Court at Versailles other than her husband; and molesting her son, the former dauphin, who had confessed to his jail keeper of his mother's heinous sins. Punishment: beheading within four and twenty hours.*
>
> *You aren't safe, my niece. No noblewoman is. I shall come fetch you shortly, within the hour, and bring you back to my home, where you shall remain for now, under my faithful protection.*
>
> *Your devoted,*
> *Uncle Nico*

André absorbed the news, the letter shaking in his hands. "The dauphin *confessed* to his jail keeper?" André scoffed. "More like the poor child was forced, by the blade of a knife, to agree to such a shameful accusation!"

Sophie was staring blankly at the floor in a state of shock, and André folded her into his arms. Looking up at him, tears in her eyes, she asked: "Has this entire world gone mad?"

André held her tight without answering her question. He couldn't—he himself did not know the answer. With today's verdict, the last ties to the old order were cut. Just a few years ago, the people had believed the queen to be a divine figure, God's anointed vessel on earth. And now, today, she was to be beheaded.

With no monarchs left to vilify and condemn, to whom might the Committee and its frenzied supporters turn next? André squeezed Sophie tighter, trying to suppress the shudder that threatened to force its way through his frame. This very day, for the first time in its history, France would be without a living monarch. And Sophie would begin her own prison sentence.

PART TWO

10

Paris

December 1793

Jean-Luc felt as though something was amiss. It seemed strange that Gavreau, his supervisor and erstwhile mentor, hadn't been invited to the Rue Saint-Honoré. Odd that he, Jean-Luc, would enjoy this meeting while his friend, the man who had first introduced him to Merignac, knew nothing about it. Odd that, in fact, Gavreau had not been included in any of the meetings to which Jean-Luc had been invited lately.

Citizen Merignac had seemed blasé when he'd first proposed the ideas—a meeting in a café to enjoy a glass of wine and discuss a current legal case; an invitation after the workday to stroll through the gardens outside the former Tuileries Palace to discuss some recent piece of legislation. A note or bottle of wine or, in one instance, a small box of snuff, sent to Jean-Luc by Merignac, but always bearing Lazare's compliments.

Jean-Luc had been flattered by the sporadic but thoughtful attention paid him by someone as powerful and esteemed as Guillaume Lazare. And his boss didn't need to know, really. Gavreau had little interest in legal debate or study after work hours; it made sense that he was not included in these outings or correspondences.

But then it had turned into somewhat regular dinners. Jean-Luc had accepted these invitations, always flattered to be receiving them, and simultaneously a bit uneasy at the fact of his manager's exclusion. And now, Merignac intended to follow through on his initial offer—he planned to introduce Jean-Luc to his patron, Guillaume Lazare.

It was a cold, windy evening at the end of the year. Jean-Luc stood on the dark street, preparing to meet the leaders of the Committee—a powerful group of Jacobin lawyers who, behind closed doors, passed laws and held the levers of power of the entire French Republic. Guillaume Lazare had personally issued an invitation to Jean-Luc St. Clair to visit the headquarters. Robespierre himself might be there.

The light of the nearby lanterns flickered on the cobblestones of the Rue Saint-Honoré as Jean-Luc approached the door. He studied a shadowed building that had the appearance of an abandoned monastery. Gothic and imposing—like so many other Parisian structures whose function had once been religious—its façade was a vast expanse of soot-covered stone and dirty windows. A mere hint of illumination gave the vague indication that life stirred within. There was little to signify that there, on the other side of the rattling windowpanes, the most powerful—and radical—figures of the Revolution assembled on a nightly basis.

The street was quiet, the muffled sound of horse hooves clopping on a parallel lane. Jean-Luc glanced over his shoulder as he climbed the two steps in front of the door. Following Merignac's guidance, he knocked three times, slowly. *Liberté. Égalité. Fraternité.* He stood still, alone in the silent evening, for several minutes. Perhaps he had been mistaken about the hour, or the date. And then, from within, the doorknob turned and the wide oak panel groaned open, away from the street.

Jean-Luc was greeted by a diminutive figure in a plain black suit and white wig. The man barely acknowledged his presence, standing stiff and straight against the wall to allow passage for Jean-Luc.

"Good evening. I'm Jean-Luc, er, Citizen St. Clair, here as a guest of Maurice Merignac."

Without looking Jean-Luc in the eye, the footman said: "Wait here." Then he retreated into the house, disappearing from the foyer. Jean-Luc, standing alone, tried to gaze farther into the interior of the residence, but the lone candelabrum that lit the space before the front door did not cast a wide enough halo, and so Jean-Luc clasped his hands behind his back and waited.

"Citizen St. Clair?" The footman reappeared several minutes later, his expression expectant, indicating that Jean-Luc should follow him, which he did. The small man, holding a single candle to illuminate their path, led

Jean-Luc into a spacious front hall, its ceiling high as a curving staircase, carpeted in red velvet, swept upward from its center. Jean-Luc followed the man into a smaller room, a parlor of some sort, off the left side of this central hall. His heeled shoes clicked heavily on a bare stone floor, but other than that, the entire space was silent. The parlor had a door on the far side of it, and it was toward that door that the footman led Jean-Luc now. Without a word they crossed the threshold, and Jean-Luc found himself in a spacious study.

It was a dark-paneled room with a low-hanging chandelier, its candles casting a murky glow on the bare walls and uncarpeted floor. In the far corner of the room sat a group of men at a small rectangular table. The dim shadows in which they sat, with books and papers surrounding them, gave their gathering a rather haunting aspect; the chandelier lit the center of the room adequately, yet they occupied the darkened corner, beyond the light, as if they shunned its illuminating effect.

Or perhaps their eerie appearance was due to the chalky whiteness of several of their faces; they wore *la poudre,* the same white powder once beloved by the noble courtiers of the old Versailles and the *ancien régime,* those same people whom they had now condemned to the guillotine.

None of them spoke a word, either to Jean-Luc or among themselves, but they turned in unison at the sound of the door shutting behind him, closing him into the room. The footman was gone. Jean-Luc, alone, hovered on the threshold, fidgeting under the blank stares of twelve sets of eyes.

"Citizen St. Clair." Merignac was one of their number, and he alone rose at the entrance of the newcomer. "Good evening." Merignac strode across the study, reaching Jean-Luc and extending a hand in greeting.

"Won't you come sit with us at the table?" Merignac, too, had his face masked in white makeup, giving him an appearance somewhat foreign from that to which Jean-Luc was accustomed. "We are just waiting for Citizen Lazare. He is resting now, but soon he will join us." And then, expectantly, Merignac reopened the door that the footman had just closed.

Jean-Luc followed his friend to the table, where the Committee members sat. On top of the glossy oaken surface, a candelabra held four nearly expired wicks, the spent wax dripping down onto the table in molten dollops. A half-finished bottle of red wine stood uncorked amid piles of papers, news journals, and opened books. A couple of the seated men wore the red cap of the revolutionaries on their heads. The Committee members to whom Jean-Luc was introduced greeted him with hushed voices and stolid stares, and he could not help but feel as though they were studying him with a restrained but intense inquisitiveness.

Merignac leaned forward and retrieved an empty wineglass, which he now placed before Jean-Luc. "Citizen St. Clair is a brilliant young legal mind. He came to Paris from outside of Marseille during the early days of our Revolution and has been working for our new Republic for over a year."

Several of the men nodded; others had turned back to their papers. Jean-Luc shifted in his chair, wondering why Merignac was speaking so softly. "You are too kind, Maurice," he said. "But the work I do is humble compared to the tasks you all have before you—ensuring the liberty of the people and facilitating the many tasks of the Republic." Humble indeed. Cataloging the confiscated furniture and artwork of imprisoned noblemen, defending penniless widows. In truth, he had little right to be at this table, in this study on the Rue Saint-Honoré, and he lowered his eyes, noticing a rip in the side seam of his pants.

"Wine, citizen?" To his left, a gray-haired man wearing a red cap tipped the bottle toward Jean-Luc. The man was seated in a wheeled chair, the likes of which Jean-Luc had only seen in journals or drawings. The man faced Jean-Luc with a blank look, turning a lever on his chair to move slightly forward.

"Please," Jean-Luc said and nodded, his voice sounding brutishly loud in the dim, quiet study. His neighbor filled the glass with the burgundy drink. "To the Republic," he offered, lifting his glass and looking around the table at his companions.

"To the Revolution," several of them offered in reply, raising their own glasses to pale, expressionless lips. Merignac drained his cup. Jean-Luc wished in that moment that he might ask them the meaning of their chalky white makeup—why would members of the democratic Committee be dressing in the fashion of the Bourbon court? But their eyes had turned from him back to the papers on the table, and so Jean-Luc sat, mimicking their wordlessness.

After a prolonged period of silence Merignac rose, and the others at the table followed him in doing so. Jean-Luc looked up, startled by the sudden movement, and noticed a new figure. There, two rooms away and framed through the opened doorways that separated them, a small man stood atop the red-carpeted staircase.

The Jacobins around Jean-Luc snapped to, standing in stony silence as the man took hold of the railing and slowly descended.

The man looked older than the rest, his frame built of narrow, birdlike bones. He was not attractive, Jean-Luc acknowledged to himself, with limp yellow hair pulled back in a ponytail, its mass insufficient to cover the entirety of his pale, balding head. His skin was an ashen shade approaching utter colorlessness, with an almost papery quality, and his light eyes were tucked back, deep-set, under a wide brow. In the hand that didn't clutch the banister he held something round and red: an apple, Jean-Luc saw. The man continued his slow, steady descent, his eyes not yet fixing on the twelve men plus Jean-Luc who watched him from two rooms away.

His heels clicked on the stone floor as he crossed the final step, and now he turned toward the study. The apple in his hand appeared unnaturally red and bright in his grip, his fingers drumming the fruit's glossy surface. How had he found such a perfect apple in Paris in December? Jean-Luc wondered, realizing that he could not remember the last time he'd had the luxury of eating such a fine piece of fruit.

Nobody spoke as the man entered the study. Merignac gestured toward the empty chair, offering a wordless, reverential bow as he did so. Pausing before the table, his pale hands resting on the back of the wooden chair, the old man smiled broadly. Jean-Luc noted that his teeth appeared slightly yellow against the stark whiteness of his skin. "Citizens."

"Citizen Lazare," the men around Jean-Luc answered in unison. Lazare's pale eyes landed on the visitor.

"A new face," he said, his voice soft, even silky. "You must be Citizen St. Clair."

Jean-Luc inhaled to answer, but Merignac beat him to it: "Indeed, Citizen Lazare. May I introduce to you Citizen Jean-Luc St. Clair, a legal counselor for our government and a very capable—"

Lazare lifted a hand and Merignac fell silent. His eyes still fixed on Jean-Luc, the older man asked: "Did I hear that you are from the south?"

Jean-Luc cleared his throat and replied, "Indeed I am, from a village just outside of Marseille."

With that, Lazare lifted a hand like a conductor leading a symphony and began to sing in a soft, barely audible voice the chorus of the "Marseillaise," the new anthem of the French Revolution. "You must be proud of your city for providing us with our nation's rallying cry."

"Yes, Citizen Lazare."

"I, too, come from the south. Near Toulon."

Jean-Luc nodded.

"But of course," Lazare sighed, "nothing of import happens in Toulon. If one wishes to be at the heart of our Revolution, or anything else, really, one must come to Paris."

"Yes." Jean-Luc nodded again, crossing and then uncrossing his hands in front of his waist. Then they had something in common, this esteemed man and himself. Jean-Luc suppressed the urge to smile.

"Shall we sit?" Lazare looked around the table, and without a word, the group assented, lowering themselves back into their chairs. No one looked at the papers now. Merignac retrieved another bottle and refilled several of the men's cups of wine, including Jean-Luc's, and yet Lazare took none himself. Jean-Luc looked at the large chandelier looming over the center of the hall, then turned back toward the cluttered table, which seemed dimly lit with only a few candles.

"I see your confusion, citizen, as to why we do not conduct our affairs directly under the chandelier."

Jean-Luc felt unnerved by Lazare's shrewd observation, but the old man continued: "Just some days ago, the Committee of General Security removed their meeting chambers into the salon down the hall, that way." Jean-Luc peered down the hallway Lazare indicated and saw only creeping shadows from the windows that looked out onto Rue Saint-Honoré.

"Citizen Robespierre likes to keep them in his sights. As do I."

Lazare, still clutching the apple in his left hand, raised the fruit to his lips and took a bite, his teeth sinking into it with a crunch that seemed to reverberate off the bare walls around them. He chewed slowly—the noises of his jaw audible. After what seemed like an interminable silence, Lazare spoke. "You work for our new government, Citizen St. Clair."

"I do."

"Then we are brothers." Lazare lifted his hands as if in an embrace of all at the table.

"Indeed," Jean-Luc agreed.

"I hope you don't mind if I cut through some of the silly pleasantries and bare my most honest thoughts to you. Our time is precious, you see. Will that be agreeable to you?"

"St. Clair always speaks frankly with me on politics," Merignac interjected, but Lazare did not divert his gaze from Jean-Luc.

"Is that agreeable?" Lazare repeated the question, and Jean-Luc nodded.

"Good." Lazare smiled, a soft smile of papery white skin and yellow teeth. He took another bite of apple. "How about a riddle?"

Jean-Luc nodded. "All . . . all right."

"Can you tell me . . . what is the one force most powerful on earth? The only force capable of driving a people, a people bound by millennia of servitude and piety, to rise out of their dark slumber and slaughter their own sovereign?" Lazare paused to chew his apple. "What storm of madness could possibly drive a people to perform this great and terrible deed?"

Jean-Luc considered the question. After a moment, he ventured: "Hope."

Lazare pressed the apple to his pale lips, smiling behind the round shape of the fruit. "Come now, citizen. The unfortunate multitudes of any nation care little for such *lofty* ideals. Hope is a luxury. I'm talking about a much more base, primordial thing. There is one force that will lead a man to kill, even murder to survive. Do you know what that is?"

"Fear?" Jean-Luc responded in a faint voice, almost a whisper.

"Close." Lazare nodded. "Now you are on the right path. But I'm talking about something even more basic. The most basic of all human needs. The need for which a newborn baby first learns to cry out. It is?"

Jean-Luc thought of Mathieu in his first moments, of Marie tenderly pulling their newborn son to her breast, and he looked down at the table. When he answered, his voice was a whisper. "Hunger."

"Hunger!" Lazare clapped, and Jean-Luc started in his seat at the sudden, giddy eruption. "There you have it! It is very simple. Hunger will bring a man into contact with his most basic instinct—the will to survive. The masses? Their interest is in their bellies, in the care of their own lands or means of industry—a constant struggle for their very survival. And while that mongrel Capet and his viperous widow dined on truffles and figs brought to them from the farthest Oriental satrapies, the poor citizens outside their gates crawled back to their hovels each night with empty stomachs. And as the days and years crept by, their pain turned to anger, and their anger darkened into hatred." Lazare raised the apple once more to his colorless lips, taking another bite. "Hunger—it drives us all. I can see that you have it within you. As do I, though perhaps of a slightly different kind."

The room fell silent as each man mulled over the meaning of this soliloquy, and Jean-Luc swore the others must have heard his heart beating within his chest.

Lazare broke the silence in the shadowed room. "Tell me, if you please, citizen, more about your work?"

Jean-Luc leaned forward, tugging on his suit coat that felt uncomfortably tight. "Of course, Citizen Lazare. I am an attorney for the new government."

"Yes, Maurice just said as much, but I wish to know what it is that you actually *do*." Lazare's soft voice held no hint of derision, merely a deep and genuine interest.

Jean-Luc cleared his throat. "I catalog and manage the inventory of confiscated goods—the property of the nobility and clergy as it is seized."

"I might dispute your usage of the term 'confiscated goods,' Citizen St. Clair," Lazare said, arching a pale eyebrow. "By what right did those noblemen come into their plush carpets and glistening porcelain to begin with? That property belongs to the people. It has always belonged to the people, and has finally been returned to them."

"Of course, I did not mean that the goods were seized unduly, Citizen Lazare, I simply meant to explain—"

"No need, I understand your point well enough." Lazare waved his pale hand and offered a conciliatory nod, his mind already turned to the next point. "So you are a glorified clerk, it would seem."

Jean-Luc felt his cheeks redden. He looked around the table and noticed the smirks tugging on several of the Committee members' lips. "I wished to serve the Revolution, Citizen Lazare. This was the opportunity that arose."

"Of course." Now Lazare, too, smiled, his light eyes darting around the table as he held the apple before his lips. "And someone must do that work. But tell me truly . . . are you an idealist?"

Jean-Luc sat up in his chair, throwing his shoulders back. "I suppose you might say I believe in the ideals of our Revolution, yes. Ideals such as liberty and equality."

"So we have an idealistic clerk among us," Lazare said. The men at the table now shared muffled laughter, and Jean-Luc got the distinct sense that few in this company ever indulged in deep, mirthful laughter.

Lazare fixed his gaze directly on Jean-Luc now, a direct, appraising look. And then, exhaling, his voice quiet, he said: "I do apologize. I meant no offense, Citizen St. Clair. I was merely making a poor attempt at humor." Lazare lifted the apple to his lips and took another bite. He chewed the apple, a series of sharp crunches. "So then, Citizen St. Clair, I suppose, like all idealists, you are acquainted with the philosophies of Monsieur Rousseau? Do you agree with his assertion that 'we are miserable sinners, born in corruption, inclined to evil, incapable by ourselves of doing good'?"

Jean-Luc tried to spool together his errant thoughts, this latest philosophical question catching him unaware. But before he could reply, Lazare continued: "And what of Rousseau's pupil, Monsieur Thomas Jefferson? I'm sure you have followed the events of the revolution in the New World?"

Jean-Luc nodded now, eyeing the cup of wine in front of him. He restrained himself from taking a drink, whether out of a habit of work or the vague feeling that he needed his full wits about him to keep up with Citizen Lazare. But then he reminded himself he had no reason to feel inadequate in the task of discussing politics or philosophy, even with a man such as Guillaume Lazare.

As Marie would have told him, had she been here: this was his life's passion. He straightened his spine against the back of his chair, meeting the older man's gaze as he answered. "I am familiar with the writings of Monsieur Jefferson, yes. As well as the writings of John Adams, Thomas Paine, and our friend Monsieur Franklin."

"Ah." Lazare lifted his fingers. "Some of the greatest disciples of the Enlightenment."

"I was but a young student at the time, but I took great heart in following the events in the former British colonies. The revolution there."

"I think that the rebels in America are falsely venerated," Lazare said, his tone suddenly expressionless. "They began with such promise. But they fell short."

"Short of what?" Jean-Luc asked, noticing with no small shock that he and Lazare were alone in speaking. The remaining men simply watched the exchange, sipping their wine and staring so intently that Jean-Luc felt as if he were speaking before a jury panel.

"Of victory, citizen," Lazare answered.

Jean-Luc couldn't help but furrow his brow, confused at this morsel of vague philosophy. Hadn't the American rebels won freedom for themselves and their nation?

Lazare held his rapidly disappearing apple in his fingers, licking his lips before he spoke. "I think that, had the Americans been burdened by a noble, despotic class of their own, and had they been gifted with the tools of Dr. Ignace Guillotin, they would not have failed to put his device to good work."

"Ah," Jean-Luc said, his mind alive now with the stimulation of this debate. "But the wonder of the American Revolution—the fact at which we all must marvel—is that, even at the moment of their unforeseen victory, their foremost champion left the arena of government and politics to retire to his farm."

"George Washington," Lazare said, his pale lips letting loose a sigh. "The ever exalted George Washington."

"They replaced the tyranny of a king with a true republic," Jean-Luc added, surprised that the older man didn't share his own enthusiasm. "Do you not think it wise to draw at least some lessons from their extraordinary success?"

Lazare shrugged. "The saving grace for the revolution in America"— Lazare paused, taking a final bite of his apple—"was that they did not have foreign kings menacing their borders from every direction, threatening their very survival. Quite the contrary—our late 'King Louis' did half the work for them. For which we paid dearly, of course."

Jean-Luc thought about this. "Well, they had one foreign king crossing their borders and threatening their revolution—King George. Surely you think that the might of imperial Britain posed a sufficient threat?"

"King George, very well. I count the armies of Prussia, Austria, Spain, and the accursed English among the growing list of those clamoring to invade us and end *our* Revolution. With such enemies outside our door, the most important thing we can do is make certain to eliminate the threat of the enemies already inside our home, hidden within our midst." Leaning forward, Lazare spoke so quietly that his voice was little more than a thin whisper. In another context he might have been breathing some comforting bedtime tale to a group of rapt children. "The wolf prowling outside your door ought to be considered much less dangerous than the one who sleeps beneath your bed."

The room was silent for several moments before Lazare continued. "For that reason, this country must be cleansed of all traitors—noble or otherwise. Now that we have been enlightened, we cannot allow any of their kind to linger on, willing and eager as they are to pull us all back into the darkness. That was why we had to kill Louis and Antoinette—you know that, yes? So long as they lived, they were a symbol to inspire our enemies, both within the nation and outside of it. They incited those dark figures who would seek to put a tyrant and his Austrian spy back on the throne." Lazare lifted his thin fingers, as if shooing a fly. "Be rid of them. Kill them all. Only their blood can wipe clean the sins of all of those centuries of robbery, abuse, and debasement—only their blood can provide for the harvest of the modern age. The era of reason over idolatry, of progress over primogeniture, of enlightenment over feudal darkness."

Several men around the table rapped their knuckles on its wooden surface in support. Meanwhile, Jean-Luc prepared his response, forcing his voice to remain steady. "You are a man of the law, Citizen Lazare." He was impassioned now, the magnitude of this discussion quickening his pulse. "Surely you would assert that, prior to capital punishment being meted, a fair and impartial trial must be pursued?"

"Perhaps we might—" Merignac interjected for the first time, but Lazare cut him off, raising a finger in the direction of the chastened secretary.

"No, Merignac. I am enjoying this." And then, turning his eyes back on Jean-Luc, Lazare smiled. "Rarely do any of these men challenge me so openly. I am so glad that you will."

Jean-Luc found this odd. Was this not a Committee appointed by the National Convention, their very purpose to debate politics and arrive at compromises that would best suit the new nation? Lazare seized on Jean-Luc's momentary distraction and said: "I already told you that I was from the south, Citizen St. Clair." Lazare leaned back in his chair, placing the used apple core on the table before him.

Jean-Luc nodded. "You did."

"Toulon, as I said. My mother was a maid. A foolish young girl who had the twin misfortunes of being both pretty and powerless. Then add to that the unfortunate fact that she attracted the attention of her employer, a viscount."

Jean-Luc creased his brow, finding it curious that he should hear such a frank confession from a man such as Guillaume Lazare.

"Perhaps you have heard, Citizen St. Clair, that I am a bastard?" Lazare's watery eyes were unblinking as he stared across the table at Jean-Luc.

"I . . . I believe I might have . . . but I don't see why that should—"

"Don't redden so, citizen. I feel no shame in giving the confession, and as such, you should feel no shame in hearing it. It was not my poor mother's fault that she was seduced at the age of fifteen and made to give birth to a nobleman's bastard child. Just as it was not my fault that my father, the esteemed viscount, sent me away—first to a hired nursemaid and then to a parish school, refusing to ever once see me. Refusing to allow me to ever see my poor mother, whom, I am sure, he continued to use as a brood-mare when his own frail wife would not welcome him into her bed. Who knows how many bastard sisters and brothers I have populating the south of France?"

The flame in front of them sputtered and then expired, the last inch of pale candle dripping onto the table in a pool of molten wax. Jean-Luc was grateful for the brief period of darkness, as it allowed him to lower his eyes and absorb the heavy news he'd just heard.

Merignac summoned the footman, who appeared as if from out of the shadows, to replenish the spent candle and refill the company's wine-glasses.

Lazare, taking a full cup of wine and raising the drink to his lips, still held Jean-Luc in his gaze. "What do you make of my brief account?"

Jean-Luc sighed, weighing his next words. "I am sorry for your mother's misfortune. And yours."

Lazare nodded, still expectant, wanting more.

"And I do believe that the nobility committed crimes against the people." Jean-Luc paused, remembering the account of the Marquis de Mont-noir in the case of the Widow Poitier. "But I think that the nobility, just like the common population, comprised a wide and varied body. There are evil men among their number just as there are good men among them. And doubtless everything in between. And so—"

"Wrong!" Lazare landed his palm firmly on the oak table between them, his voice rising above a hushed tone for the first time that evening. Jean-Luc couldn't help but start slightly, and he kept quiet, allowing the older man to continue.

"The nobles of this country have been inbred for centuries, and now all virtue and humanity have been drained from their ranks." Lazare paused a moment, blinking, regaining his composure, bridling the volume of his voice. But his eyes still burned with the intensity behind his words. "Any man, Citizen St. Clair, who is born into a castle full of servants from the time he is a babe . . . who is told that he will never once have to put in an honest day of work in his entire life . . . who is made to believe that any skirt that passes before his powdered nose may be lifted at his request . . . Why, any man in an environment such as this would lose his ability to care for his common brother. The very institution of a hereditary nobility predisposes, no, *guarantees,* that a nation's leadership will sink into profligacy, abuse, and licentiousness."

"But look at Lafayette, himself a marquis," Jean-Luc said. "He eschewed the wealth of his noble birth and sped to America to fight for their rebellion, nearly paying with his life in the process. Why, we owe our esteemed Declaration of the Rights of Man to himself and Monsieur Jefferson, drawing much of it from the Virginian's own pen."

Lazare's voice was tight as a bowstring as he retorted: "A vain, self-serving dandy who showed his true treachery when he attempted to save the lives of Louis and Antoinette. If he had remained in France, we would have sent Lafayette to the guillotine as well. He was right to flee, like the rat he is."

Jean-Luc swallowed hard, feeling it wiser not to speak too strongly on behalf of a denounced marquis declared an enemy of the nation. He sat motionless and offered no reply.

Lazare continued. "You say that these aristocrats deserve fair trials. Did my mother have a fair trial before being damned to a life of shameful bodily enslavement?" Lazare asked, still looking only at Jean-Luc. "Did I have a fair trial before all of the beatings I received at that horrid school in which my father, the viscount, enrolled me?" And now, inexplicably,

Lazare smiled. "No. A fair trial is only a right for a free man. But these *nobles* . . . their rights are forfeit. They are criminals, all. Complicit and culpable, stewards of a criminal system that we, as free men, have finally undone." Lazare took a long, slow sip of wine, the red liquid blindingly bright against his colorless skin. The table was, once more, quiet.

It was Lazare who again broke the silence. "But now it grows late, and I fear that I have filled our time with such heavy matters. What is the hour?" Lazare looked to Merignac. Jean-Luc could not have guessed the time—whether an hour or ten hours had passed since he'd entered this strange, dimly lit study with these pale, wordless men he did not know.

"It approaches ten o'clock, Citizen Lazare," Merignac answered.

"Ah! The time has gone so quickly with our spirited discussion." Lazare looked around the table, his tone suddenly light, even cheery, as his eyebrows moved up and down on his chalky white face. "And now I must go, or else Maximilien will be kept waiting."

It was Robespierre to whom Lazare referred, Jean-Luc realized.

"Citizen St. Clair." Lazare fixed his eyes across the table. "I hope I have not overwhelmed you with this frank discussion. I am always eager to acquire a proper sense of a man's character, as well as his ideals, should he have any. It was a trial by fire, you might say, but you held up quite well. Quite well indeed."

Jean-Luc nodded, lowering his gaze. What did one say in such an instance?

"I quite enjoy a good debate, and I've enjoyed ours immensely."

Jean-Luc offered a slight smile in reply.

"Maurice and the rest of my protégés are constantly trying to introduce me to bright young minds. Trying to find my next *petit projet*. I always say: 'I'll meet anyone once. But a second time? That is up to the man himself.'"

Jean-Luc nodded. "Thank you, sir."

"Not 'sir.'" Lazare shook his head. "'Brother.'"

"Indeed," Jean-Luc answered, his voice quiet, his throat dry.

Lazare spread his thin lips in a smile. "Maurice told me that you live across the Seine, on the Left Bank."

"I do, Citizen Lazare."

"And how do you intend to get home?"

"I thought I'd walk, citizen."

"No." The old man shook his head. "I am going that way to meet Citizen Robespierre. Won't you please join me in my coach?"

"I would not wish to trouble you."

Lazare waved a bony hand. "It is no trouble. It's the least I can do for such an idealistic young clerk who counts furniture and silver plates so diligently for our Republic."

Jean-Luc swallowed hard as his cheeks flushed shades darker than his pale companion's. "If you are certain that it is no trouble, then I thank you."

Lazare rose from his chair, smoothing the front of his coat with his long, thin fingers. "The rest of you, carry on with your work. I need not remind you that our soldiers are fighting, our people are hungry, and our enemies dwell amongst us. The world is watching."

Inside the carriage, Lazare looked out the window, his narrow frame bouncing and jostling as the horses pulled them over snow-slicked cobblestones. He did not speak, so neither did Jean-Luc.

Lazare fixed his gaze on his guest as they turned the corner, approaching Jean-Luc's street. In the dark shadows of the carriage, Jean-Luc could just barely see pale lips and blond eyebrows against an unnaturally white face. The older man broke the silence. "I meant what I said."

"Oh?" Jean-Luc met his stare.

"That I appreciated your spirited debate. None of them"—Lazare waved his hand—"none of them will ever engage with me. It's as if . . ." He paused, sighing. "As if they are bridled by fear, or something else. . . ." His voice trailed off.

Jean-Luc could have gasped in laughter—finding it fairly obvious that of course they were frightened of their leader, and understandably so. But he let Lazare continue.

"I commend you for engaging with me. I hope that we can do it again. I relish a challenge." The carriage slowed and rolled to a halt in front of Jean-Luc's building. "I relish a challenge indeed," Lazare repeated, turning toward the window again.

"This is my stop, citizen." Jean-Luc leaned forward in the carriage, glancing up at the window of his garret. The light from inside spilled out onto the street, a gentle glow, and he could see a woman's shadow moving within. Marie was probably chasing Mathieu around in an attempt to lure him to bed.

The footman opened the carriage door and, to Jean-Luc's surprise, Lazare stepped out first. Jean-Luc followed him. Standing opposite each other on the cold, snow-lined street, the two men were silent for several moments.

Lazare, his face now illuminated by the nearby streetlamp, smiled. "I hope you've benefited from our company tonight, citizen." His words came out with a visible mist of warm breath.

"Very much so, Citizen Lazare. It was an honor to meet you."

"I hope that you will return, and soon. I should very much like to see your talents utilized to the fullest extent. For your sake, and for the sake of our nation. I could arrange to have you work a more prominent role."

Jean-Luc's eyes widened ever so slightly, and he suppressed the smile that such frank praise from a man like Guillaume Lazare elicited. "You're too generous, citizen."

"A man is unworthy of admiration until he earns it. One must embrace the chaos of this world and shape it according to his own will." Lazare paused, oblivious of the snowflake that had landed on his nose, the stark white crystal disappearing against the pallor of his face. "I believe you desire to achieve more than you let on, St. Clair."

"Oh, well," Jean-Luc stammered, shuffling from one foot to the other. "I thank you for the interest you've shown in my future." Of course he wished to move up and out of a department that had him cataloging furniture. He wished to move Marie out of this dingy neighborhood. And this man certainly seemed capable of helping him with all of that.

But Lazare's mind seemed to have drifted toward other thoughts, and his eyes reflected that as he stared down the street. "As for me, I might have my greatest conquest yet." At this cryptic statement, another one of his characteristic riddles, Lazare's voice trailed off, his breath filing out of his nostrils in two thin clouds of vapor. "Yes, my greatest conquest yet. If I can take this one down, I will know I could have crucified Christ himself."

Jean-Luc tensed involuntarily, his brow creasing at this odd declaration.

This sudden change in topic. "But . . . Citizen Lazare . . . would you have *wanted* to take down the Christ?"

Lazare glanced up now, meeting Jean-Luc's gaze with his eyes. They were expressionless when he next spoke: "I would tear down any man guilty of the people's false worship. Our late king was but the first." He leaned in closer to Jean-Luc and spoke in a hushed tone: "There will be more to come." His eyes seemed to glow with a zeal that Jean-Luc had rarely seen in other men.

Just then, Mathieu leaned out the window, the light spilling into the street as his voice called out. "Papa!"

Both Jean-Luc and Lazare lifted their stares to the sound issuing from the window above. "Mathieu!" Jean-Luc frowned, seeing his tiny son's face bathed in the warm glow of their rooms. "Step back away from that window! And do not lean out of it again."

"Yes, Papa!" The little boy, despite his father's stern voice, remained at the opened window.

"I will be right up," Jean-Luc insisted, before hollering even louder: "Marie?"

From within, Marie's calm voice was barely audible. "Come here, my darling. What have I told you about the window?" And the little boy's face disappeared from sight, leaving Jean-Luc and Lazare standing in silence on the cobblestones below.

"A beautiful boy." Lazare's gaze still rested on the brightly lit window, now vacant of Mathieu's frame. The sound of Marie's playful tones, mixed with the little boy's joyful laughter, just barely reached the street, and Jean-Luc longed to be upstairs, in that warm room with his family.

"Your son?"

Jean-Luc nodded. "He has his mother's looks; for that I am grateful."

"In that case, your wife must be quite a beauty," Lazare said, turning his eyes back on Jean-Luc. There, in the cold night, Jean-Luc shivered, tucking his hands deeper into the pockets of his overcoat and wondering if his sudden chill was due entirely to the frigid December air.

11

Paris

February 1794

Remy lay on his back, sprawled across André's bed in the boarding-house in the Saint-Paul quarter. Together, the two brothers were crafting a letter for their mother, though they had little idea of whether it might actually reach her. They had not heard from her in well over a year, a fact that gave André grave concerns, though he did his best to conceal them from his younger brother.

"I'm not going to mention that we're being sent back to the front," André said, concluding his letter with the promise of their continued love and devotion.

"Probably for the best," Remy agreed.

André blotted the ink and allowed the words to dry before folding the note and sealing it with wax. He would send it to London, to the one ad-dress from which he had received a letter, so many months prior.

"So, do you think we'll get to see this boy general when we get down there?" Remy asked, propping himself on his elbows on the bed.

"Bonaparte?" The room around them darkened with the coming eve-ning, and André lit a second candle as he considered his brother's question.

"Yes. They say he's unlike any of the other generals. He's the only one who's defeated the English, and on our own soil. They say he's better than all the rest," Remy said, a tinge of awe apparent in his voice. "It would be something to catch a glimpse of him."

"I'm certain we will see him at some point, even if we are not encamped with him. You might be more likely to, since he comes from the artillery."

"How far away is Saorgio from Nice?" Remy asked, referring to the two different camps to which the brothers were to be assigned.

"I'm not sure," André said. "Nice is near the Piedmont border, that much I know. So I shouldn't be too far from you."

"I wonder what Italian women are like."

"You'll know soon enough—of that I have no doubt."

Just then, there was a hurried knock on the door. Remy sat up.

"Come in." André rose from his chair in time to see a cloaked figure glide into the room. "Sophie?" He was surprised, even if delighted, to see her. And then he looked around, embarrassed; she had never been to his room before, and it was far from tidy.

But Sophie did not seem concerned with her surroundings. She stood for a moment and looked at him, a heavy cape of dark blue wool around her shoulders, a hood pulled close around her blond curls to ward off the winter chill. Her cheeks were flushed from the weather, and her face bore a troubled expression. "André." Her voice was hoarse as she panted, striding to him and collapsing into his arms.

"What is the matter?" He brought his hand to her face, sliding the cape back so that he might see her more clearly. When she looked up at him, he noted that her eyes were dry of tears but full of fear. "My darling, what is it? We weren't supposed to meet until later."

"I had to tell you." Her breath was ragged, and it was clear that she had run here. "News has not yet reached the streets."

"What is it?" André asked, his own pulse quickening.

"It's General Kellermann," Sophie said. "My uncle has denounced him to the National Convention. He has been formally charged."

André's hands fell to his sides, and he faintly noticed Remy standing beside him now. "Kellermann denounced?" Remy repeated the statement, incredulous. "But that's absurd. No one would ever dare question his loyalty to—"

"He's been arrested, thrown in jail," Sophie continued, shaking her head from side to side in small, tight gestures. "He's being held at Le Temple prison. Robespierre himself signed the orders."

"On what charges?" André asked.

Sophie bit her lower lip. "My uncle has reported the details of several conversations, going back as far as a year ago. Apparently Kellermann has, on occasion, referred to the deceased . . . er, monarch . . . by his former title rather than the correct one of 'Citizen Capet.'"

"Please, Sophie, you know you can trust us. You don't have to watch your words in here." André put a hand on her arm.

"My uncle referred to Kellermann by his full title in the charges."

"As a count," Remy said. "Made guilty by his noble birth."

"But your uncle is noble himself. What a hypocritical—" André choked off his insult to Sophie's uncle, instead mumbling: "This is madness."

Sophie nodded. "He's drawn up a full list of charges. Apparently Kellermann was critical of some of the Committee members for their decisions on the battle plans in the Rhineland. He accused one member of interfering with the army and called him a foolish Jacobin schoolboy."

André paced the room, running his hands through his hair. "I'm sure he said it in the heat of the battle, when his men's lives were being sacrificed by incompetent, meddling fools. Any general ought to be able to assert his own military expertise when making battle plans, rather than taking the orders of a few self-righteous lawyers who sit safely in Paris, surrounded by books."

"Lawyers are some of the worst scum I've ever met," Remy mused. "And now they run this country."

"It's not just the Committee's military mistakes," Sophie replied. "Apparently, on a number of occasions, he has expressed disapproval of their other decisions."

"Such as?" Remy asked.

Sophie paused, as if afraid to repeat the damning words. When she spoke, her voice was so quiet that André barely heard her. "He did not agree with the decision to behead the king and queen. He told my uncle as much."

"A conversation spoken in confidence to a friend."

"But now repeated to the Committee," Sophie said, shaking her head.

André clenched his fists, feeling as though he would strangle Murat, if he could only find him. "But that's absurd! Even if Kellermann did say that, Murat can't prove it."

Sophie sighed. "What proof is required these days? You've seen what the Law of Suspects has led to. Do you suppose that each man and woman paraded to the guillotine today was convicted on proof?"

"But this all seems completely fabricated. Kellermann will be able to clear his name."

But Sophie did not seem to share André's optimism, and she put a hand on his shoulder. "I am sorry. I know how you admire him."

"He'll find a lawyer and will be back with his men before the spring campaign resumes," André said, his tone carrying perhaps more conviction than he truly felt.

"That's just it." Sophie edged closer to André. "That's what I've come running to tell you. I fear that Kellermann might not be able to find a defense counsel."

"Why not?" André asked.

"Because my uncle has arranged for the best legal team in Paris to convict Kellermann."

"Who? Who would possibly build a case against General Kellermann? He's a hero, for God's sake," André said.

Sophie's face dropped, her eyes growing hopeless, as she pronounced the name: "Guillaume Lazare."

André absorbed the news, his shoulders growing heavier as understanding seeped in. Guillaume Lazare. The man who had tried and convicted his own father, the Marquis de Valière. And the king. Lazare was the most feared statesman in France. After his recent consolidation of the Committee, no one would go up against Guillaume Lazare; not even Danton or Robespierre himself could challenge him at this point.

André's birthday dinner was meant to be a festive occasion, a final evening with Sophie before he, LaSalle, and Remy were sent to the Italian front. She had snuck out after Parsy retired to sleep for the night. LaSalle had invited Henriette, with whom he claimed to be enamored, and Remy had invited Celine, the ballerina who had seemed to hold his interest longer than any previous lover. The group had taken a table toward the front of Le Pont Blanc, the same café where André had first dined with Sophie.

But news of the Kellermann imprisonment had darkened all of their spirits, and no one felt much like celebrating that evening.

Remy did his best to remain cheerful throughout dinner, ordering what the tavern keeper swore was champagne for his brother. "A toast to you, big brother. Cheer up; there is no way a tribunal would condemn General Kellermann, the hero of Valmy."

André shrugged, gulping his drink. If indeed it was champagne, it had been so diluted that it tasted like a distant relative of the drink.

"The mob would storm the Bastille again, this time taking arms against the Convention itself, if the Committee convicted our man," Remy predicted, his speech slowed after several bottles of wine.

But the journal reports and street gossip in recent days showed a clear and disarming bias toward the Murat and Lazare faction.

It was troublingly clear to André, as he read the countless articles pronouncing le Comte de Kellermann a "traitor to the Revolution," that public sentiment had shifted. The old hero, the brave officer with gregarious manners and unimpeachable integrity, was no longer the darling of the people. Paris, these days, venerated a different sort of man. The angry mob looked for men who offered decisive judgment and quick punishment for the enemies of the people. Men who accused their fellow men of dark and treacherous motives, men who understood how hungry the people were—not just for bread but for blood as well.

Everywhere, so-called enemies of the Republic were being sniffed out and summarily denounced. Paris was all too quick—even eager—to see evil anywhere it was suggested. Proof, as Sophie had pointed out, no longer carried much weight in the courts of the dreaded Revolutionary Tribunal.

The group separated shortly after dinner. André, who had sipped far too much wine at dinner as a tonic against his gloom, felt unsteady on his feet as he offered to escort Sophie home.

"I think it's *I* who shall need to see *you* safely home tonight," Sophie remarked. They had just wished farewell to Remy and LaSalle.

"Perhaps I was a bit too generous with the wine." André nodded, trying to shake off his oppressive drowsiness as they paused before the glistening Seine, its surface shivering like the cold passersby. "But I remember my honor, and I shall still see you safely home, Madame Vincennes. Shall we?"

"No," Sophie replied, hooking her arm through his. "No, I don't want to go home tonight." She looked up at him eagerly, expectantly.

"Well, where do you want to go?" André asked, his mouth suddenly dry, his fuzzy mind sharpening into focus; did she mean what he hoped she meant?

Sophie looked up at him. "Take me to your house."

"Are . . . are you certain?" André stammered. Sophie nodded, a wordless reply.

His heart racing, André guided them in the direction of the Marais and his boardinghouse. After a few minutes, feeling suddenly playful as he walked beside her, he asked: "What will poor old Parsy do if she discovers that you are not in bed?"

Sophie laughed, nuzzling up against André for warmth against the whipping wind of late February. "Perhaps sweet old Parsy is not as innocent as she appears. She was young once, after all."

When they reached his lodgings, André shut the door and locked it. He noted with fresh embarrassment that he had not tidied up, hardly expecting that Sophie would be in his room. But there was nothing to be done about that now. He hurried to build a small fire and then lit two candles. When the room had warmed, Sophie slid out of her cloak, tossing it over the back of his desk chair. He liked that; seeing her items among his. It felt undeniably right.

"Here we are," she said.

"Here we are," André repeated. "I wish I had some wine to offer you."

"I think we've both had enough wine tonight."

"Perhaps you are right."

Sophie stepped closer to him, lacing her fingers through his. André lifted her hand to his lips and placed a kiss on its soft surface. And then he kissed the top of her head, catching a whiff of the sweet fragrance of her hair. He shut his eyes, overwhelmed by her presence. By the fact of her, here, in his room.

Glancing up at him, she asked: "So, what would you like for your birthday?"

André laughed, bringing his hands to the small of her back. Making an exaggerated show of considering the question, he looked down at her. "I have an idea."

"Oh?" Her head fell to the side, her face angling up at him with an expression that André found enthralling.

André looked into her eyes, feeling as though he could never grow tired of the clear, light blue of them. When he leaned forward, she met his kiss, eagerly. Their lips pressed into one another, and their bodies followed. Her hands so much surer than his own, she pulled him free of his coat and began to unbutton his shirt. André thought he would go mad when he felt her soft hands on his bare skin, and he drew her in even closer, craving closeness now with every inch of her body. She pulled him down onto the bed, and he forced himself to stop for a moment. "Wait," he said, his voice raspy between his even breaths. "You know, I would marry you, Sophie, if you would have me. I would marry you tomorrow. I would have married you yesterday."

"I know you would have," she said, breaking from his gaze. She remained still, silent. Eventually, she sighed. "But we can't. At least, not while my uncle is around."

"Sophie." André took her chin in his fingers and lifted her eyes once more to meet his. He wanted her to understand how truly and entirely he meant his next statement: "Know that I am devoted to you, as devoted as ever a husband could be."

"I know." She looked at him now through a thin veil of tears. "I've been married before, you remember. I know how little it can mean." She took his hand, using his fingers to wipe her tears.

"Why are you crying, my love?" André asked.

"I finally know," she sighed, pressing her face into his shoulder, moistening it with her tears. "I finally know how I should have felt on my wedding night."

12

Paris

April 1794

The news pulsed through the city that day like the drumbeat of execution.

Haven't you heard?

But can you believe it?

How can it be?

Christophe Kellermann had found himself a defense counsel.

The journals printed the story on the first page, devoting paragraphs to speculation as to who might have been the man foolish enough to go up against Guillaume Lazare. Whoever it was, he had accepted the job willingly, the papers knew, and so it was clear he was not a man of particularly good judgment; as such, the papers wrote, events were already progressing poorly for the general.

Though many of the papers seemed firmly behind Lazare and Murat, the city itself seemed more evenly divided. Half of Paris still recalled that Kellermann had saved the city and the very Revolution in its early days, when the Prussians had been encamped mere miles from the capital. Kellermann had been the man to fight for the values of liberty, equality, and fraternity when they were still only words, a nascent rallying cry of the Revolution.

And so, while public sentiment split on the question of Kellermann's guilt, all of Paris united with the same confusion, fixating on a singular

question: who was the man who had signed on to argue against Guillaume
Lazare?

"Have you gone absolutely mad?" Gavreau stood over Jean-Luc's desk, his
face red and the veins of his neck swollen. He let out a loud grunt as he
threw the front page of *Le Vieux Cordelier,* the popular paper penned by Camille Desmoulins, down on the desk. "Defending the man against Guillaume Lazare? Do you *hope* to make Marie a widow and Mathieu an orphan?"

Jean-Luc pushed himself from his desk, leaning back in his chair as he
folded his hands together in his lap. A position of perfect ease. After a
pause, he answered the question with a question of his own: "To what,
citizen, do you refer?"

"Don't feed me bullshit, St. Clair, I know it's you. Who else would be
mad enough to gamble his professional reputation—hell, his very life—
against the likes of Lazare? I just wish to know if you're trying to take our
whole damned department down with you."

Jean-Luc looked down at the news journal that his boss had hurled in
front of him. On the front page, the latest report indicated that the lawyer
who had taken up Kellermann's case was a young man—a man who had
never spoken before either the National Convention or the Revolutionary
Tribunal. An unknown amateur, whose only experience thus far had been
the work of a midlevel clerk buried in one of the many overcrowded administrative buildings on the Right Bank.

"I know it's you," Gavreau said, raising a finger to Jean-Luc's face. "I
could call in some favors. I could get you out of it. But we don't have much
time."

Jean-Luc sighed, perusing the rest of the article. "I have no intention of
taking you up on that offer, generous as it is."

"So you admit it! It *is* you?"

Jean-Luc looked up at his boss, tilting his head to one side as if to admit
his guilt.

"I always knew you were a damned fool."

"Why is it so terrible that General Kellermann have someone to defend
him?" Jean-Luc asked, his voice remaining calm.

"He'll have someone to defend him. I just don't want it to be you."

"Why not? Have you so little faith in my abilities?"

"Faith? Ha! I could have all the faith of heaven and earth in your abilities, but faith doesn't mean a damned thing. 'Specially not in times like these, or with people of this sort. What I *know* is that you're about to make a very powerful enemy."

"Of course I believe in the Revolution, and in justice. I just don't see why you need to thrust yourself onto such a dangerous stage." Marie was irate that night. She had given Jean-Luc her reluctant approval—if not her blessing—days earlier, when he had confessed to her his desire to represent Kellermann. However, having seen the explosion with which the news broke across the city, and having read the copious articles and pamphlets outlining the many reasons why this young lawyer stood no chance in court, her opinion had shifted dramatically.

"I'm terrified that they're going to label you an enemy of the Revolution. You know how easy it is to denounce someone these days. And how quick the mob is to heed that denunciation. All it takes is one person to sniff you the wrong way and they can send you to the guillotine."

Jean-Luc sat with her at the table. Their dinner had long grown cold, neither of them touching their food. Mathieu was, for once, allowing them the peace to discuss this in private, as he played in the corner, happily preoccupied with a new wooden figurine.

"Guillaume Lazare respects men who challenge him. He told me so the first time we met."

"Fine." Marie shrugged. "But even if *he* respects you for taking the case, what about the hundreds of other rabid Jacobins who will now focus on you as the man defending an accused royalist?" Marie's dark eyes smoldered. "You know better than anyone, Jean, how dangerous it is to draw attention to yourself, especially as a champion of a perceived traitor."

Jean-Luc rested his head in his hands, his mind weary and his convictions being assailed like a ship's mast facing a strong headwind.

"It's not too late, Jean. The papers haven't found you out yet. You could withdraw."

Jean-Luc sighed, a forlorn, defeated sigh. Both of them looked to the dark-haired little boy playing in the corner, his rosy lips slurring out the marching orders to his tiny wooden soldier.

Jean-Luc turned back toward his wife. "Marie, someone has to defend him. Otherwise, what was all of this for? Our whole Revolution would be a sham."

"Someone, all right, but why you?"

"No one else will do it. Can't you see that?"

She glowered, her full lips pressed in a straight, unyielding line.

"Marie, I've waited days, weeks, hoping and praying that someone would come forward. Someone with more experience and influence than I have." Jean-Luc shrugged. "But no one has come."

"You must realize, Jean, there's a reason for that. Are you to be the only one foolish enough to take this job?"

"I have to do it, Marie!" Jean-Luc landed a fist on the table, and he instantly regretted the force of the action. Mathieu looked up from the corner, scared. Marie's eyes dropped, filling with tears.

"I'm sorry." He reached across the table, taking her hand in his own and raising it to his lips. "What is all of this for?" He looked around—at the tiny apartment in this squalid neighborhood, their paltry dinner table that rarely had meat. "Why are we here? What are we fighting for, if not justice? I have to believe that our new nation is a place where an innocent man gets a fair trial. Where the rights of a man are upheld by the law. Where fear and hate are not yet more potent than justice and truth."

He wanted to continue. To beg her forgiveness. To promise her that he would do whatever he could to keep them safe. But he was overcome, and the words caught in his throat before he could utter them. He lowered his face once more into his cupped hands.

She made a low, guttural noise, before reaching across the table and taking his hands in hers. "Jean-Luc St. Clair, why must you always be so damned decent?"

He met her eyes, pausing a moment before answering. "I have to be."

She offered a sad, resigned smile. "But why?"

"To be worthy of you."

She sighed, a joyless sound, as she looked down at their intertwined hands.

"But perhaps you're right, Marie, perhaps it is foolish to put our entire family in danger. Perhaps you and Mathieu should visit your father. Spend some time back in Marseille. Only while the trial is ongoing, just until this chaos has passed. It might make sense for you to be far enough away in case—"

"Oh, you can stop right there." She raised her hand.

"It would be prudent."

"Don't you say another word, Jean-Luc St. Clair." Her tone was suddenly stern and authoritative. "If you think you will be shipping us out, if you think we'd leave you behind at a moment such as this, then you are not as intelligent as you think you are."

"Papa?" Mathieu was by his side now at the table, tugging on the jacket of his father's frayed suit. "Papa?"

Jean-Luc collected himself with a long inhale and looked down at his son. "Yes, my boy?" He put a palm on the top of his son's soft brunette curls.

"Papa, don't be sad."

"I'm not sad, my dear boy," Jean-Luc lied.

"Here, Papa, you may have my new toy." Mathieu extended a chubby hand toward his father, offering the wooden figurine. Jean-Luc took the soldier in his hands.

"This is a very nice toy, Mathieu." Then, looking up at his wife, he whispered: "How did we afford this?"

Marie rose, taking the two cold plates between them to clear the table. "I didn't buy that," she said. "I thought you did."

Jean-Luc was confused now and looked back at the toy—its glossy paint, its fine features carved with expert artistry. "Not me. How did he get it?"

Marie was scrubbing the dishes, her back to them. Jean-Luc turned to his son. Had his little boy stolen the expensive figurine from somewhere? "Mathieu, where did you get this?"

Mathieu took the figure back in his hand, hugging it close to his tiny body as if he feared he might have to surrender it. "The nice man gave it to me."

The words, as vague and garbled as they were coming from his toddler's mouth, sent a chill through Jean-Luc from the crown of his head down to the base of his gut. "The nice man?" he repeated the phrase. "Who is the nice man?"

Mathieu shrugged, bored of the questions. Marie turned around from the dishes, listening now with keen interest.

Jean-Luc put his hands on his son's shoulders, looking from his wife's worried expression back toward his child. "Mathieu, where did you see this nice man?"

"Downstairs." Mathieu pointed in the direction of the street, of Madame Grocque's tavern, of the wretched neighborhood.

"You mean Monsieur Grocque, the tavern keeper?"

"No, Papa." Mathieu shook his head. "He comes in his carriage sometimes."

"Do you know his name?"

Mathieu shook his head. "But he said he would come back. He promised me."

Marie was by their sides now, leaning forward to speak to the little boy. "What did he look like, Mathieu?"

The boy considered the question, his little brow creasing in thought. "I don't know, Papa. Old. A very white face."

Jean-Luc exchanged a tortured look with his wife before pulling his son close to him, his heart tightening as if constricted by a noose. He clung to Mathieu, needing to enfold the child in a safe, protective embrace. As he did so, a feeling somewhere deep inside him told him that he was foolish to think that he could protect anyone, or anything. Not in this world.

Marie spoke again, clutching her husband and son. "Mathieu, you listen to your papa. This man in a carriage—you are never to speak to him again unless you are with your mama or papa, do you hear me?"

Mathieu nodded, his sweet, soft features impervious to the fear that unnerved his parents. "Don't worry, Mama. If you don't wish me to see him, I'll ask him to disappear."

"What do you mean, my darling?" Marie asked, looking at Jean-Luc.

"Because, Mama," Mathieu explained, "he told me that he can make people disappear."

❧

Jean-Luc had taken to staying late at the office; there was always more work to be done than hours in which to do it, and it wasn't until the rest of his colleagues had left for the evening that he found he could accomplish most of his tasks. That, and it was easier to get home after Marie had already gone to sleep. Living alongside her nervous presence, avoiding her short, detached comments, was growing more and more difficult. He hated being at odds with her, hated seeing her so unhappy. Especially when he knew his own actions had inspired her anxious looks and the evasive turning of her back when he tried to embrace her. It was better, he had decided, that they see as little of each other as possible until after the Kellermann case had been decided.

Outside, the ground had thawed and spring had bloomed across Paris. The trees lining the Seine hung heavy with chestnut blossoms, and the days stretched out so long that the sun did not set over the western barrier of the city until only a few hours before midnight. It was a cruel taunt on the part of Mother Nature, to see the city so ripe with beauty and promise, so full of new life, all the while knowing that these very streets were a cauldron of death and destruction.

On a night in early summer, Jean-Luc sat at his desk before a pile of papers and a nearly expired candle. Hours had passed since his last colleague had left. The days were approaching their longest of the year, and the time was now that delicate hour in Paris during which the sun and moon hung simultaneously, sending a faint, milky glow through his window that made his eyelids heavy. He sighed. He felt as if he was retreading the same barren ground, hour after hour, night after night, seeking desperately for some fertile plot from which to coax some seed of hope for his client, Kellermann.

The trial approached, and, still, he had found nothing. Not knowing what proof the accusing team might produce, Jean-Luc had yet to develop a plan to counter the charges. Since the Law of Suspects had been decreed the previous September, a mere rumor of a man's royalist leanings or support for the antirepublican clergy was substantial enough to send him on a tumbril ride to the guillotine. And Jean-Luc's interviews in the old general's dank prison cell had only discouraged him further; Kellermann seemed undaunted, bent on telling the full truth as if the act of preserving his own life meant nothing to him.

"Yes, I questioned the necessity of beheading Louis and Antoinette. Since when has it become a crime to ask a question aloud?"

Jean-Luc did not know how to answer his client. Especially when he himself had wrestled with the same questions as Kellermann. But Reason and its sisters, Mercy and Integrity, were poor pillars upon which to build a defense these days. Possessing any one of these character traits might earn you a death sentence; Kellermann had all three. It *was* a crime to question, at least now. The Committee had ruled that any questioning of the actions taken by the Revolutionary government was sedition punishable by death.

A knock on the door interrupted Jean-Luc's gloomy musings, bringing his attention back to his shadowy office where his candle had nearly expired. "Come in." He looked up, unsure of what time it was. The face of the office errand boy appeared at the threshold.

"Two letters for you, Citizen St. Clair."

Jean-Luc waved the boy forward and took the letters from his hands. "Thank you. What time is it?"

The boy shifted his weight. "It's two hours until midnight, citizen."

Jean-Luc sighed, noticing for the first time that the world outside his window was now fully enveloped in the dark of night. "You better go home, boy."

"Are you certain, citizen? Orders from Monsieur Gavreau are to stay until you . . . er, until the last clerk has quit the office."

"I'm certain." Jean-Luc nodded, waving the boy out. "Go home."

Left alone, Jean-Luc opened the first of the two letters, seeing a handwriting he did not recognize. Holding it beside the flickering flame of candlelight, he read:

> *Citizen,*
>
> *Please allow me to introduce myself. My name is Captain André Valière. I am currently encamped with the Army of Italy.*
> *The cause for my letter is to inform you that I have served previously under General Christophe Kellermann. I think myself guilty of no exaggeration when I assert that no finer man or officer exists in*

the Army of the Republic. I hereby offer myself as a willing character witness, should you require any, in the upcoming trial for his life.

You have, no doubt, reckoned with the risks that you yourself have assumed by rising to the defense of the general. I, too, have wrestled with the question of whether to come forward, and, in so doing, render myself exposed to his critics, of which there appear to be a great number.

I confess that for a period I was disinclined to write to you. I had settled on the course of inaction. But as I recalled, night after sleepless night, how the general saved my life and the life of our Republic at the Battle of Valmy, and as I reflect on the irreproachable character and integrity of the man who has devoted his entire life to the service of our people, I cannot accept the course of inaction. Every virtue of his stands out as a censure against my own hesitancy and desire for self-preservation.

He must not die. Not now, not by the hands of the citizens of France. We must stop the Republic from committing this crime, a crime which would surely come back to haunt her. While there are men who are still willing to stand up for what is right and good, I cannot watch idly.

I will look for a response from you. And I extend to you my sincerest gratitude for your willingness to serve as defense for General Christophe Kellermann.

> *I remain your humble servant*
> *and fellow patriot,*
> *Captain André Valière*

Jean-Luc read the letter twice, the second time proving more difficult as a lone tear obscured his vision and splashed onto the words of this captain, this Valière.

By the end of the second reading, Jean-Luc was overcome, and his head collapsed to his desk. At last, someone who understood his own senti-ments. Someone who, rather than discouraging and censuring him, had taken the measure of his own beliefs and had come to the same, duty-bound conclusion: the shame of inaction outweighed the risk of action. These words felt like a hand extended to someone lost at sea, just moments before the final wave threatened to pull him under. They filled Jean-Luc with a renewed will to fight, the will to struggle against powerful forces in defense of an innocent man.

He sat for several minutes, reading and rereading the words. The man had offered himself as a character witness. What good this particular character witness might do, Jean-Luc did not know, not when the prosecution was certain to provide any number of witnesses who would claim to have heard disparaging and unpatriotic remarks coming from the general.

It may not be much, but it was something.

Jean-Luc turned to the second letter. On this paper, the handwriting looked vaguely familiar, but he could not immediately place it. He tore the wax seal and read the note. It was short, much shorter than the missive from André Valière. His heart lurched up into his throat as he placed the handwriting.

> *I see you've finally decided to try for glory. I look forward to the* contest. Bonne chance—*good luck.*

There was no signature, but no signature was necessary. Jean-Luc instinctively knew, by the blood throbbing in between his ears, who had written this note. He put the letter down, far away from him on his desk, as if the paper posed some threat to his work, to his very well-being.

Lazare had made no contact since Jean-Luc had accepted the case, and the two men had exchanged no correspondence. How Jean-Luc wished, now, in this dark office, that he had never opened the letter.

At the very bottom of the page lurked a curious postscript, also in Lazare's handwriting. Jean-Luc lifted the paper once more and read it:

> *Recall what I once told you: I would tear down any man guilty* *of the people's false worship. Keep your eyes on the journals in the* *coming weeks. I think you shall happen upon some news that may be* *surprising. Even wildly entertaining. A word of advice: I would avoid* *any contact with the Jacobin Club, if I were you.*

Jean-Luc found this last statement bizarre, incomprehensible. And yet, it stayed with him for the days to come. Each morning, when he arrived at the office and looked at the morning's journals, Jean-Luc sought out some news that might make sense of Lazare's veiled and strange prophecy.

It wasn't until weeks later, on the morning of July 28, that Jean-Luc finally discovered what Lazare had meant. There, on the front page, the words leapt out at him. Illogical words. Impossible words. His legs collapsed into his chair before he could master them.

> Maximilien Robespierre, Leader of the Jacobin Club, Guilty of Treason and Traitor of the Revolution, Will Be Guillotined Today!

13

Paris

Summer 1794

Andér returned to the capital the evening before the trial of Christophe Kellermann. The guards at the southern barrier had been ornery, unhappily marching out of their guardhouse into the rain that had pelted André for hours. One of them held up a lantern, inspecting André's leave papers, turning his gaze back and forth to inspect the stranger. The other, a large pike held in one arm, chewed on a piece of soaked bread. André was doubtful that either of them knew how to read.

With a wordless grunt and a half-hearted salute, the guard with the lantern waved André through, and his horse splashed through the mud under the gates and into the city. Hoping he was not too late, André made his way directly to the large Right Bank building near the Palais de Justice, where Jean-Luc had told him he would be working, preparing the case for the next day.

"I can't tell you what a relief it is to finally meet you, Captain Valière." Jean-Luc's dark hair was disheveled, his eyes sunken with fatigue, but André had the distinct impression that his was a face he had seen before. He blinked, trying to pluck the receding image back into the fore of his mind from behind the gossamer veil where it lurked. And then he knew: a year earlier, the night he had first kissed Sophie, on the footbridge spanning the Seine. But before he could say so, Jean-Luc was speaking: "I've seen you before, Captain Valière."

"Please, call me André."

"It was at the Café Marché. Months ago. Years even, perhaps. You were escorting a drunken man out."

André laughed. He knew exactly to whom the lawyer referred. But the night could have been any number of occasions. "My brother, Remy."

"Ah. Well, I remember only because it was the first night I met Maurice Merignac—a work associate, I suppose you could say. He was rather . . . opinionated about it." Jean-Luc smiled. His face was open and earnest, betraying no glimpse of design or intrigue, and yet the man clearly possessed an active mind. "Please, come in, André." With that André slipped off his drenched riding coat and placed it on a hook on the office door. He set his tricorn hat on top of his coat and took in his surroundings. Jean-Luc's office was littered with papers and opened books, dimly lit by a lone candle on the desk.

"Can I offer you anything to drink?"

"Just a bit of coffee, if you have any," André said, his entire body damp and aching from the long ride from his quarters in the south.

"Of course."

Each of them settled with a mug of coffee at the large desk, its surface a battleground of papers, spent inkwells, quills, envelopes, and cups in varying degrees of fullness. "I work amid chaos," Jean-Luc said, picking up a quill and dipping it into the inkwell.

Perhaps that was correct, André mused, but his expression was one of grave determination. André took a liking to him immediately.

Together, the two men discussed André's statement for the following day. André was under no circumstances to get into a political debate with the opposing lawyers. Especially, Jean-Luc pointed out, given the fact that he himself had noble blood. "Nothing we can do about that, if it comes up," Jean-Luc said with a sigh.

"Believe me, I know." André nodded, sharing the story of his father's fate. The menace of his noble lineage was like a serpent he wore around his neck each day. Calm for now, but André would have been a fool not to wonder if and when it might stir to bite him. Particularly as he faced off against a legal team headed by the same attorney who had convicted his father.

Jean-Luc listened to André's story, his eyes earnest and attentive. Pausing briefly at the end of André's account, Jean-Luc sighed. "We must assume, since it's Lazare, that your noble lineage will come up. He will come at you with everything he can muster."

André rubbed his brow and nodded slowly.

"Just remember that you were present at Valmy; you witnessed what General Kellermann has done for this country. You denounced your own noble birth and you faced the enemies of the Republic and, with the general, you saved it. I would not say that he is above reproach, not these days, but if any man can show that he has sacrificed and risked more for the Republic, then I would like to hear from him. Keep returning to these points: Valmy. Prussians. Imminent defeat. Rallying cry for the army."

André nodded, trying to absorb each of these pieces of counsel.

After a long pause, both men seemingly lost in their own thoughts, Jean-Luc looked up. "You're going to be excellent." The lawyer stared at him with an intensity that the young captain found somewhat unsettling, yet André felt confident all the same. This was a competent man, a passionate man. Even if every fact of fate and fortune were conspiring to work against him.

"All I can recommend now, sir, is to get a good night's sleep. Wear your uniform. Oh, and if I may suggest, be sure to wear a tricolor cockade prominently on your coat."

"Yes." André nodded. He supposed that this lawyer was just a few years older than he himself, but there was a shrewdness about him that André respected. Perhaps this was a man who took himself a bit too seriously; then again, these were not times for the lighthearted. It was undoubtedly encouraging that Jean-Luc seemed to possess a fire within. André hoped it would reveal itself during tomorrow's trial.

"Very good." Jean-Luc had already risen and was riffling through a stack of papers on his desk. Sensing the attorney's urgent need to work, André rose from his chair.

"I would say to you, St. Clair, to get a good night's sleep as well, but I very much doubt that you would heed my advice," André said, offering a wry smile.

"I'll sleep after tomorrow, when, God willing, justice has been served and a good man is set free." Jean-Luc reached forward to place a palm on André's shoulder. "Captain Valière." Jean-Luc paused, looking into André's eyes. "Thank you. Truly, thank you. On behalf of General Kellermann, and all those who still hold out hope for a tattered nation. God bless you."

André swallowed, hoping his trembling voice would not betray the true depths of his feeling as he answered: "The man saved my life."

Jean-Luc nodded wearily. "And perhaps, tomorrow, you will save his."

Darkness hovered over the narrow streets by the time André reached Sophie's apartment. It was his first time back in the capital since the death of Robespierre, and the city was now under the control of the new legislature. In a backlash against Robespierre's gang, now out of favor, the Jacobins were being hunted down or driven from the city. Membership in the club was banned, on punishment of death, and an eerie, tenuous calm had descended over the city.

Bread was still unaffordable for many, and the foreign wars had bled the coffers even drier. With the monarchs dead, the nobility ravaged or fled, and half the leading political party butchered, it remained to be seen who might next pay with their own blood for the grievances of the masses. Not a person in the city, André felt, could take tomorrow's sunrise for granted.

Sophie stood by the window, awaiting his arrival, when Parsy announced André's name. "André!" Sophie ran to him, folding herself into his arms in a prolonged hug.

"My darling." He lifted her chin for a kiss. He hadn't seen her since his departure for the front in February. Despite his bleak mood, his heart raced, remembering their last night together, so many months earlier—the night they had celebrated his birthday and then returned, the two of them, to his room in the boardinghouse. The memory—along with the hope that they would be together again soon—had sustained him throughout their long separation, when he'd slept outside in the cold, nights so bitter he lost the feeling in his limbs. Mornings when he awoke to musket fire from an unseen enemy. Every day had felt like a week, and every month was a year. Now it seemed almost impossible that he was back, looking into her eyes again.

She clung to him. So much time had passed, but she looked even lovelier than the memory he had held. Her hair framed her face, loose and undone, and she wore a simple dress of lilac silk. "What kept you so long? I had begun to worry."

"I had to take care of something. No need to worry, my darling." He kissed her again, but he sensed the hesitancy in her embrace. Sophie tilted her gaze, looking toward the maid whose presence André had completely forgotten about.

"Thank you, Parsy. You may leave us," she said. The maid fidgeted in the corner before reluctantly turning to leave.

When Parsy had shut the door, Sophie turned back to André, her eyes suddenly beguiling and full of desire. "We have a lot of time to make up for."

Later, they lay in bed, listening to the sounds of the Parisian evening that rose up from outside Sophie's bedroom window. A café across the street was crowded, its patrons spilling out onto the lane in various states of intoxication. A pipe player was alternating between offering his melodies to the passersby and imploring the crowds to drop a bit of change into his threadbare cap. From a nearby alley, a dog barked.

Their bodies intertwined, a fire warming the room, André and Sophie did their best not to think of the coming day. They filled the hours telling each other about the past six months. Sophie told André that her uncle had stayed in the city, tormenting her with his surprise visits and stern curfew. André told Sophie about his campaign outside Saorgio and their constant expectation for the orders to cross the Alps into Italy. He also told her of his meeting, hours earlier, with Jean-Luc St. Clair and his positive impressions of the passionate young lawyer.

"He's a good man. His outward appearance might not betray it, but I think he has some fight in him."

"Certainly brave if he'll take on Lazare and his Committee," Sophie said.

André traced a line with his finger down the soft creamy skin of her back. They lay still in silence for several moments before Sophie shifted, propping herself up on her elbows. She brought her palm to André's cheek, grazing the raised scar tissue.

"You've never told me."

"About what?" André asked.

"This scar. How did you get it?"

André sighed, quickly removing her hand and holding her fingers gently in his own palm. After a pause, he answered: "This one came from Valmy."

"An Austrian?"

"Or Prussian. Whoever he was, the tip of his bayonet sliced the side of my face. He would have killed me, in fact. If not for . . ." He paused.

"If not for?"

"If not for General Kellermann. He saved my life." André blinked, his vision suddenly blurry as he recalled that day at Valmy.

Sophie, sensing his difficulty, spoke before he had to. "And now you're back here. And hopefully you shall do the same for him."

André nodded. "You know Remy is back in Paris for the trial as well?"

"Hmm?" She seemed to be distracted now, her head resting on his chest.

"Remy is here. He is going to come to the trial tomorrow."

"How is dear old Remy?" she asked, propping herself up on her elbows again.

"The same as ever. Frustrated that he didn't see any action while in Italy, but more than making up for it now that he's back in Paris. He tells me he plans to propose to Celine."

"Celine the ballerina?" she asked.

"Celine the ballerina. I think she's done the impossible; it appears that she's tamed my brother's restless heart."

"I've been thinking," André said, his voice shifting to a serious tone. Sophie looked at him more intently now, her loose curls tumbling forward to frame her face. He tugged a strand of her blond hair away from her face, holding it gently in his fingers. "Sophie, what if you and I got married?"

She cocked her head to the side as if to say: *This again?*

"No, I mean it. Listen to me."

"André, I told you—"

"Just listen."

"My uncle would kill you first."

"What if he didn't know?"

This silenced Sophie's protests. She considered what André had said, her brow crinkling in thought. Eventually, she spoke: "You mean a secret marriage?"

"Precisely. We could do it before I left for the front again. Remy could be our witness."

The words hung between them for a while, Sophie's eyes distant as she considered the proposition. When she looked back at him, a smile tugged her rose-colored lips upward. "You wish to marry me?"

André nodded, pulling her toward him. "I wish for nothing more in this entire world than to marry you."

She slid on top of him now, her body pressing onto his. The bed was warm and her cheeks were rosy. Surely she felt how much he desired her. She tilted her head down and kissed his neck. "Tell me yes," he said, closing his eyes as her lips touched his skin.

"But do I wish to marry you, André Valière?"

"Yes, you do," he said, pulling her face back toward his so that he could kiss her. "Regardless of what happens tomorrow, whatever the outcome may be, I am going to marry you before I leave the city."

"I think I need a little more time to decide," she teased.

"Nonsense. It's decided. Now be quiet and let me make love to my fiancée."

14

Paris

Summer 1794

A ndré had hoped to arrive early, but the courtroom he walked into was filled beyond capacity. He gave his name to the nearest bailiff. The man, considering André's military uniform and declaration that he was to serve as a witness, directed him to a bench one row behind where the defense would sit. One other person already sat there.

"Madame Kellermann." André tucked his chin and nodded toward the elegant woman he had met at the Christmas ball. He was about to reintroduce himself when she spoke.

"Captain Valière, how good to see you." Christianne Kellermann, to André's surprise, recognized him. She extended a gloved hand. "Thank goodness you've come." Her hair was laced with quite a few more strands of gray than the last time they'd met, and her features bore the drawn, pinched quality of sleepless nights and perpetual anxiety, but she offered him an attempt at a smile. "Please, won't you sit beside me?"

"It would be my honor, madame." André took the seat and surveyed the room, every inch of it buzzing with bodies, whispers, and roving eyes. The crowds were especially thick in the gallery above, where row after row spilled with curious spectators who vied and jockeyed for seats. It was a swarm of dirty faces, red caps, and tricolor cockades. Many of the women sat knitting while the men exchanged the latest news, and the children pulled one another's hair, avoiding their mothers' slaps and giggling as they leaned over the balcony. Also mixed in with this lot were soldiers.

André recognized some of the enlisted men, their bodies packed tight in the rafters. He saw the round face of Leroux and several of his companions. It filled André with a small measure of pride: these men were here, like he was, to support the general who had led them to victory at Valmy.

Also in the crowded gallery appeared several chalky white faces: a cluster of men from the various legislative committees, André guessed. These men, like Lazare, had skillfully ridden the wave of growing dissatisfaction from ruling party to ruling party, surviving while so many of their colleagues had been condemned to the guillotine. Now they sat in silence in the gallery of this crowded courtroom, their postures tilting away from the hordes, though there was not sufficient room on the benches for them to distance themselves much. In contrast to those surrounding them, these stern men did not exchange gossip or even speak to one another.

On the lower level, several soldiers and uniformed officers sat on Kellermann's side. A few rows back André spotted LaSalle, and beside him Remy. André nodded at them. Another group of National Guard soldiers stood toward the front, holding muskets with their backs to the wall, casting unpleasant glares at the men on Kellermann's side of the aisle. Though they had fought under the same flag, one could not help but feel the mutual hatred that cast a chill over the chamber. One of the soldiers standing toward the front lowered his musket, leered in Remy's direction, and cast a wad of brown spit onto the wooden floor. LaSalle threw an arm across Remy's chest and shook his head as Remy muttered a stifled curse.

At the back of the court hung a massive flag, the new republic's tricolor. Along the wall a large white banner brandished the words "Liberty, Equality, Fraternity" scrawled in blood-red paint. The main aisle cut through the middle of the courtroom, not unlike a church or cathedral. Indeed, for many, these courts had taken on a solemn, even religious function in the new Republic.

Sophie sat across the aisle on the prosecution's side; André had made her promise that she would do so, when she had insisted on attending the morning's proceedings. Seeing André enter, her eyes rested on him for just a moment, a flicker of acknowledgment and support, before she returned her gaze to the front of the room. All around her sat the supporters of Lazare and Murat: surviving Jacobin lawyers, a half dozen members of the Committee, ambitious advocates hoping to make a name for themselves in the new government. A man in an unnaturally orange wig sat right behind the table where the barristers would take their seats.

At the front of the hall rested a long table draped in red cloth, its surface bare save for a cluster of papers, a quill and inkwell, and a haphazard arrangement of dripping white candles. Five judges sat at this table, facing the room and the prosecution and defense. They wore the traditional black robes, two of them with red caps atop their heads. The judge in the center, appearing senior in both age and authority, wore a large black hat with a red plume jutting out. But, in reality, there was only one true authority in this proceeding; the people would serve as the arbiters, swaying the judges to choose either life or death.

A door at the side of the room opened and in walked Jean-Luc St. Clair, his eyes cast directly in front and his arms full of papers. A loud murmur arose from the hall as he made his entrance. The central judge, who had been writing with his quill, barely looked up to acknowledge the appearance of the defendant's attorney. The other judges leaned back in their chairs, their eyes tracking the path of the young lawyer.

A few moments later, the whispers of the crowd buzzed louder as the prosecution—Guillaume Lazare and his chief witness, Nicolai Murat—entered from the other side. André's heart lurched in his chest. He noted that Lazare had two disciples with him, trailing behind the old lawyer into the courtroom. Murat, with his general's uniform starched and immaculate, took his seat with a loud exhale, casting a glance across the room at the defense's table. André clenched his fists and couldn't help but cast a sideways glance toward Sophie, who offered a barely perceptible nod by way of answer.

Several minutes later, the door on the defense's side of the room opened and General Kellermann appeared, escorted by two thick guards in army uniforms. He looked thinner than the last time André had seen him, but his overall bearing remained strong and commanding. He, too, was dressed in uniform. As Kellermann strode into the courtroom, the whispers and murmurs grew to full-fledged cheers and jeers as the crowds, buzzing with an anticipatory hum a minute earlier, surrendered any final shreds of composure. All five judges looked up at the gallery where the soldiers were on their feet, pounding their fists and cheering. Beside the soldiers, the crowd of red-capped revolutionaries jeered even louder, hissing with narrowed eyes as several children began to cry. Only the Committee members sat quietly, their features pale and unmoving.

"Order! Order, I say!" the central judge barked as guards in the gallery separated a half dozen soldiers and civilians who seemed poised to brawl.

André fidgeted in his seat, turning back to the front of the room to see Kellermann settling into his chair. Beside André, Kellermann's wife clutched her handkerchief in her hands, twisting it between clenched fingers. André offered her a sideways glance, an encouraging nod, but her eyes were fixed forward on the broad, uniformed back of her husband.

Kellermann, for his part, appeared unmoved by the commotion, even calm. As he turned to glance over his shoulder, André saw on the general's features a hint of defiance. His eyes lingered for several minutes on his wife's face before turning briefly to André and then to the rest of the men and women who sat on his side. André gritted his teeth, heartened by Kellermann's show of composure—whether it was genuine or not. This should not come as a surprise, André realized. A man with General Kellermann's experience, who had spent his years fighting on the bloody battlefields of Europe, would surely not be cowed by this rabble of red-faced revolutionaries and their shouted threats.

The central judge rang his bell ever louder and continued to call the crowd to order. The guards escorted several of the more vociferous audience members out of the gallery and, after a prolonged attempt, the judge managed to wrangle the packed hall into a manageable quiet.

"This Tribunal Court is convened in the month of Thermidor, in the Year Two of the Republic of France."

André calculated the date in his head: July of the year 1794. He had still not adjusted to this new and, to his mind, strange way of tracking the months and years.

"On trial is Christophe de Kellermann, known alternatively as le Comte de Kellermann or General Kellermann." A mixture of cheers and jeers greeted these titles, and the judge cast an ornery glance upward at the gallery before continuing.

"The defense is accused of royalist sympathies and acts taken to undermine the Army of France in their operations on the Rhine. The charges are brought forward by General Nicolai Murat." Cheers sounded at the pronunciation of this name. The old judge paused to clear his throat, emotionless as he read through these facts, no more than administrative details to a man who had grown accustomed to condemning men and women— even children—to death.

"I call the attorney for the defense, Jean-Luc St. Clair, to rise and answer these charges."

Some in the gallery above hissed as Jean-Luc stood, straightening his vest to smooth it of wrinkles. The audience seemed to lean forward and crane their necks in one motion, the benches creaking under their combined weight. André took in a silent breath, as curious as every other soul in the room as to how the young lawyer would respond to the charges. The prolonged silence filled the already rapt room with a palpable tension.

When Jean-Luc spoke, it was with a clear, confident voice. "I thank you, Your Honors." Jean-Luc nodded at the five robed men before him. "Citizens and citizenesses of Paris." The lawyer turned, his gaze and his hands sweeping upward to the gallery. That was where the contest would be lost or won, André knew. That was the crowd that must be swayed, for their voices would ring loudest, telling the justices how to vote.

"My client, the hero of the Battle of Valmy, General Christophe Kellermann, has been accused of sympathizing with the deposed and decapitated tyrant, Citizen Capet. And of undermining the efforts of the French army in the campaigns on the Rhine. Charges that we, this very day, shall hold up before the infallible lights of evidence, reason, and justice. Charges that you, the good and honest people of the Republic of France, will examine and scrutinize yourselves. And charges that you, the good and honest people of the Republic of France, shall find as preposterous as they are untrue, before this court is adjourned."

Listening to this calm, cogent opening argument, André felt his taut muscles soften slightly; the young attorney was perfectly confident, his words unequivocally competent. More than competent, even. Good. His mannerisms were sure and forceful without surrendering any graciousness. His language was clear and direct. He did not stumble over a single word as he rolled out his client's case.

It was a story of a young man who, given everything by his noble birth, eschewed the privilege that those of his own social order told him was his right. A young man who, after disavowing the leisure and riches that might have been his birthright, instead sought a career in the army, rejecting a life of inactivity and profligacy. A young man who served with valor and duty and, as a result, climbed upward through the ranks, becoming a trusted officer and seasoned general. A leader of men who had aligned with and even aided the people when they had risen up against a system of tyranny and undue privilege. And a champion who had rushed to the defense of the nascent Republic when a foreign enemy crossed the borders of France, ready to invade and stamp out the new Revolution.

"These two men." Jean-Luc was striding before the front of the courtroom, his two arms now spread between Murat and Kellermann. "Both heroes. Both generals. These two men who have been friends for longer than some of us in this room have been alive—these two men have fought alongside each other for France. You must ask yourself: would a man such as Nicolai Murat, who has put his very life in this man's hands, and vice versa—would he have done so had he not trusted General Kellermann? Had he not thought him an honest, worthy, and patriotic citizen?" Jean-Luc paused, and André sensed it was more for effect than necessity. The young lawyer forced himself to break momentarily, André saw, even as he was ready to glide forward on the building swell of his argument. He took a sip of water and continued.

"Let's think of this time not two years ago." Jean-Luc's tone was calm yet authoritative, the tone of a schoolmaster laying out a series of complicated facts for a room full of pupils. "This entire city, this entire nation, was hoisting this man, General Kellermann, the hero of Valmy, atop its shoulders. This man had risked his life in order to preserve the promise of our free nation. His words, his rallying cry of '*Vive la nation,*' had driven our brave soldiers to repel the Prussian invasion at Valmy.

"Now the calls for General Kellermann's head are just as loud and ubiquitous as were those earlier cries of praise. Why is that? What has changed?" Jean-Luc shrugged his shoulders as he allowed his eyes to move over the faces of the gallery.

"Is it perhaps"—he lifted a finger, cocking his head—"that *we* have changed? Have we become so inflamed by our good and righteous desire to steer this Revolution forward, so overburdened by the arduous task of rooting out our true and real enemies, that we have become temporarily overzealous to condemn?"

Jean-Luc did not look at Murat but kept his gaze on the people in the gallery.

"Paris, trust your better instincts, your *true* instincts. You know this man, General Christophe Kellermann. You know him as a defender of the people. He has not changed." Now Jean-Luc's voice rose gradually in volume as he lifted his arms, as if beckoning the people in the gallery forward to him. "Do not allow yourself to be moved by the barbs that come from a quarrel, personal in nature. Old friends who have reached such heights that, when they are at odds, one of them has the power to bring the entire government against the other."

The crowds in the gallery were beginning to murmur, sounds of tenuous agreement and assent. Jean-Luc allowed this side noise to occur before he spoke again, his voice calm.

"The past two years have seen many guilty men earn their tumbril rides to the guillotine. Some here now say that General Kellermann deserves such a fate. What is their proof? What is his crime? If uniting the soldiers and people of France, and leading them bravely against our *real* enemies, is a crime, then yes, General Kellermann is guilty. If beating back the foreign hosts, driving them back to their own borders, is a crime, then yes, he is guilty.

"But I must ask you: do these sound like the actions of a man who *sympathizes* with a dead and deposed tyrant?"

The crowd was now muttering audibly, their responses clearly in the young lawyer's favor. Someone in the gallery, a red-capped revolutionary who had arrived this morning eager to condemn the accused general, now shouted out: "*Vive* Kellermann! Long live Kellermann!" and the entire gallery erupted in applause.

Down below, André glanced at Sophie, and he couldn't help but smile. The soldiers around him, too, were shifting in their seats, bolstered by the sympathy that the defense's attorney had managed to carve out among the crowd.

Across the aisle from André, Lazare exchanged a meaningful look with Murat. What was his expression—annoyance? Acknowledgment of defeat? André felt a flicker of hope in his chest, and he guessed that, beside him, Madame Kellermann felt the same.

Jean-Luc raised his arms and the volume of his voice, driving his argument forward on the wave of the crowd's enthusiasm. "My friends, you *know* Christophe Kellermann. You are the very patriots who hoisted him atop your shoulders! Who declared him, rightly so, to be the Savior of our Revolution! And so I say to you: if and only if fighting and shedding blood in defense of the Republic is a crime, *then* my client is guilty!"

The crowd now broke out into applause. At this Murat stood up, thundering: "Pretty words from a young lawyer fresh out of the schoolhouse. How much blood have *you* shed for France?"

Hearing this insult, the crowd erupted in laughter, momentarily distracted from the stirring rhetoric of the defense. André looked to the judges, fearing that all the momentum built up thus far might be lost if order wasn't restored quickly.

"Out of order!" The central judge clanged his bell while the crowds continued to laugh and carry on their side conversations. "This court will come to order now, or be dismissed." The room fell quiet.

"All right." The elderly judge glared at the room, his plumed hat off-center and his face red. "I think we've heard enough from the defense. Have you anything more to add?"

"That is all, Your Honor." Jean-Luc bowed his head.

"Good." The justice puffed out his cheeks, exhaling. "The defense rests."

Turning on his heels, Jean-Luc marched toward the table and took a seat beside his client.

"Right, then, let's hear from the prosecution. Citizen Lazare?"

Lazare stood up, slowly, clearing his throat. His pale hair, almost as colorless as his powdered face, was pulled back in a tight ponytail, and he wore the tricolor cockade on his lapel. "Your Honor, stating our case will be one of my legal deputies, the attorney Guy Mouchetard."

"Very well. Citizen Mouchetard?"

With that, one of Lazare's disciples, a man with a protruding chin and beady eyes, pushed back from the table and rose to his feet. Another good sign, André thought; surely Lazare himself would be speaking if the case was worthwhile or truly significant to him. The defense stood a much better chance against this surrogate, and surely Lazare knew that—and yet he had allowed it.

The man, about the same age as Jean-Luc but several inches shorter, walked slowly to the center of the room, his heels clicking on the wooden floor. Pausing, he turned and looked out over the crowd. He took a pair of spectacles from a front pocket and slid them up his nose, pausing a moment before the waiting audience. When he spoke, his voice was loud, yet also quite shrill compared to Jean-Luc's.

"At the outset of this new and noble Republic, we arrested a tyrant and his lascivious wife. The tyrant was brought to justice by this same court, the same people. The people of Paris. The people of France." The lawyer's mannerisms were jerky, his cadence irregular.

"Centuries marked by crimes, debt, terror, and usurpation were exposed. When the ermine robe was removed from Capet's royal person, we saw him for what he was: a spoiled and incompetent brat, exploiting the French people. Growing fat off the misery of those he professed to love."

The crowd hissed, agitated by this memory of their former king. The lawyer continued, his voice growing louder.

"*That* was the moment that united us as a people. That heroic stand of the French citizens against the tyranny of the monarchy and their aristocratic lapdogs. When we, the new Republic, put a tyrant on trial and demanded an end to the lies and abuse! It took extraordinary courage and bloody sacrifice on the part of this city to do that which had never before been done in history." The lawyer seemed to be gaining confidence, and he slid the spectacles farther up his nose, nodding at Lazare before continuing.

"When we demanded justice, and we sent those two necks to the guillotine, it was the moment of glory for our Revolution!" Now the crowd was whipped up into a frenzy, reminded and proud once more of its regicide. André watched, alarmed, as he sensed the momentum shifting back to the opposing side.

"Today we are looking at a man who, no doubt, has served this country. No one would question the Comte de Kellermann's skill as a warrior. Many even called him a savior." Mouchetard did not glance at the man about whom he spoke, but instead kept his eyes fixed on the gallery as he crossed his arms.

"Most of us are but common people. We have little use for the lofty rhetoric and high-flung ideas so often summoned in the defense's legal statements. We have even less use for those who preach to us as if we were attending a sermon." An emphatic laugh came out from the balcony. "Like many of you, I'm a humble man; some years ago, I began as a pruner of fruit trees. And as such, if there is one thing I do know quite well, it is the proper tending of a garden. Might I share with you one of the basic principles of this occupation? It is this: when a weed grows too tall, at the expense of every other life around it, it must be thrashed and cut before it threatens the well-being of those that languish under its shadow." He made a cutting gesture with his arm and, as he did so, the crowd erupted in roars and fist thumpings.

"Objection!" Jean-Luc rose up. "Why must we hear this lesson in horticulture? Of what relevance is this analogy?"

The judge interceded, ringing his bell irritably. "Out of order—await your turn, defense!"

"Your Honor, I'm not sure what the lesson in gardening has to do with the prosecution of General Kellermann," Jean-Luc said, his jaw twitching as he kept his tone composed. "For my part, I've heard that most gardens grow fertile with water, rather than blood."

"Order! Defense, you have had your say. The prosecution holds the floor." The judge turned toward the prosecution's table. Mouchetard stammered, momentarily thrown off his argument. The crowd, sensing the hesitation, began to buzz.

"Well?" The judge arched an eyebrow at the speaker.

"Well, I was making the point that . . . er—" he sputtered, fumbling for words but having lost his thread. Those in the balcony began to murmur, sensing the prosecutor's weakness, losing interest in his aborted analogy. André felt the faint embers of hope stirring once more. If only Jean-Luc could recapture the energy of the crowd.

And then Guillaume Lazare stood up. Lifting a hand, he asked: "May I, Your Honor?"

The judge nodded, and the room went quiet. As the younger lawyer retreated to his seat, the older lawyer glided across the front of the courtroom. Tracing a hand around his mouth, he cast a look at the defense, the hint of a smile appearing on his face. Finally, after what felt like several minutes, he turned and faced the crowd. When he did at last begin, Lazare spoke very quietly, so that everyone in the gallery was obliged to lean forward to hear him.

"I ask Citizen St. Clair, and all the citizens present in this assembly one question: how were the ancient monarchs empowered to rule this land, if not through violence and force, even bloodshed?"

Thoughtful silence stretched across the hall until Lazare continued. "How did the princes and lords of past years come into their noble seats of power? Or better yet, how was King George III, England's tyrant, expelled from the colonies in the New World? How do a people throw off the mantle of tyranny, if not through righteous force?" Lazare paused, knitting his thin fingers together in front of his narrow waist.

"Would you have had them wait patiently? Pray? Philosophize?" Lazare smirked. "*Hope* that the despot would one day wake up and decide to trade in his scepter for a constitution? Will patience mean anything against a tyrant's henchmen and cold steel bayonets? When the king's minister told our people to eat grass, should they have obliged his scornful remark?"

The crowd began to jeer, answering Guillaume Lazare's questions with their approval. André wished Jean-Luc would stand up and cry out his objection again; how did this history lesson in any way relate to Kellermann? But the defense's lawyer simply sat in his seat, listening politely. The central judge looked on at Lazare, his gaze attentive as the old lawyer continued.

"History shows us a great many tyrants who have slaughtered others to gain their power, but very few who have willingly handed away that same power. When has it ever benefited a ruler to yield to a usurper? Will a tyrant not fight his people, even *butcher* his people, to maintain his authority?"

Jean-Luc now ran a hand through his hair, wanting an opening, but the crowd listened with rapt attention to Lazare's soliloquy.

"That is the threat we face, every day, to our new Revolution," Lazare said. Then he turned toward Jean-Luc. "A young, well-meaning idealist cannot be wholly faulted for his *optimism*." The word was laced with condescension. "But, my friends, naïveté will not protect us! At this very hour, foreign tyrants are poised at our borders, seeking a way to invade and crush our young Republic. Our new freedom is fragile—more fragile than we'd even like to believe. All it takes is *one* man, one of our very own, to betray us and open the floodgates for these foreign mercenaries. One man who's decided that his aims no longer align with ours, and just like that!" Lazare's fingers spread around him, mimicking the piercing of a bubble. "The Revolution is over. The tyranny of a king, reimposed. All of us—all of our liberties—dissolved."

At this point, Jean-Luc stood up. "Your Honor, I'd like to beg your permission that these vague and theoretical soliloquies be put to rest so that the court may proceed to the business at hand, which is to establish the truth through the means of facts and testimony."

"Granted," the judge answered. "Citizen Lazare, please be seated."

The old lawyer bowed low, his lips curling upward in an obliging smile.

"Citizen St. Clair?" the judge continued.

"Your Honor, the defense would like to call its first witness."

"All right," the judge agreed.

"Your Honor, I call Captain André Valière."

André heard his name and rose, feeling the sudden focus of hundreds of eyes on his person. He walked forward, taking the seat offered to him before the judge's table. His eyes fell for a moment on Kellermann, and he thought: how odd that the general nods at me, giving me a fortifying glance, when it is I who should be bolstering his spirits.

Jean-Luc let André settle into his seat before he approached. "Citizen, please state your full name and rank."

"André Martin-Laurent Valière, captain in the Army of the French Republic."

"And how is it that you are acquainted with the defense?"

"I served under General Kellermann at the Battle of Valmy and the campaign of the Rhine in the summer and autumn of 1792. Er, I mean the first year of our Republic."

With André's help, Jean-Luc laid out the facts and circumstances of the Battle of Valmy, entirely for the crowd's benefit. The threat of the Prussians, the clear route for the Habsburg alliance into Paris. General Kellermann's decision to turn and give battle on that field at Valmy when the outcome of the campaign, and the nation's very survival, still hung in the balance.

Asking André to deliver his own account of that day, Jean-Luc listened, as did the crowd. The hundreds sat quietly as André reached the climax of his tale, the moment when a barrel-chested Prussian stood over him, wrestling to lodge a bayonet tip in his skull. And Kellermann appearing suddenly to cut down the man who, seconds later, would have taken André's life.

When André had concluded, Jean-Luc sighed. An audible sigh. An exhale intended to be heard, and felt, by the crowds in the gallery.

"And so, Captain Valière, you would say, unequivocally, that General Kellermann saved your life that day?"

"I would."

"And you would say that General Kellermann rallied the army that day, leading the decisive charge that finally broke the enemy's lines and won France her victory?"

"I would."

"And has he ever, in the time you've known him, spoken a false word against the Republic?"

"He has not."

Murat fidgeted in his chair, whispering something in Lazare's ear. Lazare nodded.

"And you recognize that, in coming here today to speak on behalf of an accused man, you put your own life at risk, Captain Valière? And yet, you come of your own accord, because your honor as a soldier and a citizen compels you to tell the people of France the truth?"

André noticed for the first time now, as he tried to swallow, just how dry his mouth was. He opened his lips and, in a loud voice, answered: "I understand that, and I willingly accept the consequences. General Kellermann would do the same for any other loyal Frenchman."

Now members of the crowd were nodding. One man in the gallery whistled his support for the defense's witness.

"Thank you, Captain Valière." Jean-Luc offered his witness a barely perceptible wink. Turning to the judge, Jean-Luc said: "Your Honor, the defense has no further questions for the witness."

Lazare raised a finger, and the judge, seeing it, nodded. "Citizen Lazare?"

"May I approach the witness, Your Honor?"

"You may," the judge replied, and Lazare rose. André felt his entire body go rigid as the image of his father on trial burst across his mind. He blinked, forcing himself to maintain mastery of his surging emotions as Lazare walked slowly toward him.

"Captain Valière, is it?"

André nodded, using all his strength to keep his voice quiet as he answered. "Yes."

Lazare flashed a quizzical expression, tapping his chin with his thumb. "What have you done with the antecedent of nobility—the 'de' that preceded your name at birth?"

The crowd began to whisper and André fidgeted in his chair, feeling it creak beneath his movements. "I denounced the noble title and lands years ago. I swore an oath to the Republic."

Lazare nodded, pacing the floor before the witness but not looking directly at him. "And your father before you, did he, too, denounce the title?"

André felt the overpowering urge to rise and lunge at his father's assailant, but he clutched the sides of his chair, holding himself in place. "My father . . . he . . . well . . ."

Lazare waited, his face now holding André's with his eyes, his features placid.

"My father no longer lives," André said eventually, his mouth dry as the words came out. His heart hammered his chest.

"Pity." Lazare cocked his head. "How, if you don't mind my asking, did your father perish?"

"He was killed."

"The guillotine, I believe?"

André nodded.

"Guillotined? Please answer 'yes' or 'no,' Captain de Valière. We must record these facts for the court," Lazare said, crossing his arms.

"That is correct," André answered, resisting the urge to look toward Sophie.

"On what charge was the late Marquis de Valière convicted?"

"Royalist sympathies."

Lazare touched a spindly finger to his ear. "I can't hear you. Mind speaking up, Captain de Valière?"

"Royalist sympathies," André repeated, louder this time. Even as the blood thrummed in his skull, André heard the buzzing once more from the gallery, and he knew that Lazare was succeeding in his aim, which was to discredit him as a witness.

Lazare nodded, recommencing his pacing. "Captain, you have served bravely. We all thank you for your service to this Republic."

André swallowed but did not reply to the compliment, certain that there was a blow to follow.

"Captain de Valière, have you ever heard the Comte de Kellermann defend the deceased tyrant known as Citizen Capet?"

"Never."

Lazare nodded. "You served at Valmy under the Comte de Kellermann. Have you seen him since the day of that battle?"

"Of course I have seen *General* Kellermann since then," André answered.

"And was it ever in an informal setting? A time when you were not under direct orders of his command?"

André thought about this. "I do not believe I have ever associated with him as a private citizen, no."

"Never?" Lazare asked. "Not even once, right here in Paris?"

André paused; it seemed as if Lazare had some hidden angle. And then he remembered one occasion. "I suppose there was one time."

"Ah, yes, you suppose there was one time." Lazare looked up at the gallery, ensuring that they'd recorded this witness's changing testimony. "And what were the circumstances of this one time?"

André paused for a moment and took a deep breath, willing himself not to grow flustered, even if the interrogation seemed to be spiraling out of control. "It was here in Paris. There was a ball given by the Jacobins shortly after Valmy. It was wintertime, just after Christmas."

"*Christmas?*" Lazare repeated, and André grimaced as he realized his error—surely the result of his nerves.

"New year . . . I meant to say the new year. Shortly before the new year," André hurried to correct himself.

Lazare nodded, allowing Andre's mistake to linger in the quiet courtroom a moment before he continued. "Captain de Valière, would you please describe for us the circumstances of that evening? Who else was there? What was discussed?"

André turned his gaze, his eyes resting for the first time on the seawater gray of Murat's. "General Murat was there with us, as was Madame . . . Citizeness Kellermann."

Lazare nodded. "And this was the night that the people decided on the execution of Citizen Capet, was it not?"

André thought about that evening. Most vivid in his memory was meeting Sophie. Standing with her outside of the Panthéon in the cold. The desire he had felt, even then, to see her again. But yes, that had also been the night they'd voted to kill the king, which was why Murat had whisked Sophie away so suddenly. "Yes, I believe it was that same night."

"You believe it was." Lazare nodded, still pacing, as he rested his chin on his thumb. "And on that night, did you three—General Murat and the Comte de Kellermann and yourself—not discuss that significant piece of news?"

"It may have come up, briefly."

"You are under oath, Captain, so think before you speak next." The lawyer's voice was cold, devoid of emotion. "I would hate for you to lie to the French people and, in so doing, forfeit your own liberty."

André fidgeted in his seat, uncrossing his legs.

Lazare pulled a paper from his pocket, which he now held at arm's length, as if it served more as a prop than a necessity. He cleared his throat, making a grand show of reading. "The Comte de Kellermann has been accused, by General Nicolai Murat, of making the following statement when discussing the appropriate punishment for Citizen Capet: 'I'm not certain that I agree with any of the executions carried out in the name of our Republic.'"

The crowd erupted in shock and outrage as Lazare's eyes slid upward, holding fast to André's. André turned to Jean-Luc as a feeling of dread gripped him; he did remember Kellermann saying that.

"Captain, do you remember the Comte de Kellermann speaking thusly?" Lazare asked, loud enough to be heard over the crowd. But before André could answer, the attorney turned back to the paper in his hands. "And one more statement, Captain de Valière. On the topic of that Austrian adulteress, the Habsburg princess whom we have sent to the grave, General Murat recalls the Comte de Kellermann saying this: 'I think that the journals have drummed up and printed many accusations that are false. . . . I believe Marie-Antoinette wielded far less influence at court than many would have us believe. And surely she was a devoted wife. Just look how many children she has given the king.' "

Now the crowd above was in a full-fledged riot. Words of support for Louis were damning enough, but a word spoken in support of the late queen, Marie-Antoinette—nothing was more likely to earn one a ride on a tumbril.

The judge rang the bell ferociously, attempting to silence the crowd. "Order! Order, I say! I *will* have order!" Guards dispersed throughout the gallery, their muskets raised aloft. After the hissing and jeers had quieted, once the women had resumed their knitting and the little children had been pulled back off the balustrade, Lazare resumed his pacing.

"Captain, now that I have refreshed your memory, perhaps you will allow me to repeat my original question: have you ever heard the Comte de Kellermann speak in favor of Citizen Capet?" He held André in his steely gaze, his eyes cold with the certainty that he would have the answer he wanted.

"It was a long time ago. I don't remember the precise words. I simply remember Generals Kellermann and Murat discussing the Revolution and its consequences—"

The crowd burst into fresh jeers and insults but André, stung by this assault on his integrity, spoke over them. "If you speak of the night of the Jacobin ball, I do recall that General Kellermann said that the monarchy should be disbanded and the king put in jail. But while I'm remembering, I also recall that General Murat said that many of the common people were fools, not yet ready to take over the reins of government."

Now the crowd was silenced, but only for a moment. And then, not sure with whom to be angry, they began to yell. A fight broke out, prompting another furious round of bell ringing at the judge's table.

Lazare waited for the rabble-rousers to be ushered out and for order to be restored before he spoke. He was done with André and turned now to face the gallery. "Citizens and citizenesses of France. There's no doubt that both of these generals have performed great deeds in the service of this land. Like any true soldier, Kellermann was not afraid to shed his own blood. But we are not here today to put his bravery on trial. We are here to determine his guilt as it pertains to loyalty and our Revolution, and whether or not he has sympathies for our dead tyrant—sympathies that would run counter to the progress of our Revolution. You hear now the very statements he has made. Statements which General Murat has sworn to, and which André, son of the Marquis de Valière, has confirmed. You know, now, what must be done."

With that, he turned to Jean-Luc and offered a curt bow, then took his seat. The court would adjourn for a thirty-minute recess.

After the break, Jean-Luc reentered the courtroom, his hair disheveled and loose from the ribbon that had previously held it in place. His features appeared strained as he conferred with his client. Across the aisle, Lazare and Murat took their seats and sat, wordless.

In his place behind the defense, André sat feeling as if his stomach were filled with stones. Rather than helping Kellermann, he feared he had helped the prosecution's case. As he admitted this to himself, he felt despair wash over him, a complete and utter loss of hope. It was a feeling he had felt only one other time in his life: on the day his father had been executed.

And today it was *his* fault. His inability to respond quickly, to swiftly deflect the charges made by Murat, had allowed doubt to enter the minds of the crowd.

The judges reentered, the central judge rapping his gavel and telling the crowd to take their seats for the closing arguments. "We will hear first from the defense. Citizen St. Clair?" The judge tilted his head toward Kellermann's side.

Jean-Luc pushed himself back, clearing his throat as he stood. He walked to the center of the room, turning to look up at the gallery. "For the closing of this defense, I call the man himself, General Christophe Kellermann."

The crowd gasped and murmured, and even André couldn't help but clutch the side of his chair as he saw Kellermann push himself to stand. Though at the center of the entire day, Kellermann had been observing. Silent. Almost forgotten.

Now all attention shifted to the silent figure, broad and composed, as he walked slowly to the front of the court. Looking out, his face resting briefly on his wife's, Kellermann smiled. Next he looked to his men, his eyes landing first on André before turning to the rest—LaSalle, Remy, and all of the soldiers who had sat silently all day. Supporting him. He offered a nod, a humble gesture, in their direction. And then he began.

"Citizens." Now Kellermann looked up at the balcony at the enlisted men, at the zealous revolutionaries who wanted to see him dead, at the Committee members who could propose one hundred legal reasons for why his head was no longer rightfully his own to possess.

"For much of my life, I served King Louis XVI." Whispers rose up in response to the name uttered aloud, but Kellermann continued on, undaunted. "I saw myself as a soldier. It was not my role to question my orders or commands; I followed the orders of my king, just as I had sworn I would do on the first day I had the privilege of putting on the French uniform." Kellermann paused, his voice catching on the words. He cleared his throat and jutted his chin out, continuing.

"But when the people of France determined that the citizen living at Versailles was no longer the true and rightful leader of this nation, it was with a free heart that I joined their fight. I was honored to be a part of the effort to gain liberty for the people of France.

"No one values the freedoms and rights that we have won these past years more than I do. I know how perilous a fight it was, how narrow a margin it was by which we won our freedom." Kellermann paused, his tone laced with emotion, as he stared at the gallery. "I would serve any lawful leader to protect those freedoms, even to the point of death. If this tribunal, and these judges"—Kellermann, without looking, gestured a hand toward the justices—"find me guilty, then that is the law of this land.

"But hear me now. If this Revolution continues to go down this path of brother denouncing brother, neighbor attacking neighbor, then perhaps a day will come when we shall hurl ourselves into an abyss. Not only will there be famine, bloodshed, and war, but indeed our very souls may become lost."

André shifted in his seat, willing the people in the gallery above to hear this reason. To heed this warning. Kellermann forged onward, striding across the front of the hall.

"Will this terror last forever? I pray that it will not. But how will it end? If we surrender ourselves to mistrust and chaos and denunciations, how will we climb back out as a people? As a nation?" Kellermann paused, and this time, André noticed, he avoided his wife's gaze, even as her weeping sounded softly from the bench on which she sat near the front of the court.

"On this day, I have been accused of undermining the Revolution. I must confess that I find this accusation to be false." Kellermann looked at Murat now. "Few have known me longer, or fought beside me on more battlefields, than General Murat. There was a time when we considered ourselves not only close friends but brothers. I would gladly lay down my life for him, as I would for all of my fellow soldiers." Kellermann paused but kept his eyes on his former friend. Murat's returning gaze was steady, unwavering.

"I cannot understand," Kellermann continued. "I may not ever understand . . . why my dear friend would level these charges against me. No, I can't understand him. But I can forgive him."

Kellermann stared a moment longer until Murat, unable to hold his gaze, lowered his eyes to the floor. "Whatever the outcome today, however you find me, I wish this to be known. Nicolai, I forgive you. And to the people of France, may the blessings of liberty be bestowed upon all men, whether born high or low, for all time."

With that Kellermann sat down, his shoulders seeming to collapse inward as he did so; as if the fortitude required to speak those words and extend that grace had sapped the last of his strength. Hunched forward, he surely heard the gasps of his sobbing wife as she wept into her handkerchief, but he did not turn. And then, André noticed, the soldiers in the courtroom, defying the order of the assembly, began to stand. As if on cue, a hand lifted, and several more followed. Then dozens more. André rose and did the same, and now every soldier and officer in the room stood, hands extended aloft in a salute to the general they loved. Kellermann, turning, saw this. André swore that he saw a lone tear in the old commander's eye.

Lazare, apparently taken aback by this unexpected and unsanctioned show of solidarity, waited a moment. The room remained quiet, with the judges and the former Jacobins in the crowd sensing, somehow, that they ought not interfere in this act of reverence. The young lawyer beside Lazare, the one who had started off the day, whispered in his superior's ear, and Lazare shook his head.

And then the judge spoke, his flat voice cutting through the charge of emotions in the hall. "And the prosecution?"

Mouchetard, the younger lawyer, rose and walked to the center of the room. Rubbing his palms together, as if to warm himself, he began. "That was well spoken, General Kellermann. But this court must not be disarmed by emotions. Emotions and sentimentality kept us in darkness, under the yoke of a tyrant for far too long. But now, we are enlightened. Now that we are a free people, those diversionary emotions shall not prevent us from doing our duty, which is the work of the Revolution. If we wish to speak of battles and battlegrounds, well, my fellow citizens, this *court* is today the foremost battleground of our fight, and here, today, we must do our duty to root out and expose the enemies of the Revolution."

The crowd, still moved by Kellermann's address, began to hiss at this Mouchetard. A woman tossed a spool from her knitting over the balcony, and it hit the lawyer in the head, knocking his spectacles loose and prompting an uproarious gust of laughter, both from the gallery and the soldiers below. Seeing this, Lazare stood up.

With that movement from his superior, the young lawyer wavered, withdrawing toward the table like a beaten dog. Lazare strode to the center and the crowd now fell silent. André was certain that, beside him, Madame Kellermann trembled. He couldn't blame her.

In his signature quiet, Lazare began: "You've heard it from the witness. You've heard it from the defense. This man, General Kellermann, thought you were wrong when you condemned the tyrant and his foreign wife before this very tribunal. He thought you were wrong to send them to the guillotine." Lazare folded his hands neatly in front of his narrow waist. "Need I remind you that since this Revolution began, we have faced enemies both within this city and outside our borders? Let's start with the latter. Armed mercenaries who would have stamped out our Revolution and put that tyrant back on the throne. Yes, those enemies are easy to identify. They wear uniforms and carry the standards of foreign kings as they march across our lands.

"But what of the others? The enemy within our borders? That is an enemy far more perfidious. Far more dangerous, because he is one thousand times harder to identify. And that enemy is the indecisive half patriot. The man who, in his heart, questions our Revolution. The man who affects to celebrate our freedom, declares himself loyal to the Republic, but in the quiet of his mind, he questions. He questions the verdicts we make. The constitution we draft. The actions we must take against our enemies.

"These are the enemies who truly cause me to tremble for our Republic. These are the foes who dwell among us, masquerading as our friends. The Prussians and Austrians are gone. But the more dangerous enemy—those who live with us, and watch us, and yet, despise us—remain ever in our midst. They are still within our borders."

Lazare paused and André noted, with a fresh pang of despair, just how silent the courtroom had fallen.

"No doubt, the defendant repelled those foreign invaders at Valmy. We thank him for that service, saving the Revolution in its infancy." Lazare turned then, nodding at Kellermann once, before turning back toward the balcony.

"But this man harbors doubts about our Revolution. He has questioned the means we have used, measures taken out of necessity in order that our Revolution may progress. You heard his statements today. He doubts whether we should have killed Citizen Capet. He doubts whether the Austrian adulteress was what we knew her to be. He doubts whether the guillotine even need be in use!" Lazare paused at this before continuing on, his tone lilting toward quiet once more.

"Citizens and citizenesses, this is no time for doubt. This is no time for hesitant and halfhearted patriots. This is no time to put trust in those who question our efforts, our sacred work. There is too much at stake. Those who don't support the Revolution are enemies of the people; it is plain as that. What is *not* plain is how we are to find and root out these enemies. That's the difficult task that falls to each patriot. And harder still is to look them in the eyes and tell them they must die. But when have the French people ever been cowed by the hard work that must be done? You are not a people who shirk your duties. You never have been. Not when you have known repression for so long, and when you know how many still roam free who would return you to that darkness.

"No, my good, enlightened people of France, you know your duty, and you shall do it. On the order of this court, the blade must fall. For the Comte de Kellermann, and all who question our Revolution, we shall be swift and decisive. It is us or them. Mercy for them today means enslavement for us tomorrow. We know this. We must not, we will not, allow this fate to befall the French people. The entire nation looks to us. Today, we do our duty. Today, and all days, we choose freedom."

When Lazare finished, no one cheered. No one clapped. No one even whispered. André looked aloft and saw how the women in the gallery had ceased their knitting and now sat clutching their children closer. The husbands had put protective arms over the shoulders of their wives.

It was not about Kellermann anymore. It was not about Valmy or Murat or any ball where an officer might have made vague political statements. It was about an unseen but ever-present feeling shared by all. The shadow felt deep in each man and woman's breast. Lazare had reminded them all of what they had temporarily forgotten: that any one of them could die in this city on any day. Defending the wrong person would make that a certainty. Saying the wrong thing would lead to the guillotine. They did not hate Kellermann; they did not wish to kill him. They merely wished to save themselves. And that, André thought to himself, was the genius of Lazare.

When the justices took their recess, the people stayed, but the giddiness from the balcony, the circus-like mood from earlier, was no more, not even among the children. The cold breath of fear had entered the courtroom, casting a frost over hearts that, minutes earlier, had been inclined toward compassion and fraternity.

The justices were out of the room for only a matter of minutes. When they reentered, the crowd was on its feet, straining and leaning close.

The middle judge read from a scroll. He read as he had spoken all day: quickly and without emotion. André, feeling his knees giving out beneath him, listened as the words were pronounced.

"The tribunal of the people of France finds General Christophe Kellermann guilty of conspiracy against the state and people of France. He is hereby sentenced to death by guillotine within four and twenty hours."

15

La Place de la Révolution, Paris

July 1794

Jean-Luc did not know where he walked; he simply knew that on that warm, black night, stillness was not an option. Marie would have heard the news by now. She would be awake, waiting, worried for him and eager to console him upon his return. But the hours had passed and, still, guilt unlike anything he had ever known hung over him, prompting him to wander aimlessly through the darkened streets of Paris. His thoughts, too, wandered, in and out of a dreamlike state. He didn't deserve the comfort of a loving wife's arms, the joy of seeing his child tucked in under a blanket, his reposing face free of worry. Jean-Luc knew that he could not go home, not when Kellermann, the man who had put his faith in him, passed his last night in a dank prison with nothing but the scaffold to greet him at dawn.

And so Jean-Luc walked deep into the night. Not another soul haunted the streets, his only companions the large linden trees that rustled in the wind. The Seine shimmered to his left, but for the occasional barge that lumbered past, bearing its cargo west on the black water, there was no noise in the Parisian night.

Suddenly, Jean-Luc heard voices. He came to, emerging from his tormented reverie, and realized that he was entirely unaware of his surroundings.

"Slide her in there, easy does it. Just like Sanson'll do it later today."

"Only then, this lot won't be melons. I heard that old General What's-His-Name is on the short list."

"Shame to waste such a good melon." Harsh laughter echoed down the silent street.

Sanson. Jean-Luc repeated the name and felt a constriction around his throat. He paused, frozen in his steps; Sanson was the name of Paris's official executioner. Known as the Gentleman of Paris, master of ceremonies, and functionary of the guillotine. Jean-Luc realized, his legs leaden beneath him, that he had wandered into La Place de la Révolution. There, in the feeble light of dawn, emerged the shapes of the massive limestone façades that hemmed in La Place, grand buildings built for the governments of Louis XIV and his heir, Louis XV, cutting a silhouette against the graying sky. And even closer to Jean-Luc stood the raised platform and sleek shape of that murderous device, its blade catching the first glints of early-morning light.

Jean-Luc didn't take a step closer, nor did he turn to walk away. Workers, it appeared, were prepping the apparatus for the day's show, a show that promised to be one of the most attended since the deaths of the Bourbon monarchs.

It was still dark enough that Jean-Luc, by remaining a safe distance back, had not been detected. The workers moved about their business diligently— scrubbing the platform, sweeping the steps, checking the nails and ropes that held the device upright. One of the men struggled under the weight of a large woven basket, filled with what appeared to be round cargo. His raspy breath was audible, even from where Jean-Luc stood, as the squat man heaved the basket up the steps toward the executioner's spot. On top of the platform now, he reached in, and Jean-Luc felt his heart begin to race, preparing him for what he was about to see. The man pulled out one of the objects from the basket, which to Jean-Luc's relief appeared to be a melon. With skilled hands that moved quickly, the man nestled the melon into the central groove of the apparatus. He must have done this many times by now.

Workers were scampering about, jumping off the platform and shuffling into a row, all eager spectators. Only the squat man remained up top.

"Ready, get in position!" One of the workers below yelled, and another man took his place on the platform behind the raised blade. He put his hand on the extended lever.

"Ready, steady, let her fly!"

Jean-Luc watched as the man, his hand gripping the lever, pulled hard and fast. That motion set free the blade, previously suspended aloft at the top of a long track. Descending downward, it dropped with a powerful and brutal force; anything in its way must either stop its fall or be sliced in two.

A whirring noise rippled across the square, reaching Jean-Luc and prompting him to shiver in dread. Then, a second later, the whir turned into a crunch. The workers applauded, hopping back up onto the platform to see the outcome of the demonstration. "Cut clean through, she did!"

"The ole girl never fails."

Jean-Luc stumbled forward and let out a muffled groan. Just then the men turned and squinted into the darkened street. "Oi, you, what you doin' here? No spectators 'til the appointed hour!"

"Maybe he just wants to try the ole girl out for himself?"

"Go on then, climb up and have a look. Mind your head!"

Bellowing laughter echoed through the square, but Jean-Luc didn't reply. He felt faint and heard only the sound of the retching that poured the bile out of his gut and spilled it out over the street. He wiped his mouth and gazed back across the square that in a few hours' time would be washed in red.

The day of Kellermann's execution dawned clear and cold. The crowd came out early, the women staking out the prime spots at the front before the platform, where they unfurled their knitting and awaited the tumbrils that would bear their ill-fated passengers across the river and into La Place de la Révolution.

As the hour approached, André felt drawn to La Place by the pull of some unseen force, as if he owed it to General Kellermann to bear witness as the great man departed an ungrateful world.

André noticed the abundance of carts and vendors present on days like this, merchants selling apples, plums, barrels of wine and ale, and even linen for dresses. The summer heat kept most people outdoors anyway, but on execution days the crowds gathered in exceptional numbers, and a crowd meant customers, business. André couldn't blame a man for trying to provide for his family, but the mere fact that it had become customary to gather and profit from the machinery of death was a sight he never accepted. A young girl, no older than five years, approached him with her hand out. She was clothed in little more than an oversized brown shift, her arms and legs stained a lighter brown. Her eyes had little light in them, and she refused to meet his gaze as she begged for his charity. With an ache of pity, André knelt and handed her a *sou,* and wondered what more executions would do to improve her life, and indeed the lives of the countless other impoverished children left hopeless and begging on the streets.

"André."

Hearing a voice behind him, he turned around and saw Sophie emerging from the crowd. Her eyes were moist with tears, and the sight of her sent a stab of pain through his chest.

"Oh, André."

He walked over to her and they embraced. "What are you doing here?" he asked. "You shouldn't have come. You don't need to see this."

"I know. I wish I could be anywhere but here, but I also know how much you loved him. How much you all loved him. We can't do anything for him now, but we can at least say goodbye." André held her to his chest; otherwise she would have seen the tears that swelled in his own eyes.

They turned and made their way to join the crowd gathering toward the center of La Place, managing to push their way toward the front, where guards with bayonets struggled to hold the hordes back. Their view of the guillotine was partially obscured by someone waving a large tricolor flag. A noise from behind drew André's attention and he glanced back; there, over the sea of fists and hands, a tumbril rolled into the square at precisely three o'clock, its arrival greeted by uproarious cheers and shouting.

There was just one carriage loaded with ashen-faced passengers. As the cart rolled to a halt before the platform, the horses whinnied in response to the noise of the crowd. The front horse jerked its head, attempting to rear up before its coachman gave it a cuff. Even these beasts, so seasoned in their daily task of bearing the tumbrils into the sea of madness, were jumpier than usual. Perhaps, André thought, they sensed the heightened energy of the crowd inside La Place today.

André and Sophie watched as the carriage gate was lowered. He was able to see the condemned more clearly now—six of them, the day's haul. Kellermann stood at the back of the carriage, the tallest passenger. He wore the gray sackcloth of the prisoner. His hair had been shorn, his familiar gray-laced ponytail gone. The crowd had seen him, too, and even though there were five figures before him, some began to chant his name.

A middle-aged man was escorted up to the platform first. His escorts turned into his carriers when his knees buckled halfway up the steps and he fell to the ground, his hands clenched in supplication. When he was jostled into position, the crowd roared ever louder. Still he cried out, begging for deliverance.

"You will have it, soon enough," André mouthed, as the man's head was fitted into the smooth wooden cradle. André joined the crowd in a collective gasp, a sharp intake of breath, when the rope was pulled loose from the apparatus. The blade whirred downward and euphoria erupted around André and Sophie when the man's head fell away from the body into the woven basket.

Two women were brought forward next—sisters, by the look of it. They clutched each other, their unnaturally thin arms interwoven like spools of braided thread. The guards wrested them apart and the first one was ushered up the stairs, her face wracked with terror as she looked back at her companion.

"Amélie!" The one who had been held back reached out a pale hand toward the platform. Her hair was the same strawberry blond shade as her sister's and, like her sister's, had been cropped short. Some guard would make a pretty fortune off those two heads of hair.

The sister on the platform was being roughly handled, pushed into place in spite of her protests. The neck rest was slicked with the other man's blood. She threw one last look out at her sister, who was shrieking and reaching for her still. "Amélie!"

The girl on the platform moved her lips fast, inaudibly, reciting a prayer. Her head was taken in Sanson's hands and slid into place under the blade. The crowd cheered ever louder when her head tumbled free, joining that of the middle-aged man.

Her lifeless frame was tossed behind the platform as her sister was led upward. André looked around, more aghast than even a moment earlier.

"You'll join her now, dearie!" A toothless man to the right of André and Sophie snickered, picking at his gums as he did so. André took hold of Sophie and shuffled her away from the man. He wished that Sophie hadn't come, and he feared that she would be sick. He had seen enough death on the battlefield as to become hardened to it, but this was something else entirely. He shut his eyes and grasped Sophie's hand with a gentle but firm grip.

The young woman's sobs were silenced by the blade as her head joined her sister's. André saw the next victim. He was a youth, fair-skinned and small in frame. André guessed that he could have been no more than twelve, judging by his smooth cheeks that had not yet grown even the hint of a beard. An innocent, surely, his only crime being born into a doomed family.

The young boy was looking to his fellow prisoner as the guards called his name. Kellermann returned his stare, and André noticed the general give the boy a touch on the shoulder. He said something, its sound and meaning immediately lost to the crowd, but the boy heard it and nodded his head.

"Enough of that—get on with it!" The same toothless man near André was growling impatient, echoing the sentiments of the crowd around them. The guard responded to this mounting restiveness and jerked the boy from Kellermann's side. The child appeared now as though he would cry, but he did not. As he neared the top of the scaffold, he turned his gaze back toward Kellermann, who offered a barely perceptible nod.

There were just two of them left now. Kellermann would go last, André suspected, and the other remaining prisoner was pulled forward: a white-haired man, much older than the others. And fidgety. But unlike the others, who had exhibited their fear openly, the old man seemed oddly at ease, even cheerful. He chattered toward the prison guards, gesturing with his bound hands as if to ask them to untie them. When the guards wouldn't untie the bindings, the man laughed, looking out over the crowd and continuing to babble as if in the midst of a riveting conversation. He tittered to himself, turning back to the guards with a discordant smile, no light of understanding in his eyes.

"Good God," André uttered, turning toward Sophie. The man had gone mad. Had it been the imprisonment? Or had he arrived at prison already spent? Whatever the case, he was still conversing with himself as he was tied into position. The guards, who had in small ways reacted and responded to the behaviors of the previous victims, were blank-faced and wordless with this man. They looked to one another, exchanging glances that André guessed—hoped—betrayed some unspoken shame.

The man was laughing as his head was fastened down. He cackled, oblivious, in the second before the blade met his neck.

Now it was Kellermann's turn. The crowd, perhaps thrown off by the previous execution, was slightly less feverish now. They seemed more intrigued than excited as Kellermann was beckoned forward. With two guards at each side, the general walked himself up the steps.

On top of the platform, one of the executioners put a rough arm on his victim, as he had done with the five before. But as he did so, the general turned toward him with a look of such force that the executioner immediately withdrew his hand, as if Kellermann's body had been hot to the touch.

The crowd grew even quieter, still enough that André and Sophie could hear Sanson when he said, with a nod of his chin: "All right, then. This way, General Kellermann." But the executioner's tone was more beseeching than authoritative.

Kellermann took a few steps forward and looked out over the crowd. André beheld his face one last time—the broad brow, the graying hair, the wide-set blue eyes. Eyes that showed not a trace of fear. Nor did they show anger. Or anguish. They showed, André realized, absolutely nothing. Was it resignation?

The quiet crowd seemed entranced now, hundreds of eyes fixed on the face of a doomed man. Without moving his body, the general's glance passed over the mob and glided beyond them, into the distance. Perhaps he caught the glimpse of a place beyond this world, a place into which he hoped to be welcomed.

And then he looked back into his present surroundings. The red-stained platform. The waiting executioner, his face still blank, workmanlike. André saw Kellermann make the sign of the cross.

The crowd was so silent now that André could hear the groaning of the wooden beams, the click of the leather straps as the general's body was fastened into place.

They stayed quiet as Sanson lifted his arm and tugged the lever. And still, the crowd was silent when the guillotine blade fell on General Christophe Kellermann, marking with collective breathlessness what Guillaume Lazare had declared "the necessary sacrifice and glory of our illustrious Revolution."

16

Île de la Cité,
Paris

Summer 1794

André did not leave Sophie's rooms the following day, lest he encounter anyone in a revolutionary spirit. If he were to witness someone making a celebration of Christophe Kellermann's death, André did not trust himself to restrain his anger.

Sophie, having received a summons from her uncle, thought it best to answer at once rather than risk Murat visiting her apartment to seek her out. "I'll return as quickly as I can." Sophie slid into her cloak, her eyes still fixed on André. "Are you *certain* you will be all right?"

"Yes," André lied. "But the sooner you return, the sooner I'll feel that much better."

Sophie kissed him and then asked Parsy to call for the carriage to take her across the Seine. Her uncle had sent a vague message inquiring after Sophie's health, but she and André had both wondered what Murat really wanted with her.

André waited in her rooms as the hour approached three o'clock. The mobs on the island had thinned as most people had made their way, en masse, across the Seine toward the Right Bank and La Place de la Révolution. The plan was that as soon as Sophie returned, she and André would take advantage of the distraction to hurry to the Palais de Justice to be married.

André felt besieged by warring emotions as he waited for Sophie on that sweltering afternoon. At the fore, he felt anger, but it went beyond that. Rage was what he felt—rage consuming his spirit, roiling within. As he replayed the scenes from the trial, he felt the overwhelming desire to throttle Murat, Lazare, and all of the others who had turned their sinister designs on Kellermann.

His rage was rivaled in its intensity only by a heavy sadness: a sense of profound and bottomless grief over losing a mentor like Kellermann, even a friend. Over the French army losing such a leader. Over the entire French nation losing such a man. But as he plumbed this grief, he found something else—something inescapable and even more unnerving: guilt. Guilt because of the part he himself had played, however unintentionally, in the man's conviction. He hadn't been able to save his hero, just as he hadn't been able to save his own father. And yet here he was, still living. Why did *he* get to continue on?

"You'll drive yourself mad. You must stop this, André." Jean-Luc, his own soul haggard following the court's verdict, had pulled André aside to tell him not to blame himself.

"But it was my testimony—"

"His guilt had been determined before you spoke a word. You did your best."

André looked at the lawyer, knowing that the man would certainly not heed his own advice; Jean-Luc would blame himself, even though it was *he* who had done everything he could. And had nearly succeeded. No, André thought, it was nobody's fault but his own. He, who had been unable to prevent his own father's execution, now had had to look on uselessly as a hero was marched to his death. And this time, he had been in some position, however small, to prevent it. But he had spoiled even that opportunity.

He sat alone in Sophie's empty apartment, running his hand through his already disheveled hair, his stomach in a tangle of grief and anguish.

And yet, in spite of everything, a part of André would not give itself wholly over to despair; there remained an inner recess in which lurked the vague yet inextinguishable embers of joy. Today was, after all, the day that he was to marry Sophie de Vincennes. In any other set of circumstances, such an event would surely overpower every other consideration, and some part of him still clung now to that happiness, to the hope of what she meant to him. It was she, after all, who had insisted that today be the day they follow through on their plan to join their lives together.

But now it was nearly three o'clock, the hour of the day's execution, and Sophie had not returned. And so another emotion entered into his mood: unease. What was taking her so long? André began to pace the room, his sense of dread growing heavier with each minute that passed.

"Parsy?" André called for the maid. He listened, and, hearing no response, opened the door and glanced into the corridor, but there was no sign of the older woman.

Several minutes later, a flurry of footsteps sounded from the hall outside the apartment and in flew Sophie, her eyes wild and her breath coming in ragged, uneven gasps. She still wore her cloak, which she did not shed as she ran toward him, but she had lost a glove. "André!"

"What is it?" He stood up, alarmed by her entrance and the shrill tone of her voice.

"He knows! He knows about us!" Sophie panted so violently that André wasn't certain he had heard her correctly.

"Who knows? Your uncle?"

Sophie nodded. "He knows you're here. That we are planning to be married today. Everything."

"But how?"

Sophie glanced around the room as if to ensure that they were alone. "Parsy," she whispered.

"Parsy?" André repeated the name, incredulous. He'd barely heard the woman speak five words in all of his visits to Sophie's apartment.

"We must leave at once! He's coming!" Sophie turned, running to a trunk in the corner of the room into which she began to throw gowns, scarves, and shoes with reckless haste.

"Where is he now?" André approached her.

"At the executions. But he'll know that I've run home to warn you. We can't lose any time; we must go at once."

"Sophie." André put a hand to her arm.

"What? Why are you just standing there? Fetch your things; we must *go!*" Sensing something in his immobility, she ceased her packing and turned to him. "What is it?"

"Sophie, *you* must go."

"And you as well."

"No."

"What is it? Gather your things; we must leave at once!"

André shook his head. "He expects me to run. He *wants* me to run. He hopes to chase me."

Now she stopped, a frown tightening her features. "What?"

"Of course he knows you will warn me. He expects us to flee together. I won't allow him to chase us down, as if we were animals to be hunted for sport."

"But we can't stay here. We can't just give in."

"It's *me* he wants, Sophie. I must stay back. That will give you time to escape."

"That's madness. Of course I'm not going to leave without—"

"Sophie, I want you to get out."

"But I'm not leaving without you."

"I'll meet you," André said.

But she looked at him, unbelieving. "I couldn't get out even if I wanted. I don't have papers to pass the barriers."

André had an idea. "Remy will take you. In a military baggage train. Anything. We'll find a way to hide you and get you past the wall."

"Why can't *you* take me?" Sophie clung to him now, her hands trembling in his.

"If I take you, your uncle will hunt us both. He'd accuse me of desertion and he would be correct in doing so. No, our best chance is for you to get out while you still can."

They wove through the crowds on the island. Even though he had been dead for a day, the ghost of Kellermann lingered over Paris, and the men and women seethed now as various factions began to face off in the streets. Crossing the bridge at a run, André and Sophie arrived at Remy's rooms on the Left Bank and found him sitting alone. His hair was disheveled and his eyes were drawn from lack of sleep, or tears. Probably both.

"What happened to your hand?" André asked, when he hugged his brother and noticed a bruise. But then he saw the hole in the wall of the room. "Never mind," André said. "Remy, thank God you are here."

"Why? What's happened? You two look like hell."

André's chest ached from the run across town. "Remy, can you clear the barrier tonight?"

"Tonight?" Remy thought about this, his brow creasing. "Well, I don't have the papers to do it on my own. But I suppose I could make up some reason, try my luck, if I needed to. Why?"

"You must take Sophie out of the city." André's voice left no room for Remy's typical humor. The younger brother looked from André to Sophie.

"Why?" Remy's entire frame went stiff, his facial features locking into stern focus. "What's happened?"

They acquainted Remy with the events of the past hour, and their decision that André stay back to give Sophie a chance to shake off her uncle.

"Can you hide her in one of the artillery wagons?"

"I've heard of it being done, to be sure." Remy leaned on his desk, folding his arms before his chest. "I've never tried." Snapping his fingers, he looked up, determination lighting his features. "But you know, now that you mention it, I imagine the federal guard units garrisoned out at Versailles might need a resupply of powder. My division is responsible for getting it to them from the city. I'll need to load up one of our transport carts and move it this very night. You're a captain." Remy's face broke out in a wry smile. "I'll write up the orders; you can sign them."

"LaSalle will sign it; within a few hours Murat will have my name on a watch list for arrest. I'm in trouble," André said, resting a hand on his brother's shoulder.

Remy noticed the pleading looks coming from his brother and Sophie, finally grasping the true urgency that drove them. "Dear God, brother, what have you done?" Remy looked at Sophie, then back toward his brother. "Never mind that. We'll go right now."

André nodded. "Where are these carts?"

"The carts are loaded with the stores from the Montgolfier factory and taken out via the western gate."

"I had better get back to the apartment," André said. "When he comes, I should be there. Otherwise he'll guess that we've both fled, and he'll race you to the barrier."

Sophie's eyes were wide with terror but dry of tears. With a deep exhale, she nodded, resolved.

"Thank you, brother." André pulled Remy into a hug, whispering into his ear. "We were supposed to be married today. I was going to come and ask you to stand up as our witness."

Remy pulled back, looking into his brother's face, the light blue of his own eyes brightening at André's news. "If I'd have known that I'd be carry-ing the ring, I would have taken better care of my hand."

They shared a brief, sorrowful laugh, and the three of them stood in silence for a moment. Remy whispered into his brother's ear: "I'll send word as soon as we've found a place in the country for her to hide. I prom-ise that I will do my best."

"You're a good man."

"Not half the man you are, André. I think it was she who once told me that." Turning back toward Sophie, Remy tried to interject some levity into his tone. "Am I remembering that correctly?"

"That was not quite what I said." Sophie sighed, stepping forward toward André. Remy turned away and busied himself with packing a small satchel while Sophie and André stood together, clinging to each other. After a hug that felt too short by a lifetime, they separated.

"What will happen to you?" she asked.

"I will be all right."

"No, really. If this is our last chance to speak for a while, I want the truth."

"I will be arrested," André answered. "But I should be allowed a trial. I am an officer in the Army of the Republic, after all. They will grant me that."

"What good is a trial?" Sophie asked, her voice drained of hope; she knew what a trial most likely meant.

"Sophie, my love, I've done nothing wrong. On what charges can they convict me?"

"But who will make them see that? If you're denounced by my uncle, who would be willing to defend you in a trial?"

André paused, trying to think of something to ease her mind, and then it occurred to him. "Jean-Luc St. Clair. I will ask him to represent me."

Sophie nodded, lowering her eyes.

"Sophie?" André tucked his fingers under her chin and tilted her face upward toward his own. "I still intend to marry you, you know."

"Good," Sophie answered. Her blue eyes glowed with an intense fire, but she blinked her lashes, keeping the tears at bay. "Don't keep me waiting too long."

The sun set over the city, and Remy made his way to the western barrier, with Sophie tucked out of sight under four half-empty bags of gunpowder. Across the city, General Nicolai Murat and a handful of guardsmen marched into Sophie's courtyard. Their boots thumped loudly as they climbed the steps to the second floor. Two of them carried torches. No one answered the door when they banged, so Murat ordered them to pound through the lock. They found André dressed in his uniform, his pistol holstered and unloaded. Parsy stepped with them into the drawing room, her eyes puffy and apologetic as André beheld her.

"There he is." Murat ordered the men to bind André in irons, and he did not protest. "You are under arrest, André de Valière." Murat stared André squarely in the face, the words sliding from his thin lips like a vengeful serpent.

"On what charges?" André tried not to wince as the men clawed and pinched the skin of his wrists into the manacles.

"I denounce you as an enemy of the Republic. You have no right to ask me any questions."

Murat crossed the room in two strides, his cavalry saber lifted, and André thought, with a brief flash of incredulity, that the man might run him through right where he stood. But then the hilt of the sword swung down swiftly across the side of André's head, and his vision went dark.

17

Paris

Fall 1794

Jean-Luc St. Clair sat in his Right Bank office late into the night, preparing his opening statement for the case of André Valière, when a knock on the door pulled his focus upward. "Yes?"

The office errand boy peeked his face in. "Sorry to interrupt, sir. Late evening papers."

"Bring them here." Jean-Luc waved the boy in. "I need a break from this damned trial, anyway. Though, of course, reading the news is hardly the medicine to lift one's spirits these days."

The office boy nodded agreeably, though Jean-Luc suspected that he had little idea of what Jean-Luc spoke about. "Thank you, little lad. Now, go home to your family. And be careful on the streets—no side alleys, you hear?" Jean-Luc tossed the boy a coin and turned to the papers, scanning the sprawl of calamitous headlines.

Paris was burning, the city turned into a war front. With Robespierre dead and the Convention now unleashing a fresh Terror on a ravaged populace, thousands of irate, hungry Parisians ran amok over the city, with no one at the helm to harness the sails of discontent, to steer the ship of vengeance into a sound harbor. Winter was coming with its promise of further starvation and fuel shortages. Their hero, Kellermann, had died to expiate their misery and fear. And yet, still they suffered. Who, then, was left to pay for the mass suffering?

Sensing the void of leadership, and the pliable anger of the mob, thousands of Old Guard royalists had now risen up in open rebellion against the Republican government. The royalists declared themselves at war with the National Convention and planned to take back the Tuileries Palace.

Rumors flew throughout the city now with an effect more powerful than the sporadic volleys of musket fire. And so the Convention decided to throttle the opposition before they could gain more power. They'd called in the army to thwart the insurrection; now the city of Paris waited, wondering if the army would answer the summons.

Jean-Luc sighed, pushing aside the papers and turning to the lone political pamphlet on his desk. "Let there be no more death meted out or received between Frenchmen," the writer urged, his voice a rare and welcome dose of rationality and clemency. This theorist, this Citizen Persephone, urged members of the government to meet in a peaceful manner with the leaders of the royalist faction, reasoning that any government composed of free Frenchmen would be preferable to foreign invaders.

Finally, a philosopher with whom he could agree, Jean-Luc mused, wishing he knew the identity of this mysterious and reasonable man, Citizen Persephone.

But his thoughts were disrupted by the sudden barking of gunfire on the streets below, followed by cries of anger and rapid footfalls outside. Nightly battles like this had become common, and yet Jean-Luc considered spending the night in his office rather than risk traveling on foot to the bridge and the comparatively peaceful Left Bank.

The trial date of André Valière had already been moved once, on account of the internecine conflicts raging in the government. Jean-Luc did not know when the new trial date would come, but the longer he sat at his desk that evening, allowing himself to be distracted by the noises below, the more certain he became that his arguments would fall short, whenever the day might be.

He had visited the prisoner several times in his shadowy, dank cell at Le Temple. Those interviews had left Jean-Luc carrying a gloom and melancholy so heavy that he had felt the blackness of despair seeping into the very marrow of his bones. Jean-Luc consoled himself with one fact: that they were holding André at Le Temple, and not at the Conciergerie, meant that he might, in fact, be granted the tribunal hearing he had been promised. The Conciergerie, everyone knew, usually held men for only one night—always their last.

And yet everything about the prison, it seemed, had been engineered to sap the hope from a man's spirits. The block of black, rock-hard bread that was slipped through a creaky slit in the door. The sunless, tunnel-like passage that echoed with the cries of the other prisoners, their beards ragged and their minds in varying states of decay. The solitude of the place, where nothing but the shadows and the rats kept a man company. Jean-Luc dreaded his trips to Le Temple but reminded himself that his duties kept him there for a mere hour or two, while his client had to remain there indefinitely.

Through his conversations with the prisoner, Jean-Luc had heard about André's father's execution as well as his mother's exile abroad. He came to understand what the loss of General Kellermann meant to André. How did this man keep hope alive while all else crumbled around him? It perplexed Jean-Luc, while also filling him with profound admiration. If André still allowed himself to hope, it was Jean-Luc's duty to demand the same of himself.

Just then, suddenly, Jean-Luc noticed a lone envelope tucked in with the pile of papers delivered by the errand boy. He lowered his eyes, reading the note:

Citizen St. Clair,

> *I write to you as the fiancée of André Valière. I beg you to tell him that I am safe, thanks to his brother. I will not tell you where, as that would be far too dangerous. I fear writing André directly, as I suspect that my uncle would prevent my letter being delivered to him. Yes, it is my uncle, Nicolai Murat, who first brought the charges.*
>
> *And yet I must write and beg that you will tell André that I am well, and that I love him.*
>
> *I hope that, someday, André and I might be able to repay you for your kindness and courage.*

> *Your faithful admirer*
> *and servant,*
> *Sophie Vincennes*

Curious, Jean-Luc thought, reading it a second time. The letter was un-addressed, with no hint as to how Jean-Luc might respond to this Sophie Vincennes. But then, her intent had been to remain unfound, Jean-Luc reasoned.

This poor woman, as hopeful as the man she loves. Fools, the pair of them, Jean-Luc thought to himself. And as he collapsed his head into his hands he felt the overwhelming desire to hold Marie. It wasn't a desire; it was a need. An urgent, implacable need. This life was too mad, too tragic, and it all might change so quickly; he couldn't allow for the recent es-trangement that had hardened between them to persist. He pushed his chair back from the desk and stood up, determined to go home and take his wife in his arms.

Outside, the chaos surrounding the Tuileries had spread so that an im-promptu assembly of city folk stood in front of his building. There were several dozen, a number of them holding muskets, a handful of others bearing pikes, saws, and fire pokers.

"Citizen, what is the latest?" Jean-Luc asked a mustached man who stood several feet apart from the men holding muskets. This onlooker ap-peared less dangerous than his companions, with his arms crossed casually in front of his chest.

The man looked at Jean-Luc and signified, with a jerk of his chin, to watch his associates. Jean-Luc's eyes couldn't help but rest a moment on the man's mustache, which had an elaborate, unnatural quality about it. The man noticed him staring, and Jean-Luc averted his eyes, gazing back toward the crowd.

Standing atop a bench, one of the apparent leaders of the gang held his musket aloft and cried out. He, too, Jean-Luc noticed, had the same dark, unnatural mustache. They all did, Jean-Luc realized, as he paid closer at-tention to the individual faces of the crowd now surrounding him. Even the women, he noticed with a quick gasp.

"We showed that countess what we thought of *her* national treasure, did we not?" the leader on the bench shouted in a raspy voice. The crowd erupted in cheers and jeers, their fake mustaches flopping about on their lips in response. Several of them began to dance, a macabre dance that looked better suited for wild bonfires than a Paris street full of free citizens.

Good God in Heaven, Jean-Luc thought, don't let them mean what I think they mean. He'd heard about the uprisings in some of the other cities—uprisings during which unspeakable acts of vengeance had been carried out against the nobility. Children being tossed from château windows and women being deflowered and then defamed, their pubic hair turned into jests and playthings for the incensed mob. But those reports could not actually be true, could they?

"Those royalists thought they could take *our* city back!" the musket-wielding leader roared from his bench.

"Citizen?" The man to whom Jean-Luc had first spoken, the man who had stood apart, was now beside him. He leaned forward, and Jean-Luc saw through the glare of the full moon that a giddy, febrile excitement colored the man's dirty face. Jean-Luc could not wrest his eyes from that horrid mustache.

"You look as if you might need some cheering up, citizen. Care to get a whiff of the dear Comtesse de Beaumonde?" Beneath the vile mustache, the man's lips spread apart into a broad, toothless smile, and Jean-Luc turned away, walking, as fast as he could, toward the river.

On the southern half of the Pont Neuf, another impromptu assembly was gathering, and Jean-Luc groaned, pausing. What hateful villainy were *these* people up to? But their gathering seemed to be of a more subdued nature. They were perhaps two dozen in number, with several small children clutching their mothers' skirts and fathers' hands.

"Citizens, what news?" Jean-Luc approached them slowly, cautiously.

"We're waiting for *him*." One of the mothers, passing her fingers through a young child's hair as if to improve his ragged appearance, turned and watched Jean-Luc approach.

"For whom?" Jean-Luc asked, pausing before the group now.

"*Him!*" Another member of the group pointed across the river in the southern direction, as if that might solve Jean-Luc's confusion.

"I beg your pardon, on whom do we wait?" Jean-Luc repeated his question, straining his eyes to peer through the nightscape of Paris. He began to hear the slow rumble of many horses approaching.

"Bonaparte," the first woman answered, her voice heavy with reverence. "He's coming!" The group was now spreading out, forming a single file along the side of the bridge to clear a passage for the approaching horsemen. It sounded to Jean-Luc like an entire squadron of cavalry.

"General Napoleon Bonaparte!" one of the fathers in the group cried, hoisting his son atop his shoulders. The little boy began to wave the tricolor flag.

Their torches appeared first, and Jean-Luc scampered back with the others to clear space as the horsemen became visible, approaching at a steady trot. At the front of the column rode a narrow figure, a nearby torch throwing enough light on his face to show dark hair and bright, delicate features, his black eyes fixed intently forward. He wore a jacket of a deep blue with golden epaulets on his shoulders, a bicorn hat on his head.

As his horse charged onto the bridge at the head of the column, Bonaparte raised his sword and cried out: *"To the Tuileries! For France!"*

In a blur, the horses approached and then passed, racing up toward the Right Bank and the siege. The group surrounding Jean-Luc roared back its response, chasing after General Bonaparte, the tricolor flag waving like a banner carrying them to battle.

Jean-Luc seized upon the momentary excitement of the crowd and slipped off, unnoticed, in the opposite direction. He had been struck by an idea, as sudden and abrupt as the frenzied dancing of the crowd. He ran toward home now, thinking that, perhaps, he'd finally landed upon the line of argument that might actually save André Valière. He could not wait to tell Marie.

At home, the garret apartment was dark and quiet. Marie would not have expected him home this late, not when he had taken to spending so many nights at the office. He found his wife and son curled up together in the corner of the room on Mathieu's small sleeping pallet, their bodies intertwined in the blissful web of sleep. Jean-Luc slid out of his shoes and tiptoed toward them. He stared down at their serene faces for several minutes, tears stinging the corners of his eyes. Mathieu was snoring, his plump little body enfolded in his mother's arms.

Jean-Luc lowered himself down beside them on the pallet. Marie shifted, sighing in her sleep, but settling back down into the arms that her husband now wrapped around her. "I love you, Marie," Jean-Luc whispered into her ear. "I love you both." Whether in her sleep or in waking, she smiled, and he kissed her soft cheek. The warmth of their bodies softened his entire frame, and fatigue pulled on him; he might actually sleep well tonight, for the first night since he could remember.

But just then, Jean-Luc's eyes landed on a spot next to the sleeping pallet, just inches from his son's head. There rested the shiny, elaborate figurine that Mathieu had been given by the mysterious, unseen "nice man." The gift that had made both Marie and Jean-Luc so unsettled; it had been an unwelcome presence in their apartment since Mathieu had first displayed it.

But that miniature was not what made Jean-Luc's heart lurch this evening. What made his heart lurch this evening was that right beside the figurine, its glossy paint catching the light of the moon, rested yet another new toy, and one that surely had not been given to the boy by his mother—a miniature guillotine.

18

Le Temple
Prison, Paris

Spring 1795

Jean-Luc had smuggled in two letters from Sophie in the past year, and that was the only word André had had from her. The first letter had been a quick note scrawled to tell André that she was hidden safely in the country; Remy had done his job getting her out of the city and beyond her uncle's grasp. As long as he heard no other news, André had assured himself that she remained safe. Hidden. Her silence had afforded him a small measure of peace of mind, in recent months, to think about and prepare for his trial.

Until this morning. On the day of André's long-awaited and -postponed trial, Jean-Luc had come to the prison bearing another letter. It had been early. André had been lying in the corner of the cell, his body curled up in the damp straw and his eyes shut as he tried not to consider the potential outcomes of the day ahead, when his counsel appeared, bearing the note from Sophie.

"I wasn't sure whether to give it to you or to wait until after the trial," Jean-Luc admitted, his brow bearing a new worry line between his eyes that André had never before noticed. "But I decided that I couldn't, in good conscience, keep this from you. I hope that Sophie's words will give you strength today."

André took the note, the paper shaking in his dirty fingers, wondering whether perhaps Jean-Luc had been correct to consider holding on to it; perhaps he *ought* to wait until after the trial to read it. Keep his mind clear, or as clear as it could be, for the day's ordeal. But then, he reasoned, if he was found guilty, the opportunity to read this letter could be gone forever.

He tore through the wax seal and unfolded the paper, his chest contracting as if squeezed by a rope when he beheld her familiar handwriting.

> *My love,*
>
> *I've left the château where Remy had installed me. I was forced to leave, in fact. My uncle found me.*

André lowered the paper, his hands trembling. But he forced himself to read on.

> *The only answer at which I can arrive is that one of my uncle's men must have followed Remy to the spot, as your brother came somewhat regularly to ensure that I was all right and to offer me news on your well-being. Always it was the same—that you were still alive, though imprisoned, and awaiting your trial. Remy told me that you had forbidden him from visiting you in the prison, out of the necessity of keeping him at a safe distance and free of any suspicion, and as such, that he could not deliver my letters. It was agony for me, but I do not wish to dwell on my suffering when you currently shoulder a burden so heavy as to render my own pains light by comparison.*
>
> *But my cause for writing now, as you've likely guessed, is due to an urgent change in my situation; as I said, I was forced to flee my hiding place. My uncle arrived at the château two nights ago. Remy had just come with fresh supplies of food and firewood. We didn't see my uncle's party until it was almost too late. Remy heard it first, the sound of hooves some distance away. We thought it was our imaginations until we saw the torches lighting their approach. The sight sent a chill through my blood.*
>
> *Remy, ever the soldier, kept his wits about him and hastened me out a back door to the stables, where we found the estate's one remaining horse. Your brother put me into the saddle and sent me into the*

orchards. From there, I was able to slip into the woods and vanish
from the grounds before my uncle's party discovered me. Given that
the stables had only the one horse remaining, and that the old,
starving beast would have been overburdened by the two of us, Remy
sent me away on that mount and assured me that he would make his
way to the front of the château, where his own horse was tied. André,
I don't know what became of your brother. I have not heard from him
since that hasty farewell in the darkened stable.

The last thing I saw, as my own horse panted through the orchard
and into the backwoods, was a great blaze, as the château was set
to fire. My very soul urged me to return, to offer help to Remy, whose
selfless actions had led him to protect me and put his own life in
danger. But I don't know if I would have brought back help or more
harm. I recalled that he had made me swear that I would keep riding
until I found safety.

Oh, André, I am so sorry that I did not turn back. My heart is torn
apart with regret. I've put both you and your brother in the way of
danger, and that inescapable fact makes me ill.

I will write you again when I have a more regular and permanent
situation. In the meantime, know that I am alive and well, though
very eager for news on what I hope was your brother's safe delivery.
He is the only reason I am able to write you this day.

And, of course, even more important than my own happiness—I
search everywhere for news of your trial. When it will be and what its
outcome is. Oh, what terrible times we live in!

> My heart remains yours,
> and I shall remain for the rest of
> my days your loving and faithful,
> Sophie

André lowered the letter, guessing from the rushed and disorderly
handwriting that Sophie had been just as distressed in this note's writing as
he was now in its reading. Sophie, hunted from her hiding place like an
animal. Remy missing, or worse. André sat or, rather, fell to the ground.

For a moment his vision blurred and his eyes failed him. He shut them and dark visions swirled in his mind's eye—his father, his general, his brother, his love—a waking nightmare playing out before him.

"André de Valière?" A stout guard, his cheeks flushed from a morning of cards and wine, stood at the door of the cell. André peeled his eyes open and blinked, looking around as if by some miracle he would wake to find himself anywhere in the world but this place. He noticed the letter lying on the damp straw at his feet and remembered Sophie's troubled words. Despite his feeling of hopelessness, he hurriedly grabbed the letter and held it close to his person, as though protecting a candle's light from flickering out.

"It's time," the guard said, jamming a rusty key into the lock and pulling open the groaning cell door.

"Time?" André stammered, remembering the trial. "Oh, yes." He rose to his feet unsteadily. "But first, a moment. I must quickly change." He glanced around his cell. "My uniform . . . my army uniform. It was right there—where did it go?"

The guard shrugged, unhelpful and uninterested. "You'll stand trial in the sackcloth just like the thousands before you."

André felt his spirits sink even lower. "But I meant to wear my uniform—"

"You'll wear a new bruise 'cross your ugly aristocratic face if you don't hurry out now." The guard lifted the butt of his musket menacingly. "Now, get out, or I might lose my temper."

One of the other prisoners peered out of his cell, staring at André, his dark eyes earnest. "May God be with you, brother. May God be with you."

God hasn't been with me for quite some time, André thought, as he shuffled through the cell door. His legs were unsteady, barely up to the task of carrying his body to its condemnation. As he walked, his thoughts turned to Sophie's letter, the news he had just read in his cell. He agonized now, one question haunting him more than even the dread of his upcoming trial and sentencing: where was Remy?

André stepped down from the wagon, hands and ankles shackled, and shuffled his way through a small passage toward the court. The sun poured down, a blinding light he had not seen in months, forcing him to raise his hands and shield his squinting eyes.

Jean-Luc stood outside the court, his face dropping noticeably when he saw his client. "André, you are not dressed in your army uniform."

André glanced down at his body covered in the scratchy gray sackcloth. Looking back up at his lawyer, he could read the disappointment in Jean-Luc's soft hazel eyes. "I'm sorry. It was gone. Taken from my cell by one of the guards."

"Murat, no doubt," Jean-Luc growled under his breath, his face momentarily shedding his constant composure. He sighed. "Very well. We will carry on regardless." He forced an encouraging smile, patting André gently on the back, his eyes taking in his client's emaciated frame. Just then, a bailiff called out the next case, and Jean-Luc and André were shuffled inside toward the front of the hall.

"The Citizens and People of the French Republic versus André de Valière, heir to the former Marquis de Valière." At that announcement, the crowd stuffed and squeezed into the courtroom began to hiss and stomp their feet. The row of jurymen, all wearing tricolor cockades and red caps, whispered to one another, their eyes fixed eagerly on the doorway where André and his lawyer entered.

Jean-Luc leaned close to whisper: "Never mind that. Just remember— you fought at Valmy, you fought on the Italian front, and you have risked your life for the Revolution. You've willingly renounced your title, your lands, and your claims to nobility. You merely wish to continue serving the Republic."

Putting a hand on André's shoulder, Jean-Luc heaved in a fortifying breath before saying: "Right, then, let's go."

André kept his eyes firmly ahead, though in truth he saw little and felt less. Nodding, he stepped forward alongside Jean-Luc, and the counselor set his gait to remain in stride with his client.

As they entered the court, the crowd turned to get a better look at the two men. Since the fall of Robespierre and the Jacobins, the tribunals had changed in many ways. Noticeable among these changes was a more mechanical functioning of these proceedings, which, to some, seemed dull by comparison. Seething emotion and rage from the gallery was replaced with a bureaucratic rigidity that, Jean-Luc fervently hoped, might give him an opening to reasonably plead André's case. But there was no certainty, for many in the crowd still remained hostile to the nobility and fearful of a royalist uprising; the scars of the Revolution would not disappear so easily.

The head magistrate rang the shrill bell, its noise falling in with the roar of the audience but restoring no order.

André took his seat, ringed on all sides by benches of spectators. The chamber was less grand than the courtroom in which Kellermann had been tried, this being a lower-profile case. All the same, the hall overflowed with the usual mass of eager, spectating faces.

André blinked, trying to overcome this paralyzing sense of numbness and detachment. The room of spectators blurred together—their humorless smiles and stringy hair blending into one tableau of concentrated hostility. Only one face stood out, a familiar set of features: gray eyes, an ink-black ponytail, a prominent mustache. Nicolai Murat sat in the center of the room, several rows back, his gaze fixed on the prisoner with singular focus.

When André saw his accuser—Sophie's hunter, Remy's tormenter—he felt a sudden wave of emotion stronger than anything he had experienced in months. His numbness gave way to a swell of anger. Pain at the thought of Kellermann's memory and unjust death. Of Sophie's fear and unhappiness. Of poor Remy, from whom he'd had no news. André felt so overcome with emotion that he struggled with a great effort to hold back tears.

Guillaume Lazare, the same attorney who had haunted André's loved ones in recent years, had been enlisted to convict him. Hired by Murat, no doubt. This, André supposed, made it all the more likely that he would be tried quickly and condemned to death. Jean-Luc St. Clair had stood up as a trial defense attorney only one other time in his young career; the outcome of that case, as everyone in Paris knew, had resulted in a good man being sent to the guillotine.

Aware of this grim precedent, and sensing the hatred his accusers had for him, André found it impossible to retain any hope. This hostile courtroom, combined with the morning's news from Sophie, had finally done what all those months in Le Temple had failed to do: André despaired, certain that he was a doomed man.

A powerful wave of resignation suddenly swept through him, overpowering his senses. The noises of the crowd, the shrill ringing of the magistrate's bell for silence, the stomping of hundreds of feet—it all receded. With this surrender came, surprisingly, a feeling of sudden weightlessness. Relief. He could finally give up fighting. He could sense the creeping shadow of death but no longer felt fear at its approach, for death would be the end of his suffering.

So consumed was André by this sudden realization of his own defeat, the recognition that, for him, the torment was over, that he became momentarily blinded to the developments unfolding before him in court.

André did not notice how Jean-Luc St. Clair—seasoned from his inaugural and failed attempt to win over a courtroom and best the masterful Guillaume Lazare—spun a narrative of the Battle of Valmy to sway the stone-faced jurors and spectators. The way Jean-Luc St. Clair spoke of a young man, having renounced a noble name that he had never chosen for himself, who wore the blue coat of a soldier before the nation had even gone to war. Had he been listening, André Valière might have supposed that his lawyer was describing Christophe Kellermann, but no, the lawyer was describing André Valière. And the lawyer was fighting this case as if his own life depended on it. André's death would be the end of him, he knew it. Just as André's deliverance would be his own salvation.

Moving with confidence and clarity through his argument, Jean-Luc St. Clair continued to the topic of another one of the Republic's recently discovered heroes: General Napoleon Bonaparte. Jean-Luc described, in vivid language, the night of the uprisings across Paris, when royalists had besieged the Tuileries and nearly taken back the capital. How he, Jean-Luc St. Clair, had been standing on the bridge when Bonaparte himself had ridden past on his way to save Paris from these enemies of the Revolution.

Pausing, perhaps as much to build suspense as to wipe the sweat from his brow, Jean-Luc went on to describe how Bonaparte had raised his sword and cried out: "For France!" The crowd throughout the hall began to murmur, even nod, when the lawyer recounted how the young Corsican general had rallied the people in the face of that threat, and when Jean-

Luc remarked that Bonaparte would now be taking that rallying cry abroad, to punish the enemies who had threatened to quash the noble Revolution, some began to cheer.

This panel of jurymen were as patriotic as the most fervent citizens in the land, Jean-Luc asserted. They knew that General Bonaparte's call for men must be answered. How then, as patriots, could they sit here and send a man, a soldier, and a hero such as André Valière to the guillotine? How could they rob Bonaparte, and the French nation, of such a seasoned fighter?

The mood in the courtroom was shifting around André, but he noticed none of this. So absorbed was he in his own musings on death—on the verdict that he had already accepted—that he did not notice the beautiful web of logic and emotion that his passionate young lawyer was spinning around him. A protective web of perfectly honed arguments, designed to strike the chords of clemency and patriotism in the breasts of his would-be executioners.

"Citizens." Jean-Luc's face was flushed, his ponytail loose, as he strode across the courtroom, weaving his final arguments in André Valière's defense. "This man before you, André Valière, was born in a château. When just a helpless babe in a cradle, he was given wealth more abundant than that which any one man deserves. For that, he ought to pay a price, even if he has renounced all of it and proven that he would give his very blood to save our Republic. He still owes this nation. On that score, I am in perfect agreement. But don't you share my opinion that that price should directly benefit that same nation? Our beloved French Republic?

"If we kill André Valière today, his head rolls and his once-noble blood spills. Where does that leave us? It gives us a show. A few minutes of . . . entertainment." Jean-Luc shrugged, pressing his palms together. "But if we take his body and put it into the service of our Revolution—what does *that* get us? André Valière becomes a servant of our people and principles. A warrior for our General Bonaparte. And not just any warrior—André Valière is well trained, battle hardened, and proven. Can we squander such a man as this, just because a few vengeful persons wish to see a fleeting show of blood?"

The crowd cried out at this point, as the jury members shifted in their seats, casting sidelong glances at one another, noting the mood of the hall.

"I, for one, would not have it so." Jean-Luc paused, short of breath, his voice now hoarse, but he held every pair of eyes in the room. "I say: make André Valière fight for this country. Put him to work. Send him to Bonaparte. There, his blood might be shed, but not without first serving our Republic." Jean-Luc pounded his fist into his palm at the conclusion of each sentence for emphasis, and each gesture was greeted with fresh cheers from the crowd.

"In that way, the wealth and riches of André Valière's family—so long squandered due to an undue title—may at last be earned back for us all. Citizens of France, I say this man owes it to us to fight for our Revolution!"

André barely heard the rousing words of his lawyer's closing argument. Barely looked up as the jury deliberated. Barely heard the voice of the bailiff who announced that a verdict had been reached after only a matter of minutes.

André greeted the reading of the verdict with a barely perceptible shrug. "André de Valière is found guilty."

But then, he felt a strange sensation, as if his mind and body had been forcefully thrown back into the present moment, when the second half of the verdict was read. He had been waiting for that dreaded word, had been expecting to hear the utterance of *guillotine*. Instead, the judge declared in an expressionless voice: "Sentence for the guilty shall be permanent exile from the Republic of France, mandatory service in the navy of General Bonaparte."

André looked sideways at Jean-Luc, the lawyer's face alight with the same disbelief as his own. They had done it; they had squeezed some small feeling of mercy from the people. André would not face the guillotine after all. André would be forced to live.

Later, outside the court, André was jostled through the crowd, a handful of guards forming a protective ring around him and Jean-Luc. "Can you believe it, André?" The lawyer was alternating between laughter and seriousness, as if he himself had not fully absorbed the news of his own victory. "Ha! God bless, your life is yours, my friend."

André nodded, still struggling to comprehend the outcome. "I have no words . . . but thank you."

"Thank *you*, for not giving in to those who tried to destroy you," the lawyer answered, his tone low and serious against the shouts of the surrounding crowd. "You know, your strength gave me new spirit, and dare I say, made it possible to build your case."

Though André had been freed of his ankle shackles, his wrists were still bound, but he and Jean-Luc clasped hands.

"It would appear, André, son of the former marquis"—Jean-Luc said the latter part quietly—"that your story was not meant to end today."

The crowd began to disperse. Some of the stragglers still lingered, hoping for a closer look at the man who had been ripped from death's grip. But as the crowd thinned, André realized they were not alone.

Waiting next to the carriage that would transport André Valière back to the prison to gather his belongings stood Nicolai Murat. The tall man's demeanor was entirely changed from that which he had shown in the courtroom, where he had appeared animated. Now his face was blank, his seawater-gray eyes devoid of emotion.

"Captain de Valière." Murat leaned up against the carriage, arms crossed before his chest. Hearing his own name uttered by the man's lips, André's entire frame stiffened; he had not known it possible to hate this passionately.

"André?" Jean-Luc shuffled closer to his client, resting a hand on his shoulder. "You've just been spared, do not . . ." Jean-Luc threw a hard gaze toward Murat. "Please get into the carriage."

"No." André lifted a hand, pausing in his steps. "It's all right." Turning to Jean-Luc, he asked: "Would you give us a moment?"

Jean-Luc shifted his weight, his eyes darting back and forth between Murat and André. The lawyer leaned close, barely whispering: "Please, watch your words."

André nodded. "A moment, please."

Jean-Luc sighed, clasping his hands in front of his waist. "I'll be in the carriage when you're ready to go." With that, Jean-Luc stepped away.

Left alone with Murat, the guards hovering nearby like nervous chaperones, André stood still and stared at his tormenter. "General Murat." But there was no deference in the young man's use of his superior's title.

After a pause, the general spoke: "I suppose congratulations are in order." Murat traced two fingers along the tip of his mustache. "Never thought that young lawyer had it in him. I must say, I'm impressed."

André clenched his jaw, willing himself to master his nerves and his temper before saying anything. He would not give Murat the satisfaction of seeing any of the pain he had inflicted.

"Not that it's certain you've escaped death," Murat continued. "No doubt you'll be sent straight to the cannon's mouth, perhaps to face Nelson and his dreaded English ships."

André offered nothing by way of a reply.

"But the young lawyer put up quite a fight, didn't he?" Pausing, Murat smirked. "Which is more than I can say for your brother."

At this, André's chest collapsed. "What did you say?"

Murat's lips curled under his mustache. "I found him skulking about in some abandoned château in the country near Le Mans, where he had my niece holed up like a rat. How dare you?" The general's eyes narrowed. He hissed the next question: "Where is she?"

André didn't answer. His vision patchy, he tried to understand what could have possibly become of Remy. After a long pause, Murat, his voice calm once more, continued: "Never mind. I'll find her. She can't have gone far. Your brother may have tried his best, but it was not enough."

André prepared to lunge forward, but he knew that by choking the man, he'd miss his chance to learn his brother's fate. "Tell me what happened to my brother."

Murat laughed—a joyless, ragged sneer, his gray eyes seething like a gathering storm. "When I find my niece, then perhaps I will tell you where to find your brother's body."

19

Paris

Summer 1795

"I suppose you've got a right high opinion of yourself now."

Jean-Luc looked up into the face of Gavreau, who hovered before his desk. The man had been circling, like a hungry dog, for a quarter of an hour and had finally decided that no invitation was necessary to interrupt Jean-Luc's work.

Jean-Luc sighed, lowering his quill. "I beg your pardon?"

Gavreau tossed the day's news journals forward, adding to the pile of papers covering Jean-Luc's desk. "Front page of the papers. This pamphlet dubs you 'the most promising young lawyer in Paris.' So, as I said: I suppose you've got a right high opinion of yourself now."

Jean-Luc threw a cursory glance at the top pamphlet, skimming the first sentence before noting, with a quiver of pride, that it was written by his favorite writer, Citizen Persephone. He looked back up at his boss, concealing his urge to smile. "Marie would never allow me to get a high opinion of myself. I suppose it's her sworn duty to remind me on a daily basis of how far I am from perfection." Jean-Luc shrugged, and his manager began to laugh.

"Then she's good for something, your wife, even if she does keep you from ever accompanying me out to the cafés at night."

"Now that," Jean-Luc said, leaning his head to one side, "I can't blame on my wife."

"But why was she at Valière's trial?"

"Hmm?" Jean-Luc looked up at his boss, confused.

"Your woman," Gavreau said. "I saw her there, tucked way in the back. It looked as if she was taking notes, or recording something for herself. Thought perhaps you've got her working as one of your clerks, now that you're too busy for one man."

"Marie, at the trial of André Valière?" Jean-Luc repeated the claim. "Surely you're mistaken. She wasn't there." Marie had never mentioned anything about attending the trial. He'd insisted she stay far away.

"She was there, I tell you. I never miss a pretty brunette."

"No." Jean-Luc shook his head, convinced of his supervisor's error. "You'd enjoyed too much wine at lunch and noticed someone who resembled her. But, speaking of Marie, I've got this pile to get through and I've promised to be home in time for supper."

Jean-Luc's workload had become insurmountable lately, so backed up he'd gotten in the months and weeks preparing for André's trial. "Say, who do you suppose he is—this Citizen Persephone writer?" Jean-Luc asked his supervisor.

"Not sure. Some reference to Greek," Gavreau said, eyeing the pamphlet. "I know it was actually a *she,* the daughter of Zeus."

"Oh?" Jean-Luc looked from the pamphlet to Gavreau.

"Come now . . . is it really the case that *I* know something that the esteemed Jean-Luc St. Clair does not?" Gavreau gloated, his ruddy face teasing. "Don't remember your classics? Persephone, the poor gal, gets dragged off to the underworld by some dark devil who fancies her. She reemerges each spring, bringing life, but then descends again each winter, leaving death and decay. The ultimate symbol of life and death. Hope and despair, the light and the dark. The fragile balance of this cocked-up world in which we live."

Jean-Luc nodded, vaguely recalling the lessons of his boyhood. "Well, Gavreau, I have to admit: I'm impressed."

"I'm not completely useless, after all. But come now, St. Clair. It's one o'clock in the afternoon." Gavreau, rather than showing signs of leaving his employee's desk, now perched himself on its edge. "Have you eaten anything all day?"

"No, actually, I haven't," Jean-Luc answered, realizing for the first time how hungry he was.

"I'll buy you lunch. It's the least I can do for the . . . what are they calling you now? Oh yes, 'the most promising young lawyer in Paris.'"

The day was a pleasant one, with golden sunlight bathing the square in a gentle warmth. They walked west along the river to the Saint-Jacques neighborhood and chose a table on the terrace of the Café du Progrés for lunch.

Gavreau ordered two thin stews, a loaf of bread with something advertised as liver pâté, and a carafe of watered-down wine. "So have you heard from the poor bastard?"

"Which bastard are we talking about?" Jean-Luc asked.

"The captain. Valière, or de Valière, whatever his name is."

"Not since he left for the coast. But I saw him off just a few weeks ago."

Gavreau leaned back as the waiter delivered the basket of bread, its crust a dark, flaky brown. "How'd he feel about everything? True, exile is not death, but it is still exile."

Jean-Luc thought about the question. "I'm not certain. He was very distracted whenever we spoke. Perhaps a bit nervous. This war . . ." Jean-Luc paused, glanced over his shoulder, and decided against continuing on. Not that he even knew how to express his own troubled thoughts on this Revolution and what had become of it.

"What's he got to be nervous about? He gets to keep his head." Gavreau tucked his linen napkin into his collar the way Marie arranged Mathieu's bib and scooped himself a generous portion of the pâté. "And from everything I've heard about his family, I'm sure his relations have a hoard of treasure hidden away somewhere."

"Not nervous for himself. Nervous because his brother *and* his fiancée have gone missing."

Gavreau raised his eyebrows, holding his knife to hover above his pâté. "Are they dead?"

"I don't know," Jean-Luc said, lost in thought. He picked up a knife and sliced himself a thin piece of bread. "Her uncle is the general. Murat. The one who brought the charges against André."

"Well now, perhaps he's in more trouble than I thought."

Jean-Luc nodded.

Gavreau, having gobbled up his half of the pâté, served himself more.

"Now the young man's fate rests in hands that are not your own, my friend. So you should stop your worrying. I've never known a man to talk himself into trouble and court misery the way you do."

Jean-Luc thought about this, realizing that, for once, he agreed with his superior.

"He's alive," Jean-Luc reasoned. "That counts for something. And I'd take my chances among the Italians or Austrians over the—" Jean-Luc stopped short and surveyed his surroundings once more. Convinced no one within earshot was eavesdropping, he continued, "I'd sooner face war with those people than stand before that godforsaken tribunal. After facing down Murat, Lazare, and the wrath of the Committee, I think Valière might welcome the sight of a foreign land."

Gavreau wiped his lips with the back of his palm. "Have you soured on our Revolution?"

Jean-Luc leaned his head to the side, looking out over the crowded square. He sighed. "Perhaps it's simply human nature on which I have soured."

"People are like the apples you find in a harvest bushel." Gavreau shrugged. "Some are right and good, and some are rotten."

Jean-Luc narrowed his eyes, surprised by his colleague's rare display of wisdom.

"And some are like me," Gavreau continued. "You just eat around the rotten parts."

"Or leave you for the worms." Jean-Luc flashed his boss a grin.

"Say, you ever hear from the big shot lawyer?"

"Guillaume Lazare?" Jean-Luc asked, his heart beginning to race.

Gavreau nodded.

"Not since André's trial." Jean-Luc pushed his stew away, his appetite suddenly gone. "I wrote him a note following it, trying to be cordial. But he never replied."

"He's probably upset that your client escaped his grasp. Not something he's accustomed to, from the sound of it."

After the afternoon meal Jean-Luc crossed the Seine to the Left Bank. His steps fell lightly on the stone bridge as he watched the gentle afternoon light glint off the river's surface, shimmering streaks that ebbed and dissipated along with the shifting current.

It was still light out when he turned onto his street. He walked slowly, feeling, for the first time in a while, a sense of ease. He would be home before his boy went to bed. He would be home in time to have supper with Marie and hear about her day.

Through the opened window of the ground floor he spotted Madame Grocque sweeping the front room of her tavern. "Citizeness Grocque." Jean-Luc tipped his hat to the thick-shouldered woman. She didn't reply but rather looked with her beady eyes toward a carriage parked on the nearby corner.

Dread shot through Jean-Luc, a cold blast of ice melting the warm glow he'd felt just a moment earlier. As if awaiting his arrival, the carriage door opened and out stepped the narrow figure of Guillaume Lazare.

"Citizen St. Clair." The man's yellow hair was pulled back in a tight ponytail, his skin blanched an unnatural chalky color. Only his lips were red, an artificial painted red, and they now curled into an unconvincing smile.

"Citizen Lazare." Jean-Luc paused where he stood. He threw a quick glance up in the direction of their garret, and he instantly regretted it. The old man's eyes followed.

"You look surprised to see me, citizen."

"A little, yes," Jean-Luc replied.

"Have I caught you at a bad time?"

"No, no, it's just . . . how can I help you?"

"Oh, I don't need your *help*, citizen." Lazare braided his long, spindly fingers together in front of his waist. "I've simply come to congratulate you on your recent victory."

Jean-Luc forced a smile, but he was certain that the old man could sense the tension in the gesture. "Thank you, Citizen Lazare. That's kind of you."

"I've always said I appreciate a challenge." The old man narrowed his eyes, studying Jean-Luc as if the young man were some dense bit of text in which the meaning was not immediately clear. After several moments, Lazare sighed. "Well, I should let you go. I am sure your wife is anxious to have you back, now that the business of that unfortunate trial is over."

"Indeed." Jean-Luc stepped up to the doorway, feeling as if he could not be done with this interview quickly enough. "Thank you again for your well wishes." He accepted Lazare's outstretched hand—as flimsy as paper in his grip, the old man's skin cold.

"Please give my best to your family." With that, Lazare threw one more glance upward toward the apartment before turning back to the carriage. The footman opened the door but Lazare paused, gazing back to Jean-Luc. "Oh, and by the way, I thought it was interesting that *she* was visiting. I had never realized that you were so friendly with Captain Valière. Perhaps it was naïve of me to think that you were simply serving as his counsel. I suppose we all have our secrets, hmm?" Lazare paused, his eyes gliding up toward the garret window, which Marie must have opened, for now the sound of Mathieu's distant laughter rained down over the street. Lazare turned back toward Jean-Luc.

"I took you for an honest man, St. Clair. Imagine my disappointment if it turns out that I have been deceived."

"Citizen." Jean-Luc, visibly shaken by that last remark, fumbled to offer some reply. "I assure you, I have no idea to what you're referring."

"Peace! All is well, my friend. I am but a man of the law; the personal affairs of others are no concern of mine." With that, Lazare put on his cap and climbed into the coach. The driver's whip cracked and the carriage lurched forward. Lazare called out from his retreating window. "Though, of course, I cannot speak for her uncle, General Murat. Evening to you and your family, citizen!"

Jean-Luc entered his apartment, his heart racing. Instantly, he knew. Knew exactly to whom Lazare had been referring.

"What are you doing here?" Jean-Luc asked, staring into the beautiful face of a young blond woman who he guessed must be Sophie Vincennes.

"Jean-Luc St. Clair." Marie stepped forward, putting her hands on her hips. "Is that any way to speak to a guest?"

"Papa!" Mathieu ran toward his father, tripping over his own feet so that he tumbled before reaching Jean-Luc. The lawyer leaned over and scooped up his son and walked toward the two women.

"I apologize; I didn't mean to be rude. It's just that I'm stunned to see you. You must be Sophie?"

The woman nodded.

"What are you doing here?" Jean-Luc repeated his earlier question.

"What has come over you?" Marie walked around the table where she had been depositing plates of dinner food and approached her husband. "Where are your manners?"

But Jean-Luc kept his focus fixed firmly on their guest. Sophie lifted her gaze, her tight facial expression showing fear, but also hope. "I had nowhere else to go. André told me you were one of the few who could be trusted."

"Papa! Mademoiselle Sophie is going to draw me a flying balloon!" Mathieu pounded his fists excitedly on his father's shoulders. "Mademoiselle Sophie, please draw a flying balloon!"

"Not now, Mathieu." Marie took her son from Jean-Luc and placed him on the floor before his toys. "First Mademoiselle Sophie is going to have dinner with Mama and Papa." And then, turning her dark eyes on her husband with a look that told him he had better agree, she asked: "Isn't that right, Jean-Luc?"

He sighed, nodding. "Yes, of course."

Dinner was a strained affair. Marie did her best to engage Sophie on lighthearted topics, such as Mathieu's refusal to eat certain foods and Madame Grocque's ongoing feud with each dog in the neighborhood. But Sophie's laughs, though polite, were forced. Jean-Luc said very little.

"Have you heard from André?" he asked as they cleared the table following the meal.

Sophie shook her head. "He's had no idea where I was for months."

"Where were you exactly?" Jean-Luc asked, as Marie listened in, stacking a pile of dirty dishes for scrubbing.

"At first," Sophie spoke quietly, evidently fearful that someone might hear her, even here, "Remy found me a place in an old château about three days' ride south of the city, outside Le Mans. The family had departed in the first wave of emigrants and I suppose those who chose to remain were . . . arrested . . . so the château was empty save for an old caretaker and his blind wife. The couple took me in, allowing me to pay for a bedroom. They didn't ask any questions."

An old château near Le Mans—had it been one of the properties he had inventoried? Jean-Luc wondered. He didn't recall a château outside Le Mans. His memory didn't hold the faces of any ghosts related with that place.

"And what became of you, once you were settled at the abandoned château?" Marie's question pulled Jean-Luc back to the room, to the dinner table.

"Remy deposited me there, then returned to his garrison outside Versailles. He would visit every few weeks, bringing any extra rations or resources scrounged from his already starving camp. And then one day . . ." Sophie's voice trailed off, and her eyes stared past her two eager listeners, through the garret wall and beyond.

"Yes?"

"*He* found me there. Or, at least, came close to finding me." At this point in her story, Sophie's voice broke and she cupped her face in her hands. Marie and Jean-Luc exchanged a glance, allowing her this pause in the narrative.

Eventually she resumed. "Remy helped me flee. That was the worst night of my life," Sophie whispered, her blue eyes turning to Mathieu as if unwilling to let him hear. "I rode through the woods all night on that horse. I didn't stop once. Just shortly after daybreak, I came out on a lane. That was about the time the horse lay down; his legs just buckled beneath us. He wouldn't get up, poor creature. If I'd had a pistol, I would have shot him dead, put him out of his misery."

Marie paused her scrubbing, allowing the wet dishrag to trickle a slow stream of suds onto the wooden floor as she listened, her face creased in sympathy.

"Do you know . . . what happened to Remy?" Jean-Luc asked.

Sophie simply shook her head, her whole body sagging in on itself as her light eyes filled with moisture. "No," she said, suppressing a shudder of tears. "I haven't seen him since that night."

Marie crossed herself while Jean-Luc sighed. Knowing what he did of Murat, he had to assume the worst. After a long silence, he looked back toward Sophie. "So how did you move without a horse?"

"I knew I had to get off the road. I had no idea how close my uncle and his men were at that point. But since I had no money, I couldn't stay at an inn. Besides, I didn't wish for word to spread about a strange, disheveled-looking woman traveling alone, so I spent the entire day making my way slowly through the woods on foot, just hugging the side of the road.

"That evening I came upon a farm. It seemed like a remote enough place and I could tell it was inhabited, so I made my way into the barn. I was so hungry by then. But even more than that, I was tired. I had ridden all night and walked all the following day. I don't know that I've ever felt so weary. I found an empty stall in the back and I lay down there and fell into a deep sleep. That was where I spent the second night."

Jean-Luc looked at Sophie, amazed. She may have been well bred—genteel even—but she had a strength that he had not expected.

"I awoke the next morning to the confused whispers of an old man. The farmer. He had a pitchfork held aloft, but I sensed from his face that he was not a wicked person. I clasped my hands together, praying for mercy, and he lowered it immediately. He brought me into the farmhouse, where I met his wife and daughter, who gently insisted that I eat breakfast."

"Thank God they were friendly." Marie sighed.

"Friendly doesn't begin to describe them," Sophie said, her voice with a choking quality even as she forced herself to continue. "Saintly, in fact. That's where I've been, ever since that day I first wrote André. Or, wrote *you*, I should say."

"He received your letter the day of the trial," Jean-Luc said, nodding. He remembered vividly how shaken André had appeared in court. He had presumed it to be the man's nerves over facing the tribunal and possibly the guillotine, and did not realize until later he was reacting to the contents of Sophie's letter.

"They weren't suspicious of you?" Marie asked. "These farmers?"

Sophie shook her head. "They asked where I had come from. I told them I was from Paris, and they didn't ask more after that. They said that everyone from Paris had a sad story these days, and that they had no need to hear a sad story. They took me in as if I were their own blood. I worked, too, of course, offering whatever assistance I could. Helped in the kitchen and with the children, and sometimes in the kitchen garden. I was so grateful just to be safe, and fed."

"Until now. What happened?" Jean-Luc asked.

"Until just a week ago," Sophie answered. "They must have been more nervous than they had let on, because just last week, they sat me down and asked me to leave."

"What reason did they give?" Marie ran her fingers distractedly through her brown hair, pulling it away from her face.

"I mentioned their eldest daughter. A sweet girl," Sophie said, a sad smile pulling on her lips. "She had a suitor, a young man from a nearby village who wanted to marry her. But he could not while there was a stranger living in their house. I think they were afraid that I might be noticed and bring suspicion on the whole family." Sophie paused. "With the new decrees passed, anyone who so much as suspected them could denounce the entire family for harboring 'traitors,' and we know what would happen then." Sophie looked as if she would be sick. For a moment Jean-Luc feared she might be, and he leaned forward as if to support her. But the shadow slowly passed and she composed herself. "I couldn't blame them, and I told them as much."

All three of them sat in silence after Sophie had finished, with only the sound of Mathieu's voice infiltrating their somber circle as he played with his few toys.

Eventually, Sophie looked up. "I had no money. No food. I had nowhere else to go. My parents are dead. Remy is missing. I knew André had been in Paris. Other than him, I have no one."

"But . . ." Jean-Luc stammered, "how did you get past the barriers?"

Sophie laughed, a mirthless laugh. "It's easy enough getting into the city. It's getting back out that's the hard part."

Later that night, after Mathieu had fallen asleep and Sophie had been provided with blankets and a small pillow for sleeping, Jean-Luc and Marie retreated with their sleeping toddler into the bedroom. It hadn't been quite the celebratory evening of family reconciliation he had been hoping for.

They undressed in silence, putting Mathieu on his tiny pallet in the corner before getting into their own nightclothes. For the first time in a long while, Marie was awake as Jean-Luc climbed into bed. She curled up in a ball and faced him, her face just inches from his on the lumpy pillow. "Is there no other way? Nothing we can do?"

"It's not safe," Jean-Luc whispered, sighing. He had told Marie that he did not think they could offer a place to Sophie in their home. That she would have to go elsewhere.

"You heard her, Jean, she has nowhere else to go. She has no money to rent a room. And not a friend to speak of."

Jean-Luc groaned, rubbing his tired eyes with his fists. "I feel terrible about it, believe me. I keep seeing André's face in my mind and I feel overcome by the urge to tell her yes, she can stay with us. But I must think about you and Mathieu. It's too risky."

Marie looked toward the door, where Sophie slept—or tried to sleep—on the other side. She turned back to her husband and whispered: "You said yourself that her uncle is gone from Paris, back to the front with the army. I know this city has turned upside down and gone mad, but how would anyone know who she was? Perhaps we can pretend she is our maid?"

Jean-Luc showed the hint of a sad smile. "That woman, *our* maid? Even if we could afford that, which we clearly cannot, no one would believe it."

Jean-Luc took Marie's hand in his, pausing. Deliberating as to whether or not to tell her. But he was tired of the distance that had grown between them; he needed her back, as his full partner. "He's seen her."

"Who's seen her?" Marie asked, her big brown eyes narrowing, holding his in the dim light.

"Guillaume Lazare. He saw Sophie arrive."

"The lawyer? What's the danger in that?"

Jean-Luc paused, as if searching for the right words. "There's something about that man that makes me uneasy. I don't trust him, at least not when it concerns the safety of those I love. Besides, he talks to Murat. I think—no, I'm certain—he will tell him."

Marie nodded, her brown eyes catching a glint of the moonlight that spilled into the bedroom, giving her an otherworldly glow. When she spoke, her voice was determined. "André Valière came forward for you when you needed him most. He stood up for Christophe Kellermann, and it nearly got him killed."

Jean-Luc nodded, reaching for her, pulling her closer and wrapping her in his arms as she continued.

"And then you stood up for André Valière. And saved his life. I can't say why, or how it happened, but one way or another, you and he have been thrown into all this together." Marie sighed. "This is his love, and she's guilty of no crime other than falling in love with a man her uncle hates. I say, if this Guillaume Lazare poses a threat to her, that's all the more reason why we will take care of her."

Jean-Luc heard the resolve in her voice and had no choice but to match it with his own, to make her see his perspective now. "Marie, it's not just her uncle or even Lazare. If anyone so much as suspects we're hiding an outlaw, they will inform the authorities. She can't stay here—"

"Jean-Luc, I won't hear it. You risked our family's safety when you took on those two trials. Consider this my turn to gamble on a worthy cause. Sophie Vincennes is a friend in desperate need of help, and we will provide it. If you won't allow her to stay in our home, you will at the very least procure someplace where she *can* stay. You must know someone, perhaps a colleague or that foolish boss of yours. All I can say is that we're not going to make that woman suffer any more than she already has."

Jean-Luc looked at his wife in silence, his own will dissipating against the breaking wall of her resolve. "Marie."

"My beloved husband, find her a place where she can stay, or I'll find one for you," she said, weaving a cold foot in between his ankles.

Jean-Luc sighed. "Oh, all right. I suppose I could look for a place." He slid his body closer to hers in the sheets. "I haven't seen you this passionate in a while." He kissed her neck, wrapping his arm around her waist as he pulled her body flush against his. "I have to say, I rather liked it."

"Good." She smiled at him as she brushed a lock of hair away from his face. They kissed for several moments before she pulled her lips back, grinning. "I believe I may have just bested the man who defeated the *great* Guillaume Lazare."

"Don't even say that name." Jean-Luc reached under the sheets for the hem of her nightgown. "The very sound will trouble my sleep." She assented and allowed him to kiss her.

But she had triggered his memory, and he pulled away from her after a moment. "That reminds me, Marie: Gavreau told me he saw you at the trial. Were you there?"

He felt her body stiffen in his arms. "I . . ." She paused. "I stopped in, just for a moment. I was in the neighborhood."

"In the neighborhood? For what?"

"Oh, just looking about. To see if bread costs less in any different quarters. You know how we could always do with saving a bit of money."

Jean-Luc's mind whirled. "But . . . who was looking after Mathieu?"

"Madame Grocque was minding him, just for a bit."

"Hmm," Jean-Luc muttered, considering this, certain that his wife wasn't telling him everything. "I'm not certain I'm comfortable with that, leaving the boy downstairs in the tavern."

"Then it won't happen again," she said, a bit too agreeably. "Now quit worrying and get back to the business at hand." She resumed kissing him, sliding his nightshirt off as she ran her hands down his back. Before he could protest, Jean-Luc succumbed, his body rousing to her long-withheld touch.

"Papa?" Mathieu's voice pierced the dark bedroom like a needle piercing an inflated balloon. Jean-Luc felt Marie's body stiffen again. For a moment they both lay still and silent, hoping their son would roll back to sleep.

But Mathieu did not oblige, calling into the dark once more. "Papa?"

"What is it, Mathieu?" Already he could feel Marie's body slipping away from his, and he could have groaned in frustration.

"Papa, I heard you say that you will have nightmares because of Citizen Lazare. But you don't need to be 'fraid of him, Papa. He tells me: 'Your daddy is very brave.' When I am playing in the tavern he brings me biscuits and tells me that he will take me to see the flying balloon!"

Jean-Luc looked down at his wife and saw in her expression the same thing that he himself felt; there, in the cold glow of the milky moonlight, Marie's face constricted with fear.

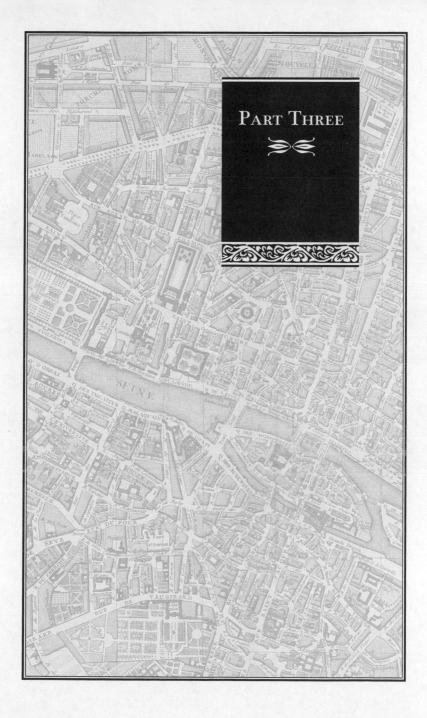

PART THREE

20

Mediterranean Coast, Southern France

Spring 1798

André had nearly gasped aloud as he saw the familiar handwriting. How on earth had this letter found him here?

It had taken ages for this word to arrive from Paris, so many times had Jean-Luc's letter been waylaid and redirected before it had reached his ship, *l'Esprit de Liberté*, in the waters off the coast of southern France. By the time the letter had arrived, it was creased and crumpled, its texture having taken on the briny air and sea—as altered from its former self, one might have said, as the man who now held it.

André, dressed in his sailor's smock and taking his break on the deck of the naval frigate, had torn at the seal of the letter, starving for the words that would come, morsels of food to his lonely soul.

> *André, my friend,*
>
> *A visitor showed up at our door, giving Marie and me quite a surprise: Sophie. She is safe with us. Mathieu seems smitten by his new "Aunt Sophie" and no longer has much time for his mother or father. We try to keep her out of sight whenever we can, and hopefully our neighbors believe us when we tell them we can indeed afford a maid.*
>
> *All is well with us. We will keep Sophie safe, and Mathieu will be certain to keep her busy.*

I hope that this letter finds you well. Or, at the very least, finds you at all; my inquiries into your destination have proven dishearteningly unfruitful. Please send word when you are able to.

> *Your friend,*
> *Jean-Luc St. Clair*

Postscript: I'm sure that I am not in fact the person from whom you hoped to hear. Enjoy.

Tucked into the envelope was a second letter, unsigned but written in an elegant, familiar hand.

My darling,

As you've heard from our mutual friend, I am safe in Paris. With my uncle gone from the city and back at the front, I don't expect to find much trouble here.

The St. Clairs have proven themselves generous and gracious hosts. Though I must warn you: if you don't hurry back, I fear that Mathieu St. Clair might be very much in danger of falling in love with me, and I with him. How can a girl resist such large brown eyes?

Writing through Jean-Luc seems the best course, for now, as I endeavor to maintain a discreet presence. Paris is much changed. The thing that struck me most upon my return was that passersby no longer seem to look one another in the eye.

Nevertheless, we have some hope—we hear, almost universally, that Napoleon Bonaparte is the leader to restore peace and order to France.

My darling, I am starved for information of you and your whereabouts. Please tell me that you are well. Are you getting enough to eat? Please tell me that you have not again found yourself in the same path as my uncle?

Please, my love, I beg you to promise me that you shall take care of yourself. Stay safe. And know that I remain your loving and devoted,

S

André clung to these letters, reading them and rereading them, glancing around to ensure that none of his fellow sailors witnessed the tears that filled his eyes. These words were a balm to a battered soul; he imagined Sophie—the guarded yet beautiful girl he had first met—now strolling around Paris under the guise of a domestic maid. The most beautiful maid the city could employ. He envied Jean-Luc, Marie, and Mathieu for their easy proximity to her, their ability to see her so often that they no longer thought much of it.

And he thought, too, of how he might ever repay Jean-Luc. Not only for his generosity in harboring Sophie, but for his bravery in simply giving them both such support and assistance. André made a note to himself: once he regained his freedom, if he survived the struggles no doubt yet to come, he would find a way somehow to thank Jean-Luc for all that he had done.

Eventually, André folded the letters and tucked them into the breast pocket of his coat, holding the words close to his heart, where their arrival had kindled a warm and comforting glow after so many months of absolute despair. How he longed to reply!

But he was allowed neither pen nor paper for writing. In the laws of the government and the Army of France, he had been stripped of his commission as an officer. He functioned aboard l'Esprit de Liberté as nothing more than an impressed sailor, his hammock one in a long line of many in the crowded sleeping quarters belowdecks. It was in this hammock each evening that he read and reread these letters, this news of Sophie, wondering when his next word from her might reach him on the vast blue waters on which he served his sentence.

As his stomach settled and his legs became accustomed to the ceaseless rocking of his new, undulating home, André adapted to his surroundings. His skin darkened. His lips—at first stinging and raw in the new climate—became accustomed to the permanent film of salt that seemed to settle on them. His days were predictable, if not a little monotonous. He was aboard one in a number of vessels ceaselessly prowling the waters off the southeastern coast of France, their primary purpose fending off the threat of a naval incursion from the Spanish or, worse, the English. They saw little action in André's squadron, and he most often did battle with the rats that haunted the holds and the gulls that pelleted the deck with their excrement, quickly rendering his hours of scrubbing and sweeping utterly wasted.

Most of André's fellow sailors, gruff men with varying accents as thick as their beards, seemed to regard him with a sort of distrustful yet civil neglect. Oftentimes, upon entering the communal quarters belowdecks, André had the distinct impression that their conversations had ceased abruptly. They tolerated his presence, yet did not invite him to share their fraternal intimacy. The arrangement suited André just fine; after so many months imprisoned in a dank cell, André did not need new friends or confidants.

As he looked out over the vast horizon of rolling blue, André regarded these days aboard *l'Esprit de Liberté* as a period akin to what the nuns in his home village had taught him about purgatory. He would keep his eyes down and his mouth shut and he would do his time, paying the penalty for whatever crime he had committed.

And yet, being out here on the sea was not such a terrible fate compared to the one he'd narrowly escaped in Paris. It was far better than serving a similar sentence in the horrid prison of Le Temple. There was food—salted and dry, to be sure, but enough of it. The maritime work was rote, but it occupied his hours and allowed him a deep, exhausted sleep each evening. His arms and legs, previously strong from youth and years of war, became even stronger, his muscles carved out in well-defined contours from hoisting and climbing. The clear, warm air had expunged the cough he had developed in the drafty, wet dungeon of Le Temple.

And, in spite of his indifference, he'd made one friend.

"You received a note from a woman." Ashar smiled as he approached André on the deck, a roguish grin that creased the dark skin around his black, inquisitive eyes. "Don't bother denying it."

Most days, André didn't mind Ashar's teasing. Most days he might have gone so far as to admit he welcomed the good-natured banter. Much in the same way he would now relish Remy's carefree company.

Ashar came from Egypt, which André had heard of, and liked to remind the others of this, often speaking with vague and lyrical language about the home he had left behind. He rarely talked to the other Arabic-speaking sailors, who came from the Barbary Coast. As an Egyptian, he would claim, he might as well be their king.

Ashar, gaining no reply from André now, continued his teasing banter: "A woman . . . I'm guessing a beautiful one."

"What do you know of beautiful women?" André quipped, and Ashar's eyes twinkled mischievously.

"Perhaps it is more correct to say I know about people." Ashar sat down beside André, glancing sideways at him. "And you? You I know much of."

"Oh?" André leaned back, challenging his friend. "And?"

Ashar studied him keenly, pausing a moment before he answered: "You, my friend, are not like the others. You are different, because of what you have suffered."

André looked out over the sea rolling before them, silenced. The view was an endless expanse of salty blue, and his thoughts teetered back and forth between feelings of his overpowering and unequivocal love for Sophie—and the hatred he carried for her uncle. He also thought of Remy and the last time he had seen him.

"You suffer in silence, which is admirable, but you suffer all the same. And now, I see something has come over you."

André sighed, trying to redirect the conversation. "And what of you, Ashar? What on earth are you doing on this ship?"

"Tut-tut, no need to be rude with me, my friend. I am simply—"

"No, you misunderstand me." André turned, taking his eyes off the horizon to look at his companion. "I mean, how in God's name did you end up here? How is it that an Egyptian philosopher such as yourself is serving in the French navy?"

"Well, that is a good question." It was Ashar's turn to be caught in silent reflection. He sighed a slow exhale before answering. "Allah, peace be upon him, has a plan for all of us. I wonder if I did not stray from his plan, displeasing him. My heart is not wicked, my friend, but I have done wicked things. So, I must submit to his will, until my fate is revealed. It is written."

André stared at his friend for a moment, not sure what to make of this mysterious statement, and decided silence was the best answer. He reflected on his own past, thinking that his heart was not wicked, so how had he earned *this* fate?

A rough smack on his shoulder brought André out of his gloomy meditations, reminding him to get back to his work scrubbing the quarterdeck. Their conversation would have to wait for another time.

Several weeks later, the crew of *l'Esprit de Liberté* were granted a week of shore leave in their port of call, Toulon.

All that week, while André strolled the cobblestoned streets, enjoying tasty bowls of fish stew and the easy hospitality of the restaurant and tavern patrons, he had noticed ever more ships docking at port, each morning bringing the arrival of yet more sails.

Each new French ship meant hordes of men pouring into the city, unshaven and rowdy. The streets of Toulon grew so crowded that André had to weave his way through a swarm of bodies simply to make it from his small inn to the harbor for his morning exercise. There were men everywhere—loud, drunk, scruffy men, pent up from months at sea and eager to visit some of the south's famous taverns and brothels.

It was over dinner on his final night in Toulon that André found his Egyptian friend. André looked up from his garlicky stew into the dark, familiar eyes. "Ashar," he said, greeting him with a genuine smile and pulling him in for an embrace.

Before André had time to offer him a seat, the Egyptian helped himself to the empty chair opposite him and ordered a second bowl of the fish stew.

André lowered his spoon, wiping his mouth. "How has your week been?"

Ashar looked around the terrace, a swarm of sweaty, loud men drinking wine and beer from mugs, circling the few women who were present. "It was . . . enlightening," Ashar said.

André nodded. "Have you heard anything about what we're doing here?"

The Egyptian lifted his hands as if to gesture for André to look around. "Haven't you noticed? Every able-bodied man in service is descending on Toulon."

"I noticed the crowds, yes, but I was unsure of the reason. Do you have news?"

Now it was Ashar's turn to be incredulous. "You haven't heard?"

André shook his head, clearing his throat. "No."

"Why, that mad devil Bonaparte is up to his game again."

None of this was becoming any clearer to André, as his friend answered with these half riddles. "What game is that?"

The Egyptian paused, pulling a parchment out of his tunic and placing it on the table. "Orders of embarkation."

André eyed the paper, then glanced at his friend with a quizzical look.

"General Bonaparte's ambitions are even greater than I had supposed," Ashar said, leaning close to whisper to André. "I've had visits with a minister from the government and an aide to the big man himself. They want me. Need me, in fact."

"I still don't quite—"

"Captain Valière, all these men you see, they are not merely flocking to the south for the women and the wine. We are all part of Bonaparte's mighty flotilla."

André surveyed the crowded terrace once more, eyeing the mass of sailors in their blue-and-white striped shirts, soldiers smoking pipes and breaking out in impromptu drinking songs. "Flotilla for what?"

"The one that will ferry Bonaparte's army to their next conquest: my homeland, Egypt."

Curious onlookers from the surrounding countryside swarmed the jetties and docks of Toulon as General Bonaparte's army and fleet—a moving fortress of thirty-eight thousand soldiers and sailors, four hundred vessels, and France's most distinguished scientists, historians, botanists, artists, and writers—boarded their vessels. Sailors scurried about above and belowdecks as the orders were shouted out under a fierce southern sun. The anchors were lifted and the sails billowed, pregnant with the Mediterranean breezes that would sweep the force farther south toward the African continent.

If not for the intelligence Ashar had provided, André would have been as ignorant as any of the others as to the purpose of their mission. From ensigns to admirals, all had been ordered by General Bonaparte to guard the secrecy of this mission with the utmost discretion.

André could guess why. Though Bonaparte had proven himself seemingly invincible on land, the British still maintained their preeminence when it came to naval power. Moving such a massive fleet of French men and ships safely through British-patrolled waters would require speed and, more important, secrecy.

On the third morning of heading in a southeasterly course through the blue-green Mediterranean, André stood alone, mopping a portion of the portside deck. He listened to the familiar sounds of the sea—the groaning ropes, the gentle *glug-glug* of the waves below that lapped the ship's hull. And then he heard his name being called. "Valière?"

André turned and, to his surprise, spotted the ship's first mate walking toward him. He stiffened, placing down the mop. "Yes, sir."

"Cap'n wants to see you on the quarterdeck."

A pit formed in André's stomach—what had he done to attract the ire of his commander? In his time aboard the ship, he had yet to be flogged, but he'd seen enough of it to dread the punishment. The worst punishment, however, would be an order to return to Paris.

"He's waiting," the first mate added, his tone tinged with impatience.

"Right away, sir." André wiped the suds from his hands and headed to the stern of the ship.

Captain Dueys leaned his stocky frame against the ship's railing, his commander's cap resting atop a head of white hair. It was a clear day, and a gentle breeze glided over the ship, bringing with it the distinct scent of tangy saltwater and the cries of hungry seagulls. All around them the sapphire waters were crowded with other French frigates and flags. Without looking up, the captain acknowledged André's approach. "Captain Valière."

André stood up a little straighter, taken aback at the use of his former rank. "Captain Dueys."

The captain still leaned on the railing, but now he pulled his eyes from the expanse of rolling sea and stared sideways at André. His white beard and breath smelled of tobacco smoke. "At ease."

André lowered his hand.

"You were at Valmy."

André nodded, surprised. "I was, yes. Sir."

The captain now turned back toward the ocean, pulling his pipe from his pocket, his thick fingers stuffing tobacco into its bowl. Captain Dueys lit the pipe and took a long puff, exhaling a fog of fragrant smoke before looking back toward André. "General Kellermann was a fine man. That business back in Paris was a damned mess, a damned bloody mess and a waste."

André felt his features tightening. "I agree, sir."

The captain spoke again, appraising André with his gaze as he did so. "Most of the men on this ship are untested. They've spent the past year mopping up seagull shit and fighting over rum rations."

Not seeing an opening for a response, André remained quiet.

"I need a man with a little hair on his chin, one who has experience leading other men in battle." The terse captain paused at that, taking another long draw from his pipe. When he exhaled, the smell of smoke blew into André's face, mingling with the aromas of salt, wood, and a cooking fire from the galley.

"Valière, I know you were a captain. Before you got into"—he waved his weathered hands—"whatever mess it was you got into back there." Captain Dueys took another puff. "That don't much concern me. This navy don't much care for the squabbles of a few lawyers back in Paris." Another long inhalation of the pipe preceded the captain's next words.

"Any man who was good enough for Christophe Kellermann is bloody good enough for me. When the shooting starts tomorrow . . . you're to stay close and take your orders from me." And now the captain peeled his eyes from the horizon and looked squarely at André. "Are we clear?"

Clear was not the first word that André might have used to describe this conversation, but he nodded. "I am at your service, Captain."

The captain nodded, tapping his chin with the tip of his pipe before eventually muttering: "Good."

They stood silently, André awaiting his orders for dismissal back to his chores. But the captain wasn't finished. "You've never led men at sea?"

"Not at sea, no, sir."

"Well, if that little general . . . that Bonaparte . . . has his way, there won't be much of a sea battle to speak of." The captain turned to André, his red brow creased. He laughed when he read the blatant confusion apparent on André's face. "Tomorrow, our General Bonaparte wants to do something that hasn't been done since before the Holy Crusades."

André swallowed, raising his eyebrows. "If you don't mind my asking, sir, what is that?"

The captain exhaled through his nostrils, sending out two lines of smoke. "He wants to capture Malta. Only problem is the current inhabitants, the Knights of Malta, have no intention of giving it to him."

21

Southern
Mediterranean
Sea

June 1798

"You know why they call it Malta?" Captain Dueys stood beside André in the bright morning light, one weather-hardened hand leaning on the ship's railing as the other held the ever-present pipe to his lips.

"No, sir." André shook his head, eyeing the island before them. "What's the meaning, sir?"

"Means *honey*. Ancient Greeks gave it the name."

André squinted his eyes to gain a better view of the steep, craggy cliffs that jutted up out of the shimmering sapphire water. Against the cloudless blue sky he could just barely make out the silhouette of buildings.

"It's strategic, sure." The captain exhaled. "But we don't need this damned rock. We could just as easily take our objective without it. I think it's the man's pride that needs this island. He wants to add one of the most sacred spots in Christendom to his loot."

Captain Dueys sighed, tobacco-tinged smoke coming out with his exhale. "We'll find out together whether God is keen on that idea or not. If not God, that salty British rascal Admiral Nelson might have something to say. From the rumors I've heard, the damned Brits are out there somewhere, waiting for the right chance to pounce."

André felt a chill run the length of his spine, in spite of the warm sunlight and mild breeze. Just then a thunderous roar clamored from one of the ships nearby, and André winced instinctively. The men aboard his ship, momentarily knocked off balance by the sudden blast, all looked in the direction of the disturbance.

"Bloody hell, it's begun already." Captain Dueys steadied himself on the railing, surveying the surrounding fleet as all around them ships adjusted their sails and slowly tacked toward Malta's harbor and its capital, Valletta. The old captain grumbled as he studied the fleet through his spyglass. "Almost time."

He lowered his spyglass and looked at André, his eyes alert with the thrill of the coming battle. Just then another cannon ripped across the sky. The siege of Malta had officially begun.

"Right, it's time. Valière, when we get close enough to the island, take one of the transport boats off the starboard side with as many men as you can fit. You see them transports rowing into the harbor? Make your way in and join them, see if we can't find out what the hell is going on here."

"Yes, sir." André nodded.

"Oh, and Valière?"

"Sir?"

Dueys looked at him intently. "Today . . . when my men are looking to you . . . you are Captain Valière. You hear me?"

"Yes, sir." André shifted on his feet, trying not to smile. "Thank you."

Dueys waved a hand. "Don't thank me. Just do your job, like you were trained to do."

André lifted a hand in salute. "Yes, sir."

The captain offered a quick salute in return before turning to bark orders at the nearby helmsmen.

As they approached the island, its gray-brown cliffs spiking up out of the sea like a natural fortress, André took a dozen men and huddled them close in the tiny rowboat that hugged the stern of their larger battleship.

A cannon roared from somewhere behind them, and the noise was followed by a cracking sound where it smashed the tall, sand-colored walls ringing the island. The men looking to André winced. The few with oars began the arduous task of rowing toward the shore.

André drew their focus back on him, trying to steady their nerves. "Right, lads, a few more strokes now and we'll ride the surf right onto the beach. Keep your muskets up out of the water—your gunpowder will do you no good if it's doused."

All around them the fire from the fortress batteries was being answered by French artillery. In every direction, André saw parties of men lowering themselves down from the transport ships and rowing themselves ashore. The island's natural harbor appeared shallow and calm, and it hugged the eastern seaside border of a narrow, hilly peninsula. As far as André could tell, none of the Frenchmen were meeting armed resistance on the sandy coast below the cliffs.

The beaches were sunlit and quiet; eerily quiet, devoid of all signs of life save for the cluster of Frenchmen who had already made landfall and the few seagulls that skittered along the edge of the shoreline.

"Come on, the rest of you." He waved his men forward and they climbed off the landing boat, clutching their muskets. Around André, the other transports were slowly and cautiously making landfall as well. No one seemed sure of what to do next. Several of the soldiers, unaccustomed to the small crafts, vomited onto the sand.

Just then, a general's aide appeared on the beach, half running, half stumbling down the seaside hill. "Officers! Officers?" The man's slender features were pinched, his voice shrill as his eyes combed the beach. André watched as several officers stepped forward, answering the summons. He, too, lifted a hand; he hadn't acted in the capacity of an officer for some time, but he had landed on this beach in command of Captain Dueys's men.

The soldier eyed André's tattered sailor's clothes somewhat suspiciously but shrugged his shoulders. "Well, tell your men to stay here on the beach. They are not to leave the harbor until General Dumas comes for them. You there"—he looked straight at André, frowning at the sailor smock—"You're an officer?"

André nodded. "Yes, Captain Valière."

"Right, then, come with me." He paused, once more eyeing André's bizarre appearance, before adding a perfunctory, "Sir."

A half dozen other officers were similarly summoned, and the aide guided them away from the beach and up a steep trail no wider than a single man. It seemed to be a goat's path carved in a meandering fashion through the rock face that hugged the coast of the peninsula. Where they were heading, André did not know.

The day was hot and André was soon sweating through his uniform. His discomfort grew with each step they took away from the beach. Where was the Maltese resistance? The higher they climbed, the more distant the shimmering blue of the Mediterranean became beneath them. Pebbles dislodged by their boots slid down the rocks, falling hundreds of feet below. Who awaited them at the top of this steep climb?

All André knew of the local army, the Knights of Malta, was that they were an ancient order, blessed by Rome since the earliest days of Christianity, and that they had fended off the threat of foreign invasion since the Middle Ages. St. Paul had walked this land, bringing the first words of Christendom with him. He had blessed the Maltese with a special place in the church, and some believed that the Knights guarded the Holy Grail itself, here on this sunlit island named after honey.

Who was this Bonaparte to think that he was somehow the heir to all of this? André wondered.

Eventually the ground leveled, the sea so far beneath them that André could see only rock behind him. All around him, his fellow officers paused. He licked his parched lips, reaching for his canteen to take a sip of water.

"This way now—we cannot stop!" The aide urged them forward; no break for water. A few steps past the end of the goat trail, the path widened, and they followed it in silence. After a tiring march they came upon an open square of cobblestoned alleys and stunning, massive Baroque buildings. Now the men halted in their steps, amazed by the grand scale of the architecture, these structures seemingly dropped down onto the top of a giant rock jutting out of the remote Mediterranean seascape.

A large red flag, inscribed with a white cross, billowed from atop a high, glistening dome. But where were the Knights? The quiet in this city square did more to put André on edge than the sight of an armed horde would have. But as the men stood there, the others seemingly as befuddled as André, he saw not a single armed soldier in Malta's hillside city. There weren't even many civilians, from the looks of it; windows were shuttered, doors shut. Several housewives crossed the square, pulling their young ones closer to their sides as they fixed their eyes on this group of foreigners. Two priests filed past, whispering to each other and casting suspicious glances toward André and his companions. And yet, no sign of the renowned Knights of Malta.

The aide who was leading them on this strange journey now paused to take a drink of water from his canteen, so André did the same. Wiping a sheen of sweat from his brow, the aide broke the silence. "Now, then, I would not have put this question to you in front of the enlisted ranks, but this is of the utmost importance: who here is of noble birth?"

None of the officers answered. Some of them fidgeted; one let out a cough, which echoed off the ancient walls and empty square. Exasperated, the aide sighed. "I assure you, on the honor of our esteemed General Bonaparte himself, this is no trap. The political concerns of Paris hold no import here; this is a matter concerning the success or failure of this mission. Now, I ask again—surely *some* of you must have belonged to the old aristocracy—who among you is noble?"

Still no one stepped forward.

"*Mon dieu!*" The aide, frustrated, pressed his hands together. "How about if I begin the confession? *I* am of noble birth. My former title was Gerald Joseph-Etienne, Comte de Landeville. Now, who else?"

One of André's companions raised a tenuous hand. "I am," he said, his tanned skin matching the chestnut tint of his hair.

"Good! Come closer to me, please." The aide waved the man to his side. "Who else?" He looked over the group. Two others volunteered their secret, stepping forward. André held his silence.

"That is all? Only *three* of you?" The aide looked intently at each of them. There was silence for several moments.

"I am," André said eventually, stepping forward.

The aide looked him up and down. "Good," the man said. "Anyone else? No? Very well, the rest of you stay here. Keep your guard up, but speak to no one. General Dumas shall arrive from the beach shortly. You are to obey his orders without delay."

And suddenly, the aide had an interest only in the four men who stood beside him. "Now then, come with me, my *lords*."

André obeyed, growing more confused with each passing moment.

The domed building was more massive on the inside than it had appeared from the square outside. Here, the insignia of the Maltese flag, the ivory cross outlined in scarlet red, was everywhere. The only symbol more ubiquitous than the flag was the crucifix, which seemed to adorn every doorway, every alcove, every gilded corner. The building was quiet, dark, and cool, and André blinked as his hazel eyes adjusted after the stark midday sunlight of the square outside. It was also, he noticed, completely empty.

They walked for what felt like ages, and yet they never left the building. The soldiers' boots clicked on the cold marble beneath their feet, echoing off walls that were covered in glossy oil paintings and ornate wooden carvings. They crossed room after room until, eventually, they came to a long passageway.

Their French guide, seeming perfectly familiar with the building and how to reach his destination, led his four confused noblemen down the dimly lit hallway, the candles tucked in sconces flickering erratically to their left and right.

At the end of the hallway waited yet another closed door. This one was as large as all the others, but entirely different, for in front of it stood two very tall men. At first André supposed these figures to be statues, so fixed were they in their rigid, sentry-like stances. But as he approached, he saw that they were, in fact, living men. Two guards who appeared to be from another age of the world, each dressed in a white satin tunic with large scarlet crosses emblazoned across their broad chests. They wore swords in scabbards at their waists and the mail of ancient crusaders on their torsos.

The aide paused before these two massive sentries, straightening his own posture but still falling short of their immense frames by many inches. "Your Excellencies." He made a grand bow. "I bring with me four noble lords of France, here as the honored guests of General Napoleon Bonaparte."

André could have fallen over. Did Napoleon Bonaparte stand on the other side of this heavy wooden doorway? And if he did, then why was he, André, being admitted to see him? Just the day before he had been little more than a prisoner scrubbing seagull waste. A captain reinstated only today—if, in fact, he had been reinstated at all. And now, a noble lord and honored guest of the Supreme Commander General Bonaparte?

André tried to stifle the expression of utter bewilderment that he was certain had fixed itself on his features. To his further astonishment, the two armed men guarding the door simply nodded, putting their massive, pawlike hands to the burnished doorknobs and opening the door in a gesture of perfectly coordinated fluidity.

"Here, take this." The aide was beside André now, and as they crossed the threshold, the man stuffed a small velvet pouch into André's hands. "Do not speak until you are addressed." André looked from the pouch to the aide, confused, but before he could open his mouth to inquire as to the meaning of the small, heavy parcel, the party was ushered through the great door into the adjoining room.

"My God." One of their party could not hold back his astonishment upon entering the great hall.

André looked around, overcome, dazzled, incredulous. Circling the ceiling was a series of colorful paintings marking the great and sacred history of the island, and André felt a brief pang of guilt for traipsing into this place, a storied sanctum, at the forefront of a conquering army. His eyes drifted to the other end of the hall, and he counted thirteen men standing before them. Twelve of them were dressed exactly alike, much like the two giants who had guarded the door to this inner chamber. They stood behind an immense oaken table, their faces lined with age, yet free of any emotion or hint of expression. They wore the same white satin tunics emblazoned with red crosses across their chests. Around their necks they wore golden crucifixes that fell just below the tips of their graying beards. They were armed with bejeweled swords and ancient chain mail, and all appeared somehow alike, as if they could have been twelve brothers. The Knights of Malta.

André could have studied these twelve men and their otherworldly appearance for hours, but it was toward the thirteenth man that he found his eyes involuntarily drawn. The thirteenth man in the room—a separate figure who looked nothing like the other twelve.

Napoleon Bonaparte was as André had always heard him described: average stature but appearing smaller as he stood next to these leonine men in ancient mail. He was dressed in a dark blue frock coat with bright red and gold trim on his collar and down the sides. His waist was wrapped in a red and white sash, and a sheathed cavalry saber hung from his belt. On his legs he wore tight-fitting white breeches. His hair, a shock of thick black, fell just above his shoulders. In his hands he held a bicorn hat, removed out of respect, and the other officers entering the room followed his example.

What had drawn André's eyes toward Bonaparte felt like some indefinable magnetic pull. It came, André realized, from the general's facial expression: a look of supreme confidence. He was young, perhaps André's own age, yet hardened beyond his years. His eyes, dark and alert, surveyed the room, taking in the appearance of the new entrants. When he saw André and his three fellow countrymen at the doorway he smiled, as if they were his oldest friends. André felt strangely buoyed by the smile, as if it bestowed an incontrovertible blessing. By stature, Napoleon may have been the shortest man in the room, and yet, André noticed, every single man in the room, even these somber knights, looked to him.

"Ah, and here they are now." Bonaparte spoke with the faint traces of his foreign Corsican accent. He held out a gloved hand, summoning the new arrivals toward him.

"Your Excellencies." Bonaparte turned toward the twelve knights. "Allow me to introduce four of my friends. Lords of France. We come bearing a precious gift as a token of our appreciation. And gratitude that you have let us dock in your harbor while we rest and replenish our supplies. Now, my friends." Bonaparte angled his small narrow frame toward André and his three flabbergasted companions. "Who has the gift?"

None of them replied, the aide having mentioned nothing about gifts. Or knights. Or General Bonaparte.

"Well, then?" Bonaparte extended a small, gloved hand, his smile appearing suddenly impatient.

The aide stepped forward from the shadows. "He does, Your Excellency." To André's surprise, the aide had placed a hand on his own shoulder. André turned to the aide, his eyes spelling out his bewilderment.

"The *pouch*," the aide whispered, and André remembered the small, heavy velvet bag in his hands. And then he understood.

"I do," André blurted out, holding up the pouch.

"Bring it here," Bonaparte said, with a quick flick of his wrist. André stepped forward, his eyes fixed on the general as he handed the velvet pouch forward. Bonaparte took the pouch in his hands. "Thank you, my lord." He smiled, his dark eyes holding André's for just a second in a steady gaze. In that moment, André was taken aback and found himself staring, mesmerized, at the short man before him, instinctively aware of the power and will in those dark, vibrant eyes.

Bonaparte turned abruptly and approached the line of knights, holding the pouch before him like a sacred object. "To the men carrying on the tradition of St. Paul himself." He bowed his head as he would before an altar. "Please accept this ancient and sacred treasure of our realm." The general placed the pouch in the hand of the knight nearest to him, offering it with another bow. The man murmured a quiet offering of thanks, his face as expressionless as stone.

When he revealed the contents of the pouch, an audible gasp rippled across the room, as all twelve knights and each of André's companions reacted in the same way. It was a cross: a massive cross, but not simply gold, or silver, or even rubies. This was a cross of large, shimmering diamonds, bordered with sapphires that shone with the same brilliance as the Mediterranean Sea below.

André felt dizzy, knowing that he had held such a precious object in his hands, if only for a moment. He knew, instantly, from where it came: the Bourbon Court. This had been a treasure fit for the world's wealthiest king. And now it was General Bonaparte's treasure to give away.

Sensing the impression his gift had made on the room, the general paused a moment, smiling. "Now you see, Your Excellencies, that we come in good faith." The knights nodded, their eyes still fixed on the dazzling cross that they now passed among themselves.

"Please accept this treasure as a token of our humble gratitude." Bonaparte bowed again. His eyes darted quickly toward the aide. If André hadn't been watching him—if he'd been distracted, as every other man in the room was, by the glimmering cross—then he wouldn't have seen it. Wouldn't have tensed. Wouldn't have reached involuntarily for the pistol at his waist.

But then, before he or anyone else understood what was happening, the doors opened with a crash and in rushed scores of soldiers with muskets and fixed bayonets. André turned in their direction, his eyes widening in shock. But it was not a group of Maltese warriors who stormed this sacred chamber, filling it like a flood. They were soldiers dressed in blue coats, his countrymen. The two massive guards at the door looked on, their eyes filled with shock as they saw their threshold breached, and the swords held to their throats rendering them powerless to stop the advance.

Bonaparte was now disinterested in the cross of diamonds, his four noble visitors, or the twelve Knights of Malta. As armed men descended on the knights, the ancient-looking men reached for their swords but quickly realized that resistance was futile.

"Do not harm them!" Bonaparte yelled. Strutting through the parting crowd as he crossed the room, he stuffed the bicorn hat back onto his head. "My lords, allow me to offer my most humble apologies for this brief display of hostility. Know that the Republic and people of France hold you and your kingdom in the highest esteem. Consider this the hour of your liberation."

With that, General Bonaparte turned to the French soldiers and officers now flooding the great hall. His hat fixed at a jaunty angle across his haughty brow, his right fist raised high in the air, he cried out: "In the name of liberty, equality, and fraternity, I claim this realm, and all of its treasure, as the property of the French Republic! The Kingdom of Malta is now ours!"

22

Paris

Spring 1798

Jean-Luc stretched his hands, straightening his cramped fingers before he drew more ink upward into his quill. The tedium of this day was, mercifully, nearly done.

"You haven't looked up once all day, St. Clair." Jean-Luc recognized the familiar voice of Gavreau as his supervisor approached his desk. "I could have paraded a line of large-breasted wenches in here and you wouldn't even have seen 'em."

Jean-Luc lowered his quill onto the top piece of parchment, his black cursive covering nearly every inch of the paper with names and figures.

"And have the good bishop's silverware, silks, and gold plate been properly cataloged for our public records?"

"I'm nearly done," Jean-Luc said, rubbing an ink stain from the side of his aching palm. His latest assignment had been an onerous one: a large and wealthy monastery to the northwest of the city had been ransacked by a band of starving farmers. Jean-Luc had spent the past two weeks buried in lists of the property's riches. Mercifully, the bishop and his household had been spared, but it appeared that, even after the looting party had taken their share of the plunder, the Directory was now owner of quite a few new gold-plated communion dishes and silken robes.

"I hate to tell you this." Gavreau leaned on Jean-Luc's desk, eyeing the lists of inventory his employee had meticulously documented. "When you've finished with this, I've got something else to show you."

"What is it?" Jean-Luc asked, certain that his features betrayed his fatigue.

"The Saint-Jacques church has been razed."

Wordless, Jean-Luc let his expression convey his confusion. Razed?

"Torn completely to the ground." Gavreau nodded, folding his arms in front of his broad belly. "All that remains is the bell tower. Seems the looters couldn't quite figure out how to bring that one down."

Jean-Luc propped his elbows on his table and lowered his head into his hands. Yet another church here in Paris, sacked and looted. More priceless relics defiled, more nuns and priests hauled off. He wondered, as he had every time before, what good would come of this?

"One might have hoped, with the number of rich nobles and clergymen whose estates have been plundered, that the poor folk of this city might at least have a bit of bread. A few spare coins to pay for simple medicines," Jean-Luc said quietly, so that only his friend might hear. "And yet, I think the poor of this city are worse off than ever before." His shoulders were cramped; his entire body felt heavy. "At this point," Jean-Luc continued, rubbing the flesh between his two eyes in slow, circular motions, "I almost hope for one of those men in the Directory, or even one of those generals, to lay down his fist and get this place in order."

"You?"

"Anything to halt this anarchy." Jean-Luc sighed. "I don't know how much more of this we can stand, beasts running amok."

"They say that Bonaparte fellow is something of a genius—and ambitious, too. At least he's whipped the army into shape."

"Well, I don't think he'll be returning today, or anytime soon for that matter." His thoughts briefly drifted to his friend André Valière, who was somewhere at sea, among Bonaparte's massive flotilla that had left from the Mediterranean ports. "Or my good friend André. Godspeed, André."

His boss heard this and cocked an eyebrow, as if Jean-Luc were losing his wits. Perhaps he was, Jean-Luc mused to himself. "Yes, well . . . Anyhow, do you have a minute for me to show you what I'm speaking of?"

"What is it, exactly?" Jean-Luc asked.

"Some of the spoils of Saint-Jacques; they've started carting over the goods. I've had them haul it into the basement with the rest of the loot."

"Very well." Jean-Luc pushed himself up from his desk, looking forlornly at the day's unfinished documents. "Let's get this over with."

✄

The basement was cool and dimly lit, with clerks and commissaries buzzing about to deposit marble statues, leather Psalters and hymnbooks, and altar vases of tarnished silver and gold.

Gavreau let out a prolonged whistle and shook his head. "These priests lived well. I'm surprised they held on to this treasure this long." He weaved through a row of marble statues as Jean-Luc followed behind. The seized sculptures—carved figures of angels, saints, and wealthy church patrons—waited in various stages of ruination, each one's condition depending on the attention it had received from the mob that had plucked it from the ancient church of Saint-Jacques.

Jean-Luc paused, looking at a marble rendition of what was surely the biblical scene of the sacrifice of Isaac. The figure of Abraham stood, his muscles carved like fine sinewy ropes, his face contorted in the agony and knowledge of his coming sacrifice. Abraham was almost entirely intact, while Isaac, the son whose blood was to be spilled by the father, had been completely battered and smashed. All that remained was the neck resting in his father's strong grip. "Christ in heaven," Jean-Luc said, stepping aside so that a worker could deposit the cracked figure of Mary Magdalene beside Abraham and Isaac.

"Allowed this to happen . . . I'd say," Gavreau said, fingering a fragment of burgundy silk that appeared to have been a priest's robe.

"God did a curious thing, granting free will to such wild creatures as we are." Jean-Luc ran his hands through his disheveled hair, gazing around at the growing cache of holy goods.

In truth, even after years of work overseeing and cataloging confiscated belongings, Jean-Luc had never quite grown comfortable with being in this cellar. He had never been able to separate these ornate treasures from the individuals who had been similarly seized, their own fates forfeited to the new nation. His imagination drifted when he saw a simple maple table and empty chairs, never again to gather a family of parents and children for supper. Food had been scarce in the preceding years, to be sure, and though families of aristocratic stock had once dined like gluttons, it was clear enough to see in this room that not all of these belongings had come from noble houses. Held somewhere within each of these confiscated heirlooms was the story and mystery of a soul that had hoped, wished, feared, and loved; most of them were now departed from this world forever.

"All this," Gavreau said, raising his hands to mark the delineation of the day's haul. "The rest you've already seen, I reckon."

Jean-Luc nodded, eyeing the rows of new inventory.

"You can't get to it all today. Come on, let me buy you a drink." Gavreau put a hand on his employee's shoulder. "You look as if you've seen a ghost."

Jean-Luc nodded, his entire frame shivering in this dark basement. "Hundreds, in fact."

Outside the office building the workers still swarmed, carrying armfuls of cloth, stained glass, and prayer books. Jean-Luc paused before a particularly arresting statue. It was an angel, easily twice the size of a tall man, the face wild and windswept as if caught in the current of some great celestial storm. The angel's arms were thick with muscle, and his hands—giant bearlike paws—were raised aloft. One hand he held out as if in blessing, the other clutched a spear. Whether it was a weapon for battle or a spear of heavenly light was unclear, perhaps intentionally so.

"Michael," Jean-Luc said, peering into the marble eyes of the angel, their expression severe, savage even, ready to carry out the Lord's fierce grace.

"Pardon?"

"Michael the archangel," Jean-Luc explained.

"Which one was Michael?" Gavreau asked.

"Come now, you've forgotten your catechism?"

"These days, who hasn't?"

"Michael was the archangel who led God's army," Jean-Luc said.

"That so? So we've come to that—even the angel of warfare falls before the mob," Gavreau muttered. "But this one's not from Saint-Jacques. All this"—the boss gestured at the nearby cluster of statues—"comes from some noble's estate nearby. Montnoir. Eh, you're familiar with that old marquis, aren't you?"

"Montnoir." Jean-Luc considered the name a moment before he remembered. "The Montnoir estate. The Widow Poitier! That place?" Jean-Luc looked at his supervisor questioningly.

"Indeed, the very same. That dreadful old lord you had removed from his castle at the same time you got that old widow put back into her cottage on his estate. Seems she's been petitioning the government ever since—years—for someone to come out and seize the old nobleman's riches. We finally got out there, and"—Gavreau let out a snort—"seems the old man had an appetite not only for his women, but for holy art as well. I'd guess this one's an altarpiece, based on the size of it." Gavreau gestured back toward the massive statue of Michael the archangel. "Anyway, you've got that old woman to thank for passing you more work."

Jean-Luc nodded, and yet he couldn't pull his eyes away from the statue: that stare, those eyes. The archangel Michael appeared alive—even responsive—conveying a judgment, or perhaps a challenge, to anyone who dared look into his face.

Gavreau fidgeted beside Jean-Luc. "Shame to stick the angel of war in the basement. The Republic might need him yet." His impatience growing, he gestured to Jean-Luc. "Come now, I need a drink."

The days were long and the evening sun pierced the curtained windows in gentle spears of light as they sat inside the café, sharing a bottle of wine. "This *Bonaparte* will name himself supreme commander of the entire army soon enough. From there, it's an easy step to king. Or emperor, even. It's the only way I see of bringing some order back to this madness."

Jean-Luc sat opposite his boss, nodding heavily. Had all of this, all these years of chaos, been for nothing more than to replace a king with an emperor? And yet, thinking about it, he could not entirely disagree with Gavreau. Perhaps the French people had forfeited their right to a democratic government, so base had been their handling of the new nation's liberties.

"He seems pretty well occupied in the Mediterranean at the moment. First taking Malta, and now sailing for Africa." Jean-Luc took a sip of wine.

"He'll take Egypt," Gavreau agreed. "But when he gets bored of war, he'll come back to Paris and find himself a crown."

"Just like Caesar." Jean-Luc sighed, looking out the window at the steady stream of passersby. It was amazing how, no matter what happened, life in Paris seemed to go on. Students still gathered in the inns for supper. Mothers still chased children through the foot traffic. Lovers still paused at every corner, exchanging kisses and promises for the future—as if they had any control over their own fates. They were willful and obdurate, the Parisians were, to continue to *live*. To do so as if the future were theirs, even when these past years had taught them that it most certainly was not.

Did they not realize that the future of their country was being decided, at that very moment, by distant actors and unseen events? That, thousands of miles away, the French fleet was sailing the Mediterranean, its sights set on war—the outcome of which would change the fate of not only their nation but also the world?

Jean-Luc wondered, as much for Sophie's sake as his own, where André was. Somewhere in the Mediterranean, with Bonaparte's fleet. Was he part of the party sailing for Africa?

"When that happens . . . when Bonaparte comes back and restores some order to this place"—Gavreau drained his wineglass—"the first thing I plan to do is recommend you for a promotion to the Directory."

Jean-Luc turned his gaze and his focus back to his employer, his eyes widening at the statement.

"Don't argue with me on this, St. Clair. I know you've bucked in the past when I've tried to recommend you. I know that the thought of working every day alongside or opposite Guillaume Lazare makes you about as comfortable as the thought of pissing over a pit of snakes. And I cannot entirely blame you for that. There's something *not right* with that fellow. I just . . . I just regret that I put you in his path."

Jean-Luc waved this last comment away. "All you did was introduce me to his colleague, Merignac. It was not your fault. It was I who sought out Lazare's acquaintance and his camaraderie," Jean-Luc admitted.

"Aye, but . . ." Gavreau hesitated. "I'm not entirely innocent, I regret to say."

Jean-Luc frowned, confused. "What do you mean?"

"Merignac . . . he came to me looking for . . . an acolyte."

"I don't understand."

"You know that Lazare. How he always seeks to have his minions. His 'Little Projects,' he calls them. His band of disciples, even if he's not Christ. Hell, perhaps he's the Antichrist."

Jean-Luc nodded, yes. He did understand, for his mind went back to the Jacobin Club on Rue Saint-Honoré, the first night he'd met Lazare, and how they'd been surrounded by a band of admirers; the men had been wordless in their subservience and attendance to Lazare, their undisputed sage and master.

"Well, Merignac came to me, saying that Lazare wanted a bright new talent from within our department. Someone he could mentor. I recommended you, of course."

Jean-Luc felt a chill pass over his body, in spite of the warmth of the café.

"Thought it would be a good opportunity for you. You were my most talented, most hardworking clerk. Ambitious, too. I regretted that the only work I could give you was bureaucratic drudgery. But now . . . well, now, I regret ever putting you in front of him."

Jean-Luc understood, in that moment, just how wrong he'd been. He'd supposed that Lazare had sought him out for the quality of his work. That the prodigious lawyer had followed his career from afar and had respected his service to the Revolution. That all this time, Gavreau had been pushed aside and not invited into the acquaintance with Lazare. But, in truth, Gavreau had been the one to pull Jean-Luc into Lazare's orbit, had been the one to facilitate the relationship—a relationship from which Jean-Luc now longed to escape.

"So, that dinner, that first time you introduced me to Merignac?"

"It was an interview . . . of sorts." Gavreau nodded, averting his eyes. "You passed, whatever that means. 'Course now, I fear that Lazare was less interested in mentoring you and more interested in molding you; I suspect you've proven a frustrating prospect to him as a result, you and your damned character and integrity." Gavreau leaned closer, his voice low and uncharacteristically devoid of jest. "Just . . . just don't let him get too close."

"No." Jean-Luc frowned.

"He's very intrigued by the work you do. He's always asking about your cases and your files. Just be careful . . . I wouldn't let him get much closer. To you . . . or your family. And whatever you do, keep him out of your office."

Jean-Luc nodded, agreeing. He wanted that man out of his life entirely. "Perhaps I should just . . ." Jean-Luc hesitated. "Perhaps this was all a mistake," he said, his tone sour. "I should pack up Marie and Mathieu and take us all back to the south where we started. The hell with them all—Lazare, Merignac, the damned Directory."

"No, no," Gavreau growled. "None of that defeatist talk. Don't turn cynic on me now, St. Clair. We're so close, at last. Hear this, the one bright spot: the days of lawyers terrorizing Paris are almost over." Gavreau leaned back in his chair. "When General Bonaparte comes back, things will be different. He'll bring the army and pack up that guillotine and restore order so that folks like Lazare won't be ruling with fear. And you'll get your promotion in the new regime. You'll finally be playing the role in this damned nation that you deserve."

Jean-Luc lowered his eyes and thought about this. *Did* he want that? Did he still crave a prominent role in shaping this nation's course? Wasn't it his ambition that had driven him into the troubles he currently faced?

"Come now, St. Clair. Surely you and Marie aren't going to give up now? Think of it: a real role in a new government. Moving out of that cramped garret. You can't tell me you haven't been thinking about your future."

"I suppose"—Jean-Luc paused, rubbing his palms together—"that somewhere along the way, I allowed myself to lose hope in what the future could bring."

"None of that." Gavreau shook his head. "You're my optimist. If *you* lose hope, what becomes of the rest of us, who had hardly any to begin with? No, no, no. This war will end and Paris will get back to itself. And when that happens, you'll be a representative in the Council of Five Hundred. You're far too good a lawyer, and man, to be squandering your talents behind a desk, counting silver spoons. Or worse, pruning lemon trees in the south."

Jean-Luc couldn't help but smile now as he stared at the ruddy, earnest face of his employer. He sat for a moment in silence, thinking it all over, before he sighed. "Thank you, Gavreau."

"It's I who ought to thank you. Not sure what I would have done had I not had you all these years."

At home, the living room was warm and the air smelled of roasting chicken. Marie looked up from the table when her husband entered. She had a small pile of papers spread before her, which she quickly folded up and tucked into a pocket of her frock. "My love, you're home!" She practically ran across the room to greet him, her brown eyes more alight than usual as she balanced on her toes to kiss her husband.

"Still reading the journals, I see?" he asked her, curious as to what she had been doing and why she had been so quick to tuck it out of sight.

"Oh, just a bit of gossip from the salons," she said, waving her hands. "Nothing important."

Jean-Luc looked around the room. "It's quiet. Where are Sophie and Mathieu?"

"I've sent them out on an errand," Marie said as she removed her husband's coat, giving him another excited kiss. "And I'm glad of this moment of peace, I confess, because I have news."

"Oh?" Jean-Luc arched an eyebrow. "And I do, as well." He planned to tell her about his conversation with Gavreau, and his hope, recently rekindled, of actually building a career in the new nation's government. "But you look so pleased and eager with yours that you ought to share yours first." He wrapped his arms around her waist, but she stopped him, instead taking his hands in her own and guiding them to her belly.

"Feel that?" she said, her pretty features spreading into the glow of a wide smile. Jean-Luc felt his heart jump in his chest.

"Really?" he asked, his voice barely a whisper.

"Really." Marie laughed now. "This tiny apartment is about to get a bit more crowded."

"How marvelous!" He picked her up at the waist, twirling her around the room.

She looked into his eyes, her own brimming with delight. "Are you happy?"

"I could think of nothing that would make me happier." He leaned forward and kissed her once more. "How can we have been so blessed?"

Marie beamed. "To think . . . another little one. *Now* will you agree it's a good thing Sophie is here, to help me?"

"When will Mathieu and Sophie return?" Jean-Luc was eager to tell Mathieu that he would be a brother.

"They should be back any moment. I sent them down to fetch a loaf for supper," Marie answered, turning to check on the chicken where it roasted over the fire.

Jean-Luc helped himself to a glass of wine and sat at the table, feeling a contentment unlike anything he had experienced in recent memory. "I told you I had news as well."

"Oh, yes, I completely forgot." Marie looked back toward him expectantly. "What is it?"

"Perhaps we won't have to be crowded in this garret when the little one comes, after all."

"Oh?" Marie smiled, the hope plain across her lovely, dark features. Jean-Luc relayed to his wife the contents of his discussion with his supervisor and his expected promotion to the Directory, the nation's governing body.

"Good news, indeed! But how soon can we move? If only we could be out before the new one arrives." Marie clasped her hands together, her features bright as she surveyed their cramped home.

"Is it really so bad here?" Jean-Luc teased, glancing around the low-ceilinged room; he had to admit to a certain attachment, even an affection, for the place. An attachment he knew had little to do with this shabby dwelling but everything to do with Marie, and Mathieu, and the family they had begun to build, together, in this home. This place that had witnessed their first years together, and all of the triumphs, defeats, and memories they had shared.

As the minutes passed and the evening outside darkened, Jean-Luc's belly filled with warmth, and he basked in the comfortable glow of their hopes in the future. The moonlight poured into the room as he helped himself to another glass of wine. And still, he and Marie waited.

"What hour is it?" he asked after a while.

Marie paused where she stood, stirring a bowl of potatoes to prevent them from sticking as they grew cold in the juices of the chicken; a rare feast, and she had clearly splurged on procuring it, in honor of her celebratory news. She checked her timepiece. "Almost eight. How long has it been since you returned home?"

"Nearly an hour," Jean-Luc answered.

At this the smile slid ever so slightly from Marie's features, replaced by a thoughtful crease of her brow. "I can't think what would be keeping them."

Jean-Luc glanced out the window over the street. "They went to the baker? On Rue de Tolbiac?"

"Yes."

"But that surely should not have taken an hour?" Jean-Luc turned back to his wife.

"No," Marie said, shaking her head.

Just then the door to the room burst open, and Sophie's trembling frame appeared in the doorway. Sophie panted, her breath uneven and her eyes frantic with a look of terror. "I've lost him!"

Jean-Luc felt cold dread freeze the blood in his veins, driving away the contentment and warmth he had felt mere minutes ago.

"'Lost him'?" Marie looked at Sophie, her own voice faint.

"Mathieu," Sophie panted. "I turned my back for one moment and he was *gone*."

"Where?" Jean-Luc rose and crossed the room toward Sophie.

"In the baker's. It was so crowded. I took my eyes off him for a moment to pay for the loaf and when I looked back, he had vanished. He's run away!"

"Run away?" Marie gasped, her face ashen as she turned to her husband. "No, he's a good boy. He would never just run away. That's impossible!" Marie shook her head violently, charging toward the door of their apartment where her cloak hung on a hook before the entrance. Sophie stood motionless, trying to place the scene where she had last seen him.

Jean-Luc looked at his wife, sensing the panic that she now shared. He should have known: his good fortune to hear of a new child and a career advancement on the same day surely would not come without a price.

Fate could not be so kind as to grant these blessings without exacting some penalty. No one had the right to feel blessed in times such as these.

He stood, crossing the room in two strides. "Marie, you stay here, in case he returns home. I shall go."

No one in the neighborhood had seen the little boy leave the baker's. Nor had they seen him on the nearby streets. Panting, Jean-Luc raced across the bridge, crossing the calm waters of the Seine where the boats glided along the surface. He could not have explained it in any logical way, but his course was set for the Right Bank. He suspected, without knowing why, that that was where his little boy would have wandered.

The air was warm and the pedestrians marched at a languid pace, laughing freely as they enjoyed the balmy evening. Along the quay heading south, Jean-Luc spotted a little boy, his small little head covered in dark curls, his light summer coat and short strides the same as Mathieu's. The boy was leaning over the embankment, endeavoring to get a better view of a barge that passed beneath.

"Mathieu!" Jean-Luc could have wept in relief. He sprinted toward the little figure, clasping a hand on his narrow shoulder to pull him back from the water's edge. "Mathieu, you are very naughty to have run away! *Maman* and I were very frightened that you'd—" Jean-Luc wheeled the little boy around and gasped aloud when he stared into a face, a set of features entirely foreign to him. The little boy, stunned by the rough treatment at the hands of a stranger, began to cry.

"Oh, I'm . . . I'm terribly sorry . . ." Jean-Luc stammered, pulling his hand away.

"What are you on about, eh, taking hold of my boy like that?" An angry housewife, stout and red-faced, stepped between the little boy and Jean-Luc.

"I am sorry, madame, I was mistaken." Jean-Luc stared at the boy, blinking.

"Mistaken indeed. Now be off with you, before I report you to the *gendarmes!*"

Jean-Luc glanced one more time at the boy before he turned and raced back along the quay. The crowds in the streets were thinning now as candlelight began to flicker behind shuttered windows. Jean-Luc's lungs ached from the effort of his running, but still he weaved his way through the streets and narrow alleys, calling out for his boy.

After a quarter of an hour of running, he turned a corner near Rue de Cléry and nearly charged face-first into a blue-coated guardsman. "Easy, there!" The man stood smoking a long pipe. He eyed Jean-Luc with a mixture of disapproval and mistrust, as if deciding whether there was something for which he ought to arrest him.

His breath frantic and uneven, Jean-Luc stammered out the reason for his frantic chase. "Please, good citizen! My boy . . . a little boy." Jean-Luc raised a hand to where Mathieu's height would fall against his leg. "Six. Dark hair like his mother's . . ."

Through a piecemeal explanation, Jean-Luc relayed the urgency of his search, and the officer promised to keep an eye out for the child. "It's highly likely, citizen, that he just wandered off looking for some mischief and, growing tired, or bored, has returned home. We see it all the time. Either way, he wouldn't have come *this* far. You're much better off returning to your own neighborhood."

Jean-Luc thought about this, considering it to be possible. Perhaps Mathieu was home right now, safe and happy as he ate some of the roast chicken that Marie had prepared for their supper. "Home? Yes, perhaps you're right. Perhaps he's gone home."

With that, he sought the officer's assurance that the *gendarmes* would search that evening for a little boy with dark hair and dark eyes. And gaining that promise, he set off toward home, sprinting back across the river.

Back on the Left Bank, his neighborhood was quiet and the streets were empty, save for a few students and a barking dog. As he came upon his building, he spotted a familiar coach. The dread in his belly thickened, and he stopped in his footsteps, gasping to steady his breath; Guillaume Lazare stood outside the coach.

"Citizen St. Clair." The old man opened the carriage door when Jean-Luc approached. "You look fatigued. Please, have a seat."

"Not now, Lazare." Jean-Luc barely paused, still marching toward the door that would take him inside his building.

"I shall not detain you for long. I have news concerning a matter that may be of interest to you." Guillaume Lazare slipped a black box of snuff from a pocket in his jacket, spilled some of the contents onto his hand, and sniffed it in one swift gesture.

Jean-Luc paused in his steps, noticing the peculiar silence of the street around him.

"Your son," Lazare said, his voice barely a whisper. "Have you found him?"

Jean-Luc turned toward the carriage, his entire frame rigid. All that was in him longed to lurch forward and take Lazare's thin, reedy neck in his hands. If he had wanted to, he could have snapped it in two. "Where is my son?"

"Come in, have a seat." Lazare retreated back into the darkness of the coach, his figure concealed in shadow as he left the door ajar. Jean-Luc forced himself to climb into the velvet interior.

"You tell me where my son is."

"Care for any?" Lazare, his white face enshrouded in darkness, extended the small case of snuff.

"No." Jean-Luc waved it away. Lazare poured another small sprinkling on his hand, which he snorted through his thin nose with two quick gasps. Sighing, he leaned his head back, his emotionless eyes holding Jean-Luc in their steady gaze.

After a pause that seemed interminable, the old man spoke. "Seems your boy stole some bread from the baker. Tried to make a dash for it."

"That's a lie." Jean-Luc leaned forward. "He has never stolen. Would never do such a thing, not when he was there with his own . . . aunt . . . who had the money to pay for the bread."

"His *aunt*, you say?" Lazare tittered, his narrow teeth glistening in the shadows of the coach as he sneered. "Well now, I'm simply reporting what I heard."

"Where is he?"

"He has been detained."

"Detained? But this is preposterous! He's just a child!"

"I am telling you what I know, Citizen St. Clair. I am a man of the law; justice is the only master I serve. You know that."

Jean-Luc narrowed his eyes, allowing himself to admit, for the first time, that this man was his enemy. This powerful, cunning man. He knew, in that moment, that Lazare would accept nothing more out of Jean-Luc than pleading. Submission. Absolute surrender.

And so that was what he, a desperate father, would give. "Please, Lazare. I will do whatever you ask. Just give him back."

"I'd like to help you, St. Clair. I believe that it's a bit . . . *excessive* . . . to detain your little boy. Why, he wouldn't last more than a month in those dungeons. If it's not the other prisoners, it'll be the malnourishment. Or the diseases, the way they spread in this heat."

Jean-Luc balled his fists so tightly that his nails dug into his palms. "Where is he, Lazare?"

"Come now, no need to be short with me."

"Tell me where my son is!"

Lazare leaned his head to the side, whistling a sigh through his pale lips. "Would you like my help?"

"You know I want my boy out of prison. I beg you to tell me: what do you want?"

Lazare's eyes were unblinking as he sat across from Jean-Luc in the shadowy coach. His face, after a long look of thoughtfulness, eventually folded upward, his lips spreading into a thin smile.

"What do I want?"

Jean-Luc swallowed, staring at the face opposite him.

"How about an exchange?" Lazare leaned forward, his voice quiet as he continued. "I shall help you get your darling son back, and, in return, you help me get something I've wanted for a very long time."

"Tell me—whatever it is, I will do it."

"It's simple. And I do believe that you are capable of arranging it."

"What? Tell me."

"Give me Sophie de Vincennes."

Jean-Luc fell silent, the impact of these words blunting his ability to reply, even to think. A trade? This man, this sadistic man, was really holding his little boy hostage in order to gain access to Sophie? Jean-Luc stammered, his thoughts awhirl with the desperate need to save his child and to find a way to protect Sophie. Before he could reply, another voice filled the street, and Jean-Luc heard it through the open door of the coach.

"He doesn't have to. I am here. I will go with you, willingly."

Jean-Luc turned and saw Sophie standing on the street. She wore her travel cloak, her face an implacable mask. "I will go with you. But not until you've returned Mathieu."

"Sophie." Jean-Luc stepped out of the coach and toward her. "This is madness. An exchange? This is utter madness. Surely we live in a land of laws. Mathieu has broken no laws. We must think—"

Sophie held up a gloved hand, resolute. Her eyes communicated her message; they both knew this was a land devoid of the law. This was a land where people in power made the choices, and people without power paid—often with their lives. "I am through allowing others to suffer . . . allowing others to sacrifice themselves for me. Not this time. Not like Remy. Not like André. No, Mathieu will not suffer. Nor will you or Marie, not after the kindness you've shown me. I will go. I go freely." She turned from Jean-Luc to Lazare, her posture rigid with her defiance. "Bring back the boy at once, and I'll go wherever you take me."

23

Mediterranean
Sea

Summer 1798

André's stay on Malta was brief. After a sleepless night in a dark, cramped upper bedroom of a private dwelling in the Maltese capital, he and the rest of the French force were ordered back to the harbor below where their ships waited, ready to lift anchors.

"André Valière?" A heavily mustached soldier blocked André's way at the top of the gangway to his ship.

"Captain Valière," André corrected him. "What do you want?"

"You are hereby placed under arrest." The sergeant nodded and two soldiers appeared behind André, taking his hands in their thick fists and clamping irons around his wrists.

"What do you think you're doing?" André struggled uselessly against their collective force, glaring at the sergeant. "Need I remind you that I am an army captain serving aboard this ship? I've been reinstated by Captain Dueys. I just took part in the capture of Malta, in the presence of General Bonaparte himself."

"Ah, yes, the young *nobleman* who played such a significant role. You held a velvet pouch, was that it?"

André knew that voice. He wheeled around to behold a familiar face—pale gray eyes and inky black hair.

"Good to see you again, Valière." General Murat stood before André dressed in a clean brigadier general's uniform, a tricolor sash across his waist, a mirthless smile on his lips. "Thought you could escape your sentence just because you were floating in the middle of the Mediterranean? Have you forgotten that our Revolutionary justice extends beyond our borders?"

"I serve on this ship for Captain Dueys." André raised his chin, speaking with an authority that belied his inner dread. "I am here on orders as a member of General Bonaparte's Army of the Orient." His words rang hollow, and both men knew it.

Murat waved a hand as if in boredom. "Captain Dueys has been . . . reminded . . . of the situation." The general smirked. "Some of my colleagues have short memories, I'm afraid." Murat stood so close now that André could smell his breath. "But I haven't forgotten. No, I will never forget. You are a prisoner exiled from the Republic, not a hero in pursuit of the glory that rightfully belongs to other men."

André struggled now, futilely writhing and bucking against the bindings that locked his wrists in place. Across the deck, he spotted the white-haired captain who looked on, his face heavy. Dueys shook his head, as if in apology, but did not step forward to intervene.

"I am the commanding authority aboard this ship right now, Valière," Murat growled, his voice low. "Take him below!" And, with that, André was swept out of the clear, sun-washed afternoon and pulled belowdecks. A door creaked open and he was tossed inside like a sack. After blinking his eyes desperately in the darkness of a windowless room, André shouted, his voice hoarse. "Let me out! Let me out, you bastards! Open this damned door!"

How was it possible he could have come all this way, survived this long, only to be back within the grasp of that hateful man? His disbelief and shock turned once again to white-hot fury and he pounded his fists on the locked door, his voice rabid as he screamed into the darkness.

On the other side André heard laughter, a high-pitched cackle from one of the soldiers standing outside the cell. That laughter sapped the final ember of hope, and André shut his eyes, allowing everything to go dark.

There was no way to gauge the passage of time in the black cell. No way to see the rising of the sun, or the appearance of distant shapes forming up out of mountainous shores and islands.

All André knew, down below, was that the slit in the lower half of the door opened twice in any given day: once, he assumed, in the morning, once in the evening. Though he groped at the door, demanding an audience with Captain Dueys each time he heard the creaky slat groan its way open, he was never answered by a human voice. His only reply was the careless toss of a hand, sending in a piece of black, hard bread and a small bowl of dirty water, half its contents spilled by the time it landed on the floor of André's cell.

Toward the top of the thick oaken door was a lattice, a small window lined with bars. If opened from the outside, it might let in a small square of light. Many times the small slit below had been pried open, resulting in an issuance of bread and water, but this upper lattice had never been opened.

And so it was the opening of this window that stirred André from his troubled, numbed reverie. He heard the noise, first, before he saw the sudden spear of light. The glow, though nothing more than a small sliver of a candle's flame, blinded him with the force of a hundred suns, and he put his hand to his eyes.

"Who's there?" André's voice was hoarse, his throat dry. He blinked, suddenly stunned after what seemed like days of uninterrupted darkness.

"Captain Valière?"

As André's eyes slowly adjusted to the garish new light, he saw an unfamiliar face through the slit in the door. The face that eyed him was stern, with large black eyes and a smooth complexion several shades darker than André was accustomed to seeing. "Are you Valière?" the stranger repeated, his accent sounding French, yet with the tinge of something unfamiliar.

"Yes?" André still held a hand to his eyes as he shielded them, feeling a headache throb mercilessly. "I am André Valière."

"If I unlock this door and come in, do you promise you will not try to force your way past me and out of the cell?"

André considered this question. "I don't think I would get very far. So I suppose so, yes."

The man ignored André's sarcasm. "Do I have your word?"

"You do."

The man fiddled with a key and the lock creaked plaintively before him. As the door swung into the cell, the rush of new light overwhelmed André, and he blinked desperately.

"Goodness, a few candles too bright, eh? How long have they had you in this wretched hold?" The man's accent was strangely foreign to André, but he wore the high-collared blue and gold coat with the tricolor sash along the waistline indicative of a French officer.

"But good God, I'd think the stench in here would do more to trouble you than a light!"

André, who had retreated back to the corner of the cell like an animal frightened by the light, felt a rush of embarrassment; this cell had served as bed, home, and toilet for him. He said nothing. As he blinked, André found his eyes adjusting and noticed that indeed all the light by which he had been stunned issued from only a few flickering candles.

"You scared of me, lad? No need for that."

"Sorry. I've been in the darkness for . . . well, I don't know how long."

"Almost four days. Damn foolish, if you ask me." The man spoke in a quiet tone, but his gestures were quick and purposeful as he surveyed the tiny cell. "Have they been feeding you in this bloody rat hole?"

"I get bread and water." André tried to swallow but found his throat too dry.

"Well, at least that's as it should be." He turned his focus back to André, his dark eyes taking in the prisoner's squalid appearance. "My name is Dumas. General Thomas-Alexandre Dumas."

André wondered why the man's name sounded familiar, and then he knew; his was the name mentioned on the beach in Malta. "I'm André Valière," he said, quietly. "Formerly a captain in the Army of the Republic."

"I know who you are." General Dumas rested a hand on his sword hilt, looking intently at André. "You testified at General Kellermann's trial."

André nodded, lowering his eyes to the grimy cell floor.

"He was a good general, and a good man. I told my wife—the day we killed him was the day our Revolution lost the side of the angels."

André chewed on his lower lip, seasoned now at hiding his true feelings, too frightful to speak anything that might further condemn him.

Dumas continued. "Kellermann was one of the few who supported my promotion to brigadier general." The more this man spoke, the more distinctly André noted his foreign, rolling cadence. "While many of the others, Murat especially, said there was no way someone so dark-skinned as me should be commanding Frenchmen . . . so much for their liberty and equality, eh?" Dumas spit in the corner of the cell. "But the past is the past. I've proven to them a time or two my mettle."

André, not knowing what to say, said nothing. But the general continued.

"You look confused, Valière." General Dumas's hard stare unsettled André. "Never seen a Negro before?"

"No, sir, it's not that. It's just . . . well, I've never seen a black general before. Sir."

"Well, that's something we have in common then, Captain," Dumas said, pacing the small cell. "I'm the son of a Haitian slave, my mother. Never mind the fact that my father was a French lord—most men only see the dark half." To André's surprise, the imposing man suddenly flashed a broad smile. "But never mind that now."

André still did not know what to make of this strange visitor. He asked the first question that came to his mind. "If you please, General Dumas, what time is it?"

"Midnight," the general answered, still looking around the cell in disgust. "I came down here to see what you were about. This is a waste—having an officer like you locked up. The British are chasing us like a sailor chases whores. We are going to face fire any day now. Whether it's the Royal Navy or the Mamelukes. Murat is a fool if he thinks we don't need every able-bodied man above, ready to fight."

André noticed the quickening of his pulse, the fire of what he was sure had to be hope filling his chest. "Dueys agrees with me," Dumas said. "That makes a general and a ship's captain against a general. We outnumber him."

André swallowed hard. What did this mean?

"Valière, I wasn't sure about it, but now it's decided. I'm setting you free."

André nearly doubled over in shock. "Free? You mean . . ." André's voice caught in his throat. He hadn't dared use the word for so long he had almost forgotten its meaning.

"I mean you are free. Come now, I've seen what it means to be a slave, and these conditions rival even that. We're less than a week's sail from Egypt. We keep you down here another week and you're likely to be dead by the time we make land. And then what? No, no, no, this won't do. We need all the men we can get."

"But . . . General Murat—?"

"You let me deal with Murat." Dumas waved a large hand, frowning. "In fact, I look forward to the chance to tell Nicolai Murat what I really think."

André could not suppress a short, guttural laugh. He was free—free to leave this dark cell that smelled of piss and filth and what would surely be his death. He could have hugged this man, this strange yet gracious General Dumas. "Thank you, General. Truly, thank you."

"Don't thank me now. Perhaps once we've gone ashore you'll prove to me that it was worth it, saving your sorry skin."

André nodded, managing a smile in spite of all of his recent misery. "Gladly."

The man paused in the doorway, leaving the door ajar behind him. Now, in the full light for the first time, André noticed just how tall and imposing this half-noble, half-Haitian general really was.

"You said your first name is André—is it not?"

"It is, sir. André Valière."

Dumas leaned in the doorway. "My wife is pregnant. She thinks it's a boy and she wants to name him Alexandre."

"Alexandre Dumas," André said, repeating the name aloud. "It's a fine name."

"I like André. Perhaps we'll shorten it and call him André."

André's good luck continued when, the next day above deck, he heard a familiar voice. "They say that Allah is good, and yet he keeps putting you in my path." André turned at the sound of this playful remark and stared into a wide, earnest smile.

"Ashar!" The two men embraced. "How are you, my friend?" André could not help but notice the man's changed appearance compared to the last time he had seen him. He was dressed in a flowing saffron tunic that hung past his knees and wore a white hood coiled about his head. It was

Ashar, free of his sailor's garb and dressed in the clothes of his homeland, as if he had been restored to a former life.

"But how have I not seen you before?"

André couldn't suppress a short, bitter laugh. "I've been belowdecks."

Ashar gave a quizzical expression as the two men walked, side by side, toward the deck railing.

"I was locked away," André added by way of explanation.

"Locked away?"

André nodded.

"But . . . why?"

André glanced over his shoulder, waiting as a pair of sailors passed before answering: "I seem to have made a very powerful enemy. One who has chased me here. All the way from Paris."

Ashar's eyes narrowed as he leaned toward André. "Who?"

André whispered the name: "General Murat."

Ashar blinked his eyes, a grave expression settling on his handsome features. "How did you do a thing like that?"

"The true reason? I'm not sure." André sighed, looking back out over the rolling horizon of azure blue Mediterranean. "But it could not have helped that I fell in love with his niece."

The summer ripened into scorching heat and the late June sun poured down onto the men, turning their skin darker with each passing day. At night, a blinding moon shone, setting the water's surface to a rolling shimmer, accented by the reflection of a thousand stars. All the while the French fleet, a traveling fortress of hundreds of ships, their sails fat with the salty Mediterranean wind, sped toward the unsuspecting kingdom of Egypt.

André, like many of the sailors and soldiers on board, was eager for information of that distant land, and no one seemed better able to provide it than the Egyptian within their ranks.

Was there really gold hidden away in the ancient tombs? they asked Ashar. Were the women truly the most beautiful in the world? Would the Mamelukes, Egypt's legendary and mysterious warriors, choose to fight or flee to the desert when the French and their fearsome commander arrived?

Ashar enjoyed fielding these questions and did his best to stoke the imaginations of the bored Frenchmen. Yes, the tombs belonging to the dead pharaohs were stocked with riches enough to put even the Bourbon court to shame; and yet, they were guarded by ancient curses and magic that no Frenchman could possibly hope to understand. Yes, the women of Egypt would bring these foreign invaders to their knees.

But for the Mameluke warriors, Ashar showed only a mystifying respect, even a reluctance to speak of them. He assured André, and once or twice admitted frankly to the generals aboard, that they would not fear General Bonaparte's reputation at all. The Mamelukes were brought up with fierce principles of courage and loyalty; fear was not part of their tradition.

Some of the officers scoffed at the Egyptian's warnings, claiming that he was a mere Bedouin Arab, enamored by the power of his overlords, and that his fears were exaggerated. But André could not help but feel unease toward this arrogant way of thinking; what had become of his countrymen who had foolishly undervalued and dismissed the opinions of peasants? And what would become of a force that disregarded the ancient wisdom of the local forces it sought to conquer?

André's main objective those days was to remain out of the path of General Murat. The general, though he had seen André several times since his sudden release, had refrained from acknowledging him in any way. And yet André, as well acquainted as he was with the general's loathing, knew it was only a matter of time before his senior's gray-eyed gaze alighted on him once more; Murat was not one to forget a grievance.

General Dumas shook the young captain's hand each time they met above deck. André suspected that it was that man, more than any other, who kept him out of irons, kept him from rotting in a cell belowdecks, and he felt full of appreciation for the roguish general. If only he could make it to Egypt, André thought. If only he could take part in Bonaparte's march through the country, he felt that he could slip from Murat's grasp and serve with distinction. All he wanted was to serve, to live, and to someday make it home to Sophie.

On the last night of June, Ashar and André sat on the forecastle, looking out over the shimmering moonlit water. A sentry yawned as he paced back and forth on the deck beside them. It was a clear night, the dark sky overhead pierced with thousands of bright, steady stars. The ship rocked in a smooth, constant rhythm, as hypnotizing as a baby's cradle. André, feeling his own eyelids growing heavy, was about to bid his friend good evening, but Ashar's voice interrupted the silence. "We are close now."

André turned to look at his companion, catching his gaze through the milky glow of the moon's light. "What's that?"

"We are nearing Egypt."

"How do you know?"

Ashar smiled, a wise, knowing smile. "My friend, if you were kept away from your land for years, dreaming of your return, longing for a homecoming that you thought you'd never be given, and then, one day, you were this close . . . you'd know as well."

Ashar sat beside him in heavy thought, neither one of them speaking for several minutes. "My country"—Ashar finally broke the silence and looked at André—"is a realm that has enticed the ambitions of men and great powers for centuries. I can't divine what will happen when we arrive there. But, André Valière, my friend, I pray to God that your fate is not written to end in my country."

The soldiers were roused before dawn and called to stand-to on deck. There, donning his newly provisioned captain's uniform, André blinked as the first hints of daylight broke over the horizon, slicing the darkness like knife blades of purple, orange, and pink. And there, for the first time in weeks, land awaited them.

"Alexandria!"

"My God, we've made it!"

"We'll make landfall by midday, won't we?"

All around him, the men on the ship muttered and fidgeted with a nervous, anticipatory energy, like hounds chafing at their leashes at the start of a hunt.

André found Ashar a short while later, leaning on the far railing, his gaze fixed over the bow and on the distant horizon. "There you are," he said. "The men have been called to breakfast. Shall we go below and eat?"

Ashar didn't pull his gaze from the nearby shore. Didn't speak, but only shook his head, no.

"Your homeland." André stood beside him, looking from the land toward his friend.

"Alexandria," Ashar finally answered, his voice charged with a stern reverence. "The city built for the great Alexander. The capital fine enough for Cleopatra herself. Called by the ancient Greeks the 'best and greatest.'"

As the ship pulled them closer to the Egyptian shore, bathed now in the ethereal orange glow of the rising sun, André gained a better view of the city. His eyes roved over the land, its shoreline sliced open in the middle by a narrow waterway that issued out into a broad, calm bay. Beyond that, André knew, the desert stretched for leagues without end, a vast dry sea of sand and punishing sun.

"And now General Bonaparte wishes to add his name to that elite and distinguished history." Ashar turned to look at André for the first time, his voice grave but calm. "He can take Alexandria. He might even hold it for a time. But Alexandria will never be his. Egypt will never be his, no matter how deeply he is seduced by her. Many others, beckoned by the myths and legends, have thought they could possess her. Even if he somehow manages to chase away the Mamelukes, which I doubt he will, there is something in these sands and within the hearts of these people that he does not understand. The deeper he penetrates, the more she will close in around him. She will strangle him with her soft, perfumed hands before he even realizes he is in her grip. You shall see."

André stared at his friend uneasily for a moment, then turned his gaze back to the city and sighed. "I have seen enough horror to last a lifetime, ten lifetimes. But, Ashar, I must admit, the way you are speaking now . . . I am uneasy."

Ashar blinked, his hard features softening into an unexpected smile. "You need not fear. At least, not on account of me. As long as I am a guest of your people, I will do all that is in my power to see that you remain alive. You may be a heathen and an infidel, but you are my friend."

24

Le Temple
Prison, Paris

Summer 1798

"You must eat, even if you have no appetite." Jean-Luc sat beside Sophie on the small rusty bench in the courtyard. He was visiting her in the prison that had once housed her fiancé. The air was uncharacteristically chilly on this summer morning, with a biting damp that felt more like late winter. They sat in a small garden reserved for the female prisoners, their bench tucked beneath the limbs of an ancient plane tree. "Eat whatever food they bring you; do you understand?"

"I would hardly call what they offer us food," Sophie said, trying to smile even though her eyes were devoid of mirth. She looked thin and pale, and her small frame shivered more than it should have, even in the damp morning air. Jean-Luc peeled off his coat and draped it over her slumped shoulders.

"All the same, you must force yourself to eat. You must keep up your health. For when you are set free."

Sophie exhaled a short, apathetic laugh. Lifting her gaze from the puddled ground, she looked up at him, her eyes encased in shadow. "Have you found out anything more?"

Jean-Luc sighed, breaking from her stare. "Seems the only things they have on you are some vague conspiracy charges of consorting with a 'criminal' and eluding your guards and captors."

"I hadn't even been arrested or charged! I was just trying to avoid my uncle because I know what he is capable of."

"On technical grounds your relations with André at that time can be construed as 'criminal.' But thankfully, according to the recent laws, your offense is not a capital one. I promised you, and I hold to it: I will do everything in my power to get you out of here." Jean-Luc paused, knitting his hands together in his lap. "Have you given any further thought to what I proposed?"

Sophie let her eyes slide away as she shook her head, a barely perceptible gesture.

"Come now, Sophie, I think it might be our best chance. Please allow me to write to your uncle."

"I told you—I suspect that he has as much to do with my being in here as that old snake, Guillaume Lazare. Who else would be charging me with 'eluding guards'? Why, he's the very man who chased me from the city."

Jean-Luc thought about this, sighing. The last couple of months had been the strangest and most troubling time since the Terror and the trials of General Kellermann and André. His mind ceaselessly returned to that night when Guillaume Lazare had appeared outside his door—the same night that Mathieu had gone missing. How the old man had demanded that Jean-Luc turn in Sophie, and how Sophie had willingly gone, exchanging herself for the little boy.

And now, weeks later, Sophie still sat in prison, enduring the stifling, pestilent-ridden summer, as neither she nor Jean-Luc came any closer to understanding how or why they had become entangled in this strange game of cat and mouse with Guillaume Lazare.

Jean-Luc stared past the prison walls and up at the patch of visible sky, closing his eyes for a moment. "It's likely, I suspect, that your uncle was angry with you for defying him, and he hoped to teach you a lesson. I think you've learned it well enough." He brought his eyes down and looked back at Sophie.

"I am certain that he wants me locked up in here until he returns home from . . . wherever it is. Where is the army now? Italy?"

"Somewhere in the Mediterranean, from what I've read, and heading toward Egypt. Seems Bonaparte wants to make a play for Cairo."

Sophie's entire face sagged. "Cairo? But that's an entire world away. Even farther than Malta. Is André there as well?"

Jean-Luc reached for her hand, taking it in his. Overhead the sun slipped behind a cloud, casting a pall over the courtyard that added to Jean-Luc's sense of hopelessness. Neither of them had heard from André in many months, but he forced a buoyant tone as he answered: "I've reason to believe he is with that army, yes. Or at least was nearby when they departed from Toulon and Marseille."

"How can you be sure he is safe?"

Jean-Luc thought about this, knowing that there was no honest way to answer her. "I cannot be completely certain, but none of the letters I've sent to him have been returned. And I always addressed them to the port of call at Toulon, where a greedy Temple prison guard tracked him for me, in exchange for a fee."

"Have you heard any news of his mother?" Sophie asked. Jean-Luc felt heavy at the question—he had put off telling Sophie, wanting to keep her spirits lifted. But perhaps it was time she knew—perhaps it would give her the determination she seemed to be losing.

"My contacts in London have replied, yes."

"And?" Sophie's eyes perked up ever so slightly. "What news of Madame Valière?"

Jean-Luc swallowed, clearing his throat. "I am sorry to say that . . . Madame Valière has . . . not survived to enjoy a reunion with her son."

Sophie brought a hand to her pale cheek. "Dead?"

"Some sort of pox, perhaps smallpox."

Sophie's stare went blank as she picked at a piece of rust on the old bench beneath them. After a long pause, she sighed. "She escaped the Terror only to perish of smallpox. Will you tell André?"

"I will try. If I can figure out where he has been sent."

Sophie nodded.

"All the more reason why *you* must take care of yourself. My dear girl, don't you see? His father lost, his brother gone, most likely dead, and now his mother. You are all that André has left to return to."

If, he thought, André ever returns at all.

Sophie nodded her distracted agreement. "I suppose you're right."

"And you *will* be free when he returns, Sophie."

"Free. Yes." But then a shadow passed over her face, bringing with it the indication of renewed agony.

"What is it?" Jean-Luc leaned toward her.

She trembled, as if unsure whether to speak. And then, her voice at barely a whisper, she looked into his eyes and said: "*He* came here again. To visit me."

Jean-Luc looked away, suppressing the curse that rose to his lips like bile. "*Bastard!*" Turning back to Sophie, he tried to smooth over his features. "Did you speak with him?"

"I did what you told me: I received him. I was cordial. But I told him nothing. Nothing of our visits. I answered no questions."

"Good," Jean-Luc said, swallowing hard. "And did he offer a reason for his visit?"

"He always seems to be coming as a friend. At least, he tells me that he's coming as a friend. That he hopes to help me."

"And the devil comes dressed as an angel. But Guillaume Lazare is no friend, Sophie. Do not believe the words he speaks."

"I know, I know," Sophie said, her eyes shutting with fatigue. "Believe me, I know."

"I'd rest easier if you were not forced to receive him when he visited, Sophie. But whatever his purpose is in detaining you like this . . . whether it's your uncle behind it or not . . . we cannot risk agitating him further."

Sophie nodded, understanding. And then she paused. "I don't like . . . the way he looks at me."

"How does he look at you?"

"I can't explain it, really. He talks of his home in the south. Of his desire to go back there, and 'return to a simple life apart from politics.' " Sophie sneered at those words. "He tells me that he never had a wife and children but that he hopes it's not too late for that. It's bizarre, really."

Jean-Luc felt discomfort rising up from his belly like water bubbling to a boil. "What do you mean?"

"I've seen men look at me before with love in their eyes," Sophie said, her voice faltering over the words, and Jean-Luc knew that she thought of André as she said it. Sophie inhaled, steeling herself to go on. "And I've seen men look at me before with hatred in their eyes. But never before—at least not until Guillaume Lazare—have I seen a man look at me with what appeared to be both love and hatred at the same time."

❧

That particular afternoon, having sensed Sophie's worsening despondency at their morning visit, Jean-Luc was gripped with dread even more tightly than usual. Outside of Madame Grocque's tavern he spotted the familiar covered coach waiting on the cobblestoned street below his window. He froze in his steps.

Perhaps he hadn't been seen yet, Jean-Luc calculated; perhaps he could slip down the nearby alley. But the thought of leaving Mathieu and Marie alone within sight of that man was too much for him to allow. Jean-Luc turned to quietly dart inside when he heard the coach door open. He turned in time to see Guillaume Lazare hop down onto the street, his aged frame appearing uncharacteristically nimble, even peppy. "Greetings, Citizen St. Clair!"

Jean-Luc clenched his jaw and nodded. "Citizen Lazare."

"Your wife is getting nice and round."

Jean-Luc's heart thumped in his chest as he stood, motionless, outside the tavern door. Sensing that he had the young lawyer's attention, Lazare continued. "Tell me, do you hope for a daughter? Or would you like another son?"

Now Jean-Luc wheeled around, turning to face the man. "What is it that you want?"

Lazare, apparently satisfied that he had succeeded in baiting his prey, smiled. He leaned back against the coach as he considered the question. He took his time before answering. "A great many things, I suppose. But where should I begin?"

"Why don't you begin by telling me why you've imprisoned that poor woman."

"Citizeness de Vincennes? The count's widow? I'd hardly call her poor."

"Good lord, what has she done wrong?"

"You know what she has done. She consorted with a known enemy of the state, citizen."

"What of it? Has that man not been tried, and permitted to leave this place and start a new life?"

Lazare sighed. Behind him, Jean-Luc heard the tavern door creak open. Madame Grocque, feigning disinterest, emerged on the street and began sweeping her stoop.

"I'll go after her"—Lazare paused, smoothing a fold in his glove—"because that will draw him back."

Jean-Luc could not conceal the concern on his features. "André? But he's serving his sentence."

"He has not paid," Lazare hissed, his pale lips curling around each word. "He's not dead, as I believe he should be. And it was *you*, Citizen St. Clair, who made it so."

"He's paying every single day; he's served our Republic for years. Why must you persecute André further? What has he ever done to earn your hatred?"

Lazare laughed, slowing his pace, reining in his features, even as Jean-Luc saw the purple vein that pulsed behind the otherwise pale flesh of the old man's neck. "Come now, I don't *hate* him. I don't even know the man. But he *was* the first one to—how shall I put this?—slip through my grasp. You managed to spare his life."

Jean-Luc was no nearer to understanding. "That was just business. Your dislike of him can't be personal."

"My dear fellow, St. Clair, it's *all* personal. Don't you understand that? Why, you'll never achieve the status you so greedily covet if you have not learned that by now."

Jean-Luc stuffed his hands into his pockets. "Then your feud should be with me. I am the one who thwarted you in that case."

"Perhaps you're right." Lazare shrugged. There was a long pause before the old man, still examining his pristine gloves, looked up. "It started out that I planned to convict the man—Valière—as a favor to a powerful general. Nothing more. Oh, not because I have any special fondness for Nicolai Murat. *Au contraire,* the man is a brute who can't help but act on his aversions and impulses, but I have indulged him because our interests have always been mutual. His hatred for the noble class impresses even me." Lazare paused, his voice dropping in volume and pitch. "But now . . . now, I must finish the work that Nicolai Murat began."

Jean-Luc rubbed his two clammy palms together, still unsure of the old man's motivations but certain of his madness. "For God's sake, Lazare, why must you do this? The poor man's father was beheaded by you and your friends, his brother was chased, I believe murdered, by the man who wants to kill him, and his fiancée has been hunted for no reason other than returning his love. When will it all end? The Terror is over. Can we not attempt to rebuild our lives and our city?"

Lazare took out his snuffbox, sprinkled a pinch onto his gloved hand, and snorted the powder. He lowered his eyes and stamped the ground with his feet. After an uncomfortable pause he looked back up at Jean-Luc. "André de Valière has managed to elude the justice of our Republic. The justice that our fallen martyrs died to bring us. Their work will continue posthumously, through me, until all of our enemies are hunted down and destroyed. That is a vow I will keep."

Now Jean-Luc couldn't help but let out a short, bitter laugh, a gesture of disgust. Of contempt. He looked directly into the old man's pale eyes as he answered, his tone biting: "You do not seek justice, citizen. You're no better than any of those monsters—Robespierre, Saint-Just, Hébert. They were murderers who ultimately received the same *justice* that they so ruthlessly meted out. Perhaps you have been fated to join them."

"You'll make me irritated, saying things like that," Lazare sneered, his voice as taut as a bowstring.

Now Jean-Luc broiled with a feeling of rising indignation. For his friend André. For Sophie, imprisoned. For the nation that had been gripped by the madness of this old man and his murderous friends. "I don't give a damn about your anger, Lazare. But take it out on me—not Sophie. You can't imprison a woman just because she loves a good man and looks at you like a plague-ridden corpse. And how can you blame her? You're barely better."

"And here I was trying to forgive you."

Jean-Luc spit on the ground close to the old man's shoes. "Piss on your forgiveness."

Lazare sighed, rubbing his gloved hands together, his voice staying calm. "So this is the gratitude I receive? For pulling you up out of the gutter, making you something greater than you were. Bringing you into the company of important men. You've thrown away my friendship over a woman and her pitiful lover?"

Jean-Luc gasped out a guttural exhale. "This is madness, and I've had quite enough." He stepped up onto the curb, shoving past the old man. But Lazare had not finished.

"I still want André de Valière's head. And I'll have it."

Jean-Luc paused, hovering outside the tavern door. He turned around, wrestling with the urge to rush toward the man and throttle him. But Lazare's words cut him short. "I *will* have it. And then, once I've done away with him, I shall begin to tighten the noose."

Lazare looked Jean-Luc squarely in the eyes now, his steady gaze impervious to the giving or receiving of emotion. His eyes spoke of one thing only: his raw, unwavering determination.

"You see, Citizen St. Clair, I will offer you one last lesson. And then I think I am quite done teaching you. Here it is, so listen closely: Murat sought simply to kill his enemies. He wanted to settle some old grievance, a feud he had with Old Man de Valière, by punishing the subsequent generation." Lazare waved a hand dismissively. "But *I, I* told him that that was much too easy. Death ends pain, you see? You do not merely *kill* your enemies; you must first make them suffer. You must take from them everything they hold dear. So, with that said, I have a question for you, Jean-Luc St. Clair: should I begin with Marie or Mathieu?"

25

Alexandria,
Egypt

July 1798

A ndré had never truly known thirst before the march through Egypt. Alexandria had fallen quickly, its sentries caught unaware and ill-equipped to fend off the French cannons and rifles that bombarded the walls of the city.

Their principal objective would be Cairo, which lay almost two hundred kilometers inland, on the southern side of a punishing stretch of barren desert. This desert was Bedouin-controlled territory, inhabited by fierce and dreaded tribes of nomadic warriors who neither acknowledged nor feared these strangely uniformed foreigners. But the most lethal enemy on that march, André suspected, would be the relentless sun. The daytime heat of the first few days was unlike anything André or any of his comrades had ever experienced.

André found Ashar on the beach the day before they were to set out from Alexandria. The Egyptian's face was blank, an inscrutable mask, as he looked out over the horizon. "Why do you side with us, the French, against your own people, Ashar?" André asked.

Ashar's dark eyes were steady, without expression, as he turned to face André. After a long pause, he answered André's question with an evasive statement: "Your general, Napoleon Bonaparte, intends to make war with the Mamelukes."

"Yes?"

"Tribal warriors, horsemen, who rule the interior of my country."

"And so I ask you again: why would you fight with the French?" Implicit in André's question, though he did not say it outright, was: *how can we trust you?*

"Because the Mamelukes are not Egyptian," Ashar answered, matter-of-factly. "They are Ottoman, or at least they come from somewhere ruled by them. They are foreign invaders, just as you are. But they rule my country as a wolf would rule a flock of sheep, taking and devouring whatever they wish. From what I have seen of them and of your people, I believe the French would show more mercy to my people than those barbarians have done."

"You must have never been to Paris," André replied with a half smile, though it quickly faded as he thought of home and all those who had perished over the previous years.

"Captain Valière!" A horseman approached, offering André a brisk salute. "Sir, you are to report to the command tent of General Dumas immediately. Your promotion orders are complete and the general would like to issue them to you personally."

"My promotion?" André stared at the man for a moment, wondering whether this was some sort of ruse.

"Yes, sir." The soldier saluted André, then remounted his saddle.

Ashar looked at him with his typically sly smile. "Perhaps your fortunes have finally begun to turn."

André ran a hand through his hair and exhaled a long, deep breath. "Major Valière."

"Yes, sir," the messenger said. "You're to be assigned to the cavalry, under Generals Dumas and Murat."

As the sun descended beyond the dunes on the third evening of July, André rode out of the city of Alexandria among a force of some fifteen thousand soldiers. They rode or marched through the night, with the sounds of howling winds and far-off cries echoing as unseen reminders that they were foreigners in this wild desert realm. As the gray light of dawn turned to day and the sun rose in the sky, the heat hovered over and around them like an unwelcome and unmoving presence, extinguishing their high morale and sapping the energy they needed to cover the miles of desert.

"Conserve your water, lads!" André ordered as they halted and made camp for their afternoon rest. He noted, with dismay, that few took heed of this command; in temperatures soaring well above anything they had ever known, this order ran counter to their every human instinct.

On the third day of their march, the first animals began to die, and this cruel omen of the desert's lethality caused some of the men to grumble and ask questions. "How much farther until the water source?" became a common query, posed nearly every hour.

André didn't know the answer. He did not know, any more than his men did, what lay ahead; all he knew was that turning back was not an option. Their only hope was to keep going forward—eventually, they had to reach the Nile. With the tricolor standard leading the way like a distant, shimmering apparition, André and his men covered mile after mile across open sand that burned under centuries of unforgiving sunlight. The men felt their cheeks scorch and blister, their lips grow puffy from sun poisoning. More animals dropped, their carcasses left in the sand to feed the intrepid buzzards that would fly this far from any oasis. And still, no sign of the lifesaving Nile.

As horrible as the days were, the nights were no better. Their evening serenades were the high-pitched trills of the nearby Bedouin warriors, encamped just out of sight, a constant companion to the French march. The presence of this heard but unseen foe was made all the more eerie by the distant glow of their camps, the scent of their fires drifting over the horizons of moonlit sand.

"War cries," Ashar explained. He had ridden up silently and now unfurled his sleeping pad beside André's.

"Do they wish to fight us?" André asked, mesmerized by the neverending glow of the distant fires.

"Perhaps," was all the cryptic reply that Ashar offered.

André shivered involuntarily in the dark, bitter desert night.

But of all the trials André faced on that march, his dreams were the worst, for they assailed his mind and his very soul. He could not say whether it was the exhaustion. Or the thirst. Or the strange sounds that seemed to float across the endless expanse of desert. But his dreams were so vivid that he woke each morning feeling as if his grasp of reality, even of his mind, was slowly slipping away from him, grains of sand sliding through his blistered fingertips.

He dreamed of many things, but without fail his dreams would end with visions of Sophie. In one of the more vivid ones, she invited him to attend her wedding—a wedding between herself and another man, aged and ghostly pale. But the worst was when she came to him, crying, telling him that Remy was dead and that she had been listed for the scaffold the following day. André would wake with a lurch, his neck clammy and his body sweating under a makeshift cover made from his saddle and saddle blanket.

On the tenth day, it seemed as if the men could go no farther. André, exhausted and defeated, did not know whether he had it in him to force them on. It was on this morning that a small group of scouts appeared, riding back from the front of the train with a fervor that none of them had felt since leaving Alexandria. "Water! Water up ahead! We've reached the Nile!"

André watched the track of the riders as they galloped past him and disappeared along the horizon in a cloud of dust. He fixed his eyes forward and shielded them, hoping to see a shimmer up ahead that promised to be their salvation.

Turning to the nearest noncommissioned officer, André said, "I want to know how far the river is. Stay here, I'm coming straight back. Keep formation, no matter what any of the other companies do. For God's sake, keep formation."

André spurred his horse forward and galloped past the miserable infantry companies. After cresting a small dune, André squinted and gazed ahead, and then he saw it: a vast field spotted with intermittent groves of fertile vegetation. At the far end of the expanse, a brilliant track of shiny blue-green. It was a glistening surface, lined by a wall of shade-giving palm trees. Glorious sight! Perhaps a half league ahead of him, the first companies were reaching it, splashing into it with the joy and reckless abandon of a prisoner unexpectedly set free. It was no mirage; they had in fact reached the Nile.

André snapped the reins of his exhausted horse and cantered back to rejoin his squadron, eager to tell them that they were indeed saved.

"They will drink themselves to death." Ashar reined in his horse beside André's.

André laughed. "I think some of them might welcome that."

"No, it is the truth," the Egyptian answered, his tone as humorless as his facial expression. "Their bodies are not meant, after ten days, to guzzle this much. They must sip this water in moderation, slowly, or they will poison themselves. I have seen it before."

The warning, and Ashar's certainty, settled on André, and he turned with a new, horrified concern to see thousands of Frenchmen glutting themselves in the water, gulping uninterrupted mouthfuls.

"Stop drinking, damn you!" The order was issued from over André's shoulder. André turned and saw the outline of a familiar figure. Nicolai Murat. André's entire body stiffened, but the general cantered past him and rode directly toward the bank. "Stop drinking, that's an order!"

André had a feeling that this would end badly, so he rounded up his men, some of them only footsteps from reaching the river. "Squadron, back into column!"

His men, stunned and incredulous at being ordered not to drink the water their bodies so badly needed, nevertheless assented, muttering unhappily under their breath as they stepped away from the river and gathered around André.

But some of the other squadrons and infantry companies already appeared as an unruly mob, abandoning their discipline to the intoxicating relief the river provided.

"Stop drinking, that's an order!" Murat, atop his horse, yelled louder at the hundreds of troops bathing in the river. Most of the men either did not hear the general or chose to ignore his orders, too feverish were they drinking and splashing in the water.

"To file now, lads, we'll drink our fill in a moment, but we must be patient." André kept his men close, even as he kept his eyes fixed uncomfortably on Murat and the chaos unfolding in the nearby river.

With a decisive movement Murat reached for the pistol holstered at his waist. He raised it and took aim. A loud crack was followed by a plume of smoke and the familiar scent of burnt gunpowder as the bullet hit a man who was stooped over the river, greedily gulping mouthfuls of the Nile. The man did not see it coming. His body fell into the water with a splash, a flow of red seeping across his back. It was as instantaneous as it was in-glorious, this man's death on the Egyptian riverbank.

All around now the other men ceased their drinking and turned in the direction of the gunfire. "The next man to drink without his commander's permission shall face a firing squad," Murat shouted, his mustache quiver-ing as he spoke. "You are soldiers in the French army, not beasts without control over your instincts. You will show moderation, or you will bring about your own death."

The men began to inch back away from the river, huddling in small groups with looks of disbelief, fear, and anger. André was as stunned as the rest of them, but he kept his men close, an organized cluster removed from the melee of the riverbank.

"Officers, control your men as they refill their skins and canteens." Murat turned his horse, not glancing again in the direction of his lifeless victim. "And someone bury that damned fool."

Ashar remained beside André at the bank of the river, his voice sage as he watched the flowing waters before them. "I've seen it before."

Later, once the column had re-formed and recommenced its seemingly unending march, they hugged the snakelike shape of the Nile on a southeasterly course. Much of the panic had dissipated, washed clean by the fact that their thirst had been sated and the water source would henceforth remain in sight, bordering the army's eastern flank for the remainder of the march. Morale rose as they continued on, bound for Cairo.

As they marched farther inland and south, André and the men got their first glimpses of villages and local Egyptians. The people were dressed simply, in lightweight cotton that hung loosely on their frames and san-daled shoes much more suitable for the terrain than the heavy leather of the French boots. Their eyes, dark and inquisitive, watched as the soldiers lumbered past. Some of the little children ran up to the moving columns, jabbering in incomprehensible Arabic as their bare feet scudded along to keep pace with the strangely dressed French.

One morning they encountered a train of Egyptians marching in the opposite direction from their lines. Several camps had begun to pop up along the banks of the Nile. Establishments that appeared temporary, as if the people were on the move.

"Where are they going?" André asked, looking at one such camp, where a group of children had broken off stalks of papyrus reed and were using them to duel one another outside a cluster of tents.

"They are fleeing," Ashar answered.

"Why?"

"They fear the Mamelukes more than the French."

It was late morning, and the column paused for a water break. André and Ashar sat along the bank of the Nile, their canteens filled, awaiting the orders to resume the march.

"What are they like?" André asked. "The Mamelukes."

"They are like the desert," Ashar answered after a thoughtful pause. "Fierce. Unforgiving. Unrelenting."

"But . . . how do they survive out here?"

"The desert is their home. It is what they know."

"They have no permanent homes?"

"Some of the Mameluke chieftains have great houses in the cities, palaces adorned with women more beautiful than you could possibly imagine." Ashar sighed wistfully, then looked back to the endless sand dunes stretched out before them. "But they are nomadic warriors. Horsemen. Their women and children move with them as they go."

André picked at a reed, tying a bow with its stalk. "Are there many of them?"

Ashar nodded. "Beyond count."

André whistled. Austrians and Prussians were a formidable enemy, to be sure, but a familiar one at least, their tactics and weapons like those of the French. These desert horsemen seemed to come from a place and time that none in their army had ever known. André eyed Ashar again, with that recurring sense that although he was familiar with his friend, he did not truly know him.

"The Mamelukes are a proud order," Ashar continued. "And why should they not be? They were brought to this country by Egyptians to be our slaves. Within a few decades they went from slaves to becoming the masters of Egypt. Now they simply have a new enemy to slaughter."

"Are we getting close to their territory?"

"My friend, look around." Ashar raised his arms, embracing the entirety of the desert. "It is all their territory."

André nodded, thinking a moment before he continued. "I have served under many generals in my time. Some were truly great; others were not. But this Bonaparte fellow is unlike anyone I have ever seen. He fears nothing and yields to no one. He moves his armies faster than many men would think possible. And the men who were with him in Italy seem to have some sort of"—André laughed in spite of himself, reaching for his words as he plucked a handful of river grasses—"some sort of inexplicable devotion to him, as though he were a god. I'm not sure how all of this will end, but I find myself thinking—*believing*—that as long as Napoleon Bonaparte leads this army, we will be victorious."

Ashar held his friend's gaze before turning his eyes back toward the flowing river. He cupped a pebble in his hand, which he now tossed into the water. "It will be up to God," Ashar said, "and the desert."

26

Giza, Egypt

July 1798

After two weeks of marching, the camp pulsed with an unmistakable hum of excitement; word spread that evening, moving among the men in hushed but urgent whispers, that they had nearly reached Giza, the riverside city of pyramids just across the Nile from Cairo.

Ashar, with his seemingly endless knowledge of Egyptian lore, was the most sought-after man around the campfires that night, where he regaled the men with tales of the afterlife and the ancient belief that each soul crossed a river at the end of his days to dwell among the immortals.

André, like dozens of others, sat before his friend, listening. Tonight Ashar was describing to the soldiers a large monument, not far from the great pyramids, that bore the body of a lion and the head of a man. "We call him the Sphinx," Ashar said, to dozens of rapt faces. "And he guards the Valley of the Kings from any who would seek to plunder the pharaohs' wealth."

"Major Valière?"

André turned at the sound of his name and saw one of the cavalry orderlies cutting through the camp. "Yes?"

"Major Valière?" The aide squinted, his face visible in the glow of the surrounding campfires. "The general has requested your presence at Commander Bonaparte's briefing, sir."

"Which general?" André asked.

"General Dumas."

André recognized only Dumas and Murat among the officers assembled in Bonaparte's command tent. The group numbered perhaps thirty, the commanders of various divisions and their aides clustered obediently behind them. General Bonaparte sat at a desk sprawled with maps, letters, and troop reports. He wore spectacles as he examined a parchment, undistracted by the growing murmur of the assembled group.

Perhaps a minute or so later, General Bonaparte removed the spectacles perched atop his narrow nose and rubbed his eyes; all side conversations ceased.

The general opened his eyes and spoke: "Citizen Fourier, what was it that you described to me earlier? Something about the mathematical genius it would have taken to build that grand pyramid that stands less than four leagues away?"

The man addressed stepped forward. André noticed that he was not in uniform like the soldiers and officers, but rather in plain clothing. He was one of Napoleon's scholars, André guessed, one of the hundreds of scientists and mathematicians selected by the general to accompany the army on this march, to explore and record what the French found in this storied desert kingdom.

Citizen Fourier cleared his throat before answering. "Sir, the ancients possessed a thorough understanding of ratios and triangles; that is to say, they had a significant understanding of geometric principles."

General Bonaparte flashed a brief smile. "Yes, Fourier, that has become apparent to many of us by now." Some of the officers laughed at their commander's quip. "But, citizen, you told me how this great structure appeared at its origin."

"Yes, sir. At the time of its creation, it would have been covered with highly polished limestone, reflecting the sun's light and shining like a jewel. The original pyramid would have acted like a gigantic mirror, reflecting light so powerfully as to be visible even from the heavens, a shining star on earth."

"A shining star on earth." The general stood up now and paced slowly before his desk. "And tomorrow, it shall be ours." Bonaparte's eyes flashed with an unmistakable zeal as he looked at the men assembled before him.

"My fellow soldiers and countrymen, we are on the eve of a battle that will be recalled by posterity among the likes of Alexander, Caesar, and Rameses the Great. We have crossed the sea of the Roman Empire and traversed the sands of Africa to meet a great and ancient foe. We are here not merely to advance the cause of France and the Republic of our people. No, we are here to enhance the glory of all civilization." The general paused, letting his words take root. The tent was silent now, and all eyes, including André's, were fixed on the young commander.

"Like our forebears of antiquity, we travel east because that is where all great men go. Great deeds are done by men who possess the boldness to travel to lands deemed unconquerable by others and master what it is they fear. Men, very soon you and your soldiers will leave your mark on history, and it is up to you to decide what that will be."

With that, the supreme commander gazed around the tent once more. Seemingly satisfied with the impact of his words, he crossed back to his chair and took his seat. "General Kléber has informed me that our fleet remains safely moored off Aboukir Bay, with no sign of the English or that bogeyman Admiral Nelson. So the unfortunate situation of our resupply should abate soon. Furthermore, our ships traveling up the Nile with Captain Perrée should be here in a day, so the mutinous talk that has plagued this army since we left the comfort of Alexandria will cease, and you as commanders will ensure it stops at once." With that, the general sighed and motioned a hand toward the assembly. "General Dumas, you look like one who has seen a ghost. Do the mummies lurking in their tombs frighten you?"

Dumas shifted from one foot to the other as, around him, small sputters of laughter popped up.

"These desert savages wouldn't harm a fellow African," General Murat said with a snicker, glancing sideways toward Dumas.

If Dumas heard Murat's goading, he ignored it, for his gaze remained fixed on the man at the front of the tent. "Sir, it is not the dead who concern me."

General Dumas took a cautious step forward. "General, with all deference due to your command . . ." Dumas paused briefly, considering his next words. "I fear that the men—to say nothing of the horses—are not prepared for this kind of warfare."

The others in the tent became suddenly silent, all stifled laughter dissipating. General Dumas lowered his voice as he continued, and André could hardly believe his boldness: "Our enemy hovers at our flanks, striking where we are weak and vulnerable, then simply vanishes back into the desert, where our men do not wish to go. Our supply lines grow more vulnerable each day, and our reserves of water are now almost nonexistent. The soldiers have marched for weeks without bread, and those who have taken food from the Arab villages have been shot. We cannot sustain this. Perhaps if we sent an emissary to Cairo we could—"

"I thank you for your report." Bonaparte raised a hand as he fixed an intense stare on his much taller subordinate. "And I will remind you again that matters of strategy are not counted among your duties. You will leave that to me."

"Sir," Dumas continued undeterred, "my soldiers and this expedition are suffering, and our situation grows worse by the day. Furthermore, it's suffering that is unnecessary and entirely avoidable. I firmly request—"

"Enough!" General Bonaparte pounded his desk with his fist, his face turning crimson. Dumas stood rigid before him, unmoving. The tension inside the tent was now almost unbearable, and André wondered whether this confrontation would turn violent. After a moment, the commander turned his head and signaled to the assembled officers. "Thank you, gentlemen, that will be all. Now get out. You"—he signaled a hand toward Dumas—"you stay."

The officers quickly shuffled out of the tent, few daring to speak even after they had exited into the cool evening. As André turned back toward his billet he could hear muffled shouts coming from the command tent. He admired General Dumas for speaking so frankly on behalf of the men but imagined any dissent to be futile at this stage.

He noticed the soft sound of footsteps trailing behind him and turned. "Who's there?"

A figure approached, concealed by the darkness of the desert night. "So it is you, Valière." The voice kindled instant recognition. Murat.

André had not seen the man up close during the long march, not since the shooting on the riverbank. He felt tempted now to reach for his sword but suppressed the urge. He took a breath and turned to face his tormentor. "General Murat, good evening."

The two men looked at each other as the shadows from the surrounding tents and campfires flickered around them. "So, now that you are Major Valière, you attend our commander's briefings. You've always seemed to put yourself into the thick of it."

André forced a tight-lipped, bitter smile. "Despite being denounced, imprisoned, and losing my family, I am still here, General."

"I must admit, a very small part of me almost admires you." Murat rubbed the hilt of his sword. "You're not easily broken."

André remained silent; he did not intend to antagonize his tormenter on the eve of a great battle, but he felt a steady surge of painful memory as he stood so close to the man who had taken everything from him. Part of him hoped that the coming storm would be final, for one of them.

Murat shifted his weight, peering out over the vast, darkened landscape. "You think I hate you because of your affection for my Sophie." For the first time since André could remember—perhaps in their entire acquaintance—Murat acknowledged the woman they both cared for, the woman whose love André would no longer deny.

André crossed his arms before his chest, the sound of her name spoken aloud stirring his blood. "In truth, I don't know why you hate me, General."

When Murat leaned close, his gray eyes caught a glint of light, shining with a hatred that disarmed André. "I won't let another Valière take my loved one from me . . . not this time. Not ever again." The general hissed this threat, but his words gave André no further understanding or clarity.

André broke from his commander's gaze, his mind spinning. He accuses *me* of taking *his* loved ones, André thought to himself, utterly confounded. Suddenly, blinking, he saw the faces of those he loved clearly in his mind's eye: His father, reading in his study, distant and dignified, aristocratic to the very end. His mother, walking with her boys in the orchards behind their estate, her laughter mingling with early-morning birdsong. Remy, smiling, a mischievous shimmer in his eye as he charmed his way out of trouble. Jean-Luc St. Clair, his friend, earnest and steadfast though all the world crumbled around him. Sophie. Always, Sophie. André had no idea where she was or how she fared in this mad world, but if she was alive, then he knew he must somehow find a way back to her. As long as he still breathed, he would fight to return to her, to the only home he had left.

Murat took a step closer, and André's thoughts clamored back to the present. Murat was just before him, his face inches away. André could smell the odor of the general's weathered uniform. "Do you have any idea what he did? What your old man did?"

Before André could stammer out a confused reply, both men were startled by the interruption of a third voice. "Everything all right here?"

Murat turned toward the approaching figure and muttered, "None of your concern, Dumas."

"Actually, I was looking for Major Valière. Major, a word, if you wouldn't mind?"

"Not now," Murat said dismissively, angling his large frame between the two men. "I am speaking to Valière at the moment."

"I can see that," Dumas said, unfazed. "Only I have orders from our high commander himself that concern the young officer. So I'm afraid I'll have to interrupt. Major, come with me, if you would."

Murat fell quiet at this, his eyes darting back and forth from Dumas to André, apparently unsure how to react. If, in fact, Dumas *did* have business with André that came directly from Bonaparte, it would not be prudent to interfere with it—even Murat knew as much. And yet, he clearly had not decided whether he believed Dumas's claim. Finally, with a low growl, Murat acquiesced, turning and skulking off into the dark camp without another word. André watched his retreating frame with relief, even though he knew that whatever business they had was far from over.

"Right this way." Dumas led André in silence until they came to a small canvas tent on the southern edge of the camp. Dumas lifted the flap and entered, waving André to follow him.

Inside, the air was hot and still. Dumas lit a candle and gestured for André to take a seat in the lone wooden chair beside the camp bed. Dumas lowered himself onto the cot.

"Join me for a moment." The general poured two small glasses of fresh water. Then, as if skimming the thoughts directly from André's mind, he spoke: "I don't actually have a message for you from General Bonaparte." Dumas gulped his water and placed his empty glass on the table. "It just appeared that you might need assistance back there with General Murat. He can be . . . difficult."

André nodded, eagerly finishing his own glass and lowering it to the table. His mind spun as he recalled the previous hour's events, the vague and indecipherable remarks by Murat. "In that case . . . thank you, sir. And thank you for the drink of water. I should go and let you—"

"Stay, stay a moment," Dumas said, raising his hand. "Was I correct?"

"Pardon?"

"Did you need saving? Back there with Nic . . . er, General Murat?"

André considered the question. "To be honest, sir, I'm not sure *what* General Murat wanted with me. I've never understood—"

"It should come as no surprise to you when I tell you that you are not one of General Murat's favorites."

André blinked, absorbing the declaration. Dumas continued, his face frank and expressionless. "You knew that already."

André nodded. "I . . . I did."

Dumas shrugged, waving his hands as if to swat a fly. "Foolish, all of it. Egypt cares very little for the grievances and grudges of a few feuding Frenchmen."

"But, sir, that's just it. I'm not certain what his grudge with me is," André confessed. "I had the . . . poor luck to fall in love with his niece, yes. But his grievance with me predates my acquaintance with Sophie, of that I'm sure. I've had the feeling that General Murat has hated me since the moment he first set eyes on me at Valmy—perhaps even before. I know that sounds odd."

"Not odd at all." Dumas shook his head, pouring himself another glass of water. He refilled André's glass as well. "In fact, you're entirely correct."

"I am?"

"Yes. Nicolai Murat has hated you your entire life. Perhaps even longer."

André did not attempt to conceal his confusion at hearing it confirmed, this bald and unequivocal hatred that he had always suspected. And by a senior officer, no less. "But what have I done? Why does he hate me?"

Dumas took a long, slow sip and smacked his lips, weighing his words. Eventually, he answered: "Nicolai Murat hates you because you are the son of Alexandre, Marquis de Valière."

The words hit like a fist to the gut, punching the air from André. When he did not answer, Dumas continued. "You might recall a bit of my story— that I am the son of a French nobleman and his Haitian mistress?"

"Yes," André said, nodding, thinking back to the first evening he'd met General Dumas, in his prison cell onboard the ship in the middle of the Mediterranean.

Dumas's mind was elsewhere now, his gaze falling on the far side of the tent as he explained: "My father's title and wealth were enough to gain me entry into society. I made acquaintances and struck up friendships among many different circles. Many of the nobles are now gone, fled abroad or lost their heads. But some remain. Some of these individuals knew your father from the royal court, others from the academy at Brienne."

"Brienne." André repeated the name: the place of his own military schooling, and of his father before him.

"Brienne." Dumas nodded. "Where all our finest officers receive their training. I myself did not have the privilege of attending. I'm an old corporal despite this uniform and all its frills. However, I did make the acquaintance of Nicolai Murat, as well as a particularly promising graduate by the name of Alexandre de Valière."

André absorbed all of this, his thoughts becoming clearer. So they went to the academy together, his father and Murat. Did Murat still harbor some schoolboy resentment from all those years ago? Was he now determined to enact revenge on his rival's son?

"But it wasn't at Brienne that the rift occurred," Dumas said, pulling André's focus back to their conversation. "You come from an ancient noble family, André. You need not be reminded of that. Why, your family has ruled vast swaths of the north going back to the Norman Conquest."

André nodded. Such talk was dangerous—life threatening, even. And yet, he trusted that Dumas did not say it in a damning way.

"My father's family is similarly ennobled," Dumas continued. "Not so with the Murat family. Their nobility is not ancient. Not even more than a generation old."

"It isn't?"

Dumas shook his head. "Murat's father bought his title; he did not inherit it. He's not what one—say, my father, or your father—would call a true noble."

"But he . . . General Murat *hates* the nobility," André replied, recalling all the times his superior had spewed his disgust against the aristocracy of the nation, and the vehemence with which Murat had persecuted and punished the noble class.

Dumas shrugged. "And now perhaps you can understand why."

André blinked, trying to make sense of it all: Murat, possessing a title, but not a *true* one, harbored a bitter grudge against a class that had never truly accepted him.

"Murat's father came up with the money for his title through trade in the West Indies," Dumas said, apparently not done with his explanation. "He owned large amounts of land there, including on my home island of Saint-Domingue, the isle of Haiti. Sugarcane, some tobacco, but mostly coffee."

"So you knew him, all those years ago?"

"I knew of him, his family at least, from the time we were young boys. And I remember when the Murat family came to disgrace in Haiti. The whole island knew they were forced to sell off their land and flee, and in a hurry."

"But . . . but why?"

"It happens that the elder Murat, our man's father, once he'd purchased his title and set himself up as quite the seigneur on the island, became much more concerned with his rum and his local ladies than with his crop. His land floundered. His business suffered. He was a brutal slave owner but a terrible steward. There was absolutely nothing left of the estate of value for him to pass on to his ambitious young son, Nicolai. The old man had accumulated such debts that he would have been run off the island. Might even have been attacked by his creditors, or else his slaves, if not for the young buyer who came forward and swiftly bought up all of his land, settling Murat's accounts and allowing the fool to retreat back to France with his tail between his legs."

"Oh?" André didn't quite understand what any of this had to do with him.

"A buyer whose business acumen—and character—were of a much higher caliber." Dumas's dark eyes caught the flicker of the lone candle. "A young nobleman by the name of Alexandre de Valière."

"Ah," André said, sitting back in his chair, his heart hammering heavily against his chest. He knew that his father had had business dealings in the

New World and that he'd spent time there years ago, before marriage and children.

"Your father," Dumas said, "had the audacity to save Nicolai Murat's family from ruin."

"And so . . . for that . . . General Murat resented my father? And now despises me? But that doesn't seem fair—if anything, he should be grateful."

Dumas shrugged. "Resented, yes. Probably envied him as well. It was certainly embarrassing for him to see his old man bailed out by a classmate of his from the academy. A young man whose wealth and title—and character—were impeccable, while his own family's name was as black as the coffee they had failed to sell. But the loathing, that came a few years later."

"What? Why?"

Now Dumas leaned forward, his voice low and grave. "I was in Paris, a young man, when I first heard about it. Heard about her. A beauty from Blois. The fair-haired daughter of the Duc de Blois—the depth of her beauty rivaled only by the immensity of her wealth. A young lady by the name of Christine de Polignac."

"*Maman*," André gasped, his chest seizing when he heard his mother's name spoken aloud.

"That's right. Your mother. She fell in love with your father shortly after he returned from the West Indies, his face kissed by the sun and his purse even more swollen with New World wealth. Everyone who saw it marveled at the pair; they were the admiration of all of Parisian society that first season they courted."

"They were?" André's mind reeled—his father and his mother?

Dumas nodded. "The king himself blessed their betrothal. Your father was probably the envy of quite a few other young noblemen when he secured Christine's heart. But there was one man—one man in particular— who had thought he had already done so. Had thought *he* would be the lucky one to marry her."

"General Murat," André said.

"Now you understand, young André de Valière, the way Nicolai Murat sees it: your father literally took everything that was ever his. His land. His family birthright. His love. . . . And you—you are the result of that. Because you exist, Murat's own sons with Christine de Polignac do not. He will never forgive you for that."

They sat in silence for a while. André gulped down another glass of water, his thoughts in a tumult; now, at least, he understood.

Eventually, Dumas's voice broke the quiet in the tent, scattering André's troubled thoughts. "By now, you cannot help but be aware of the man's feelings toward you. But between the two of us, be sure you take caution tomorrow."

André blinked, returning to the present. It was the eve of a great battle. He needed to go—needed to try for at least a few hours of rest. He rose from his seat. "Yes. All of this talk . . . it nearly made me forget the enemy."

Dumas nodded and rose, standing before the entrance of the tent. The nearby candle sputtered, its wax nearly expired, causing the glow of its flame to dance across the general's darkened face as he whispered: "Tomorrow will be chaos. Men will be scattered and dispersed, and fire will be coming from all directions. Bonaparte, he's got a sharp mind for combat, but this is unlike anything we've ever attempted. The man . . ." Dumas waved a hand. "He may be small of stature, but his ambition . . . his ambition soars to unlimited heights." Dumas sighed. "In any event, mistakes will be made. Or, perhaps, crimes committed and made to look like mistakes. Tomorrow, if you are wise, you will watch out for the enemy, yes. But, even more important, be sure to keep an eye behind you as well."

27

Paris

July 1798

J ean-Luc heard a knock on the door.

"Yes?" Opening the door, he peered into the face of one of Madame Grocque's older boys, a dirt-stained, scrawny youth of about fourteen years.

"Letter for Monsieur," the young man said, lifting a paper but not his eyes.

"Thank you," Jean-Luc said, confused; he had just returned home from work. He broke the wax seal and tore the letter open. Instinct sent a chill deep into the recesses of his gut before he'd even registered the familiar handwriting, or the meaning of the words he now beheld.

> *St. Clair—*
>
> *My old friend, it is with profound regret that I must carry out the actions you have forced me to undertake. I only ever wished for your friendship. But, if I am to depart this life, my only wish is to leave my impact upon the world so that my work endures when I am gone. Is that not my due, after a long and tired life of sacrifice for this Republic?*
>
> *For this reason, Sophie de Vincennes and her beloved Marquis de Valière cannot be allowed to carry their noble bloodlines into the new world we've created. I will see to it that they shall not.*

But my masterstroke will be this: the whole world will blame you. They will learn how the feeble lawyer fell in love with his own client's fiancée. How else does one explain her presence under your roof all that time? Quite suspicious. And why else would you take the trouble to call on her in prison each day—your eyes fixed on hers, whispering and promising?

The people may even sympathize with you for your weakness; her beauty is so maddening they will understand why you had to have her. Perhaps even André de Valière himself would understand that. But, ultimately, they will despise you all the same. With disgust, they will learn how your affections were scorned, and you had no choice but to destroy her.

There was no signature. No address from the sender. But Jean-Luc did not need one.

"What is it?" Marie was already in bed, and she rolled over now, calling out to him. "Jean-Luc?" She clutched her full belly, wincing as she did so.

Jean-Luc swallowed nervously, trying to keep the panic at bay as he folded the letter and stuffed it into his coat pocket. "It's from Lazare." His voice was faint.

"What does that old goat want?"

"I . . . I'm not certain. Something about Sophie."

"Sophie?" Marie's features went taut. "Is she in danger?"

"I—" He faltered.

"If she's in danger, you must go to her. Immediately."

Jean-Luc nodded but then looked more closely at his wife, noting the flush of her face. The fact that she tried to hide a grimace. "Are you ill?"

"Just a bit tired." She blinked.

"I cannot leave you like this." Jean-Luc took her hands in his, kneeling beside her. "Can it be labor pains, already?"

She propped herself up on her elbows, her thick curls clinging to her sweaty neck and cheeks like wild vines. "I don't think so. Not yet. Perhaps just an early prelude, false labor, they call it. That can happen with the second child."

"How can you be certain?" Jean-Luc demanded. "Should I not run and fetch a midwife, someone?"

Marie smiled, the skin around her brown eyes creasing into the familiar pattern that Jean-Luc adored. She appeared to be lit up from inside. "I am fine. Just a passing cramp."

Jean-Luc hesitated. "I should stay. I don't know what Lazare's letter means. Perhaps it's only an idle threat. I don't think I should leave you, in case—"

She cut him off. "You must go," she said, shaking her head. "We both know enough of that man to know that he is never idle in his threats—or his evil. Go. Sophie needs someone to protect her. She has no one but us."

Taking his wife's sticky hand in his own, Jean-Luc kissed it. And then, reluctantly, he said: "I will be quick. But are you certain I can't fetch the midwife before I leave?"

Marie shook her head. "Go—the sooner you go, the sooner you return."

Jean-Luc lifted her hands to his lips and kissed them once more. "I don't tell you enough, but you're stronger than I could ever be."

"Nature made women hardier than men for a reason," she quipped, smiling. "Now, go! Give Sophie my love and tell her that I would like to have her back here—what with another little one to arrive soon, I could use her help."

"Yet another reason I am trying my hardest to see her released." Jean-Luc reluctantly rose from beside the bed, still looking at his wife. "You are *certain* you will not need the midwife?"

Marie nodded, and Jean-Luc sighed. "Then I'll ask Madame Grocque to check in on you and Mathieu. I will return as soon as I can—in less than an hour."

"Right. Now go, let me rest." Marie smiled, then shut her eyes.

"I'm here to see Sophie de Vincennes." Jean-Luc panted before the confused prison guard, a young man Jean-Luc had never seen before. "I must see Sophie de Vincennes at once!"

"Calm yourself, citizen. Your personal bothers don't supersede protocol." The guard gave Jean-Luc a reproving look and lifted a large parchment from his desk, checking the names of his wards. He hummed softly as he scanned the long list.

"Citizen St. Clair," Jean-Luc gasped out, impatient with the formalities of a new and rigid guard. "I must speak with my client, Sophie de Vincennes, at once. She's being held in prison cell number twelve, east wing."

"Just a minute, citizen." The guard still looked at his paper, a confused expression clouding his face.

"If you please, I am here every day. I know where her cell is; I can let myself in." Not waiting for the guard's approval, Jean-Luc moved toward the long, candlelit corridor that would take him to Sophie. But the guard raised a hand to block him.

"Citizeness de Vincennes ain't back there," the man said, his eyes rising from the paper to Jean-Luc.

"What do you mean she's not back there? Where else would she be?"

The guard scratched his head, taking entirely too long to respond. "Says here that Citizeness de Vincennes was set free this afternoon."

Jean-Luc looked down at the paper, incredulous. Seeing that same notice, he staggered backward until his back found the wall. "But . . . but she's my client. If she were to be freed, I would have known. It would have been my doing. Where is she?"

The man shrugged. "She was released. Now that I think on it, I remember. Blond lady? Real proper-like and pretty, that one? Yes, I remember her. Walked out on her own. Didn't look as 'appy as I woulda suspected, seeing as she was set free and all."

Jean-Luc still studied the guard, his mind a swirl of confused thoughts.

"There was a coach waiting for her. A big covered coach and a man who come to get her. Friendly enough fellow, even if he was a bit odd looking. Bright orange hair. Gave the name of Marnioc. Or Merillac. Something to that effect."

Jean-Luc clutched the cold, damp wall of the prison, swallowing hard. He thought about it, about the strange letter that sat in his coat pocket. "Merignac."

"That's the one." The guard nodded, satisfied that they had resolved the predicament. He looked back down to his papers, eager to be done with this interview.

Jean-Luc, however, felt no relief. All he felt was the paralyzing clutch of fear; he was too late. Lazare had her.

28

Giza, Egypt

July 1798

Their march began well before dawn, the soldiers setting out from their camp at Warraq al-Hadar in the frigid dark, André shivering in his blue coat as the army headed south along the river. The soldiers, tired and cold, grumbled as they watched their campfires recede over their shoulders. As cold as it felt now, it would be that much hotter once the sun peeked out over the desert horizon.

They marched for hours, stopping only once, while it was still dark, for a quick breakfast. As dawn approached, André could make out the Nile to his left, could see that it was widening, growing fuller and faster.

The horses began to whinny, and even André's temperate gelding began to jerk his head, bucking against the bridle. André had shaken off his fatigue by now, his eyes and senses alert with the knowledge that dawn was almost certain to bring a number of dangers. Just then, as the French army left the river fork behind them, the sun's first rays sliced over the eastern shore, cutting through the darkness and casting the first spears of light over the ancient landscape.

André shifted in his saddle, examining the faces of those around him. Several paces back, Ashar rode, speaking with one of the French dragoons who rode at his side. He saw André and waved his right hand. André motioned for his friend to join him at the head of the column.

"You always seem to appear when something important is about to take place, my friend. So tell me, what shall we expect for today?" André asked.

The Egyptian looked up, his face aglow in the orange light of the sunrise. "Giza is as sacred a land as any, Major. By God's grace, your general has managed to see us this far." Ashar took in a deep breath and closed his eyes. "But now, we must simply wait for whatever fate God has chosen for us."

"Are they really that impressive, these mausoleums?" André asked, skeptical. All the men were abuzz with the excitement of beholding the great pyramids, but Paris had the Panthéon—their own massive mausoleum—and stunning cathedrals that had been the envy of all of Christendom for centuries; surely these tombs would not outshine the French capital.

Ashar considered the question before answering: "Every pharaoh who lived and died wished for Giza to be his eternal resting place. I might tell you of their splendor, but you shall behold them with your own eyes soon. And then, you may answer your own question."

Just then, André's horse started, snorting and pawing the ground. He stroked the beast's neck to soothe the nervous animal, but when he squinted, his eyes forward, he saw what had spooked it. Up ahead, bathed in the gentle rays of the early-morning sun, was a massive rising cloud, a grim shadow forming from out of the earth. "Dust," André said.

"Mamelukes," Ashar added, his voice steady.

André clutched his reins, his horse jerking nervously beneath him. "Steady, now," he said, soothing the beast. He narrowed his eyes and willed them to give him a better picture of the foreign army. "Good God, how many are there?"

The men around him had gone quiet. Most had not slept all night. They'd marched several miles in the frigid dark of predawn, on stomachs empty of anything but bits of fruit that did little more than upset their insides. And now, in the distance, it appeared as if the entire desert was slowly surging toward them.

André peered into the distance once more, sharpening his gaze to focus on the figures beneath the massive plume of dust that rose to the heavens. It looked like an entire nation on horseback.

The Egyptian nodded as he beheld the scene before them. "Each Mameluke warrior has a servant to carry his weapons while on the march. A cluster of tambourine players to serenade his horse's steps. They have their children and women. War, for them, is not an event separate from life. War is life."

André turned from the distant scene to survey the French forces all around him. Just then, French scouts rode past André and out beyond the front units. On all sides of his squadron, the infantry continued its advance to the shrill notes of the fifes and the deep rhythm of the drums. Tricolor flags waved in the morning breeze, and men who could barely stand just minutes ago held their heads high and marched in time, fueled now by fear and adrenaline.

Nearby, General Bonaparte sat atop a gleaming white horse, his expression haughty, his body alert, surrounded by a dozen aides, attendants, and general officers as he bent over a map. The massive tricolor flagged billowed above him. General Dumas was there as well, as were Murat and several other officers.

The French, coming from the north, had the river on their left flank, the desert on their right. In front of André now, the infantry were forming up and closing ranks. The five division commanders, who had been given their orders from General Bonaparte, were peeling their soldiers off and forming what André saw to be massive squares. The divisional square was a new feature of Napoleon's genius, an impenetrable wall of soldiers and their rifles and bayonets. It stood six ranks deep at the front and rear, three ranks deep on the sides. In theory, but yet unproven, no cavalry charge could defeat this because a horse would not willingly impale itself on a wall of steel.

Men formed the outer perimeter of each square, while in the middle, the soldiers were tossing luggage, supplies, packs, and ammunition for the guns. On the corners of each of the four flanks were placed the cannons. Each square was a small fortress, their gun barrels and bayonets facing in any direction from which an enemy could attack.

General Bonaparte rode out, pausing in front of his army. André sat up a bit taller in his saddle.

"Men, today, our enemy will finally meet the soldiers of France!" Napoleon held his reins in one hand; his other held his bicorn hat aloft. "Remember, from atop those pyramids, forty centuries of history look down upon you. For the Republic! For France!"

André looked past the figure of their high commander toward the south, toward the wall of Mamelukes, assembling before a range of desert mountains. And then he realized: those were not mountains behind the Mamelukes. Those were buildings. Jagged, mountain-like buildings, rising up to the heavens in a proportion that defied reason and belief—that defied anything André would have ever believed achievable by mankind.

"The great pyramids," André gasped. Earth-colored fortresses that housed the remains of Egypt's ancient pharaohs, leaders who had slept in their massive tombs since time immemorial. And now, on this day, these unfathomable structures would stand impassive, witness to a desert landscape where more men would join the pharaohs in permanent rest.

29

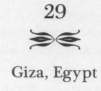

Giza, Egypt

July 1798

Daylight shone strong enough now to make clear the army they faced: a host of thousands of Mamelukes. The fighters sat atop lean Arabian horses, a massive and uninterrupted wall stretching across the southern horizon. The river formed the French army's left flank and the shimmering heat of the desert their right. Beyond them, barely visible in the distance, loomed the Great Pyramid of Khufu and its sisters. To André, they seemed out of place, too sacred for this gritty and soon to be bloody battlefield.

The Mameluke line glistened in the distance; unlike the French, covered in dark blue with red and white, the Mameluke horsemen were a rhapsody of color. Armored plates were strapped across their chests, inlaid with sapphires, rubies, emeralds, and other precious stones. Egret feathers rose from elaborately turbaned heads. Gilded helmets caught the rays of sunlight, glinting brighter than the Nile. The warriors brandished spears, sabers, lances, daggers—each one encrusted in precious stones and elaborate jewels.

"Valière!"

André turned to the familiar voice of General Dumas. "Yes, sir?"

"Your squadron will fall in with Desaix's square, on the western flank."

"Yes, sir." André directed his men, ordering them to fold into the massive square.

"Good, now you'll come with me," Dumas roared, and then rode off without looking back to ensure André followed. They raced farther to the west, André unclear of what he would be doing.

Dumas joined a party of about fifty horsemen—dragoons and chasseurs. As André tried to blink away the glare from the shining breastplates, he saw out of the corner of his eye that Murat was there. He wore his usual stern expression, his eyes gazing out over the scene unfolding before them. André saluted. "General Murat." The general touched the front of his hat to acknowledge the salute.

André turned back toward the river and the waiting Mameluke horde. Over the sound of the French bugles and the shouts of French officers rose another more frightening sound: the trilling of the Mameluke warriors, readying themselves for battle.

Their leader now emerged from the ranks of his horsemen and presented himself for both armies to see. As he rode out in front of his army, he paused, unsheathing his scimitar. When he faced his army, his sword whirling above his head, his fighters began to roar with frenzied war cries. Horns blasting from across the Mameluke lines added to the din, and André wondered if there was a soldier among the French who was unmoved by this spectacle.

Perhaps one among them remained entirely undistracted, entirely focused on the French movement; as the enemy worked themselves into battle lust, Napoleon Bonaparte steadily eyed the sea of horsemen in front of him. He ordered the French to put three hundred paces between squares, a distance large enough to mitigate friendly fire concerns but narrow enough to create the deadly crossfire that would pour into the Mameluke lines from both directions as they tried to encircle the French. General Bonaparte lifted his sword and gave the signal.

The massive French squares began to march. As the drummers and fifes kept time, the soldiers moved in perfect unison, the great squares advancing forward in one steady motion. Dust churned at their feet as they moved toward their enemy; André marveled at the discipline required to carry out this complex maneuver and wondered if even some of the Mamelukes were transfixed by this bizarre configuration marching toward them.

Not to be outdone, the Mameluke leader lifted his scimitar over his head and, in one fluid motion, dropped it to his front. At this, a tidal wave of Mameluke horsemen began speeding down the gently sloping sand, racing toward the French squares. André was gripped by a momentary feeling of helplessness; this cavalry charge appeared unstoppable, the proud Arabian horses carrying thousands of bellowing warriors directly to the French line, their armor and swords glistening in the stark white sunlight.

As the wave of Mamelukes chewed up the gap between the two armies, the French squares stood fixed, a wall of flesh and steel. Steady. Individual soldiers shook with fear, but the formation held firm. And then, as the Arabian horses thundered less than fifty paces from the French squares, the order was shouted and a deafening burst ripped out from the front of each square. Muskets cracked in unison and the cannons positioned at the corners of the squares poured a devastating hail of grapeshot and lead into the charging horde of men and horses. Horses screamed and fell, many of their riders trampled by the ranks thundering past them. Those beasts that hadn't been hit began to buck and swerve at the sight of the French bayonets so densely stacked together. The lucky riders who were yet unhurt weaved their horses between the squares and were caught in ruinous crossfire that tore into them from both sides. Now, they became stranded as the French shifted to funnel all of these riders toward the reedy banks of the river.

André watched this unfold from within his square, astonished by the carnage of this first assault. On the French left flank, the soldiers nearest to the river were dispersing the square. The battalions wheeled slowly apart and formed back into three conventional infantry lines. There, under the commander General Bon, the division formed up for a counterattack. Like sheepherders, Bon's division fenced in the disoriented and scattered Mamelukes, funneling them and their horses toward the river. This was the tactical genius of Napoleon Bonaparte at work; he had harnessed not only thousands of men and tons of steel but even nature itself to his purposes. Rifles and bayonets stabbing outward, the division offered the Mamelukes a grim choice: be gutted by French steel or throw themselves into the flowing waters of the Nile.

A large part of the Mameluke cavalry took their chances with the Nile, spurring their skittish horses into the river. Those who chose to stand and fight were methodically felled with bayonet thrusts.

Along this bank of the river stood a small cluster of clay buildings, a deserted fishing village from the looks of it. The attacking Frenchmen now swarmed this outcropping of buildings, taking cover behind the structures to fire on the Mamelukes who struggled in the nearby river. The horses splashed and plunged like sea serpents as the glorious glint of all of those precious stones went dull in the dark water. Hundreds were pulled under by the current. It appeared so far to André as if not a single Frenchman had perished, while the Mamelukes were literally being carried away in the current.

"All right, men!" The sound of General Dumas's voice pulled André's attention from the distant carnage back to his immediate surroundings. "Enough spectating. It's our turn." The general's eyes flashed with a wild light as he spoke.

"If we let that rear group retreat"—Dumas pointed his sword to the south, near the base of the mountainous pyramids—"they'll regroup and attack us later." Sure enough, in the distance was a cloud of dust, churned up by the band of Mameluke cavalry that had survived the squares and had splintered off to flee to the relative safety of the southern desert.

"Cavalry, advance!" Dumas shouted, kicking his horse in the sides. André, Murat, and the others followed. The cavalry hidden inside the squares now began to emerge and rode to join Dumas's charge. The horsemen cut a wide arc around the periphery of the French line, approaching the pyramids from the west.

From up close, the ancient structures appeared even more staggering— impossible in their width and height. André could not help but gawk as they approached the base of the nearest pyramid. But his eyes were quickly pulled from the pyramid to the desert in front of him; a group of enemy horsemen who had lain in wait behind the pyramids now rode out, taking the French completely by surprise. At this close distance, the ferocity of their battle cries was even more chilling. The numbers here were more favorable for the Mamelukes, with no river to fence them in against French rifles and bayonets.

"Follow me!" General Dumas raised his sword and turned his horse to meet the oncoming enemy. The front of the French squadron smashed into the Mameluke cavalry. In this melee, sand and dust churned up in all directions. André wiped his stinging eyes in order to see the enemy before him.

The first two enemy horses flew past him before he had time to swing his saber. A third slowed his pace as he rode toward André. He met the Mameluke's scimitar and just barely parried the strike, slashing back as his horse sidestepped another rider racing past.

The warrior struck again, this time swinging overhead, and André fended off the enemy's slash with his own saber. His horse lurched back, knocking André temporarily off balance. André looked down, surprised by the sudden movement, and saw that a Mameluke pistol shot had struck his horse in the chest.

André swore as he felt the horse stumble, struggling desperately to stay on its feet. Capitalizing on this distraction, the Mameluke slashed at André, the blade just barely missing his right shoulder. Beneath him, André's horse grunted in agonizing pain, pawing at the earth with legs that André knew would soon give out. He wheeled his horse around, willing it to carry him out of the melee. If he fell here, he would be easy prey for the slashing blades and crushing hooves that thrashed all around him.

With a painful effort, the horse obeyed. The horse limped for several paces, clearing mount and rider from the clash of flesh and steel. At a distance André deemed safe enough for a quick pause, he dismounted and looked at his beast. The creature was screeching in agony, losing blood at an unsustainable pace, and so André pulled out his pistol and took mercy on the poor animal. Now he was without a horse in a mounted engagement, far from friendly lines. At least he still had his pistol and his saber. He dropped to one knee, panting as he quickly loaded another ball, dropping it into the barrel of his pistol and ramming it into place.

He took a quick survey of his surroundings. His best chance, he decided, was to find some high ground, perhaps on the side of one of these massive structures, and wait for a mount to become available. It was only a matter of time before one of the nearby horses lost its rider in the mayhem. But before he had taken a dozen paces, he saw another Mameluke rider approaching. The man looked down on him with black eyes, his mouth opened wide as he trilled out his war cry.

André rolled to his left, ducking at the last minute out of the horse's path. He stumbled to his feet but realized he had dropped the pistol as he dodged. He clawed at the sand, hoping to find it somewhere in front of him, but there was no time, for the warrior had turned his light-footed beast and was charging again. This time, André did not move quickly enough, and the blade of the warrior's saber slashed his right leg, cutting through layers of pants and flesh. André buckled, clutching his thigh. Now he surely could not out-duel this man mounted on an Arabian. Instinctively he reached for the pistol on his belt. Empty. A cold sensation settled over him—he would die on this sand.

"Valière!" André looked up and saw General Murat approach, his own pistol held aloft. The general aimed the weapon at the enemy and fired. The Mameluke rider sat upright for a moment, then a sudden spasm shook his body. He slumped sideways, slowly sliding off his exhausted horse. André shut his eyes, relief washing over him, momentarily forgetting the excruciating pain in his thigh. The Mameluke was dead and André was wounded but saved—by General Murat, of all people.

"Valière, you're wounded." Murat hopped down from his horse and helped André up. "Can you make it onto the horse?"

André looked down at his bleeding leg; standing was a sudden agony, and he abandoned the idea of jumping into a stirrup.

"Fine." Murat walked with the reins in one hand and guided André, hoisting his other arm over his shoulders, toward a narrow lane alongside the massive pyramid before them.

"Wait." André turned. Seeing his saber not ten feet away, he hobbled over and picked it up, sliding it into his scabbard.

Each step was excruciating, and André fought the urge to cry out in pain, but he allowed himself to be carried by the general farther from the tumult and into the dark, shaded space. He noticed they were near some sort of entryway to the sealed pyramid. Here the sunlight was blocked out and the air was moist. Centuries of shadow had made the stones cool.

"Drink." Murat was panting but appeared entirely unharmed from the battle. He held out his waterskin, which André took, noticing, as he did so, how parched his lips and throat were.

"Thank you, sir." André gulped the water greedily, allowing himself to be distracted by this cooling drink so that, for just a moment, he forgot about the bleeding wound in his right thigh.

After he had drunk his fill, he lowered the waterskin. As he did so, he saw the pistol pointed directly at his face. Behind it stared the sea-gray eyes of Nicolai Murat, filled with the look of hatred that André had seen so many times before. Only this time, they were alone—just the two of them, in this dark and hidden doorway, out of sight or earshot from the rest of their countrymen. So, André realized, Murat had simply saved him so that he could be the one to finish him off.

"I've waited years for this moment," Murat said, his voice low but animated, a grim sneer showing beneath his mustache. "Make peace with your God, if you have one."

André acted on instinct, throwing the waterskin at Murat. His aim was true, mercifully, and it knocked the general in the face as André ripped the pistol loose from Murat's grip. The weapon fell to the ground, firing as it did so, smashing against the impenetrable stone of the building. Disregarding the pain in his leg, André threw himself at the general, knocking him backward as they both fell to the ground, a tangle of limbs and sweat.

Murat was strong—stronger than André had expected—and certainly strong enough that André, with his incapacitated leg, struggled to contain his writhing frame.

"I'll kill you, Valière," Murat hissed, his face just inches from André's, his lips contorting in a menacing snarl beneath his thick mustache.

André cried out in excruciating pain when Murat groped the wound in his leg with his sandy fingers, gnashing at the pulp of flesh and blood.

Just then three Mamelukes rode into view, no doubt drawn by the sounds of André's cries. Both André and Murat froze as they saw their tall frames carving out dark silhouettes against the daylight. The horsemen saw the two Frenchmen struggling on the stone floor and muttered a few words to one another in a foreign dialect. They dismounted.

André and Murat pulled apart, each one of them now thinking about his own defense against these three warriors. One of the Mamelukes muttered something in his native tongue, causing the other two to laugh, a mirthless, spine-chilling sound.

One of them, a giant with a red turban and rubies adorning his earlobes, charged André. André pulled his sword from its scabbard and parried the blow. To his right, he saw that two of them had engaged Murat, probably believing the Frenchman with the bloody wound in his thigh to be the easier prey.

André screamed, lunging desperately with his sword. The thrust was easily dodged with a quick movement by the Mameluke. Up close now André saw the man's features: an ageless face, a hard face, black eyes, and a long beard that swayed as he lunged.

His sword locked with the Mameluke's and André moved his left hand quickly, taking it off the sword to reach for his waist. Groaning against the effort of holding the Mameluke's sword back, he reached with his free hand for his dagger. With one quick motion he raised the dagger, thrusting it into the Mameluke's belly. The man dropped his sword with a loud clamor onto the stone floor, stepping back from André, his black eyes wide in disbelief. And then he fell, his body landing next to his dropped sword.

André saw that Murat and the two Mamelukes were still struggling, the general fighting savagely even as he was being backed up against the wall. André remembered Murat's dropped pistol; he looked around, spotting it several paces away, and lunged for it.

One of the Mamelukes had pinned Murat against the wall and was trying to stab him in the neck. There was blood coming from Murat's arm; the general had been injured in the fight. André loaded the pistol quickly, aimed, and fired. One of the enemy stiffened before collapsing on top of Murat. Both Murat and the surviving fighter turned and saw from where the bullet had issued. The third Mameluke, stunned by the shot, bolted from this entryway, leaving the bodies of his two dead friends.

André watched the man ride off, hoping that was the last Mameluke he'd ever see. Now, he stood facing Murat, alone in the entryway. I just saved your miserable life, André thought to himself, his hatred mixing with the salt and dust that parched his mouth. Murat's shoulder was bleeding and his face was confused as he took in the scene. He panted, appearing more like a crazed animal than a brigadier general.

André kept his sword in his hands, noticing that Murat, too, was still armed. The general looked now from the two corpses to André. There it was, still. That burning hatred. André stepped back several feet, backing away from the interior of the entryway. "Murat." He took another step backward. Soon he would be off stone and back onto the sand. Who knew what other foes waited out there in the desert, and how the rest of the French forces had fared? But he could not remain in here, alone, with Murat.

"When will this end?" André panted.

Murat strode forward, stalking him slowly, his eyes still intent on violence. "It will end, André de Valière, when I've killed you. Like I killed your brother before you. He took down three of my men, but I gutted him in the end. I saw the life leave his eyes—as I will now with you."

André cried out in agony, emotional as well as physical pain, and he hoisted his sword, though his body was drained of all strength.

Murat growled, parrying André's blow, his face coming close as their swords locked in a stalemate. "You shall be my last," Murat snarled.

"Why?" André demanded, rasping for breath, stepping back from the man, his sword still lifted protectively. "How many have you taken? My brother, my father. Your friend Kellermann. The countless others condemned to death. Why must you do this?"

Murat laughed now, a mirthless laugh that brought no joy to his features. " 'Why *me*?' You're all the same, all of you spoiled noblemen. 'Who could possibly hate *me*?' Kellermann was the same way. You believe that anyone can be bought with your purse, charmed with your smiles. You act the humble hero, even as you allow the people to worship you."

"Please." André stumbled. There was no reasoning with this man. André limped out of the entryway now, and his eyes were flooded by the blinding desert light. The heat enfolded him and made him even dizzier, but he forced himself to focus on the man standing in front of him. "Hasn't there been enough death?" His voice was hoarse, his leg throbbed, and he felt increasingly light-headed from the pain and loss of blood.

"Soon it will be enough. But before I kill you, André de Valière, there is one more thing you should know." Murat and André were hugging the base of the pyramid. From a quick glance, André saw that they remained alone. "Something about . . . *Sophie*."

André's frame froze at the maniacal smile on his superior's lips.

"You'll never see Sophie again. You'll never have her!" Murat laughed, the cackle of a madman. "I've found a punishment far worse—for both of you—than beheading by the guillotine."

André lowered his sword, feeling his body slacken. He was so tired, weighed down by a fatigue that seeped beyond his limbs and throbbed into the depths of his very soul. But then he thought of her. *Sophie*. She loved him. She waited for him. He raised his sword once more.

"You see, my sweet little So-So is never going to be yours," Murat continued, his features writhing and covered in sweat as they stepped, in unison, along the side of the pyramid's base. "I've given my blessing for her to be married to my old friend."

"Who?" André asked, his voice faint, his throat choked by dryness.

"Guillaume Lazare."

André remembered the man: The lawyer who had tried to have him killed. The man who had convicted Kellermann and his father.

André stopped edging backward. Now, as he raised his sword, he lunged forward. He cried out in pain as he did so, and Murat easily sidestepped. Seeing the weakness in André's legs, Murat turned and shuffled back a few paces. The blocks of the building beside them were broad, like steps, and Murat climbed a few so that he had the high ground.

André was undeterred, driven mad by his will to be rid of this man and carry on living, or else die in the attempt. He stepped forward, ignoring the pain as he lifted his sword and tried to hack into the general's legs. Murat, on the high ground, parried the blow.

Murat answered by hammering down on him. André kept his gaze upward toward his enemy, but the midday sun shone directly behind Murat, blindingly bright. André parried several blows but knew he could not hold this position much longer.

Murat lifted his sword, his arm perfectly framed by stark sunlight, and André blinked. Just then, a gust of wind picked up, whipping the sand like a cloud around them. Murat, facing outward while André was sheltered by the pyramid, paused momentarily, shielding his face. As he did so, André took his sword and slashed at the man's shins, cutting through leather boots and breeches until he reached flesh and bone. Murat cried out in pain, buckling forward. André raised his sword and slashed a second time, this time tearing across the man's kneecaps.

Murat, doubled over now, limped backward but his boots slipped on the sand-slicked stone. He fell to all fours, his knees buckling beneath him. He cried out in torturous pain as his wounded legs broke the full weight of his body against the sand and stone.

Unbelievably, however, Murat lifted himself to stand. Disarmed, and with both his shoulder and knees bleeding, he used his last weapon: his body. He threw himself down from the ledge, jumping onto André, his face bent on destruction, determined to destroy André, even if all he had left were his bare hands. As Murat flew down onto him, André lifted his sword so that the flesh of his attacker's stomach met his steel blade. Murat fell onto André, knocking both of them backward. The sand broke André's fall; André's body and upturned sword broke Murat's.

Stunned, André rolled the general off of him. He clambered to his knees, pulling his sword from Murat's abdomen. André wiped the red blade clean on his pants and looked down at the general, the man's mustache twitching as his features contorted in pain. It sounded as if he were trying to speak.

And then, after a few moments of tortured gurgling, the noises stopped issuing from the throat of Nicolai Murat. Those eyes, so cold and determined in life, looked back at André now with no hint of the hatred they had so long held; their gray, the color of the sea, seemed entirely out of place in this parched desert.

André collapsed, breathless, beside Murat. His entire body ached with exhaustion, and his leg throbbed as he tried to stand. Failing at that, he reached for his waterskin, but it had been torn off in the fight. His eyes watered and his vision began to blur. His body was oppressively heavy, and he felt an overwhelming desire to close his eyes and rest. He stared up at the sun and thought of home. As he slipped out of consciousness, he heard the rumble of hoofbeats; they sounded distant, as if in a dream. He could make out voices, unintelligible, but speaking his language all the same.

When André blinked his eyes open, he saw a familiar face hovering over him. "I always seem to appear when something important is about to happen—isn't that what you said?" Ashar waved over two dragoons, and together they lifted André onto his friend's horse, racing back toward the French lines, splashing water on him to keep him conscious.

As he bounced in the saddle, his body racked with pain and his mind as battered as the sandy battlefield, André carried one thought: Murat's final words about Sophie. He cried out, and his companions assumed it to be the pain from his wounds. In truth, it was a pain much worse than any physical ache; was he too late to save not himself, but Sophie?

30

Le Temple
Prison, Paris

July 1798

"Answer me!" Jean-Luc paced the small prison hallway, his tone frantic. "Did you see which way the coach carrying Sophie de Vincennes went?"

The guard stared back at Jean-Luc, mute and unobliging.

Driven mad by frustration, Jean-Luc grabbed the guard by the collar of his coat. The man, stunned at this rough treatment, shut his eyes. "I don't know," he answered, his voice like a whimper. "Looked like they headed south, in the direction of the Hôtel de Ville, is my guess? But I didn't get much of a look."

Jean-Luc released his grip on the man, stepping out of the prison. Outside, the evening was warm. He felt a drop of moisture on his forehead, instinctively looking up. Just the time for the rain to start. He had taken several steps toward Rue Réaumur when a woman in a threadbare gown that barely covered her shoulders approached from the side alley. "All I ask is for enough to get a little something to eat, monsieur. I'll make it worth your time, I will."

Jean-Luc shook the woman's hands away and wove down the narrow street toward the river. He sped up his pace, scowling, as the drizzle grew heavier.

The letter—the wicked, taunting letter—had implied that, whatever Lazare was planning to do to Sophie, he would orchestrate things in such a way that it appeared to be Jean-Luc's doing. Would he take her from the city? Would he force her to marry him? Would he go as far as to harm her? Jean-Luc did not have any answers, nor did he know how much time he had. Enough time to check one, perhaps two locations. After that, he might be too late.

But how could he be sure where Lazare would go? The old Jacobin Club, that building on Rue Saint-Honoré where he had first met the old man? Or La Place de la Révolution? Or perhaps someplace closer to the city's barrier? But there was one other place—a place that suddenly made sense to him. Jean-Luc recalled the warning words of his friend Gavreau: *whatever you do, keep him out of your office.* With an instinctive gamble, Jean-Luc made up his mind and ran toward his office in the administrative building next to the Palais de Justice.

The old man knew where Jean-Luc worked. He would also know that, this late in the evening, the building would be empty of clerks and administrators. He would have the privacy he needed to torment the poor woman, and in a location where Jean-Luc could be made to look responsible. Jean-Luc sprinted until he reached the building, climbing the front steps at a leap.

"Damn!" The front door was locked. As hard as he yanked, he could gain no entry. He knocked like a madman, but of course there was no one to let him in; if there had been, Lazare would not have chosen the location.

Jean-Luc was struck by an idea. Running to the side of the building, he arrived at the entrance of the narrow, covered alleyway. There, he froze in his tracks; the archangel Michael, the same oversized statue he'd first found so arresting with Gavreau, loomed in the shadows. Too heavy to move without several strong horses and too tall to fit through the doors into the office building, the angel had been left in this lane. His fierce gaze burned, unseen, as the walls of the surrounding buildings cast their darkness onto this angel of war. Jean-Luc stood, mesmerized, staring at this imposing figure—the arms raised high, one offering a blessing, the other, eternal damnation. Michael held aloft a spear of light, ready to be hurled toward some celestial nemesis.

Jean-Luc forced himself to peel his eyes from the fierce, righteous angel and found the side door at the bottom of several steps. This entrance was locked, too, so he cracked the glass of the door and turned the lock from the inside. He took a breath and stepped into the darkness of the interior.

He was in the cellar—the cold storeroom where the plundered treasure of the victims of the Revolution sat, forgotten. He blinked his eyes, his vision patchy in the darkness. He blinked again, as the outline of a large open space cluttered with objects began to take shape. The hall was filled, nearly every inch of it, with the spoils of noble and Catholic dynasties, the objects' decorative splendor now obsolete and appearing ridiculous as the cache sat collecting dust. Jean-Luc thought he heard a whimper from some unseen corner of the massive warehouse, as if one of the statues had called out. There it was again, another muffled cry. His heartbeat quickened.

Rows of seized goods—marble statues, furniture shrouded in sheets, cracked mirrors, smaller items of a personal nature such as ivory combs and satin shoes—all obstructed his sight and slowed his movement as he cautiously made his way closer to where he had heard the cry.

"Sophie?" he called out, wincing as his voice echoed loudly off the cold walls of the dark, damp storeroom. Another whimper sounded as his reply. "Sophie!" Jean-Luc cried out again, his heart smacking against his rib cage now. "Sophie, it's Jean-Luc! Where are you?"

A shriek, muffled, followed by the sound of china tableware crashing to the ground. Jean-Luc darted up the row of statues, glancing from left to right, but her whimpers seemed to be receding from him. "Sophie!" He sped up. At the end of one row of goods he paused, debating which way to turn in the shadowy maze of wasted splendor. He wheeled left and nearly tripped over a footrest covered in plush red velvet, before racing down another row. Why did it have to be so damned dark in here?

A shrill cry, like that of an animal caught in a trap, sounded from his right, and Jean-Luc clambered over a pile of rugs to move toward the noise. "Sophie, I'm here!" He rounded the corner past a tall candelabra and saw her at the end of a long row of statues.

Sophie was on the floor, a heap of disheveled hair and a ripped dress. Bound and gagged, her blue eyes wide in terror. A line of crimson trickled down her left cheek, matched by another wound on the opposite shoulder. And what was that on the white flesh of her bare forearm, Jean-Luc wondered—a bite mark? Clenching his jaw, a growling sound escaping from his lips, he sped toward her, unsure of where her tormenter lurked.

And then a dark object came flying at him, just barely missing his temple as Jean-Luc ducked his head instinctively. When he turned, he saw Lazare, his yellow hair wild and his light eyes illuminated by a savage glow. In his left hand he held a fire poker, which he now lifted to swing once more. He missed Jean-Luc again, the poker smashing violently against a bust of a plump-faced nobleman, shattering the plaster. Shards of statue rained down over both Jean-Luc and Lazare, showering them with a cloud of white dust. Lazare lifted the poker again, and this time its point found the flesh of Jean-Luc's thigh.

Jean-Luc roared as the pain ripped across his thigh, causing him to keel forward to clutch the bleeding wound. Lazare, seizing on his target's momentary shock, let go of the poker and ran forward. He pulled a knife out of his coat. Brandishing this weapon, he approached Sophie. "Stand up! Stand up now, you slut, or I'll slit your throat!"

Sophie struggled, faltering for a moment as she tripped on the folds of her torn dress, but she obeyed. Pressing the knife to her belly, applying enough pressure to make its presence known, Lazare snarled. "With me. Now!"

The old man dragged Sophie away with a quickness that surprised Jean-Luc. He craned his neck to follow their movement, but they hurried along the confiscated furnishings, disappearing from his sight. Jean-Luc was still bent over, pressing his palm to the mangled flesh of his leg. Pushing back against his agony, he seized what looked to be the coat of a small child and tore off a small strip of fabric, tying it around the top of his thigh. He had no training in medicine but knew enough to try to slow the bleeding in his leg.

He looked back up, listening for any sign of Sophie, but they were gone. He could not even hear their receding footsteps. Clutching the discarded fire poker in his hand, Jean-Luc rose, limping in the same direction that Lazare had run off. Each step was fresh agony—like a new gash to his leg—but he forced himself onward.

Now he heard Sophie. Her voice, high-pitched with pain or terror, or both, was shrieking, but she was slipping farther and farther away. Jean-Luc forced himself to quicken his pace as he hurried up the stairs from the cellar.

He stumbled into the front hall of the building, its shuttered windows admitting only a pallid, muddled light from the outside. There, across the hall on the second floor, were the two figures Jean-Luc sought. Glancing over his shoulder and spotting his pursuer, Lazare cursed and sped up his pace, half-dragging Sophie toward a corridor that was lined with empty administrative offices.

Jean-Luc, growling in response to the burning in his leg and his anger at the sight of that old man, forced himself into a run. Lazare tried to quicken his pace, but Sophie was stumbling, tripping over her ripped dress as he practically dragged her by her bound arms.

Sophie was slowing him down, deliberately so, but Lazare refused to release her. He flashed the dagger, holding it before her face as a menacing threat. Jean-Luc, still lumbering forward, had closed the gap now and extended the poker, hooking its curved end around the old man's legs. Lazare tripped and fell to the ground, his grip releasing both the knife and Sophie as his face cracked against the hard marble floor. His body lay prone, lifeless.

"Sophie." Jean-Luc knelt down beside her, pulling the rag loose from her gagged mouth.

"Is he . . . is he?" Sophie, eyes wide, stared at the motionless frame of her captor.

"Not dead. Unconscious." Jean-Luc stood over the man, eyeing the pale face. Holding the poker aloft, his entire body trembling with the pain of his wound, with the rage he felt for this sadistic tormenter, Jean-Luc groaned. This was his chance. He could kill Lazare now and be done with it all. As Sophie looked on, Jean-Luc lifted the poker, preparing to bring it down with a fatal blow. But in that moment of hesitation, Marie's face flashed before his mind—then Mathieu's. André's. Kellermann's. Even the image of his unborn child, swaddled in his wife's arms. The better angels of this mad nation. What was he fighting for, if not for justice over lawlessness? Reason over rage? He lowered the poker.

"Come, we must run." Jean-Luc took a firm grip of her hand and helped her up. "Are you terribly hurt?" But even as he asked, he saw the multiple places her skin had been torn and her blood had been shed.

"I can run," Sophie said, her tone resolute. "Where?"

"To the prefect of the National Guard. Let this madman face a trial and die in La Place de la Révolution, like so many others he's sent there. Come." They took off at a sprint across the hall, Jean-Luc guiding Sophie toward the front entrance. But when he pulled on the door, the same door through which he had tried to enter, it didn't budge. He remembered: it had been locked. And he had no idea where the guard's key would be kept. Behind him, the figure of Guillaume Lazare began to stir, a snake uncoiling from its slumber. They couldn't get out this way, nor could they stay where they were.

"Come with me," Jean-Luc whispered, still gripping Sophie's arm. He had an idea, and he guided her back through the hall and toward the central staircase. He didn't know if Lazare had seen them run past, but he could hear the old man stirring, his shoes clicking on the marble floor of the hallway. Jean-Luc quickened the pace.

"Can't we go back out through the cellar?" Sophie asked.

"No." Jean-Luc shook his head. "We'd have to run right past him to get to the steps down. Best if he doesn't know where we are."

"Then where are we going?" Sophie asked, panting as they raced up the stairs.

"To my office."

"Where?"

"Upstairs—he won't find us in time. I will call down for help from the window, or better yet, we can climb out."

Sophie's eyes betrayed fear, but she kept his pace as they climbed the steps. When they reached the office, they paused at the door. Lazare's voice gave the two of them a moment of paralysis.

"You always thought you were so clever!" The old man, his voice high-pitched but steady, climbed the stairs after them. "But you've left a trail. Didn't you learn—always cover your tracks?"

Jean-Luc looked behind him and, sure enough, both his and Sophie's blood had dripped as they had run, leading their pursuer straight to them. "Damn it," Jean-Luc spat under his breath. "Hurry, come in." He pulled Sophie into the office. Propping a desk against the door, he reassessed the situation.

"Please?" Sophie turned and offered her hands, her wrists rubbed raw from the tightness of her bindings. Jean-Luc used the sharp point of the fire poker to slice through the rope and release her.

"Thank you," she said, massaging her wrists.

Jean-Luc, hearing the old man's steps approaching the doorway, looked to the window. "Come, this way." They ran to the windows, the glass panes as tall as doors and running the full length of the wall. In the summer heat, the window was swollen and stiff, hindering Jean-Luc's attempts to open it. With Sophie's help, they eventually pried it open, just as Lazare began to bang against the door.

His entry was momentarily blocked by the propped desk. "Oh no, it's not very nice of you to lock me out. Won't you let me in?" The old man's voice bore the mad determination that drove him on in spite of his injuries and old age. He banged again on the door, and the desk began to slide.

"Stay away," Jean-Luc shouted, his voice hoarse, but he saw the desk moving and knew that Lazare would soon gain entry. Jean-Luc's vision began to blur, his blood slowly draining from the wound in his thigh, but he forced himself to remain upright.

"It's too high to jump," Sophie said, looking out the window at the little alleyway that hugged the building. The same alleyway through which Jean-Luc had entered.

"Yes," Jean-Luc said, agreeing. "Hello! Anyone?" He called out to the dark street, to the abandoned alleyway, but his yell was met by only the bark of a dog. Now the door to the office burst open and Lazare entered, his mouth spread in a fiendish smile, his hand wielding the knife.

Sophie, with a desperate bravery, charged at the old man. Before Jean-Luc could react, Lazare dodged her charge and pulled her into his arms. Turning her to face him, he punched her hard across the face with the handle of the dagger. She fell to the ground, her body limp. He turned his gaze on Jean-Luc.

Jean-Luc lifted the poker to lunge, but Lazare still wielded the knife he'd held earlier. Seeing Sophie lying on the ground, Jean-Luc's anger threatened to overtake him. "If you touch her again, I'll kill you."

"You know, citizen, there was a time when I took a liking to you." Lazare's voice was a quiet hiss as he slowly stalked toward Jean-Luc. "I offered you a place on the world's stage, and instead of cooperation, you chose to thwart me at every turn. But your short, pitiful story is over. When I am through here, you will not even have a family left to mourn you."

The old man lunged, the knife held aloft. Jean-Luc parried the thrust, swinging the poker violently, smacking the old man's hands. To his dismay, he saw that Lazare still held the knife. The old man regrouped and charged again, straight at Jean-Luc's abdomen. His ferocity caught Jean-Luc off guard; all he could do to avoid the knife was step back. Now he had his back nearly against the wall. He was cornered, and both he and Lazare knew it, judging by the gleam in the old man's eyes. All that was behind him was the tall open window. He could jump to the street, but that would mean certain death as well.

Lazare lunged again, this time slashing the blade at Jean-Luc's throat. Jean-Luc sidestepped, but his thigh was in such severe pain from the earlier wound that he was unsteady and he banged into his desk. He groaned in agony, clutching the bleeding gash as his vision became mottled, his gaze dizzy. The poker fell from his grip just as Lazare's knife grazed the side of his waist, tearing through his waistcoat and the flesh just below his ribs. It was a superficial wound, not fatal, but it served to stun Jean-Luc. Now, unarmed, he stared in horror at the knife-wielding madman before him.

Jean-Luc's thigh burned from the wound and his side bled. He had no weapon and nowhere to run. His vision blurry, Jean-Luc slumped to his knees and crashed to the floor. He reached a hand out desperately to the old man, but his strength failed him and he blinked, fighting to stay conscious. Lazare approached him slowly, cautiously, as one would a wounded—but not yet dead—beast in a trap. The old man arched his back as he skulked toward Jean-Luc. He stood before the open window, his figure a black silhouette against the sky.

And then, before either of them knew it was happening, Sophie stood and charged the man, her arms bent and bracing. With a shove that took the entirety of her strength, she screamed and pushed her tormentor's frame toward the large window. He hadn't expected the assault from that direction, and he dropped the knife, turning his confused gaze to her. She was struggling to wrap her arms around him, and the two of them were caught in a tenuous embrace.

Sophie's face was contorted and flushed, her eyes burning with the frenzied, primordial instinct to survive; Lazare was stronger, but still surprised and disoriented by her unexpected ferocity.

"You filthy whore!" Lazare spat at her, lifting his hand to strike her across the face. Staying low, Sophie looked up into the man's eyes. Using her last bit of fight, she shoved her body against his once again. The force with which she knocked into him sent him flying backward, toward the opened window. He slipped on the pool of blood that had collected beneath Jean-Luc's gaping wound and lost his footing. Sophie, in a flash, capitalized on the old man's unsteady balance and gave him another push. At the moment Sophie lunged forward, Jean-Luc stirred and saw through his blurred vision Lazare reeling back, his frame thrown by the momentum. His eyes wide with shock, his arms groping at the air, he flew backward out the window.

Jean-Luc struggled to pull himself to the window to watch the man's fall. Lazare careened toward the street but was stopped suddenly short. Before his body could smash onto the cobblestones, the spear of the archangel Michael met the man's back so that he landed impaled on the blade of divine vengeance; it tore through his flesh and rose out the top of his gut as the old man writhed, losing his blood and his life, coloring the pristine white of the statue a bright, brilliant red.

The few pedestrians on the street in Jean-Luc's neighborhood eyed him and Sophie with a mixture of fear and ghoulish interest; why were they covered in blood, their clothes tattered, their faces hollow? Jean-Luc did not acknowledge their shocked expressions or muted utterances of alarm. He had no time to pause to answer their questions. He had left Marie hours earlier and needed to get back to her.

Jean-Luc limped up the stairs toward his garret, his arm around Sophie's shoulders for support.

"Marie?" He burst into their apartment, and it was there he found the thick figure of Madame Grocque. The woman sat beside the bed, holding a small bundle of linens, a pink face of wrinkled flesh. The baby had come, and now it began to whimper.

"Oh, God have mercy! The baby is here, already? Healthy? But it's so small. It arrived so early." Jean-Luc gasped, surveying the scene. Marie was in bed, asleep. The baby, unbearably tiny, was swaddled snugly in the tavern keeper's arms while Mathieu sat in the corner. The boy wept, undoubtedly upset after what he must have witnessed during the birth, Jean-Luc realized. Sophie rushed to the boy and took him in her arms.

"Oh, thank you, Madame Grocque. Thank you ever so much." Jean-Luc crossed the room, looking down at the fragile body clutched in the woman's embrace. But Madame Grocque said nothing, staring at Jean-Luc in dumb silence. What was the meaning of such an expression on her face? Jean-Luc wondered.

"Oh, Monsieur St. Clair, I'm so sorry. I tried, I did. But it all happened so fast. I didn't even have time to fetch the midwife." Just then, the infant began to cry, its wail surprisingly strong given the newness of its lungs.

"Well, the baby sounds perfectly healthy, madame, even if a bit early," Jean-Luc said, approaching the bed. "A little hungry, perhaps." He looked down at his child, and there was no mistaking that he had a daughter. The baby's face was a mottled pink, a rosebud with a shock of her mother's chestnut hair. "As beautiful as her mother," Jean-Luc said, momentarily consumed by the first sight of his daughter. "And I think she ought to be named for her, as well. Hello, Mariette. Little Marie. How do you like the sound of that?"

The old woman, still holding the baby, shook her head and did something Jean-Luc had never seen her do before: she began to cry.

"Why, Madame Grocque, what is the matter? I know that it must have been frightening, but you've done wonderfully well. Surely there's no need for any tears, unless they be tears of joy."

"You don't understand, monsieur!"

"What don't I understand, Madame Grocque?" Jean-Luc looked from the woman to the baby, then to his wife, where she lay sleeping in bed. And it was in that moment that he noticed the unnatural paleness of Marie's cheeks. The eerie plum color of her lips—lips that had always shone red and warm. Her brown eyes shut, and remaining shut, even as her baby wailed and her son whimpered in the corner and her husband clamored about.

He noticed for the first time the pile of papers by her side, and he leaned over to inspect them. Political pamphlets. All of them signed by the same mystery writer, Persephone. Beneath them were the originals, all written in Marie's familiar handwriting. And then on top, a note. Also in Marie's handwriting.

Hands trembling, Jean-Luc read her words:

> *My darling Jean-Luc,*
>
> *You know that I have always been your greatest admirer. Carry on with our noble work, for there is still so much more to be done. I shall stand beside you, always, in the two children you will raise, two children who could never have a more loving and devoted father. Do well for them, do well for our free nation, and you shall do well for me. I know you will.*
>
>
>
> *Yours, with love for eternity—*
> *Marie St. Clair*
>
>
>
> *Postscript: You've always been worthy of me—though perhaps a little less wily.*

"Marie?" Jean-Luc looked from the note to the motionless figure of his wife, his lungs collapsing, his chest squeezed tight by a noose. "Marie? No! This can't be! Wake up!" He leaned over her, tears rushing to his eyes as his wife, his beloved, failed to respond to the crying out of her name.

"*Maman!*" Mathieu, too, joined in, but his mother's eyelids remained shut, impervious to the supplications of her son, her husband, her new daughter. That was not something Marie would ever have done. Marie had never once ignored the cries of her son. She would never have been deaf to the pain of her husband. To the plaintive yelps of her newborn daughter. There was only one explanation: Marie was no longer there.

And when Jean-Luc took her hand in his own, he knew it to be true, for her soft flesh was cold.

31

Outside Cairo,
Egypt

July 22, 1798

André woke to a strong odor in his nostrils and a throbbing in his head. He sniffed the air and recognized the faint but familiar smell of sulfur. Stronger still was the smell of burning flesh. His neck ached as he lifted his head, and he saw that he was no longer in the desert but in the middle of a crowded tent with a dozen others. Cots lined the space and a pair of physicians tended to groaning men.

One of the camp doctors noticed André sitting up and walked over to his cot. Thin eyeglasses perched on the edge of his sunburned nose. He leaned over, pressing his hand to André's forehead. "Your fever has passed. And some of your color has returned. I believe the worst is over for you. You're luckier than some of the others."

André parted his parched lips. "Is there . . . water?"

The man walked across the tent, returning with two skins. "General Bonaparte has ordered us to be generous with the last of the wine rations. No, take the water first." André gulped greedily at the water, letting it run down his bare chest. "Slowly, sir. You've lost a good deal of blood and will be weak for some time."

As André caught his breath, he held out his hand for the wineskin. The warm drink burned slightly as it dripped down his throat. He closed his eyes as he savored the taste. "Thank you."

"Save your gratitude for that Egyptian fellow." The doctor smiled faintly at André. "You would have bled out onto the sand if he had not brought you back."

André thought back to the battle, recalling only confused flashes. He remembered the French squares shooting deadly fire into the enemy horsemen. He recalled the massive pyramids as the cavalry pursued the fleeing Mamelukes. A cold, shadowed doorway. A struggle for a gun. *Murat*. The madman had tried to kill him. But here he was, in spite of it all, alive and in one piece, for the most part. Had he killed Murat?

"You know, shirking duty is a crime punishable by death, Major Valière."

André turned toward the familiar voice and saw the tall, dark figure of General Dumas standing in the open flap of the tent. His face was stern, his uniform weather-beaten. His boots were caked in mud and silt. André gawked for a moment, unsure of what his superior had meant by that remark. The general took several steps toward him and flashed a sudden smile, his broad face handsome and relaxed. "Don't you know there is more work to be done, soldier?"

André made to sit up but Dumas put a hand to his shoulder, motioning him to remain as he was.

"From the looks of everything, I take it we've won the battle, sir?"

"We did not defeat our enemy, Valière," General Dumas replied. "We annihilated them. They've bolted into the desert with their survivors, abandoning Cairo. Our commander believes that twenty thousand of them perished in the battle. Between us, I think that may be something of an exaggeration. Still, he has already written his report to Paris, trumpeting the glorious miracle of the Battle of the Pyramids." As he said this, General Dumas appeared tired and somber, not proud like one who had taken a central role in an astonishing victory.

"You do not seem convinced of our success, General."

Dumas stood in thoughtful silence for a moment. He put a hand through his dark hair and sighed. "We have won the battle, of that I have no doubt, but what follows concerns me. These desert tribes will never yield to our rule. And Admiral Nelson and the British Royal Navy will descend upon us within weeks, even days."

Dumas glanced at André and smiled weakly. "But you need not concern yourself about any of that now. You have survived a smart little wound and deserve a rest."

André nodded, his thoughts returning to Murat. "Did we take many casualties? At least, anyone important?"

"Less than a hundred killed. Perhaps two hundred wounded. I suppose we should be thankful for that." Dumas studied André for a moment before adding: "General Murat was killed. Took a blade to the gut. Seems to have gotten himself entangled in some side skirmish, away from the main fighting."

André stared at the general, his heart beating sharply in his chest as grisly flashes of memory burst across his mind. A moment that felt like an eternity passed between them. Did Dumas know—could he hear the clamoring of André's heart?

Dumas nodded once, clasping his hands as a sigh of finality passed his lips. "So, his story is over. He will be mourned in Paris like all the others who have fallen bravely in the service of their country."

André exhaled, shutting his eyes, feeling as if an enormous weight had been taken from his shoulders. The oppressive cloud of fear, hatred, and death that had plagued him since he walked into that tent in the Valmy woods years before had passed away. He lay back and collapsed onto his cot with a careless crash.

Dumas lingered beside the bed a moment longer. "I suppose there are certain souls who have despaired of this world and are determined to drag down as many as they can. I admire you, Major, for fighting for your own life."

André's thoughts drifted back to Paris. "I swore to survive for those whom I've lost, and those I will not accept losing."

"And so you have. And you shall continue to do so." General Dumas looked at André, an admiring gaze, before nodding and placing his bicorn hat back on his head. He stood tall and arched his back. André sat up and offered him a salute.

Later, André woke from a deep sleep, bolting upright in his cot after being startled by a commotion inside the tent. He looked around and saw a cluster of soldiers standing in the opposite corner. There, in the center, stood one man, slightly apart. André nearly lost his breath when he caught a glimpse of the red sash about his waist, the tricolor cockade. "General Bonaparte, sir." He saluted, trying to keep his mouth from falling open in dumb shock.

"Major Valière, is it?" General Bonaparte approached the cot, his short-legged stride buoyant and jaunty. "At ease now. You've got to heal a bit still." The high commander stood beside the bed, staring at André with his intense, dark eyes before asking: "Anything we can do for you, Major?"

André, his mouth painfully dry, his brain feeling as if it were filled with cotton, answered with the simple, honest reply that came to him: "Sir, I just wish to go home."

"Ah, in due time, Major." Bonaparte's voice took on a heavy, imperious tone as he stared off to the far corner of the tent. "There are yet more enemies to fight, more battles to be won. The citizens of the Republic will learn of the Battle of the Pyramids a hundred years hence. This Army of the Orient will be remembered as the worthy successor to the soldiers of Alexander and the legionnaires of Rome."

André stared at his commander, wondering if he was, in fact, serious. He appeared to be. André nodded slightly in deference, suddenly feeling pain and fatigue in every part of his body.

"But you rest now, Major. You've earned it. I assure you, our surgeons are the best." Bonaparte smiled, nodding once, and then suddenly clasped André by the shoulder. As he did so he leaned forward and said quietly: "Courage, Major. Home will always be there, but glory—glory is fleeting and must be seized while it lies before you."

André's thoughts turned to Sophie, and he felt a pang of longing that outweighed the pain of his wounds.

"We have won a great victory," Bonaparte continued. "No man, alive or dead, can ever take that honor from you."

An aide passed the general a curved saber and a silver eagle pendant hanging from a blue ribbon. The general took the pendant and draped it around André's neck. The sword he placed on the cot at André's feet. Before André even understood what was happening, a scroll was unfurled and the orders for an award were read aloud to the tent by one of Napoleon's adjutants. "For intrepid gallantry in the face of the enemies of

France, the Award of the Grand Saber is awarded to Major André Valière on this day, Ivraie in Thermidor, Year Six of the French Republic."

With that, Napoleon Bonaparte offered one more nod in André's direction. "Congratulations, Major."

"Thank you, sir," André stammered, fingering the medal that hung heavy around his neck. *Glory is fleeting and must be seized while it lies before you.* Funny, André thought to himself, he would have said the same thing about love. About his very life. And now, suddenly, he wanted nothing more than to return to France and, at last, begin living that life.

32

Paris

Fall 1798

André Valière had not been directly heard from in more than a year. In that time, Jean-Luc had saved Sophie from her imprisonment and torment by Lazare. The old man had perished in the deed, but the relief that Jean-Luc should have felt from the release of that vicious citizen's torments was wholly replaced by the shock of Marie's passing. She had been through all of Jean-Luc's struggles, both successes and failures, and her journey made all the more difficult by her exclusion from his work. She had been left to raise their child, tend to their home, and share in the strain of Jean-Luc's labors, all while carrying out her own work for the Revolution in silence and in secret. She, as true a patriot as any, had had no legal or public authority to share her gifts on behalf of the nation. No rights as a citizen, even. Even in his grief, Jean-Luc reflected on this for many days after her passing. How a woman was expected to obey the laws and thrive in society, with virtually no say in the very existence and promulgation of those same laws or that society. Was that not itself an injustice, Jean-Luc wondered, itself perhaps worthy of a revolution? But he had had enough of that word for now, and his thoughts turned to his remaining family. He would leave Paris.

Sophie decided to remain, to wait. She said farewell to Jean-Luc and the children with a promise that she would send word—as soon as she had any, if she ever had any—of her fiancé.

Once he had loaded the carriage—the children, the luggage, his wife's casket—they made their quiet departure from the city. Near the barrier, Jean-Luc looked back over his shoulder at the receding silhouette of the capital. Paris, the place to which he had come so many years ago, a young lawyer who believed in his countrymen and his nation and the principles of liberty and equality and fraternity. All of that was before; before the guillotine had been installed in La Place de la Révolution, before the king had lost his head and a movement borne of the Enlightenment had taken a turn down a dark path.

There, against the distant backdrop of the city, Jean-Luc made out the French tricolor flag that hung over the wall, its three-colored cloth flapping in a strong breeze. Red and white and blue. The flag billowed back and forth—shifting, wavering, as the sun's rays rippled over it with the soft glow of coming dusk. Tenuous, and yet somehow durable. A thin, fragile symbol, its presence hopeful, its shape as illusory in the breeze as the ideals for which it waved. From his vantage point, Jean-Luc paused, transfixed. He stared at the city he had called home these many years, half of it covered in the veil of the evening's darkening shadow, the other half illuminated by the last rays of the vanishing sunlight, glorious, a burnished mirage of so much beauty that it gave Jean-Luc a final ache in his breast.

Jean-Luc was alone when they buried Marie, her body gently dropped into the soft earth. He had left Paris and brought her home, as he had promised; back to her beloved south, where the air smelled of the sea and of the citrus groves and the faint perfume of lavender. A priest read from the Book of Wisdom, and Jean-Luc tried to remember her as she had been—warm, bright-eyed, blooming with strength and vigor—and not as he had found her, cold, limp, in a stained bed on the day she had brought his daughter into the world.

After her burial, Jean-Luc had returned to the home of his father-in-law and wrapped his two children in a long embrace. Something inside him told him it was better to stay here, where his children might bathe in the sea and the warm light of the Mediterranean sun, and learn more of their mother than they ever could in Paris.

Did he still believe that liberty and equality and fraternity could guide the people of this new nation? Jean-Luc wondered. Would he tell his children with pride or with shame that he had served in the Revolution? He didn't know; he couldn't answer any of that on that day. All he knew was that Marie would have her way: he would raise her children, he would love them and keep them safe. He would teach them to be honest and kind and brave, as their mother had been. He'd honor the woman she'd been, the wife she'd been, the mother she'd been, the citizen and thinker she'd been. He'd raise her children in the belief that, as long as there were still men and women willing to stand for justice and for truth, there was still reason to hope for their nation and, indeed, for all.

And in that, Jean-Luc St. Clair would be performing a service more sacred than any he had yet done.

Epilogue

Cathédrale
Notre Dame
de Paris

December 2, 1804

The frigid winter weather—falling snow, bitter wind that skittered off the Seine—did nothing to discourage the Parisians. They gathered by the hundreds of thousands, perhaps as many as a million, outside the magnificent cathedral, newly restored after the ravages of the Revolution, its Gothic spires rendered all the more glorious by the snowfall. Notre Dame stood proud once more, triumphant, signifying to all who looked on that God himself blessed France and the emperor she had chosen for herself.

Jean-Luc glanced around, holding more tightly to his son's hand as his daughter bounced on his hip. He marveled at the spectacle of it all—the sheer size of the crowd, the volume of their cries, the fact that they'd come out in the cold and dark, assembling before the first light of dawn. He blinked, forcing out the memories of so many crowds before this one; today, their faces were not fiendish and vindictive, calling for blood. Today, they were hopeful and euphoric as they lined the entire parade route from the Tuileries across the river and along the island to the great Gothic entrance of the cathedral, waving the tricolor, shouting *"Vive Napoleon!"* as others sang the anthem. Today, the people were bestowing a crown rather than seizing one; making an emperor rather than destroying a king. As ever, they were ravenous, shouting, demanding a show.

Napoleon himself had seen to every detail of his own coronation. The people wanted a pageant, a majestic spectacle, and there was no one more fit and willing to give them one than the man who believed himself to be destined by God to carry forward the virtues of the Republic, now an Empire, in the style of Alexander the Great and Julius Caesar. Great men who, like Napoleon, had fashioned themselves into living gods. Every detail—from the decorative eagles lining the parade route to the hot-air balloon that would take flight from the square at the conclusion of the coronation Mass—reinforced his claim to the imperial throne.

Jean-Luc had read in *Le Moniteur* newspaper how Napoleon had ordered a crown made especially for the occasion, one to replace the medieval diadem destroyed in one of the Revolution's many orgies of devastation. In wearing a crown modeled after Charlemagne's own from centuries ago, Napoleon would silence those bold critics who dared to point out that the general, a Corsican, was not in fact of French noble blood—or French blood at all, for that matter.

All morning long, the gilded carriages rolled past—mayors of far-reaching French cities, army officers, naval admirals, members of the Assembly, distinguished judges, men of the Legion of Honor, ministers of the government. The people of France, having shivered along the parade route for hours, met each passing dignitary with an ever more fervent cry.

Jean-Luc noticed a mule approach, its rider bearing a magnificently bejeweled crucifix, and he supposed that this must be the papal procession approaching. Indeed, Napoleon had summoned Pope Pius, and Pius had come, bringing his most powerful cardinals and bishops from Rome to Paris. Everyone, even God himself, it appeared, now obeyed Napoleon. After years of sacking ancient churches, seizing holy relics, and defiling the very image of Jesus, the French people were willing to return to God, return to the church, and that was because Napoleon said they would.

Of course the pope would not be crowning Napoleon; Napoleon would not answer to Rome, nor anyone. He would crown himself, and Josephine, too. The papers had been abuzz with the scandal of it all—how Napoleon's mother had refused to attend because of her dislike of her daughter-in-law, and how Napoleon had sat his siblings down, threatening his three sisters with exile until they finally agreed to attend the ceremony and walk behind Josephine as her humbled trainbearers.

As the carriages flooded the square now, the government ministers and royal dignitaries were ushered into the grand cathedral, where golden tapestries decked the walls, glittering against the backdrop of thousands of candles. Not one but two full choirs, accompanied by two full orchestras, sang the holy words of the music composed especially for this day, and the blasts of the trumpets, the clamor of the cymbal and the timpani, now spilled out to where Jean-Luc stood in the packed square.

But the glorious music from inside the cathedral was drowned out when Napoleon's imperial cavalcade finally appeared. Preceded by his brothers, his sisters, and his closest generals and advisers, the emperor's coach stood apart, pulled by eight white horses and emblazoned with a large "N" across its gilded exterior. Napoleon stepped out with Josephine, each of them in white silk trimmed in gold, impossibly long capes of ermine and plush red velvet. The large "N" of his imperial cape was visible from within a web of elaborate golden stitching. The gold and velvet and ermine had cost at least 50,000 francs, the papers reported, and that was not saying anything of Josephine's jewels, but the starving people of France didn't seem to mind what this celebration cost them, because Napoleon would improve the lives of all France's citizens. No one dwelled on the fact that more than 300,000 of their fellow countrymen had died to establish the Republic—a Republic that, today, became an empire once more.

Standing beside Jean-Luc St. Clair, silently observing it all, was his old friend, André Valière. The former soldier was accompanied by his wife, Sophie, and their two young sons, Remy and Christophe.

"Are you glad you traveled back for this?" Jean-Luc turned to André, shouting over the chaos of the crowd. Though André had retired from the army and moved north, making a new life for his family on the lands that had once belonged to his ancestors, he, like so many other Frenchmen, had traveled with his family to the capital for this historic moment.

André considered the question, his mind wandering back to a dusty tent in the desert. Pain in his side, a hard cot under him, a saber placed at his feet. "He's wearing a few more jewels today than the last time I saw him, but I am not surprised it has come to this," André answered. After a moment, he added: "It was in his eyes; it always showed in his eyes. He appeared as one who could look past you and the present moment. As if he could not only see the future, he could shape it."

"And in that future, no doubt, images of his own glory stretch out before him," Jean-Luc said, and he exchanged a wry smile with his friend. They'd both heard the rumors—Napoleon's desire to take his glory beyond France. Plans to conquer England, Austria, and even the vast lands beyond. So it would mean more war for the French people.

Jean-Luc had had enough of all that. He, too, had returned to Paris from the south only in order to see this historic event and briefly reunite with his old friends. In Marseille, he dealt with the civil disputes of private citizens. It was small, uncomplicated, humble work. Just as he liked it.

A tap on his shoulder pulled him from the sights of Napoleon's procession. He turned to see a man dressed in a black coat, stern faced, looking at him expectantly. After a brief look at the man, Jean-Luc guessed him to be a government official, based on the formal lace of his cravat and a small but distinct Napoleonic Bee insignia on the left breast of his coat. "Jean-Luc St. Clair, is it?"

"Yes," he replied, surprised to be identified by this stranger in a crowd of thousands.

"For you. From His Imperial Majesty."

The man pressed a sealed parchment into Jean-Luc's gloved hand, the symbol of the eagle emblazoned on it. Napoleon's imperial crest. Jean-Luc blinked, deaf to the roars of the crowds now as, on the far side of the square, Napoleon saluted the cheering thousands. All Jean-Luc saw was the paper, the simple words that appeared large in his trembling hands:

> *By formal request of His Imperial Majesty, the Emperor*
> *Napoleon I of the French:*
>
> *Your talents are requested in the service of France.*

Jean-Luc lowered the paper, stunned. The service of France. Wasn't that how it had begun?

Would he really answer this call a second time, allowing himself to be pulled back into the maelstrom of Revolution?

"What is it, Papa?" Mariette asked, studying him with her large eyes— dark, knowing, so much like her mother's that it caused his heart to lurch in his breast.

"A letter, dearest one."

She cocked her head to the side. "From a friend?"

"I don't know yet. We shall see."

Where the Light Falls: Authors' Note

The process of writing this novel and bringing this story to life has been a long and winding journey, both an incredible challenge and a great joy. In many ways, it has been the realization of a dream to see this story brought from the realm of ideas and fantasy into a tangible, real book. As co-authors, we both ventured into uncharted territory in writing this together. It was something neither of us had ever attempted, but we both agree that this has been a genuine and rewarding partnership. We believe that this story is better because of it.

The tale, as the reader by now is surely aware, unfolds in the midst of the French Revolution. Even beginning to examine the conditions and events that led to the French Revolution, the Terror, and the period of its aftermath is a monumental task to which many have devoted entire careers. Delivering a definitive and exhaustive historical account of one of the formative events in modern Western history was not our intention in writing this book; what we did want to do was tell a compelling story that managed to capture some of the feelings and spirit of this momentous and tumultuous period.

Our quartet of protagonists—André Valière, Jean-Luc St. Clair, Sophie de Vincennes, and Marie St. Clair—are all fictional characters, though their stories and struggles are certainly inspired by real events. One will find no shortage of disenfranchised young noblemen fighting in the ranks of the Revolutionary army, idealistic young lawyers serving in the new government, aristocratic widows struggling to evade the guillotine, or politically minded female writers within the cast of flesh-and-blood individuals whose lives fill the pages of history. But the exact likenesses of these four characters never walked the streets of Paris.

Our story's primary antagonists, Nicolai Murat and Guillaume Lazare, are also fictional. However, like our protagonists, the villains of this story are inspired by the true-to-life people who brought their particular brand of Revolutionary vengeance to the citizens of eighteenth-century France. In fact, Nicolai Murat is directly inspired by a real man, General Adam Philippe, Comte de Custine. The real-life Comte de Custine was a noble-born officer in the French army who had previously served in the American Revolution; his soldiers affectionately called him General Mustache. He was present at the Battle of Valmy and later in the Revolution did in fact accuse his former comrade, General François Christophe de Kellermann, of "neglecting to support his operations," after which Kellermann was called to Paris to defend himself before the National Convention.

Guillaume Lazare is also a fictional character very much based on real historical figures. His fervent advocacy for "the people" and his endorsement of state-sponsored terror in pursuit of their interests are based on the figure of Maximilien Robespierre. His willingness to call for mass bloodshed of the noble and clergy classes is based upon the speeches and pamphlets of Jean-Paul Marat. Lastly, the deep-rooted feelings of anger and injustice, even rage, are based on Jacques Hébert and his "enraged" wing of the Revolutionary government. There are other notorious figures of the Revolution who would actively carry out mass executions across France on behalf of the government, but we cannot list them all here. The Committee that we meet in our story, over which Lazare presides, is based on Robespierre's Committee of Public Safety.

Christophe Kellermann, one of the early heroes of this story, was a real figure. François Christophe de Kellermann was an Alsatian general from Strasbourg, widely celebrated throughout France (for a time) as the primary hero of the Battle of Valmy. As stated above, he was in fact denounced by his former partner, Custine, and imprisoned for thirteen months in Paris during the Revolution, due in part to his reluctance to commit mass executions in the rebellious city of Lyon. However, with significant but we believe necessary dramatic license, we see our fictional Kellermann executed at one of our story's turning points. Although the real Kellermann was never executed, many French generals were recalled to Paris and condemned to death under dubious, if not controversial, circumstances. Many political and civilian leaders would find themselves on the wrong side of the Revolution's justice.

On the topic of Revolutionary justice, several points should be addressed. First and foremost, the use of the guillotine in La Place de la

Révolution (now Paris's Place de la Concorde, renamed by Napoleon) was certainly an important feature of the Revolution's Reign of Terror. Depending on which source you go by, it is estimated that as many as 20,000 people were executed by guillotine (approximately 2,500 of those individuals in Paris), and nearly 30,000 would be enacted by other means throughout France. The Terror was state policy, organized and enacted by the Committees of Public Safety and General Security. These officials oversaw every aspect of government from economic policy and formulation of laws and special courts to military policy and taxation.

The Revolution began in earnest in the summer of 1789 when the "Third Estate," or the class of common and bourgeois individuals of the Estates General Convention (by far the largest portion of the population), decided to oppose the much more powerful and tax-exempt First and Second Estates: the clergy and nobility, respectively. Starving and strapped by crushing taxation, the representatives of the common class used the gathering of the Estates General Convention in Versailles to demand greater representation and legal rights. King Louis XVI proved intransigent in the face of these demands, reluctant to compromise and thus appear to diminish his "divine right" authority.

In response to these events at Versailles, located just outside Paris, the outraged population of the capital rose up against the government of the monarchy and took down the formidable and reviled Bastille prison on July 14 (now celebrated as Bastille Day). Over the course of the next three years, a growing feeling of patriotic and revolutionary fervor was inflamed across the country, and the unpopular king and queen—along with their aristocratic allies—became increasingly isolated and threatened by the likes of ambitious young men such as Maximilien Robespierre, Georges Danton, Jean-Paul Marat, and Camille Desmoulins. Spreading their pamphlets across cities and giving speeches to enthusiastic crowds, these popular revolutionaries demanded more concessions from the king and more power for the people, especially those with like-minded political sensibilities.

In June 1791, amid growing hostility toward the very idea of an all-powerful monarchy, King Louis XVI and his family tried to flee the country. This action, known as the failed Flight to Varennes, sealed the king's fate. In the eyes of the people, Louis and his Austrian-born queen had abandoned their country and were clearly in league with foreign dictators to crush the new liberties won by the people. Thus, they no longer had the authority to rule. Louis would be executed a year and a half later, and the Reign of Terror would truly begin in the winter of 1793.

Our story begins in the winter of 1792. By then, the king and queen had already tried to flee, and the country had passed into the third year of its Revolution. However, the Reign of Terror, as history has come to call it, had not yet begun. In fact, the guillotine was not permanently moved to La Place de la Révolution until May 1793, so we took a liberty in having tumbrils transporting condemned prisoners there at the start of our story.

The Terror was halted in the Thermidorian Reaction of July 1794, during which time Maximilien Robespierre and twenty-one of his political allies were executed. (It is referred to as the Thermidorian Reaction because the month in which it occurred was Thermidor by the Republican calendar.) Intermittent violence and war would continue to affect France for many years to follow.

What would follow was known as the Period of the Directory. This government replaced the Revolutionary government, and it consisted of an upper and lower house and an executive body of five members. It is the lower house, the Council of Five Hundred, to which Gavreau intends to nominate Jean-Luc. It was also this elected body that Napoleon Bonaparte would overthrow in 1799, conferring onto himself the title of First Consul.

Before he was First Consul of France, however, Napoleone Buonaparte was a young Corsican officer in the French army whose career prospects looked anything but extraordinary. With the outbreak of violence in Paris in 1792, which a young, horrorstruck Buonaparte witnessed firsthand, the future was clearly going to bring change to everything and everyone in France. In 1794, outside of the southern port city of Toulon, Napoleone— then known simply as Captain Buonaparte—would first make his unusual name famous. Using the personal connections he had made with Maximilien Robespierre's younger brother, he was asked to assist in the siege of Toulon, which had been blockaded and occupied by the British and Spanish navies with help from sympathetic royalist French citizens. Assuming command of French forces in the region, young Buonaparte requisitioned supplies and reinforcements from the surrounding countryside and systematically dismantled the British hold on the city, eventually liberating it in the name of the French Republic. This event catapulted a poor, obscure young captain to nationwide fame, and the rank of general. And this was the famous "boy general" to whom Remy refers when he asks André if they might get to see him—an ambitious twenty-four-year-old from Corsica who would rise to staggering heights and change the course of world history.

In 1795, after a period of restlessness and desperation, General Bonaparte, having by then Gallicized the spelling of his name, again threw himself into events that would bring him even more fame—and infamy. The episode in Chapter 17 where Jean-Luc flees from a macabre street scene in horror and runs into a crowd chanting for General Bonaparte in Paris is based on a real event known as the episode of 13 Vendémiaire (using the Republican calendar for October). General Bonaparte took charge of a situation in which royalist sympathizers were attempting to storm the government buildings and overthrow the government. With ruthless and devastating effect, Napoleon turned cannons on the mob and butchered hundreds, saving the government and winning acclaim across France. The meticulous reader will note that this event occurs a year earlier in our novel than it does in the historical record. We ask your forgiveness if this caused confusion; it was, we determined, a necessary use of the artistic license afforded to us as writers of fiction, in order for this significant scene to work within our fictional plot and with our many characters and events.

After a year of stunning and unlikely victories with his "Army of Italy" against the Austrian empire and their allies, Napoleon Bonaparte had officially risen to the prominence he had coveted his entire life. His extortionist treatment of conquered Italian cities led to a steady flow of gold, silver, and all manner of treasure into the French coffers. The desperate financial situation France had found itself in since the years leading to the Revolution was now over. The popular general quoted his hero Alexander the Great when he stated that "fortune favors the bold," and he was now in a position to act boldly in charting the course of his own grand destiny. After the failure of his plan to sail across the English Channel and invade France's greatest enemy, Napoleon set his sights on a new prize, one that would challenge Great Britain's naval supremacy and threaten their colonies as far abroad as India. Napoleon would conquer Egypt.

With André Valière in exile, we pick up his story off the coast of southern France where he is serving as a deckhand on *l'Esprit de Liberté*. Soon after, we learn that he is to join General Bonaparte's expedition to the ancient kingdom on the Nile. The Egyptian campaign unfolded much as it does in the novel, with a two-week march across blistering sands during which hundreds, if not thousands, of French soldiers would perish. Much of the blame has to be put on a young General Bonaparte, who many believe underestimated the logistical and human toll a march across three hundred miles of North African desert would take on his army. The Battle of the Pyramids was a great victory for the French over the superior numbers of Mameluke warriors. However, in history, the French army would then be stranded without ships after a losing battle against the British navy under Admiral Horatio Nelson. Most of the surviving soldiers would not arrive home until they were captured by the British and returned to France in 1801.

One note on our use of French names and an accompanying decision we had to make on style: in French, generic words denoting squares, streets, names, and the like are written in lowercase, whether used alone or with a specific name as part of an address. For instance, one would read about la place de la Révolution. We have elected to refer instead to La Place de la Révolution, as that is likely the more familiar style for readers of English, and, we felt, would be less likely to cause confusion. With the heavy burden we are already placing on the reader to wrangle this complex history and occasionally slip with us into French phrases and names, we figured this small stylistic decision to make things just slightly less complicated might be appreciated.

This is a tale that feels very significant to us, not only as lovers of history but also because of our family's deep roots in France. Allison has lived in Paris and Owen has lived in London (where he made use of the short "chunnel" train ride to Paris). We have many relatives still living in Paris and throughout France, so we consider this history to be a part of our own heritage and family tapestry.

Like the American Revolution, this was a conflict that, at times, brought out some of the highest ideals of humanity. Many of the most celebrated aspects of French culture today—the national anthem of France (the Marseillaise), the tricolor flag, and the slogan "Liberty, Equality, Fraternity"—all originate from this seminal and tumultuous period.

However, we also see the events in France spiral into chaos, fear, and out-right butchery.

In our story we hope to convey both extremes, the better angels of human nature and the horrifying excesses of violence and extremism. The light and the dark, the hopeful and the hopeless. And we hope that this novel of historical fiction can be educational and enlightening for readers while also providing a compelling story and worthwhile experience. After all, it's through history that we might better understand not only the past but also our present and future.

Acknowledgments

We are so grateful to the many family, friends, and colleagues who have helped us to create this novel. Special thanks go to: our literary agent Lacy Lynch and the team at Dupree Miller & Associates; our editor Kara Cesare, as well as Susan Kamil, Avideh Bashirrad, Leigh Marchant, Loren Noveck, Sally Marvin, Maria Braeckel, Andrea DeWerd, Emma Caruso, Michelle Jasmine, Samantha Leach, Allyson Pearl, Gina Centrello, and the entire team at The Dial Press and Random House; Lindsay Mullen, Katie Nuckolls, Jordan Dugan, Alyssa Conrardy, and the whole Prosper Strategies crew.

To the numberless historians, curators, translators, and biographers who have helped to make sense of and shed light on (pun intended) one of the most dramatic, volatile, and complicated periods in modern Western European history: our perpetual admiration and gratitude are yours.

We have generous and supportive friends in abundance, as well as loving family members who have urged us on at every turn. For those who have been interested and supportive of this project, especially those from the very beginning, you know who you are, and we are eternally grateful. It also feels appropriate, at the conclusion of a book considering the idea and nature of light, to say: Lilly, you shine brightest of all for your parents.

While the following does not comprise an exhaustive or proper bibliography, we did wish to provide the curious reader with a list of books and works that proved particularly inspiring and helpful to us during our research of French history and culture:

A Tale of Two Cities by Charles Dickens

Danton by Andrzej Wajda (film)

French Revolutionary Infantry: 1789–1802 by the Osprey Men at Arms Series

Les Misérables by Victor Hugo

La Révolution Française: Les Années Lumière (film series)

La Révolution Française: Les Années Terribles (film series)

Napoleon: A Life by Andrew Roberts

Napoleon Bonaparte: A Life by Alan Schom

Napoleon's Egyptian Campaigns: 1798–1801 by the Osprey Men at Arms Series

The French Revolution, A History by Thomas Carlyle

The French Revolution and Napoleon by Leo Gershoy

The Black Count: Glory, Revolution, Betrayal, and the Real Count of Monte Cristo by Tom Reiss

The Origins of the French Revolution by William Doyle

PHOTO: © TRICIA McCORMACK

ALLISON PATAKI is the author of the bestselling novels *Sisi, The Traitor's Wife,* and *The Accidental Empress.* Her novels have been translated into more than a dozen languages. A former news writer and producer, Pataki has written for *The New York Times, ABC News, The Huffington Post, USA Today, Fox News,* and other outlets. She graduated cum laude from Yale University with a major in English and spent several years in journalism before switching to fiction writing. A member of the Historical Novel Society, Allison Pataki lives in Chicago with her husband and daughter. To connect and learn more, please visit:

AllisonPataki.com
Facebook.com/AllisonPatakiPage
Twitter: @AllisonPataki

PHOTO: © SARA KERENS

OWEN PATAKI graduated from Cornell University in 2010 with a degree in history. He served as a first lieutenant in the United States army, with one deployment to Afghanistan. Following his service in the military, he attended film school in London. He has also worked for the Weinstein Company and assisted on several film productions. He now lives in New York City, where he is working as a screenwriter and filmmaker. This is his first novel.

owenpataki.com
Find Owen Pataki on Facebook
Twitter: @owen_pataki

About the Type

This book was set in Dante, a typeface designed by Giovanni Mardersteig (1892–1977). Conceived as a private type for the Officina Bodoni in Verona, Italy, Dante was originally cut only for hand composition by Charles Malin, the famous Parisian punch cutter, between 1946 and 1952. Its first use was in an edition of Boccaccio's *Trattatello in laude di Dante* that appeared in 1954. The Monotype Corporation's version of Dante followed in 1957. Though modeled on the Aldine type used for Pietro Cardinal Bembo's treatise *De Aetna* in 1495, Dante is a thoroughly modern interpretation of that venerable face.

About the Type

This book was set in Dante, a typeface designed by Giovanni Mardersteig (1892–1977). Conceived as a private type for the Officina Bodoni in Verona, Italy, Dante was originally used to compose work by Boccaccio. In fact, it was first used in an edition of Boccaccio's *Trattatello in Laude di Dante*. It was through the matrices supplied by Charles Malin that Mardersteig produced the fount of Dante, followed by the italic and semi-bold roman series. Dante was re-cut for mechanical composition by the Monotype Corporation in 1957.